FLOWER AND THORN

ALSO BY RATI MEHROTRA

Night of the Raven, Dawn of the Dove

FLOWER AND THORN

RATI MEHROTRA

WEDNESDAY BOOKS
NEW YORK

First published in the United States by Wednesday Books, an imprint of St. Martin's Publishing Group

FLOWER AND THORN. Copyright © 2023 by Rati Mehrotra. All rights reserved. Printed in the United States of America. For information, address St. Martin's Publishing Group, 120 Broadway, New York, NY 10271.

Designed by Jen Edwards

www.wednesdaybooks.com

Library of Congress Cataloging-in-Publication Data

Names: Mehrotra, Rati, author.
Title: Flower and thorn / Rati Mehrotra.
Description: First edition. | New York : Wednesday Books, 2023. |
    Audience: Ages 14–18.
Identifiers: LCCN 2023024887 | ISBN 9781250823700 (hardcover) |
    ISBN 9781250823717 (ebook)
Subjects: CYAC: Magic—Fiction. | Flowers—Fiction. | Fantasy. |
    LCGFT: Fantasy fiction. | Novels.
Classification: LCC PZ7.1.M46776 Fl 2023 | DDC [Fic]—dc23
LC record available at https://lccn.loc.gov/2023024887

Our books may be purchased in bulk for promotional, educational, or business use. Please contact your local bookseller or the Macmillan Corporate and Premium Sales Department at 1-800-221-7945, extension 5442, or by email at MacmillanSpecialMarkets@macmillan.com.

First Edition: 2023

10 9 8 7 6 5 4 3 2 1

Sweet white jasmine to cure the ill
Bloodred hibiscus to bend to your will
Blazing sunflower to find and to hold
Priceless pansy for wealth untold.

Starry bluestar to counter the red
Gracious green rose to hear what is said
Silver spider lily to win all wars
Blackhearted chrys to open strange doors.

But as for the flower that rules all the rest
The pretty pink blossom I love the best
That blooms when clouds burst over the ground
The sacred lotus must never be found.

FLOWER AND THORN

CHAPTER 1

The man had been dead for a while, as was obvious from the stench. He lay spread-eagled on the cracked white earth of the salt desert, his skin burned reddish brown by the sun, the buttons of his faded shirt straining against the bloat of his stomach. In the hollow of his outstretched palm, in ludicrous contrast, glowed a bluestar, bright and impossible.

Irinya leaned forward and stared at it, her gut churning, wishing she could leave it alone but knowing she would not. Flowers were rare in the Rann of Kutch. Years of overharvesting and destruction of the hives they depended on had nearly wiped them out. This bluestar would be worth a gold mohur at least.

Fardan poked her shoulder, making her start. "Go on. It's not like he's going to jump up and throttle you."

She shot him a glare. "Why don't *you* get it?"

He took a hasty step back, raising his hands in mock horror. "I made lunch."

As if there was any comparison between making a few rotlas and plucking a flower from an extremely dead man's hand. "Some flower-hunting partner you are," she muttered under her breath. She set down her potli and wiped the sweat trickling down her face with the edge of her dupatta. They'd seen bodies in the salt flats before—men who'd come for the magic flowers of the Rann and met death instead. The monsoon rains washed their remains out to sea every year.

But they'd never seen one with an actual flower. Nor had they seen one who was so obviously a foreigner, from the strange cut of his clothes to the light-colored eyes and hair. The elders would not be happy about this. It meant that knowledge of the magic flowers had leaked beyond the boundaries of the Indian subcontinent. A complete outsider had managed to find a bluestar—although he had not managed to stay alive.

The baniya would not care one way or the other as long as he got his flowers. He'd been hectoring them more than usual lately, demanding the rarest blooms, threatening to raise the interest rate on their debt if they didn't meet his quota. He knew how flower hunting worked, knew how difficult it was to procure a single flower, and yet he acted as though it was their laziness to blame for the scant pickings.

Villain. One day, she'd pay off the debt and free the kul from his grasping hands. That was the vow she'd made to herself when she became a flower hunter, even though it seemed an impossible goal. She put the greedy moneylender out of her mind, wrapped her dupatta around her nose and mouth, and approached the body. The smell grew worse. *Just a decaying shell,* she told herself. *Nothing to worry about.* She crouched beside the outstretched hand, breathing through her mouth, and reached out.

The fingers on the hand twitched.

Irinya yelped and scooted back.

"What?" said Fardan in alarm, leaping to her side. "What?"

"Nothing." She stared at the hand. She hadn't imagined it. It was as if the flower had *pushed* the fingers aside, revealing more of itself. "Are we sure he's dead?"

"Of course." Fardan wrinkled his nose. "He smells worse than my grandmother."

"Fardan!"

"I'm serious. She never bathes. But, I mean, look at his face."

She looked. Short, salt-encrusted brown hair and beard, gaping mouth, stiff jaw, eyes staring sightlessly into the glare of the pale blue sky. "I thought I saw him move."

"Bodies do that sometimes," said Fardan with a knowledgeable air. "It's all the gases inside them. You'd better hurry if you don't want it farting on you."

That was enough to galvanize her into action. She scuttled forward, snatched the bluestar from the dead man's hand, and was about to scuttle back when she noticed the lone petal left in his palm. Inwardly, she cursed. The flower was worth more when it was whole.

Take me, said the petal.

She blinked. Flowers spoke to her sometimes, just like they'd once spoken to her mother. Or she imagined they did. A magical connection or a figment of the mind—did it matter which? The noonday sun beat down relentlessly, making her head throb. The sooner they got back to the camp, the better.

"You making friends?" said Fardan from behind her.

"Very funny." She retrieved the petal and pocketed it in a small, furtive movement so Fardan wouldn't notice, trying not to think about what she was doing. Stealing from the dead. Not that it belonged to the dead man in the first place. He had no business here in the Rann. Still, she would not withhold the words of farewell from him. She rose and backed away, joining her hands together. "May you find water and rest in the garden of death." Fardan echoed her words.

She showed him the bluestar, the elegance of its four slim petals marred by the obvious absence of the fifth. It gave off a faint stench of brackish water—quite unlike the white jasmine with its rich, sweet fragrance. "You think the baniya will write off a full gold mohur for this?" she asked.

He took it from her and examined it, his face falling. "No chance. One of the petals is missing."

"Still got to be worth at least ten silver tankas." She grabbed her potli, took the last gulp of water remaining in her waterskin, and strode away, not waiting for Fardan. Why had she hidden the petal from him? Did she mean to keep it for herself because it had spoken to her?

Each petal of the bluestar could counteract the effects of the red flower—the hibiscus that compelled obedience. But no one was about to waste a precious hibiscus on the likes of her. She had no earthly use for it.

Fardan caught up with her. "This means riches," he crowed, his hazel eyes sparkling. "Maybe I will leave the kul and become a famous artist in Ahmedabad. And you will miss me with all your poor, sad heart."

"Use your brains, if you have any." Irinya pointed at the flower in his hand. "Ninety percent of that will go to paying down debt. The baniya will be happy for five seconds before he asks for more. We'll get a few miserable jital if we're lucky. And you'll spend your share on parchment, like you always do."

Fardan sighed. "A man can dream."

She glanced at him sideways. Anyone less like an artist was difficult to imagine, with his mischievous eyes, dimpled chin, unruly black hair, and hefty build. But Fardan's large hands were capable of surprisingly delicate work.

He caught her gaze and grinned. "Missing me already?"

She snorted and focused on the landscape. The Rann stretched flat in every direction as far as the eye could see, salt crystals glittering in the sun. Not a single blade of grass broke the hard white featurelessness of the salt flats. Yet it was the only place in the Indian subcontinent—perhaps the entire *world*—where magic flowers grew. Jasmines loved the hollows of dead trees, roses preferred black volcanic rock, hibiscus were drawn to fossils, and sunflowers hid in the base of thorny bushes.

Nor were they defenseless. Each flower had its own kind of thorn that produced a unique poison. There were no known antidotes, but Irinya had been building her immunity to their poison for years, giving herself tiny pricks, widely spaced apart, so she could handle them safely.

She spied a lone desiccated tree, wrapped by a withered vine, and trudged toward it, tingling with anticipation. Like jasmines, bluestar favored dead trees.

Fardan followed. "Where are you going? We already have the flower."

"I want the thorns."

She reached the tree and inspected it. Sure enough, black needles as long as her index finger rose up the vine in a menacing column. A bluestar's thorns. This must be where the unlucky stranger had found his flower. Much good it had done him.

"Are you planning to do away with the baniya?" A thoughtful tone entered Fardan's voice: "Actually, that's not a bad idea."

"Hush." She withdrew a white cloth from her potli and plucked the thorns, taking care not to touch them directly. Eighteen—not a bad haul. She wrapped them in the white cloth and tucked them in her bag. She would treat them when she had the time, converting them to poisonous little darts for her blowpipe. One thorn she would reserve for pricking herself.

"What are you going to do with them?" asked Fardan, leaning toward her with open-mouthed interest.

"Poison you." He knew about the blowpipe she'd inherited from her mother, of course. But no way was she telling him about the darts. That was her secret.

"Ha," said Fardan. "Good joke." His brow furrowed. "Wait, you're joking, aren't you?"

Her lips twitched, and she turned her footsteps south. In the distance, white salt and pale blue sky blurred until you could no longer tell which was which. But somewhere in that haze, the desert ended and the grasslands began: Banni, their home for much of the year. She drew her dupatta farther down over her head, blinking in the glare of the sun, and caught sight of a raptor circling overhead. A black vulture, drawn, no doubt, by the prospect of a feast. There would be little but bones left of the dead man by the time the rains came. Despite the heat, she shivered.

"You're going to prick yourself, right?" Fardan caught up with her. "But why do you need so many thorns? They're dangerous. I should tell Bholi," he added in a sanctimonious tone.

"Bholi Masi would sooner listen to a bleating goat than to you," said Irinya, quickening her pace across the salt flats. Overhead, another vulture joined the first. She had no desire to witness their meal.

Fardan winced. "Your aunt hates me. Why does she hate me?"

Irinya threw him an exasperated glance, half-glad of the distraction his prattle provided. "She doesn't *hate* you. She just knows you too well, you good-for-nothing rascal."

That had been his nickname since childhood when he accidentally set fire to a supply tent. He had others: useless scribbler, lazy loafer, or simply *that boy*.

"I'm no longer a good-for-nothing rascal," he protested, nearly tripping over a small black rock jutting out of the cracked earth. "I'm a fine, upstanding member of the kul."

"You're the reason the camels stampeded on the way back to the village last year," she said, extending an arm to steady him. Not that he needed her help, the lummox.

"How was I to know my flute playing would spook them?" he said, aggrieved.

"Your flute playing would spook the dead." She dropped her arm and scanned the sky. They'd left the vultures behind. Overhead and all around was only the eye-dazzling emptiness of the Rann. "And you lost a goat the one time you took them grazing."

"I was drawing! I bet she fell in love with some wild boy-goat and is now the proud mother of several kids."

Irinya bit back a grin. "That goat was eaten by wolves, and you know it."

He scowled. "I'm not cut out for herding."

"Or storytelling." Fardan's great-uncle Chinmay was the kul's story-teller, a position that guaranteed a place in the council as well as in the hearts of the people. Everyone in the kul had grown up listening to his stories. It had been his fond hope, ever since Fardan was born, that he would take his place one day. Fardan regularly dashed those hopes. "Or milking, or flute playing, or camel training."

He threw up his hands. "Flower hunting, that's my job. And I'm the best."

Boastful boy! Irinya flicked her gaze upward. "Second best to me. And Pranal, Ayush, and Jai are just as good as you."

"Are not," he said indignantly. "I found the bud of a silver spider lily."

That stopped her dead. She spun around. "Liar."

Spider lilies hadn't been seen in more than twenty years. The sul-tan's men had posted flyers in every village of Banni, offering huge rewards for a single specimen. It was every flower hunter's dream to find one—especially now, with Portuguese invaders ravaging the Mala-bar Coast and the sultanate armies scattered in defeat.

Fardan crossed his arms, his face tightening. "I'm not *lying.* Come with me and I'll show you. But you must promise not to take it. It's only a bud, and it needs a couple more days to open."

"Impossible." She shook her head, her thoughts scrambling for pur-chase. He must have made a mistake. If anyone was going to find a silver spider lily, it was *her.* "You must've seen a jasmine bud."

"You think I don't know the difference?" he countered. "I've been flower hunting since I was twelve. Five years, same as you. And I've found as many as you, too."

This was, though she hated to admit it, true. "If it's a real spider lily," she said, the enormity of it sinking into her, "it would change everything." Not just for them, but for the entire sultanate.

He dropped his arms and gave a sheepish grin. "Actually, I was thinking of leaving it there."

"What?" She couldn't believe her ears. "*Why?* We could pay off the debt of the entire kul. And the sultan could kick the Portuguese out of India."

The silver spider lily helped defeat enemies. By law, it belonged to the sultan of Gujarat, Mahmud Begada. A century ago, his great-grandfather Zafar Khan, the governor of Gujarat, had used its power to declare independence from the Delhi Sultanate and bring Kutch under his control. She was unsure of the details. Had he eaten the petals? Drunk an elixir? Brandished the flower at his enemies like a magic weapon?

The only thing that was certain was the result: the birth of the Gujarat Sultanate and its insidious expansion, year after year, into the territories that surrounded it.

But the spider lily was long gone, and the current sultan was old, sick, and dying. He'd fallen ill after his defeat by the Portuguese at the Battle of Diu last year. The palace had bought all the jasmine in the market, but the healing flower had not helped the sultan. He'd nominated his daughter, Zahra, as his heir, much to the dismay of his court and his great-nephew, Imshan Khan. Not content with being the wazir, Imshan Khan coveted the throne itself.

At least, that was what the rumors said. And rumors had a long way to travel from the booming capital of Ahmedabad to the desolate salt flats of the Rann.

Fardan shrugged, not meeting Irinya's eyes. "What do we Kutchis have to do with the sultan? Why should we help him?"

She gave him a flat stare. Kutch was nominally under the rule of the Jadeja clan chiefs, but they owed allegiance to the sultan of Gujarat. "If the sultanate falls, Kutch will not be far behind. Besides, even if you don't care about the sultanate, you care about the kul, right? The baniya would write off all our debt for a spider lily."

His mouth set in an obstinate line. "You don't know that. And my mother used to say that sometimes a flower needs to return to the earth to replenish its magic."

How would she know? Irinya nearly shouted. *She wasn't a flower hunter.*

But she didn't. Fardan had doted on his mother, had been devastated when she died of marsh fever four years ago. An extract of jasmine could have saved her. But those who hunted flowers couldn't afford to keep any for themselves, or what would they eat? Besides, it brought bad luck. Irinya had heard stories of tents burning to the ground, entire families perishing because one of them had been greedy enough, or needy enough, to keep back a flower. She thought of the lone blue petal she'd hidden in her pocket, and guilt and unease flooded her. Was she inviting misfortune by holding on to it?

"Fine," she said, pushing aside her disquiet. "Show me. If you've really found a spider lily, I'll admit you're as good as I am."

Fardan smirked. "*Better.*"

She rolled her eyes. As if she'd ever do that. It would turn out to be a jasmine bud, and she'd never let him forget his mistake. "How far is it from here?"

"An hour." He waggled his eyebrows. "Think you can manage it without passing out?"

"Shut up and walk," she snapped, wishing she'd brought more water. Her mouth was dry, her throat parched. She could barely keep her eyes open from the glare, despite the dupatta on her head. From the position of the sun, she judged it was close to one in the afternoon—the most dangerous time, when the Rann stretched in an infinity of life-sucking heat in every direction. Time for every sensible flower hunter to head home. Instead, Fardan struck out northwest, and she followed—two fools after a flower that most had given up as extinct.

If they kept up their current pace, an hour would take them farther into the Rann than she'd ever gone before. At least he appeared sure of the way. Few markers existed in the salt flats apart from the occasional desiccated tree and thorny scrub, scattered like the last survivors of an apocalypse.

But a flower hunter learned to make do with what she had. A dead tree pointing an accusing finger at the sky. A patch of scrub that concealed a single sunflower within its thorns every season. A mound that transformed into a tiny island during the monsoon. The ruins of a boat abandoned when the floodwaters retreated. These were the things that saved you when the sun was overhead, your waterskin empty, and your head throbbing from the heat. Irinya drank in the landscape, filing away in her memory every rock and scrub.

Ahead in the distance, an Agariya woman dressed in the characteristic red and yellow robes of her tribe walked with a large basket balanced on her head, going home from her family's salt pans for a midday break.

The Agariya were salt farmers. Irinya felt a kinship with them; they harvested salt and she harvested flowers. But their lives were much more difficult than hers. Gopal Masa, who was Agariya, had told her horror stories of his childhood, of summers spent under the scorching sun, leveling salt beds with his bare feet.

The hard crystals cut into the flesh, he'd said. *They rot the skin and poison the blood. It's a rare salt farmer who has a long life.*

It was a rare flower hunter who had a long life, too. The Rann was a harsh mistress. Intruders were few and far between, and she wondered anew who the dead man was, whom he worked for.

"What are you thinking?" asked Fardan, glancing at her sideways.

"The foreigner," she said. "How did he manage to get a flower?"

Fardan shrugged. "Luck? The Rann did not let him keep it."

But where there was one, more would follow. She knitted her brows. Where had he come from?

Fardan bent to peer at her face. "*Now* what are you thinking?"

She pushed him away, annoyed. "I'm thinking what a fool you are."

"I knew it." He gave a satisfied smile. "You're always thinking about me, even when you're frowning. It's my handsome face, amazing personality, and—"

"Maybe you hallucinated it," she interrupted, mainly to make him stop. "We're going to waste the entire day trying to find an imaginary flower."

His smile faded. "You want something bad enough, you can will it into being."

She laughed. "And this was what you wanted so bad? A spider lily you have no intention of harvesting?"

He was quiet for a moment. "Remember your promise to leave it alone."

"I didn't make any promise," she teased. "I'd do anything to free the kul from debt, and you know it."

He stopped and turned to her, his face taut. "I mean it, Irinya. You're not to pluck it or tell anyone else about it."

She stared at him, surprised. She'd never seen him look so serious. "I swear by salt and sun, I won't take your precious flower. Happy?"

His shoulders relaxed and he nodded. They continued without speaking, conserving their energy. Crystals crunched under their feet, and the sharp, familiar tang of salt rose in the air. In the distance, a mound of earth topped by a straggly bush resolved into view.

Fardan pointed. "It's on top of that hill."

Despite herself, excitement stirred within her as they neared the mound. She tried to tamp it down. *Probably a jasmine,* she told herself. That was why she'd been able to make such a promise so easily. A promise by salt and sun was a promise to the Rann, after all. You couldn't break it without consequences. A sharp pebble dug into her sole through her flimsy sandal, and she winced.

"Prepare to be amazed," Fardan announced with a flourish. "Need help, weakling? It's a bit steep." He extended a hand to her.

She swatted his hand away. "Don't be silly."

"Okay." He went ahead, planting one large foot after another. She gazed at them with envy. His sandals weren't in much better condition than hers, but he must have the hide of a buffalo. Nothing could blister those massive feet.

"Are you admiring my backside?" he called. "I know it's shapely, but we're in a bit of a hurry."

Her cheeks warmed. She should have been used to his ridiculous flirting by now. They'd grown up together, and he'd been like this for ages, often making her want to smack him. If not for the excellent lunches he cooked and shared with her, she might have picked Jai to hunt flowers with instead. "I'm wishing I had your thick skin," she retorted. She clambered up, using both hands to anchor herself.

Fardan was waiting for her at the top. Beside him was the bush, spiky and waist-high. She got to her feet, wiping her hands on her ghagra. "Where's your wondrous flower?"

He beckoned. "Look from this angle, right where I am."

She stood next to him and leaned over the bush. Thin black branches pricked with gray thorns spiraled up from the ground—gray thorns with hooks at the ends that she'd never seen before. Her breath caught. "I don't see the flower," she said, her voice uneven.

He placed his hands on her shoulders and gently pushed her a few inches to the right. "Look at the heart of the spiral."

She peered at it, ready to yell at him if he'd made a mistake.

He hadn't. In the middle of the spindly black branches, surrounded by a protective circle of thorns, was a silvery white half-open bud. Not small and plump like a jasmine, but long and slender like a wand. Irinya clutched Fardan's arm, dizzy with disbelief. *A spider lily.* And she'd sworn not to take it.

"Beautiful, isn't it?" he said.

Irinya found her voice. "Yes. Yes, it is. And you're going to leave it here?"

He scratched his head. "I'm pretty sure if we leave it, we'll get another next year. Maybe more than one. Wouldn't that be something?"

It would be *everything.* For them and their kul and for the whole of Gujarat.

But there was no guarantee they'd get another next year. Magical flowers followed their own inscrutable rules of growth, quite different from ordinary plants. If they didn't harvest this spider lily, they might be losing the only opportunity they'd ever have to free their kul from debt and free the sultanate from the Portuguese in one go. Worse, if Kutch got dragged into the conflict, they might not be able to even access the Rann.

"Listen, Fardan—" she began, but he interrupted her.

"No," he said, his voice flat, his face set. "We're not plucking it."

"Suppose someone else finds it?" she tried, frustration welling up inside her.

He shook his head. "Pranal, Ayush, and Jai don't come out this far. None of the flower hunters do. You'd better keep your word, Irinya, or I'll never forgive you."

"Fine, *fine*." She narrowed her eyes at him. "If we don't get another next year, though . . ."

"We will," he said with more confidence than she thought was warranted. "You'll see. Um, are you going to keep hugging me like this?"

She released his arm, irritated. "I wasn't *hugging* you. I guess you don't know what a hug is."

He gave a huge sigh. "I guess I don't. It's my motherlessness."

Irinya sniffed, her gaze going back to the graceful spider lily. "If *my* mother was alive, I would show her this flower. And she would tell me a story about it." Twelve years now, and she still ached at the loss.

Fardan's gaze softened. "You miss her, don't you?"

She shrugged, not wanting to reveal how much. "I miss her stories more than anything else." Stories she remembered word for word, when so much else about her mother had faded, as if the stories were a substitute for the real thing.

"Chinmay knows some good ones," he offered. "Like the story about the king who sold his heart for a spider lily."

"Yes," she conceded. "If only he didn't fall asleep while telling them."

Fardan chuckled. Chinmay had told them stories of every flower and variations of every story, but he was getting on in age. "You're the one who ought to inherit his post. The kids love your stories. And you're the only one who remembers them all."

She snorted. "The only person less likely than me to become a council elder is *you*."

In truth, she enjoyed the storytelling as much as the kids did. When she was telling a story, she wasn't just Irinya. She was every person who'd told the story before her. It made her feel connected to her mother, to Chinmay, and to all the storytellers who had preceded him.

Neither spoke on the journey back home. Heat shimmered above the desert, turning it now to a lake, now to lava. None of it was real.

But the spider lily had been real. She hadn't dreamed it.

CHAPTER 2

Four hours past noon, with the sun at their backs having lost none of its fierceness, they finally neared their camp. Treetops appeared in the distance, rising out of the lush grassland. Relief flooded Irinya. Already she could taste the sweetness of water on her tongue.

Fardan whooped. "Banni, beautiful Banni! Let me kiss your sweet grass and never leave again."

He said that every time they returned from the salt flats. "What'll you do, milk the cows? Churn butter? Or perhaps you prefer embroidery?" said Irinya.

"Me with my thick fingers? No, Irinya, *you* do embroidery. How much have you collected for your dowry?" He shook with laughter. Her hatred of embroidery was well-known in their kul—the group of families that migrated together across the Banni grasslands for eight months of the year and returned to their ancestral village for the four months of the monsoon.

"Enough," she answered sweetly. "And you—have you begun saving for a bride price? You'll never be able to afford a human girl. Better settle for a goat."

"Ah, but she will be the most gorgeous goat of Gujarat," proclaimed Fardan. "With long eyelashes fluttering over limpid eyes, smooth skin, and—"

"Hush," hissed Irinya. The ground beneath her aching feet softened to grass. A cluster of tents came into view, strategically placed beneath the kharijal trees that the kul depended on for food, medicine, fuel, and fodder. Camels and cows sat chewing their cud, goats nibbled the fresh green grass, and a lamb bleated, butting another.

Pranal was waiting for them under the shade of a kharijal tree. A tall, thin beanpole of a boy with round eyes and expressive hands, he'd found more jasmines than any of them in the last few years. Lately, they'd all been swooped up by the royal apothecary of Ahmedabad in a vain attempt to heal the sultan. You couldn't buy jasmine in the flower markets of Gujarat for love or money these days. Odd, how the palace persisted in exhausting the jasmine supply, as if the next flower might work when the last hundred hadn't.

Pranal waved his hands, beckoning them. "You're late. Did you find anything? I scored a jasmine! There's a stranger in the council tent who wants to speak to all the flower hunters. Bholi is on a rampage. She's going to murder you, Fardan." He spoke fast, as if afraid someone might cut him off.

"How wonderful," said Fardan bleakly. "I look forward to it."

Irinya drank the last sip of Fardan's water and passed the empty gourd back to him. Black spots danced before her eyes. "What stranger?"

"A rich one." Pranal hopped from foot to foot. "Come on; everyone's waiting."

"Don't be absurd," said Irinya. "I need to wash and eat something first or I'll pass out."

"But the stranger—"

"Can damn well wait," she snarled.

"Of course I can wait," came a mellow voice.

She whirled around.

A slim, attractive young man stood behind her, regarding her with an amused smile. He had an elegant pencil mustache, warm brown eyes, and a firm chin. Around his neck was a gold chain with a blue enamel locket. With his crisp white dhoti, richly embroidered kurta, and stylish safa adorning his head, he seemed out of place in their camp—as surprising as a flower in the desert.

His smile deepened and she realized she was staring. Her face heated and she dropped her gaze.

"Who are you?" demanded Fardan.

The stranger bowed. "Kavi Kampilya at your service. I am here on behalf of a highly placed noble in the court of Sultan Mahmud Begada, may he live forever." He spoke Kutchi fluently, with only the trace of an accent.

"Isn't the sultan dying?" Irinya blurted out, then wished she hadn't. The sultan was as mortal as any peasant, but you were supposed to pretend something as ordinary as death couldn't touch him.

The stranger did not appear offended. "We are fortunate he has ruled Gujarat for fifty years. He will live on in the hearts and minds of his people."

"We are far from the civilized court of Ahmedabad." Fardan's voice gained an edge. "What brings a sultanate nobleman to the wilds of Kutch?"

Irinya dug a warning elbow into his side. Why was he being so rude? Like it or not, Kutch was under sultanate rule. Relations between the two were peaceful, but there was no question who the overlord was. A few years ago, one of the Jadeja clan chiefs had attempted to break away and had been roundly defeated in battle by Mahmud Begada, his lands divided among the remaining chiefs. It would be dangerous to antagonize anyone representing the sultanate.

Kavi gave a self-deprecating wave. "Hardly a nobleman. I am but a messenger. As to what brings me here, I will discuss this in the council tent." His eyes lingered on Irinya, making her uncomfortably aware of her sweaty, disheveled appearance. "Please, do not hurry on my account."

He bowed again and walked away, leaving them staring at his retreating back.

Fardan scowled. "What a peacock. How did he find us?"

"He came to Bhitiara in a fancy carriage," said Pranal, naming the nearest village, a day's trek away. Bhitiara was the current source of the kul's water supply. "He asked the headman for directions to the nearest flower-hunting camp, then hired a camel and a guide."

"But why is he here?" persisted Fardan.

"We'll find out soon enough," said Irinya, though she was wondering the same thing. City folk didn't venture this close to the Rann—not unless they were after the magic flowers. But if he was from the court of the sultan, he should already have access to the best flower markets of Gujarat.

Fardan's brows knitted. "Two strangers in the space of a single day— one dead, one alive. Coincidence?"

"What? Who's dead?" demanded Pranal.

Fardan looked at Irinya and she nodded. It was okay to tell Pranal. They would have to make a full report to Miraben anyway. The matriarch of the kul would contact the baniya and arrange the sale of the bluestar.

Now was the time to come clean about the petal hidden in her pocket, before Fardan went to Miraben with the incomplete flower. But she couldn't make herself do it. The petal had *spoken* to her. And flowers never spoke without a reason.

Like the time two years ago a jasmine had urged her to *run,* and she'd obeyed. Glancing back, she'd spied a black-and-orange cloud of killer wasps right where she'd been standing. The jasmine had saved her from being stung, perhaps from dying. She was going to keep the petal until she understood why she needed it.

"We found a bluestar in a dead man's hand," Fardan told Pranal, not a trace of levity on his face. "A *foreigner.*" Pranal gaped at him, speechless for once.

"I'll see you in the council tent." Irinya walked away, leaving Fardan to give Pranal the gory details of their find. She was dirty, tired, and hot. Seeing that city man in his pristine clothes had made her feel even shabbier in comparison. She longed for a drink, a bath, and fresh clothes. She headed for the tent she shared with her aunt and uncle—a simple affair of cotton canvas held up by wooden poles that sheltered the family's quilts, rugs, camel saddles, and pots and pans—and stopped short.

Bholi Masi was standing outside, blocking the entrance, glaring at her out of narrowed eyes. Her heart-shaped lips were pressed together in a grim line, and her thick ebony hair was falling out of its bun.

Irinya summoned her meekest expression and approached her aunt. Irinya wasn't short, but Bholi stood half a head taller than her and twice as wide—all of it muscle, she was fond of boasting.

Before Irinya could speak, Bholi Masi grabbed her shoulders and shook her. "Two hours late! You really have a gift for making me worry. What do you have to say for yourself?"

Irinya opened her cracked lips. "I'm dying for a drink."

Bholi unslung a waterskin from her shoulder and thrust it at her. "Don't gulp it down all at once."

Irinya removed the stopper and took a few reviving swallows.

"Help with the animals and do embroidery like the normal girls of our kul. Leave flower hunting to the boys. Again and again I tell you this, but do you listen?" grumbled Bholi, flicking aside the tent flap and pushing Irinya inside, barely giving her time to remove her sandals. Gopal Masa, hunched over a camel saddle in one corner of the tent, raised his head and gave Irinya a conspiratorial wink. She suppressed a grin. Her uncle knew it was pointless to say such things to her. She was a flower hunter both by choice and by necessity. How else could she dream of paying down the kul's debt?

"And why should you listen, when your mother never did?" Bholi continued, forcing Irinya to sit on a small wooden stool and unraveling her foot wraps. "Look at the state of your feet!" She squatted before Irinya and kneaded them one by one, her touch deft and sure, soothing the tired muscles. Her tone became wistful. "Urmila used to find a bluestar, a hibiscus, or a pansy every season."

A familiar tightness gripped Irinya's chest. Her mother, Urmila, had been the best flower hunter in the kul for generations. She'd known the Rann better than anyone else. Maybe that was why the Rann had taken her. She'd gone into the salt flats one misty night and never returned. Even children knew better than to stray too far from the campfire at night. As for those rare evenings when mist swirled above the ground, children weren't allowed out of the tents at all. The mist blurred the edges of the world, making everything unreal, creating monsters out of your worst fears. It was too easy to lose your way, to be lured by Chir Batti, the ghost light, to your doom.

But thinking of this only brought pain. One day, Irinya would be a better flower hunter than her mother had been. "We found a bluestar," she said.

Bholi dropped Irinya's feet and leaned toward her, wide-eyed. "What did you say?"

"We found a bluestar," Irinya repeated.

"A bluestar?" said Bholi, to confirm.

"Yes."

Bholi clasped her hands over her bosom. "Praise be! The goddess has not forgotten us. Perhaps this will get the baniya off our backs for a bit. He's been demanding hibiscus and bluestar for the military for months now."

Irinya had seen a flower that could end the war in days. She wished she hadn't promised Fardan she wouldn't take it; but then, he might not have shown it to her. Perhaps there was some truth to what he believed, and flowers needed to return to the earth to replenish the Rann's magic. But how could he choose to withhold *this* flower that could lift their kul from poverty and save countless men from dying? "What difference will a bluestar make?" she muttered, thinking, *It's not fair.* He'd found the spider lily, yes, but it shouldn't be solely his decision whether to pluck it.

"Every petal makes a difference," countered Bholi. Guilt stabbed Irinya anew at the thought of the petal she'd hidden. "Forces allied to the sultanate are fighting the Portuguese all down the Malabar Coast. The commanders want bluestar to protect themselves and hibiscus to control their men—or their enemies, in case they're caught. Prices have gone through the roof." Her gaze became steely. "But I'd rather have you safe and sound than have a bluestar. You were out in the heat for *hours.* You want to die and leave me all alone?"

"You have Gopal Masa," Irinya pointed out, getting up and wetting a rag with some precious water from an earthen pot to scrub her face and hands. A proper wash would have to wait until the weekly supply camel returned from Bhitiara.

"*Him?*" Bholi Masi snorted. "He spends half his time asleep and the other half playing pachisi and drinking hariya with the other useless men of this kul."

"I'm right here," said Gopal Masa in an injured tone, looking up from the camel saddle he was mending. A thin, sad-eyed man with a drooping gray mustache, Irinya's uncle had taught her more about the Rann than anyone else.

"But you may as well not be," said Bholi Masi. "Irinya, promise me you will not go to the Rann again without my permission."

Irinya peered at her aunt. "I promise, as long as you promise not to try to stop me." Gopal Masa chuckled.

"Irinya!" Bholi Masi's thick eyebrows drew together.

"Masi, you must know there's a stranger from the court of the sultan here to speak with the flower hunters. I should go."

Irinya grabbed a clean ghagra choli and ducked into a partitioned area of the tent. As she changed, her aunt continued to berate her. It was a familiar sound, as soothing as monsoon rain. She let it wash over her as she transferred the iridescent blue petal from one pocket to another, pausing to admire its sheen. *Thief,* said her conscience. *It's just one petal,* she told it, combing her hair. *It won't make a dent in our debt.* Still, her conscience continued to complain. She'd never kept anything from her aunt before. Or Fardan, for that matter. She couldn't shake the feeling that she was doing something wrong—something she would have to pay for. Still, the jasmine had saved her by telling her to run. Perhaps the bluestar petal would save her, too, in some way.

Did she look presentable now? She uncovered a pot of water to check her reflection. A skinny, dark-skinned girl with overlarge eyes, a long nose, and a pointed chin stared back at her. Striking, perhaps, but not pretty at all—not to someone who was used to the beauties of the sultan's court.

Her face warmed and she covered the pot, annoyed with herself. She'd never been bothered about her lack of prettiness before. Had the arrival of a handsome stranger from the capital unhinged her? What did it matter what she looked like? She was an accomplished flower hunter and a secret blowpipe expert. That was the important thing. She slipped out of the partitioned area, prepared to escape the tent.

But Bholi Masi blocked her with a speed that belied her size. "Eat something first; the stranger will not leave before tomorrow at the earliest."

She thrust a bowl of khichdi and yogurt into Irinya's hands. And although Irinya chafed at the delay, she was grateful for the food and felt better once it was inside her.

— ⚡ —

The communal tent was roomy and colorful, the floor covered with worn rugs, the walls decorated with richly embroidered wall hangings donated by the women of the kul. This was where the men held their "meetings," which meant it was where they played pachisi. But it was also where Miraben settled disputes and welcomed guests along with the rest of her council.

Not that they'd ever had a guest as distinguished as this one. For all his protests that he was no noble, Kavi was the closest thing to royalty any of them had ever seen. He sat straight-backed and graceful in the center of the tent, reeking of courtly wealth and power. Fifteen men and women surrounded him, gazing at him with avid eyes. Irinya, who was the last to enter, sat near the draft of air at the entrance.

Miraben, a stout, gray-haired woman in her sixties with piercing black eyes, sat on a cushion in the place of honor with her son, Vimal, on her right, and her husband, Devesh, on her left. Next to Devesh was the council of elders: Rishabh, the kul's recordkeeper; Shweta, the healer; Tammi, the priestess; and Fardan's great-uncle Chinmay, the storyteller.

Vimal had been a flower hunter in his teens, but he'd grown out of it. Most boys did if they wished to live beyond their twenties. Now he was the kul's chief camel herder, a task he performed with stolid competence, mostly by ensuring that Fardan was nowhere near them with his flute.

A few other former flower hunters were present who stuck to herding these days as a safer occupation. Apart from Irinya, the only active hunters in the kul were Fardan, Jai, Pranal, and Ayush. They didn't venture into the salt flats every day; that would have been inviting an early death. They went twice a week at most, and never alone, but in pairs or threes. Those were the rules—always had been, even when flowers were not so scarce. There was plenty to do in the camp on the days they didn't hunt flowers: foraging for berries, gathering firewood, mending tents and clothes, cleaning equipment, caring for the animals. Irinya didn't love it the way she loved going into the Rann, but she did her fair share—unlike Fardan, who got out of chores by doing them so badly that no one asked for his help more than once.

Jai, a stocky young man with a broad face and pugnacious chin, was the eldest of the flower hunters at twenty. He was the calmest of the lot, and the others listened to him, although Fardan often took the lead when it came to flower hunting. Ayush, Pranal's brother, was the youngest at fifteen. Short and slight, with bright eyes and a mischievous smile, he sat between Jai and Pranal, leaning forward in anticipation. Like everyone else, his eyes were glued to Kavi.

Kavi inclined his head at Irinya. "Thank you for coming. I trust you have eaten something?"

Everyone turned to look at her. She flushed under their combined scrutiny. "Er, yes."

"You were out in the desert for several hours," he continued. "Did you see anything interesting?"

Her gaze went to Fardan, sitting across from her. He gave her a lopsided grin. They'd seen multiple things of interest, but only one was safe to reveal. She wouldn't give away the silver spider lily, and they couldn't bring up the dead man, not in front of a stranger from the sultanate. It would invite scrutiny and lead to questions, perhaps even an investigation.

"We found a bluestar," she said. "The first we've seen in two years."

Kavi gave her a warm smile. "I have been told. That is a rare find indeed, even with a petal missing. It is of greater value when it's whole, of course."

"You two sure you didn't tear a petal off by mistake?" Miraben frowned at them.

Irinya swallowed. The sneaky petal was in her pocket. Was guilt written on her face?

"Of course not," said Fardan indignantly. "What do you take us for?"

"Fardan Hajani, I trust you as far as I can throw you," pronounced Miraben. "Be happy Irinya was there at the time."

Irinya's chest tightened. How quick Fardan was to defend her. He wouldn't dream she'd withhold a petal from the kul. None of them would. How would they react if they knew what she'd done? Their belief in her would be shattered.

Fardan scowled and muttered something under his breath.

"What did you say?" Miraben cupped a hand to her ear. "Speak louder."

"He said, 'I found the bluestar, you decrepit old crone,'" said Pranal helpfully. Ayush sniggered.

Miraben's face swelled, and she opened her mouth to lambast the cowering Fardan.

Kavi cleared his throat. "If I may, I'd like to begin, now that all the flower hunters of the kul are here. You have so far found three jasmines and one bluestar this season, correct?"

"Yes," said Fardan, looking relieved at the shift in conversation. "Last year, we scored four jasmines, a sunflower, and a rose—barely enough to make the baniya's minimum quota of six to eight flowers, depending on the variety."

"How much do you get for a jasmine?" asked Kavi.

"Two silver tankas is the going rate," said Miraben. "But sometimes, if a family is desperate, the baniya gives only one tanka and a few jital. He doesn't actually *give* us any silver coins. Most of what we earn goes toward paying down debt. In bad years, he lends us money to buy grain so we do not starve."

Kavi frowned. "You each deal with the baniya individually? Do you not see how this works against you? The baniya can say, 'I will only buy one flower, and I cannot pay more than one tanka. If you don't give me the flower for this price, I will go to this other person in the kul, who will.'"

They were silent. This was a scenario that had played out in the past, although flowers were rare enough now that it was impossible to imagine having two of the same kind at the same time.

"By dealing with the baniya in this way you are allowing him to set the price," Kavi continued. "You are giving him power. Why not sell your flowers directly to those who need them?"

Irinya pursed her lips. He spoke as if it was a simple solution. And in an ideal world, it would have been. But if they didn't pay the baniya with their flowers, he had the legal right to seize all their possessions, including their precious herds. Without their herds, who were they? No longer nomads, for sure. They traded the milk, butter, and wool from their animals for grain, oil, and pulses. If the animals were gone, they could not survive in the grasslands. They'd struggle to find enough food to eat. It would be the end of flower hunting. They would be forced to settle in their ancestral village—a thought that filled her with dismay. In the village, she was just another girl who milked cows and churned butter. In the Rann, she was a botanical expert.

Around her, she saw similar thoughts reflected on everyone's somber faces.

"We are in the baniya's debt," said Miraben heavily. "My mother was in *his* father's debt. It has been so for three generations, ever since my grandmother had to take a loan to pay the land revenue. That was a bad year for the kul. Sickness took half our herds and drought took the rest." Her face twisted. "But the revenue collector does not care for such things."

Kavi nodded. "I understand. But by selling your valuable flowers for a few miserable tankas, you are ensuring that you and your descendants will always be in debt, always be poor. You live difficult lives. You face danger every time you venture into the desert. And all to fill the coffers of a greedy, unscrupulous middleman who won't even blink if you die."

The truth of his words stabbed Irinya. "What else are we to do?" she demanded. "We must keep paying the baniya. Besides, we're nomads. This is where we belong. Who else could we sell the flowers to?"

Kavi's eyes glinted. "This is where I come in. I told you I represent a noble in the court of the sultan—someone very *close* to the sultan. It was his idea to deal directly with the flower hunters. He knows something of the hardship you people face. He suggested that you form a cooperative."

Irinya knitted her brows at the strange word. "What's that?"

"Exactly what it says. You *cooperate* instead of compete." Kavi held up his hand and spread his fingers. "This is you, as five individuals. Weak, easily broken." He closed his hand into a fist. "Together, you're strong."

"You mean, we all beat the baniya until he gives us a better price?" Pranal scratched his cheek. "He has bodyguards. *Big* ones."

Kavi gave a tiny sigh. "I do not advocate violence unless you act in self-defense. But as a cooperative, the five of you will collectively own the products of your labor. *You* set the price, together. You deal with your buyer as a single entity, not as five separate people."

Vimal cleared his throat. "Can it only be five people? Suppose someone else wants to join?" Miraben glared at him. But some of the other ex–flower hunters perked up as well.

"Membership should be open to all active flower hunters," said Kavi. "That is only fair. Current members can decide the rules for admitting new ones. But it's not enough if only your kul does this. Each kul should have a cooperative, and you can all set similar prices. The baniya will have no choice but to meet your terms."

Vimal rubbed his chin, looking thoughtful. Irinya knew they were all weighing the risks and benefits of going back to the Rann.

"What will we do when the baniya demands his flowers?" asked Miraben.

"Please discard from your minds the absurd notion that the flowers are *his*," said Kavi. "They are not. All flowers that you collect belong to your cooperative. The baniya can bid on them, but I doubt he will match my price. I will give you the rate he gets from the apothecaries in Ahmedabad. And you can use that money to pay down your debt."

Ah. So he *did* want the flowers, and he wanted to bypass the middlemen. Did he have the approval of the court, or was he acting out of his own self-interest? Did this mean a shift in the way flowers would be bought and sold in the future? "How much would you give for a jasmine?" asked Irinya, more to test him than anything else.

He smiled. "Half a gold mohur."

Everyone gaped at him. Irinya's head reeled. "You're joking." A gold mohur was equivalent to fifteen silver tankas or five cows.

He shook his head. "Joking's the furthest thing from my mind. An untreated jasmine goes for half a gold mohur in Ahmedabad's Khaas Bazaar. A hibiscus or a rose is worth four gold mohurs. A bluestar—well, it's negotiable, and the one you have is incomplete, but still. I would say six or seven gold mohurs at least."

These were riches beyond dreams. No one in their kul had seen a gold mohur. Even silver tankas were rare. They dealt in the lowly jital: copper coins with just a trace of silver in them.

"We could pay all our debts," said Miraben in a tone of wonder.

Excitement rippled through the tent. "It would be a fresh start," said Chinmay, rubbing his hands. "At my age, a fresh start!"

"We'll be rich," said Vimal happily.

"What's in it for you?" Fardan asked Kavi, a note of challenge in his voice. "You're not doing this out of charity."

Exactly what Irinya had been about to ask him. She studied their visitor. Would he feel insulted by the question?

But Kavi chuckled, not appearing in the least put out. "I get an assured supply of authentic flowers for the palace apothecary."

"You are acting on behalf of the palace?" asked Irinya.

"My employer is, yes," said Kavi. "You have no idea how many brokers try to pass off ordinary flowers as magical ones, even when dealing with the palace."

"They deserve to hang," said Miraben with rare venom. Unlike ordinary flowers, the magical flowers of the Rann stayed fresh for months and weren't as fragile. There were subtle differences in the shape and length of the petals and sepals. Beyond that, there were chemical tests to identify each magic flower, which could be preserved for decades by drying and pressing. But unscrupulous con men always found the greedy or the desperate to prey on.

A hard look entered Kavi's eyes. "The ones who are caught are executed; you can be sure of that. Now, more than ever, we must be careful that the flowers we use are genuine."

"Because of the Portuguese," said Irinya. "Right?"

He nodded. "If we'd had a silver spider lily, we'd never have lost Diu to them last year."

Goose bumps prickled Irinya's skin. *We have a spider lily now.* She looked at Fardan, but his face betrayed nothing. Diu was an island off the southern coast of Gujarat. It had been one of the sultanate's most important ports before they lost it to the Portuguese.

"If we had more jasmine, we could heal our soldiers of their wounds," continued Kavi. "Green rose would help our commanders communicate with the front line. The pansy would give us wealth to buy supplies needed by the army. The palace needs trustworthy flower hunters—not middlemen who fatten their purses at the expense of the poor. Now, do we have an agreement? You will be paid from the royal treasury. I am not, you understand, carrying vast sums of money on my person, but I can give you an advance for the bluestar and the jasmine." He removed a soft leather pouch from his belt, undid its strings, and withdrew a large gold coin from it. "I trust this is acceptable?" He leaned forward and placed the coin before Miraben.

Nobody moved. The gold coin shone brighter than the sun itself. It spoke of royal mints in distant lands, of elegant nobles in aristocratic courts, and of foreign ships tossing on strange seas, their holds full of spices and silk.

"Why us?" Irinya tore her gaze away from the gold mohur. "Why not some other flower-hunting kul?"

"So suspicious." His lips twitched. "You're the first one I found. I do plan to visit a few more to talk about setting up cooperatives."

"How do we know you're who you say you are?" Fardan demanded.

Kavi raised his eyebrows. "I will bring a letter stamped with the royal seal when I return with the rest of your money. Hopefully, that should remove the last of your doubts. Come, I'm on *your* side. This is an opportunity. Seize it!"

Miraben's mottled hand closed over the gold coin, and a cheer went up. Vimal pumped a fist into the air. Pranal, Ayush, and Jai clapped each other's backs. Only Fardan still looked unconvinced, a slight frown marring his face. But Irinya couldn't help the rush of hope flooding into her heart. Kavi had answered all their questions with sincerity. And there was that gold coin, irrefutable proof of his good intentions.

Kavi gave Irinya a conspiratorial smile, and something sparked between them, like summer lightning in the Rann. It made her feel like running out of the tent and submerging herself in a cold stream.

Given that the only water body close by was a stagnant green ditch, she contented herself with giving him a stiff nod and leaving the tent. The evening sun shone into her eyes, as if trying to burn away the spell his words had cast.

But she barely noticed the glare. She spent the rest of the evening imagining the rosy future while stitching her clandestine blue petal into a corner of her dupatta. It didn't matter that she'd sworn not to take the spider lily or kept a bluestar petal for herself. With the prices Kavi was offering, her kul would be free of debt within a couple of years. They wouldn't need to take loans from the moneylender ever again. They might even be able to use some of the flowers themselves. To heal your loved ones with tincture of jasmine, find lost things with a sip of sunflower tea, or speak to someone far away using rose vapor—it was the stuff of dreams. And only the rich could afford to dream.

But suppose that changed? Suppose the stories that it was bad luck to use the flowers you plucked were only that—stories designed to keep flower hunters in poverty?

That night, the kul held a communal feast under the starry sky in
honor of their new patron. To Irinya's delight, the supply camel from
Bhitiara showed up a day early, laden with water, grain, oil, and pulses.
Bholi got an extra pot of water, which Irinya finagled for her own use.
She washed in the partitioned area of the tent, using a bit of their precious soapberry essence to scrub a week's worth of salt and grime out
of her skin and hair. As she detangled her hair with a wooden comb, she
wondered what women in Ahmedabad used to clean and groom themselves. Of course, they lived in proper houses in a city. They probably
didn't get dirty in the first place.

"Are you dreaming, Irinya? I need help crushing the berries," called
Bholi Masi.

"Coming." Irinya tied her hair in a knot, soaked the week's dirty
clothes in the remaining water, and emerged, feeling fresh and clean.

Bholi Masi peered at her from behind an enormous pile of purple
berries. "You look nice. It's time to think of your marriage."

She'd been saying that for years. "And who will help you make phalsa
juice when I'm gone?" Irinya dumped a handful of berries onto a thin
cotton cloth. She would crush them and strain the juice into an earthen
pot. It was hard, time-consuming work, which was why phalsa juice
was reserved for festive occasions.

"You don't have to *go* anywhere; you could bring a husband to the
kul, like I did." Bholi gave her a beady-eyed look. "You're not thinking
of settling for that useless scribbler, are you?"

Did she mean *Fardan*? Irinya gazed at her, astonished, and broke
into helpless laughter. They were childhood friends and flower-hunting
partners, and she couldn't imagine life without him. But neither could
she imagine being married to him. They would squabble all the time.
"Masi, don't be silly. There's nothing like that between us."

Her aunt let out a deep breath, shoulders relaxing. "There better not
be. He's terrible marriage material. Even Miraben thinks so."

"I don't see what Miraben has to do with my marriage." Irinya
squeezed the berries and watched the purple juice trickle into the pot
with satisfaction. "I don't see what *anyone* has to do with it. My mother
didn't marry."

Bholi stared down at her hands. "We don't know that. Maybe she
did."

Irinya held her tongue. Her mother had run away from the kul when she was seventeen—Irinya's age—and returned a year later, pregnant and unrepentant. She never told anyone what happened or who the father was. Once, when Irinya asked about him, she laughed and said the sky was her father, the desert her mother. *And you?* Irinya had asked. *Who are you?*

Your guardian, her mother had answered, swooping down and kissing the top of her head.

It was a good memory, and Irinya held it close. She had so few of them, apart from the stories. Her mother had often been absent, flower hunting in the Rann. When Irinya was five, she'd vanished forever into the salt flats she loved so much. Irinya had waited for her, sitting at the edge of the grassland, refusing to move, until she fainted and had to be carried inside.

That was not a good memory, and she pushed it aside. *Some guardian you turned out to be.*

When they had finished crushing and straining all the berries, she carried the pot of phalsa juice to the communal tent, where it would be stored until feast time. The solid remnants of the berries would be fermented or fed to the cows. Nothing was ever wasted.

Dusk darkened the sky, and the first stars peeped out. "A clear night," pronounced Miraben, peering out of the tent. "No fear of Chir Batti, right, Irinya?"

Irinya placed the pot of juice on the floor of the tent and straightened, smiling. "None at all."

Ever since she was a child, Irinya had been able to sense the ghost light before anyone else in the kul. Even on clear nights, long before mist rolled in to dim the sight and cloud the mind, she could stand at the edge of the salt flats and judge whether it was safe to be out. Tonight was safe, and it was a full moon—a fine night to celebrate.

Fardan and Pranal made a bonfire of dead wood, and the children laid woolen rugs in a large circle around it. Men brought out pots of their best hariya, fermented from the sweet, peppery fruits of the khar-ijal tree.

The women had made stacks of rotlas to be served with jungli ja-lebi chutney and freshly churned butter. There were karonda and ker pickles, boiled kharijal leaves, and a huge pot of spicy dal, cooked by Miraben herself. Orange rashbhari, golden yellow khirni, and dark, sweet, melt-in-your-mouth khajur glistened in mouth-watering mounds before the fire.

As the guest, Kavi was served first, his leaf plate heaped with food, his protestations that it was too much ignored. After him, it was Miraben's turn, and then the four council elders. Once the elders had been served, Irinya helped herself to a plate of food and a cup of her hard-earned phalsa juice. She sat with the other girls of the kul, watching Kavi.

He didn't look her way. And why would he? He was surrounded by the kul elders. Chinmay was telling him a story of how the jasmine defeated Black Death. His once-rich voice had a quaver in it, and he had to pause to remember the right words, but Kavi listened with perfect attention and courtesy.

Saira, who was Bholi Masi's cousin's daughter, nudged her with an elbow. "He's so polished, isn't he? Not like our boys."

"He's a city man," said Irinya drily. "Probably never done a hard day's work in his life."

He glanced at her, as if he'd heard what she said over the din, and he gave her that same conspiratorial smile, like they shared a secret. Her stomach flipped.

Stop it, she told herself, staring at her plate. *He'll be gone tomorrow.*

Saira prattled on next to her. Irinya didn't hear a word, and she barely tasted the food on her plate.

Chinmay finished his story of the jasmine and launched into another of how Chir Batti protected the Rann from demons of the underworld. When he was done, Kavi clapped, making him flush with pleasure. "I am an old man now," Chinmay said with a sigh, "and my voice is not what it was. One of these youngsters will soon replace me." And he looked, not at Fardan, but at Irinya. He winked, nearly making her drop her plate. She bowed to the elderly storyteller, suppressing a grin. His hopes for Fardan must be well and truly dead if he was looking at *her* to succeed him. She'd certainly be better at it than Fardan, although that wasn't saying much.

The storyteller's post was an important one; the entire kul had to reach a consensus on who would fill it. Irinya wasn't sure she was the right person for the job, or whether she wanted that kind of responsibility. But she did love both listening to stories and telling them, giving them little tweaks of her own. And she was the only person in the kul who had memorized Chinmay's hundreds of stories, as well as the ones she'd heard from her mother. The kul could do worse than pick her for the job. It gave her a warm glow that Chinmay thought she was worthy of consideration.

Jai, Pranal, and Ayush joined the group around Kavi, peppering him with questions. Fardan hung back but sat close enough to listen. *Still suspicious,* thought Irinya, exasperated. Perhaps he would thaw once Kavi returned with a letter stamped with the royal seal. Even Fardan would not be able to argue with that.

Kavi answered their questions with an easy air, but he didn't talk much about himself. He talked instead of the beautiful city of Ahmedabad, with its gardens, lakes, and palatial buildings. He described the fortifications of the city, the carvings on the many gates, the bastions and battlements for its defense, the stately mosques within its walls, the sights and sounds of Khaas Bazaar, and the broad, tree-lined streets, crowded with people and palanquins. Listening to him, a longing took hold of Irinya to see Ahmedabad for herself. She loved the Rann, of course, and she loved nights like these out on the open grassland, when the moon appeared so big it might swallow the sky.

But the arrival of Kavi had, for the first time, made her yearn for something more.

CHAPTER 3

The baniya showed up the next morning like a piece of bad news. Irinya was hanging clothes out to dry on a loonuk bush when she heard raised voices from the direction of the communal tent. She flicked a wet blouse over a woody stem and hurried over.

A crowd had formed outside the tent. In the middle of the circle was the baniya: a portly, middle-aged man with a shiny forehead, dressed in a pristine white dhoti and cream-colored shirt. Behind him stood his two clerks, Harpal and Lattu: beefy, scowling men who doubled as his bodyguards.

"What do you mean, there are no flowers?" he shouted. "My men heard talk of a bluestar."

Irinya's heart sank. Someone must have talked to the man from Bhitiara last night. The baniya had wasted no time in rushing over.

"Sorry, Mahajan-ji, but we have sold it already," said Miraben with iron calm.

The baniya recoiled as if she had slapped him. "How dare you." His voice shook with outrage. "I've been asking you for bluestar for *months*. How dare you sell my flowers to someone else?"

"They're not your flowers." Miraben jutted out her chin and glared at him. "They're *ours*."

Around them, the men and women of the kul murmured agreement, their faces defiant. Kavi's offer had given them the courage to resist the baniya. Irinya wanted to applaud, even as her throat tightened with anxiety.

The baniya mopped his forehead with a silk scarf. "After all I've done for you, all my family has done for you, it has come to this. It is as my father said. The more concessions I give you people, the more ungrateful you become. Have you forgotten your debt? Each one of you owes me more money than you could earn in your miserable lives. How can you say the flowers do not belong to me? Did I not pay for the wedding of your niece the winter before last? Three years ago, when drought killed the grass and your cows were starving, did I not arrange for fodder and water? Last year, when you didn't have enough to pay the revenue collector, was it not I who gave you the missing amount?"

Miraben opened her mouth to speak and hesitated. Irinya's blood boiled. The worst thing about the baniya was how he pretended to be their benefactor when he was nothing but a leech. "You *gave* us nothing," she snapped, unable to hold herself back. "You lent us money at the same high rate of interest you have always done." Opposite her, Fardan gave an approving nod, a grim smile on his face. Bholi Masi frantically shook her head and put a finger to her lips. Irinya pretended not to see her.

"Two percent a month!" The baniya scoffed at her. "You call that high? In the city, my brother lends money to nobles at twice that rate." He rounded back on the matriarch of the kul. "Shame on you, Miraben, for turning on your patron."

"No, Mahajan. Shame on *you* for cheating this kul for so many years." Kavi's voice, quiet and cold, cut through the baniya's words like a blade. He stepped out of the crowd, looking as handsome and graceful as if he'd stepped out of a carriage on his way to a dance performance.

Harpal and Lattu glowered at him. "Watch that tongue, or we'll pull it out," snarled Harpal. Kavi gave him a chilly smile.

Irinya's heart gave a little swoop of fear for Kavi's safety, even as she admired his courage. She crossed her arms, trying to slow her pulse. Why was she afraid for him? He was a stranger whom she'd met for the first time yesterday. They'd barely exchanged a few sentences. But the thought of him being harmed by the baniya's men was unbearable.

"Are you the thief?" the baniya bit out, glaring at him. "Hand it over."

"Certainly not," said Kavi, his voice steady, his jaw set. "I've given them an advance, and it's mine."

"We'll see about that." The baniya snapped his fingers. "Get him," he ordered his men. Irinya's stomach seized. Before she could throw herself between them and drag Kavi to safety, Fardan and Jai broke out of the circle and blocked the men.

"He is our guest; you will not harm him," said Fardan, his eyes blazing with anger. Irinya's throat went dry. Thank goodness for his muscular build. Even the bodyguard-clerks would think twice before trying to tackle him. Still, her nerves thrummed with fear. Fardan and Jai were tough enough to win a fistfight, but suppose the men had knives? And Kavi didn't look strong enough to take a single blow, let alone land one.

"Have you all taken leave of your senses?" shouted the baniya. "You have been fooled by this stranger; he has filled your ears against me. I will complain about this; see if I don't. The law is on my side. And when the revenue collector shows up next year, don't come begging to me for help."

"They won't," said Kavi calmly. "I will pay them enough for their flowers that they won't need to borrow money ever again."

"Is that so?" the baniya sneered. "And what of their debt? I *own* them. And I will have my bluestar." He turned to his clerks. "What are you waiting for?"

Harpal and Lattu advanced, and Irinya tensed. Fardan and Jai fell into defensive stances in front of Kavi.

"Wait," said Kavi, and such was the power of his voice that the men stopped. He placed a hand on Fardan's shoulder and moved him aside. "Wouldn't you like to know the name of my patron?" Without waiting for a response, he said, "Malik Ayyaz, the most formidable captain of the west coast. Perhaps his name means something to your provincial ears?"

Wonder bloomed in Irinya, warm and fluttery. Kavi had said he represented a powerful noble close to the sultan. But she hadn't dreamed it was Malik Ayyaz, the governor of Junagadh and Diu, and the sultan's right-hand man. Around her, everyone murmured in astonishment and awe. It was Malik Ayyaz who had led the sultan's forces against the Portuguese in Diu. They had learned this in their travels across Kutch the previous year. Traders and soldiers had passed through their village, carrying tales of his daring and prowess in battle. He might have lost Diu, but he was still revered, not just in Gujarat but across the subcontinent. What other surprises did Kavi have up his embroidered sleeve?

The baniya's jaw dropped and his eyes widened. "You're lying." He mopped his forehead again and darted a look sideways, as if seeking escape.

"Try it," said Kavi, unsmiling. "See what happens to you, your brother, and your entire family if you lay hands on me."

"What of their debt?" demanded the baniya. "Not even your patron can deny that I own every stitch of clothing, every utensil, every—"

"I will buy their debt from you," interrupted Kavi. "Go to the governor's office in Junagadh and ask for the sarraf Amal Baderiya. I will send instructions to him. Make sure you bring all the paperwork."

A susurrus went through the crowd at his words. Miraben's hand flew to her mouth. Fardan and Jai stared at Kavi, their faces incredulous. Irinya clutched herself, light-headed. All her life, she had dreamed of freeing her kul from the baniya, even while knowing how impossible it was, no matter how many precious flowers she found.

I will buy their debt from you. With that one sentence, Kavi had turned everything upside down. How could he afford to make such an offer? Did he hold that much power in the governor's office?

"Junagadh is a journey of at least two weeks," carped the baniya.

Kavi raised his eyebrows. "Ahmedabad is midway between here and Junagadh, and surely you have business there several times a year. It will be well worth your while. You'll get everything you're owed. Unless . . . that's not what you really want?"

"What do you mean?" The baniya licked his lips, and Irinya almost felt sorry for him. He'd been a fixture all her life, and yet, what a small and unimportant man he was in the big scheme of things. He was being cut down to size in front of the very people he'd bullied, each one of whom was watching the exchange with avid eyes. Chinmay's lips were moving soundlessly, as if he was memorizing the conversation for a future story. Miraben had a fierce grin on her face that was more like a snarl. Of them all, she'd suffered the most, having to deal directly with the baniya and his demands. Only Fardan still had a frown on his face, as if he couldn't quite grasp what was going on.

"The flowers are an important source of income for you, are they not?" Kavi gave the moneylender an appraising look. "You buy them for next to nothing and sell them at a huge profit in the markets of Ahmedabad. I'm guessing this is how you sustain your loan-making to the nobility. A risky endeavor, but one with rich rewards. I wonder what my patron would find were he to order an audit into your accounts."

The baniya was sweating heavily now. "He has no jurisdiction."

"No?" Kavi's voice hardened. "He has the ear of the sultan."

"What do you want?" the baniya burst out. "Why are you doing this?"

"All I want is to buy flowers at a fair price, and for you to leave this kul alone." Kavi spread his hands. "Why make it difficult?"

This kul, as if it was special to him. It gave Irinya goose bumps, even though he'd said this just happened to be the first kul he'd visited.

The baniya directed a hate-filled glare at him. "Come on, you louts, let's go," he muttered to his henchmen. As they walked away, a collective sigh of relief went through the kul. Jai pumped his fist, and the elders embraced each other, half weeping, half laughing. Irinya's knees wanted to buckle.

"Go after them," said Kavi in a low voice to Fardan. "Make certain they leave."

Fardan hesitated and caught Irinya's gaze, his brow furrowed. Why was he hesitating? Did he still not trust Kavi, even after the way he'd stood up to the baniya on their behalf? *Go,* she mouthed. He gave a small grimace but obeyed. Pranal, Jai, and Ayush followed him.

Miraben found her voice. "Thank you, Kampilya-ji." She walked toward Kavi and held her hands out, gazing at him with soft eyes as if he was their savior. The council elders gathered around her.

Irinya understood how she felt. Weren't they all feeling the same? She blinked back tears, surprised at herself, at the depth of emotion roiling within her. They'd never have to deal with the baniya and his underlings again. They'd pay off their debt to Kavi and finally be free. *Free.* She wiped her eyes with her dupatta, smiling.

Kavi clasped Miraben's outstretched hands. "Please call me Kavi," he said warmly. "You are my elder."

She cleared her throat, as if she found it hard to speak. "This calls for another celebration."

"You do me too much honor," said Kavi, dropping her hands and giving a modest bow. "It is my own self-interest that brought me here. My self-interest happens to match with yours, that is all."

"That is not all," said Miraben, her voice heavy with emotion. "You have come into our lives like rain after years of drought. If there is anything we can do to show our gratitude, anything at all, please tell us."

"Yes," said Tammi the priestess, making the sign of blessing with her right palm facing out. "It would be our honor to fulfill any wish of yours."

Kavi straightened and gave a hesitant smile. "I do have a small request, but I don't want to inconvenience you in any way."

"Speak," said Miraben, waving an imperious hand.

"I would like to visit the Rann," said Kavi in a rush, as if embarrassed at his request. "I have heard it is beautiful, especially at sunset and sunrise, and I wish to see it before I return to Ahmedabad."

A surprised silence greeted his words, and everyone stared at him.

"Visit the Rann," Miraben repeated in an uncertain voice, as if she hadn't heard right.

Rishabh, the kul's recordkeeper, scratched his head. "Only flower hunters and salt farmers venture into the Rann. It's too dangerous."

But it made perfect sense to Irinya. What had they to offer him but this? "I'll take you," she said, before anyone else could.

Heads swiveled to her. Bholi Masi's face swelled like a thundercloud. "One of the boys—" began Miraben, but Irinya interrupted her. Like Bholi Masi, the elders didn't approve of her being a flower hunter. They didn't actively oppose it, because her mother had been the best in generations, and Irinya was a skillful hunter herself. Still, they would not be happy at the prospect of her venturing into the Rann with an outsider, even if it was Kavi, their benefactor. But she couldn't pass up this opportunity to spend some time with him. Who knew if she'd ever get it again?

"I know the Rann as well as any of them," she said, keeping her face and voice bland, even as butterflies created havoc in her stomach. "I'll be careful."

"Thank you," said Kavi, directing a warm smile at her, squashing any further objections Miraben could have raised. "I look forward to it. Dawn tomorrow?"

"Yes," she said, trying to quell the butterflies. "Dress in layers. You can peel them off when it gets hot." She realized what she had said, and her face heated.

He pressed his lips together, as if suppressing a laugh. "Of course." He turned back to Miraben and the elders to discuss their migration route so he would know how to find them later in the season. Thankfully, Bholi Masi was drawn into an argument with Gopal Masa and Rishabh on the best route to their next stop, giving Irinya a reprieve from her scalding glare. She went and sat on the grass some distance away, watching them all argue, while Kavi stood in the middle, a polite smile on his face. Warmth radiated through her chest. He might be an outsider dressed in fancy clothes, but right then, it didn't matter. He looked like he belonged here with them.

Fardan and the others returned to report to the elders that the baniya and his goons had left. "I played my flute, and their camel bolted," Fardan announced to general laughter. He walked up to Irinya and flopped down on the grass next to her while Jai, Pranal, and Ayush joined the group around Kavi. He eyed her. "You're fidgeting, Irinya. You never fidget."

Was she? Irinya stilled herself, clasping her hands together and placing them primly in her lap.

"And you're grinning from ear to ear like your sweetheart proposed," he continued, scratching his head. "But I can't remember doing that."

She punched his shoulder. "I'm just happy, okay? Think, Fardan. We're going to be free of the baniya!"

Fardan gazed in Kavi's direction, levity gone. "Are we? Somehow I can't believe it."

Was that an edge in his voice? "I'm taking Kavi to the Rann tomorrow," she blurted out. "He wants to see it."

His brows knitted. "Oh. Want me to come along?"

"No need," she said, suppressing a wave of guilt. "I can handle it." She would get Kavi to herself for a few hours, and she didn't want to share him with anyone, not even Fardan. She might never get another chance to be alone with him, to find out if he was anything more than a kindhearted stranger who had saved her kul from generations of indebtedness.

Fardan's mouth thinned. "I'm sure you can. Carry extra water."

She rolled her eyes. "You don't have to tell me that. Come on, all this tension has made me hungry. Pick berries?"

He hunched his shoulders, not looking at her. "If you want to."

As they foraged for the sweet purple berries of the phalsa shrub, she wondered why she felt bad about saying she didn't need him around. She said that all the time anyway.

But this time was different. It had made Fardan unhappy. Why, though? Was it because *he* wanted to be the one to take their guest on a tour of the Rann?

Good thing Fardan hadn't been around when Kavi said he wanted to see the desert, or Irinya would never have gotten a chance to volunteer.

Then a part of her wondered if Kavi had timed it deliberately so the other flower hunters *wouldn't* be around. The thought made her feel hot and cold and shivery all over.

Don't be silly, she scolded herself, rubbing her arms. *It doesn't mean anything.* But she couldn't help the flutters in her stomach.

CHAPTER 4

The wind sang outside the tent, an eerie yet familiar song from the Rann that whispered of magic, moonlight, and mist. The candle flame flickered, making shadows dance on the thrumming tent walls. A night for Chir Batti, if ever there was one. Irinya had already warned the kul. Their camp was too close to the salt flats to take the risk of being outdoors, and everyone had decided to turn in early. That suited her. She had to get up at dawn to accompany Kavi on his trek across the salt desert.

Bholi Masi was, predictably, still upset with her. "Why you?" she grumbled as they unrolled their rugs in the middle of the tent. Gopal Masa was already lying down on the lone pallet in one corner, mumbling under his breath. "Why not one of the boys? It's not seemly."

"Nothing about me is seemly," Irinya pointed out, shaking the quilts and laying them on the rugs. "You ought to know that by now."

Her aunt sniffed as she fluffed a pillow. "You act so brash, but inside, you're as naive as a flower about to be plucked. Be careful. Men like him have a mistress in every village."

"How nice for them," said Irinya sweetly, seething at the absurd floral comparison. "I can be his mistress of the Rann."

"Irinya!"

"Don't worry, Masi. I'm not a flower to be plucked." She lay down and drew her quilt up to her neck, glad of its warmth. Beside her, Bholi

Masi did the same. Nights were cold in the grasslands, especially windy nights like this one. "If he tries anything, I'll leave him to die in the desert, okay?"

"No! Not okay." Bholi Masi raised herself on an elbow and glared at her. "You can't let him die. The entire future of the kul is at stake here."

Irinya laughed. "Make up your mind. Should I allow myself to be 'plucked' or not?"

"Irinya!"

"Can't a man get a bit of sleep in his own tent?" complained Gopal Masa from his pallet.

"You be quiet," snapped Bholi Masi. "Why don't *you* escort our honored guest to the desert?"

"Me with my bad leg and weak lungs?" Gopal Masa wheezed. "It's a widow you're wanting to be."

"It's all the hariya you keep drinking with your useless friends," said Bholi Masi with a complete lack of sympathy. "It's rotting you, brain and body."

"I drink to dull the pain," said Gopal Masa. "But I don't expect you to understand, you shamelessly healthy woman."

"Why, you—"

"Hush, you two," Irinya interrupted. She'd get no rest if they got into one of their endless squabbles. "I'll make sure nothing bad happens to either of us."

Bholi subsided, muttering under her breath, and Irinya leaned over and blew out the candle. Peace and quiet returned to the tent, the only sound that of the wind. Irinya stared up into the darkness, going over her preparations. She'd packed extra waterskins and a roll of rotlas in her potli and laid out clean cotton rags for her sore feet. She hoped Kavi had sturdy shoes for walking, given that he wasn't used to the salt flats.

She was sure she wouldn't be able to sleep from the excitement, but at some point, she dozed off, then woke in a panic that she would be late. But it was still dark, the predawn chill permeating the tent with its icy fingers. She stepped over Bholi Masi, sprawled on the rug-covered floor next to her, and lit a candle. Her uncle snored on his pallet, vibrating the tent walls. She got ready as silently as she could, wolfing down leftover millet porridge and a glass of buttermilk. Then she wrapped a thick shawl around herself, hefted her potli on her shoulder, and stepped out.

It was clear and cold, stars still visible in the sky. A faint pink light in the eastern sky was the only hint of daylight. The camp was quiet apart from the usual snuffles and snorts from the animals in their makeshift pens and the tent flaps thrumming in the breeze. Kharijal trees stood like isolated sentinels in the grassland, their leaves rustling. No trace remained of the mist, which was a relief. It was safe to be out now.

She thought she would have to wait for Kavi, but to her surprise he was already awake, leaning against an acacia tree near the communal tent and blowing on his fingers to warm them.

"Have you been waiting long?" she called, hurrying toward him.

He pushed himself off the tree and smiled at her. "Just a few minutes. Is this the time you usually leave for flower hunting?"

"Yes." She led him away from the camp to the edge of the grasslands, keeping her pace brisk. "We have a few short hours before the sun begins to burn the skin and throat."

"How hot does it get?" he asked, leaning toward her, eyes glowing with excitement.

She looked at him, amused. He wouldn't be quite so eager when the sun was overhead. "You could cook a rotla on the surface of the salt."

"That means the right footwear is important." He glanced down at her feet and came to a halt. "You're in *sandals?*"

She flushed. Why was he looking at her feet? Surely he realized that none of them could afford proper shoes or boots. "I'm wearing footwraps," she said, keeping her voice flat.

He crouched before her, examining her feet. "That's not good enough. The salt can penetrate those thin wraps. In the long term, it will lead to health problems."

She stepped back from him, trying to curb her anger. Yes, he was right, but he knew nothing of the hardships nomads faced if he was criticizing her footwear. She'd wear her sandals until they fell apart, and Gopal Masa would help her stitch them back together. A decent pair of shoes from a leatherworker in Bhuj cost the same as an entire month of grain for the kul. "I'll be fine," she retorted. "Probably won't live long enough to have 'health problems.'"

His eyes widened, and she regretted her words and tone. She didn't want him to think her rude. Even more, she didn't want his pity. But all he said was, "Give me a minute. I need to get something."

He rose and strode back to the camp, leaving her to stew over his abruptness. Was he upset with her? Did he really need to "get something," or had he decided he wanted someone else to accompany him to the Rann—someone with better footwear and a better attitude?

But he returned a few minutes later, holding something bulky in his hands. *Boots.* Long matte-brown leather boots with matching laces, an air of warmth and comfort about them.

Irinya narrowed her eyes. "No."

"Please," he said, holding them out to her. "It's an old pair with good, thick soles. At least try them on. I don't think our feet are that different in size and shape."

Her cheeks burned. The problem wasn't the difference in the size of their feet but in their circumstances. How could she accept his charity? "I don't need your shoes."

"Of course you don't," he said gently. "But it would make me happy if you tried them on. Please?"

It was the "please" that did it, the implication that she would be doing something for him by accepting. And wasn't she? If the tragic state of her footwear made him feel guilty and uncomfortable with his own privilege, she was doing him a favor by trying them on. Not that she would have done such a favor for someone else. But this was Kavi, who had faced down the baniya and his men, who had offered to buy their debt, and who was—admit it, why not?—the most handsome and well-spoken man she had ever met. She wriggled out of her worn sandals, trying to control the flush in her cheeks, and held her hands out for the boots.

He knelt on the grass. "Allow me. These laces are kind of fiddly."

She was so flabbergasted, she didn't object when he grasped her right foot. Her breath caught. She could feel his fingers through the footwraps, light yet sure, as he slid her foot into a soft leather boot. He closed the flaps and deftly laced them up, intent on his task, oblivious— she *hoped*—of her stuttering pulse.

"Fits like a dream." He looked up at her and beamed. "Other foot, please."

Wordlessly, she allowed him to slide her left foot into the second boot. A mix of conflicting emotions roiled within her. She was wearing *his* boots, shaped by his feet, which he himself had laced up for her. It was intimate in a way that would have had Bholi Masi squawking about the naivety of flowers.

He stood and tilted his head. "How do you feel?"

Like I want to run away and hide. She took a deep, calming breath. "Feels strange," she said, keeping her tone light. She grabbed her treacherous sandals and shoved them into her bag. "I'll take them off if they bite. But thanks."

He gave a small, satisfied nod. "Glad to be of service."

She looked at the horizon so as not to look at him. No one had ever touched her like that. No one's touch had made her *feel* like that—as if the air were trapped inside her chest, making it difficult to breathe. She'd have to be careful she didn't betray her reactions to him. He'd think her a gauche, provincial girl who was swayed by the smallest kindness, the most casual touch. "The sun will rise soon," she said in a clipped voice. "Better hurry."

They walked across the no-man's-land between grass and desert, salt crystals crunching underfoot. The cold wind whipped her shawl and tugged her hair. She felt as if she were walking on air, and the boots were only part of the reason why. She was where she belonged, in the company of a man who'd turned all their lives around. Of course, he would leave soon for the capital, but he would return. She would see him again as they worked together to supply flowers to the palace apothecary. Perhaps they would become friends—or more. The thought made her skin tingle.

They continued in silence for a while, and she watched him watching the sky, as if every new shade of pink and orange were a painting to be admired. *Why are you here, Kavi? Is it only for the flowers? What do you think of this place, of the people?* And, unaskable: *What do you think of me?*

The sun's fiery orb peeked above the horizon, casting a glimmering reflection on the white salt, and the wind sang its ghostly song, drowning out their footsteps. Irinya bent her face against the wind and gazed at the cracked, glowing earth. Sunset and sunrise, two sides of the same coin, one heralding day, the other heralding night. How could you say which was which? You could mistake one pink and purple sky for the other. And by the time you were out on the salt flats and the moon slid into the sky, it was too late. Too late to turn back, too late to remember why you shouldn't be out here, because Chir Batti had you in its thrall. Perhaps that was what had happened to her mother. If only she could remember the night her mother went missing more clearly. But her memories of that time were hazy, like the mist itself.

Kavi glanced at her. "What are you thinking?" he asked, a teasing note in his voice. "You look so serious."

"About how easy it is to lose your way," she replied, glad of the interruption. She didn't want to think of her mother, not now. She had only a few hours with Kavi, and she wanted to enjoy them.

He gave her a smile that warmed her. "I am lucky to have you as my guide."

She smiled back at him to take the sting out of her words. "Why are you here, Kavi?"

He fingered the blue enamel locket that hung from his chain, frowning. "My patron—" he began, but she interrupted. She didn't want to hear about his patron or for him to repeat his official reasons. She wanted to know why he had chosen this mission and why he had asked to see the Rann. What was in it for him personally?

"No. Why are you *here, now?*"

His face relaxed. "That's a very deep question. I'm afraid I don't have an answer."

"Maybe I should give you mine, so you understand what I mean," she said. "I am here because this is where I belong. I am here because I aim to be the best flower hunter of the Rann. And I am here because of my kul. The salt may eat into my skin and the sun may take my sight, but one day, I will free my kul from debt." She bit her lip and made herself say it. "Yes, even from *you.*" When all was said and done, they still had to pay back Kavi. The kul might be free of the baniya, but they were still in debt. They would pay Kavi in flowers, and Kavi would give them a far better price than the baniya ever had, but it would still take time and hard work. They would also have to continue to set aside a sizable sum for the revenue collector each year.

His gaze darted to her and then away, as if he was ashamed at the prospect of being their creditor. "I hope I'm not as bad as your baniya," he murmured.

She laughed. "No one can be as bad as him. Now that you have my answer, you owe me yours. Why are you here?"

He was quiet for a while. The sun rose higher, filling the Rann with its golden light, turning the sky around it a pale yellow. In the early-morning light, his fine-featured face was both somber and beautiful. At last he said, "My parents were flower hunters, too. They died in the desert, within days of each other."

Surprise pooled in her stomach, robbing her of speech. *Flower hunters?* She stared at him, waiting for him to continue, wondering which kul in Banni his parents were from.

He gave a wry smile. "It's not something I normally talk about. But I think you will understand when I say this is a pilgrimage for me."

"But how . . . how did you . . . ?" She fumbled to put her thoughts into words. *How did you get from* here *to* there? The difference between the Rann of Kutch and the court of the sultan was like the difference between sky and earth.

"How did I reach my current position?" His face turned inward. "I changed hands a few times. My parents weren't part of a kul, and relatives gave me away to a village temple, not far from Bhuj. I spent my days listening to scripture, sweeping floors, and being beaten. One day, a childless merchant and his wife visited the temple to pray for a son. They liked the look of me and offered to take me in. A couple of years later, their prayers were answered, and they had a son of their own. They no longer needed me, so they gave me into the service of their patron, Malik Ayyaz. I was bright and quick, and he must have thought I would be useful."

"That sounds awful." Irinya couldn't imagine being shunted about like that, as if you were an object, not a child. Even though Irinya was an orphan, Bholi Masi loved her like her own daughter. True, Bholi didn't have children of her own, but even if she had, she would still have cared for Irinya.

Kavi chuckled. "I have been lucky. Perhaps I would still be at the temple, sweeping floors, if the merchant hadn't adopted me. I owe them a great debt."

"You are kinder than I am." Irinya made a face. "I would have cursed the merchant and his wife and son."

"Not the baby, too," he teased. "It was hardly his fault for being born. And if not for him, I would be an ordinary merchant."

Instead of someone who could command the governor's sarraf to buy an entire kul's debt. A frisson ran through her at the thought of the power he wielded and the generosity he had shown. "Is it hard being in the service of Malik Ayyaz?" she asked, eager to know more about him and his life, so different from hers.

"He's an exacting master but has always dealt fairly with me," said Kavi, pausing to peel off his woolen coat. The wind had dropped, and the sun had strengthened as they talked. The sea of salt around them glittered white, already harsh to the eyes.

"I owe everything I am to him," he went on. "He's a foreigner from Russia, a cold land far north of here. He was beginning his rise to power in the sultan's court when I entered his household. I learned counting and numbers from his sarraf, Gujari from his servants, and reading and writing from his own son's tutor."

"But you remember your parents, and you make this pilgrimage for them," said Irinya, an ache in her throat. He'd been through so much as a child. She might have lost her parents, but she still had Bholi Masi, Gopal Masa, and her entire kul to depend on. Kavi had no one.

He dipped his head in acknowledgment. "In a way, I am continuing their quest for a flower that might or might not exist. My mother was convinced she'd found a silver spider lily."

Irinya's stomach flipped. The spider lily again. Kavi continued, "She went every day into the Rann, watching it grow, waiting for the right moment to harvest it. My father tried to stop her, to tell her it was dangerous, that she must take a break. She didn't listen to him. One day, as he had feared, she didn't return. He went into the desert to search for her and found her body instead. After that, he became obsessed with finding the spider lily. He took it into his head that her spirit was trapped in the flower, and if he could only find it, he could release her."

Irinya swallowed the lump in her throat. "That's so sad."

His mouth twisted. "We people are full of sad stories like that, aren't we?"

We people. As if they were the same. And weren't they, in the things that mattered?

She hesitated and plunged ahead. "I too lost my mother to the Rann." She'd never talked about her mother with a stranger before, and the words felt awkward in her mouth. But Kavi was no stranger. Not anymore. And she wanted to share how similar their beginnings were, even more so than he might have thought. "She went flower hunting on a misty night, even though she knew the danger of it. She must have followed Chir Batti, for we never saw her again."

He slipped a hand into hers and squeezed. "I'm sorry. I had no idea. Chir Batti—the ghost light? Elder Chinmay told a story about it the night before last."

She nodded. "Chir Batti is the guardian of the Rann. But it's a double-edged sword. You break the rules, you bear the price. And one of the rules is, you don't venture into the Rann at night." His hand in hers was warm and comforting and exhilarating—all at the same time. Could he sense her quickening pulse? She tried to smile. "When I'm here, though, it feels like she's still with me."

"I too feel closer to my parents here." He sighed, gazing into the distance. "If I could find that spider lily, I could set them both free."

His unhappiness smote her heart. The words slipped out before she could stop them. "I can't give you *that* spider lily. But I can show you another, if that helps."

He turned and faced her, frowning. "What do you mean?"

She bit her lip. She'd promised Fardan she wouldn't take that flower. But she trusted Kavi, and if seeing the flower helped him to lay his parents' ghosts to rest, why not? "Fardan found a silver spider lily. But he made me promise not to pluck it. He thinks if we leave it there, it will replenish the magic of the Rann. And we'll get another next year— maybe more than one." *If* the war didn't spread to Kutch.

Kavi's eyes blazed, and he gripped her hand so hard, she winced. "Sorry," he said, releasing her. "But are you sure? No one's found a silver spider lily in years. They're almost as mythical as the black chrysanthemum."

"I'm sure," she said. "At first, I couldn't believe it, either, but it's certainly not a jasmine."

"Can you please take me there?" He took a deep, shaky breath. "It would mean a lot to me. I swear not to pluck it."

"It's far," she warned him. "I can take you there, but returning safely is another thing. I am accustomed to the desert; you are not."

"I was born in the grasslands. My mother used to take me into the Rann strapped on her back." He gave a grim smile. "The desert is in my bones, even if my flesh has forgotten it."

She nodded. "Tell me if you feel light-headed." She led him across the salt flats, setting a quick pace. Good thing she'd memorized the route. The sun blazed down, and she covered her head with her dupatta. She was grateful for her new footwear. It made walking across the hard, salt-cracked earth much easier.

The desert shimmered, endlessly white under the burning sun. She made Kavi stop and sip water every now and then, checking him for symptoms of heat sickness. He complied each time, smiling at her concern, but his eyes were distant—distracted, she guessed, at the prospect of seeing a spider lily. When they neared the mound where the spider lily grew, she halted and scanned the area for killer wasps.

The flower eaters were nowhere in sight. Many years ago, alarmed by the attacks on humans, locals had burned their hives. A few still survived, but they were rare now—as rare as the flowers.

"The plant is full of poisonous thorns," she cautioned as they scrambled up the little hill.

Kavi wiped the sweat from his brow, panting. "I won't touch it."

For a moment, she was afraid the flower would be gone—that someone had taken it, or it had never been there in the first place.

But the silver spider lily glowed in the heart of its spindly black nest, radiating beauty. It was half-open, stretching long fingerlike petals toward the sun, as if to catch the light.

"By salt and sun." Kavi's voice trembled. He leaned forward, his hand hovering above the thorny plant.

Irinya caught his hand. "Careful. You can die if a thorn pierces your skin."

He took a step back and shook his head, as if awakening from a dream. "Sorry. I . . . I can't believe this is real." His lips quivered, and he dashed a hand in front of his eyes.

"Come with me," she said gently, moved by the depth of his emotion. She led him down the slope to sit a safe distance away from the plant, glad that she'd brought him here.

"You must eat and drink something." She passed him a rotla wrapped around dried mango pickles, and he accepted with a murmur of thanks and the same distant look in his eyes, his thoughts elsewhere. They ate in silence as the sun beat down on their heads. Irinya considered the route back, how much time she should allow him to rest, and whether it would be wiser to wait until afternoon before making the arduous journey home.

He turned to her as she packed the remains of the food in her potli. "Do you know what it would mean for the sultan to possess this flower?" he said, his voice raw.

She'd half expected him to bring it up—he was here on behalf of the palace, after all—and yet his words raised her hackles. Fardan might forgive her showing the spider lily to an outsider, but he'd never forgive her plucking it. She sat up, her back stiff. "I promised not to take it. I only showed it to you because of what you said about your parents."

"I understand," he said, holding her with his gaze. "And it means a lot to me. Thank you for trusting me enough to bring me here. But I want *you* to understand, too. Do you know how the war with the Portuguese is going?"

She shrugged, wariness flooding her. "Badly?" Why was he bringing this up? Did he want to guilt her into breaking her promise? She understood what a spider lily could mean for the war, but the flower was not Kavi's to take. Or Fardan's to keep for that matter, but still. He'd been the one to find it, and she'd sworn by salt and sun. "They've occupied the island of Diu, right?"

He took a deep breath. "Yes. The Portuguese viceroy is building a fortress there, may he rot in hell. And it's not just Diu, not just the sultanate. The Portuguese control most of the Malabar Coast as well as the Strait of Malacca. They've captured Kochi and Ceylon, attacked Calicut, and are poised to take Goa. They've set themselves up as the rulers of the Indian Ocean. No ship can enter or leave without one of their cartazes."

Her heart sank at his words. The situation was worse than she had imagined. "What's a cartaz?" she couldn't help asking.

"A Portuguese trade pass," he said. "If they encounter a ship without a cartaz, they seize the cargo and sink the ship. It's a way to force everyone to pay tax to them, to acknowledge them as supreme rulers of the trade routes."

She filed away the information, even as it filled her with dismay. "Can't the sultan's armies hold them off until next year?" she asked. "His allies—"

"Were all defeated in Diu," he said, his voice hard. "The Portuguese naval power is far more advanced than ours. The sultan's forces led by my patron, Malik Ayyaz; the Mamluks under Amir Hussain; the Venetians; and the zamorin of Calicut all together could not withstand them. Most everyone on our side was killed. Amir Hussain fled to Cairo and the sultan was forced to sue for peace. The remnants of our armies are fighting the Portuguese all down the coast, but morale is low and casualties are high. Next year, it will be too late. The sultanate will have fallen."

Her spirits plummeted. Somehow, his telling made it come home to her in a way it hadn't before. "Why are you telling me this? My kul has nothing to do with such matters." But the words rang hollow to her own ears. The fate of Kutch was tied to the fate of the sultanate.

"Is that so?" His gaze narrowed. "Why do you think the Portuguese are here, so far from their own country?"

"Greed," she said after a moment. "It's always greed."

He nodded. "Europeans crave spice, are willing to pay its weight in gold. Peppercorn from the Malabar Coast, cinnamon from Ceylon, cloves, mace, and nutmeg from the Maluku Islands. Tomorrow it will be something even more precious from the Rann."

Irinya's mind flew to the dead body they'd found, clutching the bluestar. Had it been a Portuguese scout? Her gut clenched. "No!"

"Yes," he grated. "How long do you think the flowers will stay a secret? The Portuguese have spies everywhere."

Perhaps the secret was already out. She bit her nails, imagining the Rann overrun by foreign invaders, its delicate salt crust destroyed by a thousand boots. Her kul would be driven away from their homeland, perhaps even killed. "The Jadeja clan chiefs would never allow it."

Kavi sighed. "They don't have the forces to fight the foreigners. And the sultan cannot help them. He is old and ill, surrounded by enemies. On the west, the Portuguese; in the north, the Delhi Sultanate; and in his court, backstabbing nobles. I hear his own wazir, Imshan Khan, plots against him. Now imagine if I were to arrive at the palace and present this flower to him. Jasmine cannot cure him, but a spider lily would save the entire sultanate. Save the Rann. Save the *people*. We'd beat back the Portuguese, evict them from India."

She shivered, torn. On the one hand, her promise to Fardan; on the other hand, the fate of the entire subcontinent. How could she compare the two? And yet, and yet. "I swore I would not pluck this flower."

He stared at the horizon, his mouth pressed in a grim line. "Weigh your promise against the cost of keeping it. Thousands of people died in the Battle of Diu. Before the battle, the Portuguese razed the city of Dabul for daring to resist them. Everyone was killed. Not just the people of Dabul, but those in the villages around the city. And not just the people, but even the cows. Even the dogs."

Irinya's stomach knotted. Kavi glanced at her, his face drawn in tight lines. "When Vasco da Gama first sailed to India, he chopped off the hands, feet, and heads of captured fishermen and sent them in baskets to the zamorin of Calicut to persuade him to surrender. On his second voyage, he seized a vessel with over four hundred Muslim pilgrims and burned them all to death—including the babies."

Her gorge rose. "What kind of cruel, inhuman people are these?"

"The kind who think they own the world," said Kavi somberly.

She swallowed, trying to unsee the horrific visions his words had conjured. "The spider lily . . ."

". . . would change everything," he said, leaning toward her with pleading eyes. "It would tilt the balance in our favor. Just one flower, Irinya. It is in your power to change the destiny of India."

"Why mine?" She met his gaze squarely. "You could try to take it." If he did, she would do her utmost to prevent it. But if he didn't, the decision was hers. It wasn't one she wanted to make. It was unfair on both her and Fardan. She found herself revising her estimate of Kavi. She'd brought him here for personal reasons, and he'd changed it to something else entirely. She didn't blame him for it; he was focused on the big picture, and he'd made it clear that his goal was to secure authentic flowers for the palace. The fault was hers for limiting her perception to one aspect of him. She'd been swayed by the story of his parents—no, earlier still, when he'd insisted that she wear his boots.

He laughed—a small, unhappy sound. "Do you think I would do that? I promised not to touch the flower, and I won't. I didn't lie. This was meant to be a pilgrimage for me, a chance to say goodbye to my parents."

She twisted the end of her dupatta, feeling trapped. "You won't break your promise, so I must break mine?"

He put a hand on hers, stilling her. "I'm sorry, Irinya. Some things are bigger than you or me. I work for Malik Ayyaz. We had to flee Diu when it fell to the invaders. Every day, I live with the reality that our ships might be attacked, our men killed, our cargo stolen. Every day, we get news of a fresh atrocity."

Irinya closed her eyes. Images of people burning danced before her, their flesh melting, their mouths open in anguished screams. If she could prevent something like that happening again, she should break her promise—yes, even one she'd made to Fardan. She would deal with the guilt; she would deal with Fardan. A spasm passed through her. "Take it," she said, barely able to get the words out. "I won't stop you."

Kavi grasped both her hands. "You must give it to me of your own free will. I will not pluck it myself."

He believed, as so many did, that those who harvested a flower could not use it themselves. She freed her hands from his and went back up the little hill. The heat was at its peak now. It lay on her skin like something physical, a layer she could not peel off. She knelt by the plant and tried to focus.

"Be careful," he shouted.

The flower nestled amid thorns, perfect and serene. She withdrew a knife from her belt and reached for the spindly black branches that surrounded it, trying not to tremble.

Are you sure? it said, and she nearly dropped her knife. *The price will be more than you can bear.*

Her eyes dimmed. Did it mean she would lose Fardan? Was anything worth that? She waited for it to continue, for things to make sense, but no more words were forthcoming, and no wisdom, either. She counted her breaths, trying to slow her pulse and clear her mind. Here, now, she had to make a choice.

She pictured Dabul, its streets awash in blood, the chopped limbs of men, women, and children mingling with those of animals. She heard the silence of a city where every inhabitant had been brutally killed, and a shudder ran through her. If there was a price to be paid, then she would bear it, no matter what the spider lily said.

She gripped her knife and began to cut away the black branches around the flower. Sweat poured down her face, and she wiped her eyes with a sleeve. It was hard, slow work. At one point, she realized Kavi was right behind her, and she made him step back before she resumed. Removing the thorns required complete concentration. She tossed each deadly branch on the far side of the plant. Gradually, the flower lost its concentric circles of defense.

At last, the silver spider lily stood alone amid woody stumps, looking bereft and vulnerable. "Sorry, and thank you," she whispered, and she reached for the stem of the flower.

Something needlelike jabbed into her palm. She yelped and snatched back her hand.

"What happened?" said Kavi, alarmed.

"Stay back." She examined her palm, and coldness filled her stomach. On the fleshy underside, where it had brushed against the ground, was an inch-long gray thorn, its hook embedded in her flesh. Already, red lines were radiating outward from the puncture. Carefully, she withdrew the thorn and threw it aside. Then she sucked the wound and spat several times.

"How can I help?" Kavi hovered above her, his face taut with anxiety.

"I'll be fine. I've been pricked before." *But not by a spider lily thorn,* she did not add. She tore the end of her dupatta and wrapped it around and above the wound. That would slow the spread of poison.

He crouched and gave her his waterskin. She took a long draft of water, and clarity returned to her thoughts. She grasped the stem of the flower, said a silent apology to Fardan, and snapped it. The spider lily floated on her palm, lovely and pure. Her heart clenched at the loss, and she held the spider lily out to Kavi before she could change her mind. "For Kutch and Gujarat."

"For Kutch and Gujarat," he echoed, accepting the flower in cupped hands, his face reverent.

She rose, made herself look away from the spider lily, and collected the fallen gray thorns. Kavi did not notice; he was too busy admiring the flower.

The journey back was a blur. The poison worked its way up her arm, making it hot and swollen to the touch. Her head felt heavy, her thoughts sluggish. She stumbled from time to time, and Kavi helped her up, keeping his hand on her good arm. The sun sank toward the west, elongating their shadows, and alarm cut through the fog of her mind. She had to get them back to the camp before night fell, before Chir Batti made its ghostly appearance and led them astray. Where was the route? Was she leading them in circles?

It would serve her right for breaking her promise to Fardan, for taking what wasn't hers. Guilt and shame wormed their way into her heart, as deadly as the poison from the thorn.

But she couldn't let Kavi take the fall with her, or who would bring the spider lily to the sultan? She drank the last of their water and focused on putting one foot ahead of another, her eyes fixed on the twilit horizon. When the distant treetops of Banni finally came into view, her knees buckled with relief.

Kavi steadied her and grasped her shoulder. "I have something for you."

She blinked the sweat away from her eyes. "What?"

He withdrew a small round jewelry box from his pocket and held it out to her with a tentative smile.

She stared at it, confused. "Why are you giving me jewelry?"

He laughed. "It's not a jewel, but something better. Open it."

She took the little wooden box from him, nearly dropping it. Even in her current state, she could appreciate its intricate craftsmanship. She'd never seen anything so beautiful. She slid open the lid and gasped.

Inside, nestled on red velvet, was a white jasmine.

"For you," he said, watching her. "I've purchased it from your kul, so it's mine to do with as I wish. I want you to use it to heal yourself. Make a tincture; it will last years. One or two spoons are sufficient to heal most illnesses."

Her eyes blurred, her heart swelling until she thought it would burst. She closed the lid and thrust the box back at him. "No, it's yours. Your patron—"

"The silver spider lily is priceless," he interrupted. "Once I have delivered it safely to the sultan, I will return with all possible speed, with enough wealth to last your kul for generations. But meanwhile, please do this for me. Please accept the jasmine. If something were to happen to you, I would never forgive myself."

His words were a river of light and comfort through the poison darkening her senses. "Nothing will happen to me," she assured him, her words slurring.

"Keep it." He closed her hand over the box and squeezed. "Don't waste time arguing with me. You can barely stand. You must take medicine and rest. And I must return to Ahmedabad at once."

She hesitated. "If you do me a favor in return." He gave her a questioning look. "Don't tell anyone in my kul about the spider lily. It was a secret. I'll tell Fardan myself."

He nodded. "You can count on me."

Somehow, Irinya managed to make it to the camp without falling. Bholi was waiting anxiously on the edge of the grassland, as was most of the kul. At the sight of her swollen arm, Bholi let out a wail worthy of a barn owl. Irinya allowed herself to be carried to their tent, only vaguely aware that Fardan was the one carrying her. Someone made her drink a bitter brew, someone else removed her makeshift bandage and rubbed salve on her arm, and yet another person unlaced her boots and helped her lie down.

The brew made her sleepy, or perhaps that was the poison working its way through her body. The spider lily thorn had its own unique sting. Still, jabbing herself over the years must have made a difference, because at least she was still alive.

"Let her sleep it off," came a familiar voice. "She's stronger than she looks."

"I will watch over her," said a second voice. "You'd best leave. What are you doing in our tent?"

"I'm the one who carried her in," said the first voice, sounding injured.

Fardan. Remorse and relief in equal measure flooded Irinya. He was here. She wouldn't lose him. Would she? *Forgive me,* she tried to say, but no words emerged from her mouth. Why couldn't she speak? Had the spider lily taken her tongue?

"Her uncle has a weak heart," said the second voice sharply. "Otherwise, I'd have made him do it."

"It's my lungs," said a third person. "Not that anyone cares."

"Oh, *you* be quiet."

Irinya swallowed and managed to sit up. Her head spun, and she had the oddest sensation of ants crawling up her arms. She scratched her arms and tried, once again, to speak. *Fardan, I took the spider lily. I'm sorry.* Once again, she failed.

Worried faces swam before her eyes, and a firm hand pushed her back down. "Hush, Irinya. You need to rest."

Irinya blinked at her aunt and uncle, bending over her. Fardan was already gone. Bholi Masi wiped her forehead with a damp cloth. "Sleep, child," she said, and Irinya slept.

—✳—

Irinya had the impression of time passing, but it was nebulous at best. Perhaps it was just one long night from which she could not wake. She dreamed she was having a conversation with the jasmine hidden in her bag, except the flower had somehow grown a face and limbs and was sitting opposite her in the lotus position.

Sweet white jasmine to cure the ill, said the flower in a melodic voice. *But are you worth saving?*

"I'll save myself," she said. "I won't waste you."

Good, said the flower. *You'll need me later.*

She woke from the dream to find her mother bending over her. Urmila kissed her forehead. "Goodbye, sweetheart. I'm after a prize tonight."

Don't go, Irinya tried to say. *Don't leave me.* But she could not move or utter a word. Tears trickled down her cheeks as her mother rose and walked out of the tent into the misty, moonlit night from which she would never return. A memory, or the dream of a memory. Why could she not remember that night? Was it so painful she'd chosen to forget?

It's all right, thief, said the blue petal, floating down to her pillow. *You still have me. Starry bluestar to counter the red.*

Guilt and grief rose in black waves within her, threatening to drown her. She put her hands over her ears and screamed, "Go away!"

But there was no one; she was alone in the tent, soaked in sweat, shivering under a thick pile of rugs.

She dragged the poem out, line by line, from the murky depths of the past. Her mother had used it as a tool to teach her about the different flowers. There was another poem Urmila had taught her—a darker one. But Irinya couldn't remember that one at all.

Did you make it up yourself? she had asked her mother.

Certainly not, her mother had replied. *I learned it from the flowers.*

Irinya had believed her, of course. Her mother had a special relationship with the Rann. Years after she vanished, Irinya still kept expecting to see her walking across the grasslands, silhouetted against the setting sun, a flower in her hand, a smile on her face.

It had taken a long time for that hope to die. Its ghost lingered still, catching her when she was at her weakest, whispering to her of possibilities.

It was a week before the poison finally left her body and she was strong enough to sit up and eat on her own. It was another day before she could keep the food down. By the time she left the tent, ten full days had passed, and Kavi Kampilya was long gone, the fate of her kul in his hands.

CHAPTER 5

It was time for the kul to move. The animals had thoroughly grazed and trampled the area. The grass was reduced to stubble, the brush stripped clean of every leaf. If they wanted fresh, sweet grass to grow here next season, they had to take their herds elsewhere. On their last night, they gathered around the fire to eat and discuss their route. Irinya joined them—the first time she had done so since her illness. She was still a bit wobbly on her feet, but she was sick of being confined to the tent.

"The Poison Princess is back," announced Pranal to general laughter. She punched him in the arm, wondering where Fardan was. Had he discovered the absence of the flower and guessed what she'd done? She'd never meant to keep it from him. She'd wanted to confess, to explain *why* she'd plucked the spider lily. But illness had kept her in the tent, and Fardan had not visited; if he had, she'd been too far gone to notice.

"How are you, child?" asked Miraben.

"I'm all right, thank you," said Irinya, scanning the faces around the fire.

"Well, *I'm* not," said Bholi Masi. "As long as there's breath in my body, you will not go to the Rann again."

Irinya patted her knee. "You don't mean that, Masi. I'd drive you up the wall."

Her aunt gave a sharp response, but Irinya didn't hear it. She'd caught sight of Fardan, sitting on the fringes of the group, looking through her, his face indifferent.

Her heart gave a little jolt. Fardan had never regarded her with such an expression before, as if they were strangers. She stared at her plate, appetite gone. She needed to talk with him and apologize. He might be angry with her, but he would see that she'd done the right thing. Wouldn't he? It wasn't as if the flower had belonged to him.

After a simple meal of rotlas, pickles, yogurt, and boiled kharijal leaves, the council elders talked of Kavi Kampilya. Irinya listened, wishing she could come clean to them about the spider lily. But she needed to talk to Fardan first. As for the rest, it would be best to wait for Kavi to come back. He'd promised to return with enough wealth to last the kul for generations. That would help mitigate her crimes—not just the broken promise, but the fact that she'd given the most precious flower in the Rann to an outsider without the knowledge and approval of the elders. The entire kul would be aghast. But Kavi would tell them he'd given the spider lily to the sultan, that their debt was paid, and the war had turned in the sultanate's favor. They would all forgive her then— even the elders, who were now warning the younger ones of the pitfalls of sudden riches.

"We must be sensible about the money," said Rishabh. "We'll pay off our debt first, then invest in our herds."

The other elders nodded sagely.

"That's it?" said Pranal in disbelief. "More goats and camels?"

"Cows too," said Chinmay, his rheumy eyes gleaming in the firelight. "Maybe even *buffalo.*"

"We could buy land in Bhuj or Ahmedabad," said Ayush.

As one, the elders swiveled to glare at him. "Foolish boy," snapped Miraben. "We're *nomads.* The entire grassland is ours. We have our ancestral village. What need have we of more land, and that, too, in a city that could be occupied by foreign invaders any minute? We're safer in Banni."

Ayush rolled his eyes but held his silence. The elders would never dream of changing their traditional lifestyle. In truth, Irinya wouldn't dream of changing it, either. The Portuguese invasion had made this resolve stronger.

The gold mohur was passed around to be admired before Miraben returned it to an embroidered pouch hung about her neck. She was taking no chances with it. They wouldn't be able to change it until they sent someone to Bhuj, the brand-new capital city of Kutch. And since Miraben trusted no one but herself, this would have to wait until the monsoon season, when they traveled to their village on the outskirts of the city. Kavi would return before then, of course, and the baniya would be long gone from their lives.

Fardan rose and slipped away, quiet as a shadow. Irinya wouldn't have noticed him leave if she hadn't been watching him. She waited until everyone's attention was on Miraben and followed him.

He walked past the camp to the edge of the grassland and halted, gazing at the desert, the chilly wind whipping his clothes and hair. It was a new-moon night, pitch dark but for the starlight.

No, not quite. Far in the distance, ghostly blue lights danced above the salt flats. *Chir Batti.* Irinya shivered and moved closer to Fardan. She would have to warn the kul tonight. She glanced at him. Most likely, he hadn't noticed the lights yet. She always saw them before anyone else.

"I can see Chir Batti," she said. "We shouldn't be standing so close to the salt flats."

He did not look at her or speak.

The shards of her broken promise cut deep, and she rubbed her chest. Was this the pain the spider lily had hinted at? "I'm sorry," she said in a small voice.

Still he did not say anything.

"Don't be like this," she pleaded, her throat tight. "At least listen to me."

He turned to her, his face hard. "Speak."

She took a deep breath, trying not to let her hurt show. "I know you're angry with me right now, but there's a reason for what I did." She struggled to form the right words. *I did it to save Kutch, Gujarat, and the entire Malabar Coast from the Portuguese. Most of all, I did it for the Rann. For us.*

"Is there?" He raked her with scornful eyes. "Did you give away our heritage for a pair of used boots? Or did he promise you something more?"

She flinched. "He did, in fact, promise to return with enough wealth for the entire kul. But that's not the reason why I plucked the spider lily."

He stared at the ground, as if unable to bear the sight of her. "I know," he bit out. "Your feelings for him were abundantly clear."

"Fardan!" Anger overrode the hurt and remorse she'd been feeling all through the conversation. How dare he assume she'd given away the spider lily for selfish personal reasons? All her explanations, all the reasonable words she'd planned to say, vanished like raindrops in the sand. "My feelings for him—for *anyone*—are none of your business."

"So you do have feelings for him," he rasped.

Heat flushed through her body. "I never said that."

His face spasmed. "You didn't have to. You better pray he returns, Irinya. Because if he doesn't, if this was all an elaborate sham, I'm going to hunt him down and kill him." He walked away in the direction of the camp without a backward glance.

Irinya gazed at his retreating back, stricken. "It wasn't a sham," she shouted. "Are you listening, Fardan Hajani? It wasn't a sham!"

But Fardan did not turn around. In a minute he was lost in the darkness of the night. She was alone at the edge of the desert, the wind singing in her ears and Chir Batti dancing on the salt flats, closer than before, beckoning her with beautiful blue-green tendrils of light. For a moment, she wanted to follow it. When you were in the thrall of Chir Batti, the entire world fell away. You forgot everything that connected you to the mortal realm and you entered a different plane of existence.

An owl hooted, and she came to her senses. *What am I doing?* Her kul depended on her, now more than ever. She couldn't afford to weaken. She cast a last look at the ghost light and trudged back to the camp to warn the others, her head bowed, her heart aching.

That night, when her aunt and uncle had fallen asleep, she lit a candle and took out her mother's old dowry bag, a small cloth purse dense with embroidery. Even after all these years, the colors were bright and sharp. Inside was the sole legacy Urmila had left behind: a slim twelve-inch-long bamboo pipe.

What's it for? Irinya had asked her once, watching her place a tiny, feathery dart inside it.

Enemies, her mother had replied, and demonstrated by blowing the dart straight into the trunk of a luckless tree.

The one Miraben has is much longer, Irinya had said, recalling a ceremonial blowpipe in the communal tent.

Ah, but this *one is magic.* Her mother had given her a secretive smile. *It only works with the thorns of the Rann.*

It was one of the few clear memories she had of her mother. As a child, she had pictured Urmila battling nebulous monsters in the Rann conjured by Chir Batti, although the blowpipe had probably been protection against *humans.* She didn't know if she would ever need it herself, but it felt good to hold it in her hands and continue her mother's tradition. It felt good to work on her thorn darts. It was a dangerous, painstaking process and just what she needed to take her mind off Fardan's harsh words. The conversation had not gone remotely as she'd hoped. He'd been slow to listen and quick to judge. But if he had a right to be mad, so did she. He'd known her all her life, but when it mattered most, he'd jumped to the worst possible conclusion about her intentions and motives. He'd assumed she liked Kavi, and maybe she did, but that wasn't why she'd given him the spider lily. Even Jai, Pranal, and Ayush would have known better than that.

Still, she'd broken her promise. She blinked back tears, angry both at herself and at him.

Stop crying, or you'll prick yourself. She gritted her teeth and focused on her task. She plucked a spider lily thorn from her pile and wrapped the thicker end in raw cotton. For fletching, she used grass flowers, gluing them on with dried acacia-tree sap.

Bholi Masi stirred and mumbled in her sleep. Irinya cast a sharp eye on her before resuming. Her aunt knew about the blowpipe, of course.

Did she know about the thorns? Irinya had taught herself how to convert the thorns into poisonous little darts and shoot them from her blowpipe. She'd been discreet about it because her aunt would not have approved, but it was the only thing she had of her mother's. When she held the blowpipe to her lips and aimed at a distant tree or a rock, she could sense her mother standing beside her, hand on her shoulder, guiding her aim. That was worth all the hours she spent collecting thorns and crafting her darts.

—⚹—

They moved early the next morning, packing their belongings, disman-
tling tents, and gathering the animals. Their next campsite was a three-
day journey southeast of here near a village called Gorewali.

Gopal Masa rounded up the cows while Irinya chased the goats to
the top of an upside-down charpoy strapped on their camel Veerana's
back. She was glad to leave. Kavi knew their planned migration route
and would be able to find them as long as they stuck to it. He'd been
gone eleven days. Even now, he might be on his way back.

No, that was too much to hope for. The sultan and his advisors would
want to question him, test the authenticity of the spider lily, and take
his advice on its use. They also had to decide how much it was worth
and how to remunerate the kul. Kavi's patron, Malik Ayyaz, would grill
him, too. It might be a while before he could make the return journey.

But he'd said he'd return as soon as possible. She wished she knew
how much that meant in actual days.

At least she was leaving the scene of her crime. She'd broken a
promise by salt and sun, which meant she'd broken a promise to the
Rann. That had its own price. Was she already paying it, or was worse to
come? She'd plucked the rarest flower of all, a silver spider lily, ignoring its own warning, and given it to an outsider. She'd done it to save
Gujarat, Kutch, and her own kul—to save the flowers themselves from
falling into the greedy hands of foreign invaders.

But did her reasons matter? She'd done what she'd done, and she
alone had to bear the burden of it. It weighed on her more with every
passing hour, bowing her shoulders.

Fardan, morose and silent, continued to ignore her, and she ignored
him too, squelching her urge to run up to him and make him listen to
her. Let him think what he wanted. Time would prove her right, and he
would be sorry. Kavi would return and tell everyone about the spider
lily and how the sultan was going to use it to protect them all.

She pictured Kavi bowing before the sultan, offering him the spider
lily with reverent hands. "A girl from Kutch gave it into my safekeeping to
help Your Majesty defeat the Portuguese," she imagined him saying. "Rise,
Your Majesty! Repulse the intruders who threaten our land and seas."

And she imagined the sultan, old and ill, rising from his throne—or would he be in bed? She wasn't sure—with new hope rushing through his elderly veins. He would accept the flower with wonder and delight. "Who is this incredible girl?" he would ask, and Kavi would tell the sultan all about her and her kul.

"Are you dreaming, Irinya?" scolded Bholi Masi. "One of the goats has escaped."

Irinya caught the errant goat and tied it with the others on top of the camel. She fitted her aunt's pots and pans on the legs of the charpoy and hustled three small children in among the goats. They'd entertain each other during the trip. Last to be loaded was her own small bundle of belongings: a few changes of clothes, a comb, and the dowry bag with the blowpipe and thorns. She kept the jewelry box with the jasmine in a pouch tied to her waist. The bluestar petal was stitched into the dupatta draped around her shoulders. She would never take it off.

The kul traveled all morning, the cows setting an unhurried pace across the lush grassland. The grass rustled in the wind, cowbells jangled, and children chattered atop the camels. Irinya walked beside her aunt and uncle, taking deep breaths of the warm, grass-scented air. It was good to be on the move.

At noon, when the heat was at its peak, they stopped to rest the animals and eat a quick meal under the shade of a grove of acacia trees. As they were finishing, a caravan of laden camels appeared on the horizon—another kul, going in a different direction. Miraben hailed them and the two matriarchs exchanged greetings. Miraben invited her to have tea with them, and she accepted. Fardan and Pranal laid mats and stools for the elders to sit on. Bholi made chai in their biggest pot, balanced on a couple of bricks above an open fire. Irinya and Saira served the other kul first, as hospitality dictated.

"Have you seen any refugees in these parts?" asked an elderly woman from the other kul, blowing on her chai to cool it down.

Miraben frowned as she accepted a cup from Irinya. "What refugees?"

"Perhaps they do not venture close to the salt desert," said a man. "But we saw them on our way here from Bhuj—a pitiful group of people without possessions or animals, looking for a safe place to settle and cultivate."

"Where are they from?" asked Miraben.

"The coast," said the matriarch. "Fleeing Portuguese invaders. Did you hear about the massacre at Dabul?"

Irinya had learned of it from Kavi, but it was news to the other members of her kul. She listened with a heavy heart as their guests described scenes of carnage: torsos and hacked limbs littering blood-drenched streets; the corpses of animals mingling with the corpses of men, women, and children.

"Did you see this yourself?" asked Fardan, leaning toward the circle of elders, his face taut. He'd been so quiet for the last few days, his voice sent a tremor through Irinya.

The matriarch touched her ears, making the sign to avert evil. "Not us. But we heard from those who did. They said the stench was so horrible, it followed them out of Dabul and into their dreams."

Irinya's stomach clenched. She'd done the right thing, giving Kavi the spider lily, no matter what Fardan thought of her, and no matter what price the Rann made her pay.

The other kul left a little later, leaving her people subdued.

"We must avoid the bigger villages," said Miraben. "Even if it means taking a longer route. It would be better not to encounter any refugees from the war."

"They won't harm us," said Irinya. "They are to be pitied, not shunned."

"I agree," said Fardan, to her surprise. "We should help them." She gazed at him, conflicted. She was gratified he'd chimed in to agree, that he felt the same as she did and did not hesitate to speak up about it. But if the plight of the refugees moved him, why did he think they should not use the spider lily to end the war?

"We cannot help them," said Miraben sharply. "We don't have the resources. The safety of the kul is paramount, and I cannot risk it. Suppose they try to steal our cattle?" *Or the mohur,* she did not need to add, as her gnarled hand went to her pouch. Irinya opened her mouth to argue, but Bholi caught her eye and shook her head. *No use,* she mouthed, and Irinya subsided. She understood Miraben's concern, but it frustrated her. True, they had little to spare, but the kul could absorb a family or two, especially if they were willing to work hard. But the more one had, the more one had to lose, and Miraben was not about to risk the gold mohur.

They continued southeast, roughly parallel to the Rann, following an ancient route their ancestors had mapped out before them. As Irinya walked, her feet encased in Kavi's soft leather boots, her heart lifted. She loved the white salt desert, but to hike across Banni with the grass beneath her feet, the pale blue sky above, the horizon remote and un-knowable was its own special joy. Roosting birds flew up from the grass as the caravan approached, and a distant herd of fawn-colored wild ass glanced up briefly from their grazing before going back to their meal.

The terrain kept changing with time. The land was alive if you could but sense it. There were the big things, like earthquakes, which created new lakes or threw up a bund where none had existed before. But there were the small things, too. A never-before-seen species of grass, a new herd of gazelles or blackbucks, or—best of all—a new pond where they could camp and water their animals.

They stopped at dusk near a watering hole and lit fires, both to cook and to keep predators away from the herds. They were far enough away from the salt flats that Chir Batti was no longer a danger, but wolves and cheetahs prowled the grassland, searching for easy prey. Everyone had a task; the men constructed rough pens for the livestock using rope and wooden poles. Rishabh counted the camels and cows, making sure none were missing. Tammi, the priestess, blessed the ground and prayed for a safe night for them all. The children fetched water and collected fire-wood, while Chinmay regaled them with stories. Irinya, Saira, Ayush, and Pranal helped Bholi and the other women prepare the food. By the time they were done, it was pitch dark and everyone was hungry.

Once the elders had been served, Irinya took her plate and sat with the other flower hunters to eat, away from the noisy cook fire and near the camels. Even if Fardan refused to speak with her, she could still talk to Jai, Pranal, and Ayush. Maybe Fardan would join in.

"What did I miss while I was sick?" she asked, squeezing between Ayush and Pranal.

"A lot of arguing," said Ayush with a grin, shifting to make space for her.

"All the old hunters want to join the cooperative," said Pranal, rolling his eyes. "Even Vimal. Miraben threatened to demote him from his position as chief camel herder, and he said he never wanted to see another stinky-damn camel in his life, and now they're not speaking to each other. His wife took Miraben's side and kicked him out of their tent, so now he's in our tent, and I hate it; he snores." He paused for breath, and a camel lowed behind him, as if to drive the point home.

Irinya laughed. "Did you all decide on rules for membership?"

"They have to earn their way in by harvesting a flower," said Jai in his calm, deep voice. "That's only fair. But they didn't seem to think so."

"They want the benefit without the hard work," put in Ayush.

"It *is* very hard to find a flower," said Irinya. "Much harder than it was in their younger days."

"It's hard for all of us." Jai set down his plate, frowning. "And not just for our kul, but for everyone. Kavi said being in a cooperative means that together we own the flowers we collect and the money we get from them. Of course, the money will be shared with the whole kul, so everyone will benefit. But the members of the cooperative decide who to sell the flowers to, for how much, and when."

"The elders want to be involved in the decision-making," said Irinya, biting into her stuffed rotla. She cast a covert glance at Fardan, sitting opposite her, but he was eating his food with stolid disregard for the conversation, his eyes on his plate. Her stomach knotted. She took a deep breath, trying not to let his indifference get to her.

"They want to poke and meddle," said Ayush. "They should stick to brewing hariya and herding cows. Flower hunting's too dangerous. I mean, look at them."

They looked. Most of the kul members were gathered around the cook fire. Vimal was beating a rhythm on his dholak. Several men and women were dancing, including, Irinya noted, Gopal Masa, his weak lungs forgotten. Bholi was yelling at him, to no avail, to sit down and catch his breath. Irinya could not suppress a giggle at the sight. Fardan cast her a sharp look and dropped his gaze again.

Jai sighed. "They won't be able to keep up. We decided that members must contribute at least one flower every year. That's the minimum to stay in the cooperative—unless you fall sick."

That made sense. "What about involving other kuls?" Irinya asked.

"I'm going to speak with my cousin about setting up a cooperative in his kul," said Jai. "You know Mugesh, the one who married and moved away. Although it won't be easy for them; they're as much in debt to their baniya as we are."

And they didn't have the luck of a patron like Kavi. "Anything else?" she asked.

"If anyone tries to steal a flower, we kick them out," said Fardan, his voice startling her. He regarded her with flinty eyes. "The flowers belong to *all* of us. The future of the kul depends on them, especially now that we've angered the baniya."

The accusation in his voice cut to the bone. *I didn't steal the flower,* Irinya wanted to shout. Her face burned with indignation. She should show them the jasmine Kavi had given her as proof of his sincerity. But then she would have to explain what she'd done. At least Fardan hadn't told the others about the spider lily, and for that she should be grateful. She longed for Kavi's return, for Fardan to forgive her, and for everything to be all right again. How many more days would she have to wait?

They slept under the stars, not bothering to put up tents for a single night. The men took turns keeping guard, for the wolves of Banni were always eager for tender goat flesh.

Irinya shivered under her rug, sandwiched between Saira and Bholi Masi, and gazed at the star-studded sky. She thought of the huge wealth the spider lily promised. Would it change their lives? Did she want it to? What about the other flower hunters? If they paid their debt and saved their money, none of them needed to go into the Rann anymore.

But what was there for her apart from the Rann, except cows and embroidery and Bholi Masi carping at her to get married? Kavi needed a stable supply of flowers for the palace apothecary. Irinya didn't want to give up flower hunting once their debt was paid. Neither did Fardan, if she knew anything about him. Pranal and Ayush might leave the nomadic life, but Jai wouldn't. She fell asleep thinking of the fabled gates of Ahmedabad, wondering if she would ever glimpse them.

Three days later, they passed the village of Gorewali and arrived at their destination: a lush green stretch of land with long, wild grass

swaying in the wind, and the occasional stunted tree resembling a leafy
exclamation mark. Elegant antlers poked out of the grass: as the caravan
approached, they sprang away, revealing a herd of gazelles.

The Rann was much farther from this campsite than it had been
from the previous one. The flower hunters would have to walk an hour
to get to the edge of the salt flats. But the advantage was the presence of
a relatively clean water hole. They wouldn't have to depend on supplies
from a village this time.

Irinya threw herself into the daily tasks of the kul: cooking, foraging, fetching water, taking care of the animals, patching tents, washing
clothes. The busier she kept herself, the less time she would have to
fret about Kavi and Fardan. She found a few nightjar feathers and ex-
perimented with using them as fletching for her darts. She practiced
at dawn before anyone else was awake, taking care to bury the spoiled
darts far away from the campsite and water hole. In the soil, the thorns
lost their poison and became harmless.

But she didn't go back to the Rann. She'd broken a promise by salt
and sun, and that meant she was no longer welcome there, no longer
worthy—perhaps no longer safe. Maybe that was her own guilt eating
away at her, making her doubt herself. *Are you sure?* the spider lily had
asked, and of course she wasn't, but she'd made her choice and must
live with it. Perhaps if she punished herself, she could atone for what
she'd done. Or perhaps she was being superstitious. Whatever the reason, she couldn't venture into the salt flats, even though her heart ached
each time the flower hunters left without her.

"Have you finally come to your senses and realized flower hunting is
a man's job?" said Pranal, his eyes sparkling with mischief as he followed
her one morning back from the watering hole. She hefted her bucket of
water and scowled at him.

"Bholi must be over the moon," added Ayush with a snigger, winking
at his brother.

She showed them her teeth, wishing she could dump the water on
their heads. But then she'd have to go back and fill the bucket all over
again. "I've harvested more flowers than either of you, so shut up and
make yourselves useful, you lazy louts. Carry this bucket to Miraben's
tent, or I'll complain to your mother."

"Irinya! You wouldn't," said Pranal in alarm.

She thrust the bucket at him. "I would. Now go."

They went off, carrying the bucket between them, grumbling under their breath.

Fardan didn't say anything to her at all. He continued to head out every other day, returning empty-handed in the afternoons, his face grim, his limbs trembling with exhaustion. Was he looking for another spider lily to replace the one she'd given Kavi? She wished she could make him stop. This pace would kill him. But when she tried to speak to him about it, he turned away from her with such scorn in his eyes that the words stuck in her throat. She went to Jai instead one evening and asked him to keep an eye on Fardan.

Jai gave her a shrewd look. "Something up between you two?"

She shrugged, her insides twisting. "Nothing much. Don't tell him I asked you. He's pushing himself too hard, and he's going alone. You know it's against the rules."

Jai nodded. "I'll talk to him. And you—when will you go back to the Rann?"

"Soon," she said, swallowing the lump in her throat. "When I have permission."

He raised his eyebrows but said nothing. Irinya hadn't needed permission to hunt flowers, not for years. He didn't realize *whose* permission she meant. Not Bholi's, for sure. But it was a plausible excuse, one that Bholi Masi believed herself. Irinya did not disabuse her. Her poor aunt would realize she was wrong soon enough.

In truth, Irinya was waiting for Kavi to come back so she could finally put aside her guilt. Only when he returned could she tell everyone the truth. And only when Fardan forgave her could she walk back into the Rann, head held high.

But two weeks turned into three, and still Kavi did not return. She began walking to the edge of the camp at dawn every day, scanning the horizon for a rider.

She made excuses for him. It had only been a few weeks. He must have been held up in Ahmedabad. Perhaps he was involved in planning the attack on the Portuguese. After all, it wasn't as if there was an *emergency* here. He'd left them a gold mohur as an advance; he'd even given her the jasmine. She couldn't expect him to guess the state of her mind, to be as anxious to see her as she was to see him.

One morning in the fourth week, she walked to the edge of the camp as usual, unable to tamp down the hope she woke with every day. It was early enough that none of the flower hunters had left for the salt flats yet. Only a couple of people were awake, milking the cows. She stood beyond the camel enclosure, gazing at the twilit landscape, her heart leaden, wishing she had a flower that could conjure Kavi.

The sun sent its first tendrils of light across the grassland, and Irinya blinked. Was that dust rising in the distance? And that rhythmic sound cutting through the wind—was that not the sound of thudding hooves? Someone was riding toward the camp. She dug her nails into her palms. *He's back.* Her eyes blurred. *Thank the goddess, he's back.*

The dust cleared, and her joy evaporated. Six men on horseback were cantering across the grassland, making straight for the camp. Long, spiky clubs bristled from their shoulders and saddles. Irinya stared, petrified. Movement returned to her limbs, and she ran back to the tents, shouting, "Intruders!"

People emerged, rubbing sleep from their eyes. Miraben hurried over and grabbed Irinya's shoulder. "How many?" she demanded.

"Six," said Irinya, panting. "They're armed with clubs."

Miraben closed her eyes, sagging. She snapped them open and her face hardened. "Wake the children," she barked, turning around. "Tell them to hide in the trees and grass away from the camp. Disperse the herds; let them graze as far away as possible. The older boys can watch over them. Vimal, Jai, Fardan—grab some stout sticks. Stand with me."

Everyone scattered to obey. Irinya ran to the tent to grab her blowpipe, her heart thudding. The tent was empty; Gopal Masa must have gone to protect his beloved camel, Veerana, although how her skinny uncle was going to stand against armed men was beyond her. She emptied her mother's dowry bag and scooped up a few jasmine thorn darts. Jasmine thorns were toxic but usually nonlethal. She inserted one into the blowpipe, trying not to tremble. *You can do this. You can protect everyone.* If she repeated it to herself like a mantra, she could make herself believe it.

Bholi Masi burst into the tent. "There you are, I was so—" She stopped, her eyes narrowing. "What are you doing?"

"Doing my bit to defend the kul," said Irinya as she tied a couple more darts into her dupatta, making her voice bright and confident.

Bholi Masi wasn't fooled. "You think I don't know about the thorns? But you are not your mother." She pointed at the blowpipe. "You've never used that on an animal, let alone a person."

Irinya swallowed. No, she hadn't. Was she capable of it? "There was never any need to. Let's go, Masi."

"You will stay here where it's safe." Bholi Masi crossed her arms and blocked the entrance, a ferocious scowl on her face.

Hoofs thundered outside the tent, and Irinya's stomach seized. Bholi Masi jerked around, her arms flailing. "Nowhere is safe while there are intruders in the camp," Irinya said. "Don't you want to see what's going on?" She summoned an innocent expression. "I promise not to do anything foolish."

Her aunt hesitated, torn between caution and curiosity. Curiosity won, as Irinya had known it would. "Stay beside me," she ordered.

"Yes, Masi," said Irinya meekly, and they stepped out together.

The sun had risen and the riders had dismounted. They were a rough-looking bunch, tall and beefy, armed with clubs and daggers. Mercenaries? Irinya's spirits plummeted as she recognized Harpal and Lattu, the baniya's bodyguard-clerks.

"Where's Miraben?" called Harpal, scanning the crowd. The men gathered behind him, brandishing their weapons, anticipation on their faces.

Miraben stepped forward, her chin out, her back straight. She looked small and defenseless next to the hefty men, and Irinya wanted to drag her back to safety. "What brings you to our camp?" she demanded.

Harpal gave an unpleasant smile. "To collect something that doesn't belong to you."

"What do you mean?" Vimal thwacked a thick stick against one palm. Fardan and Jai stood on either side of him, armed with cudgels, their faces taut. Irinya's heart gave a little swoop of fear for them all. "We keep nothing that's not ours, nor do we let anyone take what's not theirs."

"I will explain once. After that, any bloodshed is *your* fault, not ours," said Harpal, pointing a finger at them. "You people sold flowers to a man called Kavi Kampilya. Flowers that belong to our employer. Since you do not have the flowers, you will give us the money you got for them. Our employer doesn't like to be cheated."

The words burned away Irinya's fear. The baniya had always acted as if he owned them—as if they were no more than cattle. "We didn't cheat him," she bit out, despite a warning glance from her aunt. "The flowers belong to us, not to him." Around her, the people of the kul murmured agreement, their faces tight, their hands gripping an assortment of unlikely weapons.

The men broke into ugly laughter. "You need to be taught your place," said Lattu with a sneer that she longed to wipe off his face. "You're in his debt, and everything you have is his."

"Kavi Kampilya told your employer to go to his patron's office in Junagadh," said Miraben, her voice steady. "He said he would buy our debt."

"Buy your debt?" Harpal's lip curled. "You've all been taken for a ride. Listen. Mahajan-ji sent a man to the governor's office in Junagadh. He met the sarraf Amal Baderiya, showed him the paperwork, and asked for our employer's money. The sarraf laughed at him. Said he'd received no such instructions and they weren't in the business of buying the debts of poverty-stricken nomads."

Shock coursed through Irinya's veins, ice-cold. "You're lying," she snapped. Fardan locked gazes with her and shook his head. *Stop talking,* he mouthed.

Harpal's voice hardened. "Give us the money. Enough to compensate for a bluestar and a jasmine."

"Just leave," growled Fardan, stepping in front of Miraben and thumping his cudgel on the ground. "We don't want a fight, but we won't let you rob us."

Harpal made a cutting gesture with his hand, and the men attacked. Irinya swallowed a scream and pulled Bholi Masi out of the way of a club-swinging mercenary. Fardan blocked him with his cudgel, and Vimal threw himself on Harpal. Jai tackled Lattu, and all the other able-bodied men of the kul joined the fray, using whatever they'd been able to lay their hands on: sticks, rocks, camel whips, tent ropes, kettles. Even Gopal Masa threw a rock at someone, although he missed. Everyone was fighting too close and moving too fast for Irinya to use her blowpipe. She grabbed hold of an iron pot that had been discarded on the ground and, her stomach turning at what she was about to do, hit one of the intruders on his head. He staggered back in pain, then swung around with a snarl, his club raised. Fardan tackled him from behind, bearing him down to the ground.

Bholi Masi pulled her back. "Come away, Irinya!" Irinya tried to break free, but her aunt's solid arms locked around her middle.

The kul outnumbered their assailants, but the mercenaries were bigger, better armed, and much better trained. Clubs smashed down on shoulders, cracked ribs, broke arms. Ayush and Pranal were knocked down and kicked repeatedly until they were dragged to safety by their shrieking aunts. Fardan got a blow on his head and fell to the ground, unconscious. Irinya's gut clenched at the sight.

"Masi, let go." She dug an elbow into her aunt's side, managing to free herself. She rushed to Fardan and bent over him, checking the wound on his head. Her chest tightened. Blood seeped through his torn scalp and trickled down his face. The club must have had nails on it. She tilted his head back and checked his breathing, praying he was all right. *Normal.* She rocked back on her heels, exhaling in relief.

One of the attackers yanked her by the hair, making her lose her balance. "Is that your sweetheart?" he said with a leer.

There was a sick thud as someone hit him from behind. He stumbled to the ground, clutching his head. Bholi Masi had brained him with Irinya's iron pot. Irinya scrambled to her feet and backed away from him, her scalp burning.

"Enough." Harpal's voice rang out, loud and commanding. Everyone who was still standing turned to him.

He crouched with his back to a tent wall, holding a wicked-looking knife to Miraben's throat. Several people gasped, and someone screamed. Irinya hugged herself, coldness creeping into her limbs. *Not Miraben.* They couldn't afford to lose her. Beside her, Bholi Masi covered her mouth and whimpered.

"Stop right now or I'll kill her, I swear," snarled Harpal. His face was covered in cuts and bruises, but the hand that held the knife didn't shake in the slightest.

"Don't listen to him," Miraben rasped. "Fight!"

Harpal pressed the knife into her throat, and her voice died in a gurgle. Irinya's hand tightened over her blowpipe. But Harpal was shielded by Miraben, and she didn't have a clear shot. She couldn't take the risk of hitting the kul matriarch.

A thin rivulet of blood trickled down Miraben's neck, and her hands spasmed. "Stop it," cried her husband, Devesh, taking a lurching step toward them. "Leave us alone. What have we ever done to you?"

"We would love to go," said Harpal. "We have much better things to do than waste our time in this godforsaken place. Give us what we came for and we'll leave."

"We don't have any money," croaked Miraben.

His eyes narrowed. "Is that so? Then we'll have to take your cattle." He raised his head above Miraben's and cut his gaze to his men. "Round them up."

"No!" Gopal Masa waved his skinny arms in defiance. The others began to shout, too, their faces distorted with panic.

Irinya froze. The herds were the life of the kul. They couldn't survive without them.

Now, whispered the blue petal stitched in her dupatta, startling her out of her paralysis.

Irinya reached within herself, past the fear, to the blowpipe expert who could hit a target thirty feet away. This was the moment she'd been waiting for. No one was looking at her, and Harpal had raised his head, giving her a clear line of sight to his face. She took a deep, shaky breath and raised the blowpipe to her lips. She'd only get one shot; she had to make it count. Sweat beaded her forehead. *Imagine it's a circle on the trunk of a tree, and you're practicing your aim.*

Like she'd done a thousand times before, Irinya aimed and blew with all her strength. The dart flew from her blowpipe with a minute *whoosh* and buried itself in Harpal's forehead. She hid the blowpipe behind her back, her heart banging against her rib cage.

Harpal broke off in the middle of a series of instructions to his men. He let go of Miraben, who collapsed on the ground, and reached up to his forehead. His hand came away stained with blood and broken grass flowers. His mouth fell open in puzzlement. "What . . . ?" he began and keeled over. Lattu and his henchmen rushed over to him as Miraben crawled away. Devesh helped her up, and they backed away, staring at Harpal as he twitched and frothed at the mouth.

The bile rose in Irinya's throat. She'd never hurt a person before. Harpal's body stopped twitching. The men shook him, shouting his name. The kul members watched in silence, casting puzzled glances at each other. Tammi said a quick prayer and made the sign to avert evil. Chinmay took a halting step forward, peering at the men gathered around Harpal as if to memorize the scene for his story collection.

Bholi Masi grabbed Irinya's arm. "Give it to me," she whispered. "They mustn't find it on you." She wrenched the blowpipe out of Irinya's grasp and hid it under her dupatta.

Lattu rose from the ground, his face split in a snarl. "Who did that?" he shouted. "Who killed Harpal?"

He was *dead*? Irinya had wanted to knock him out, that was all. That was why she'd chosen a jasmine thorn. Her limbs went numb and her thoughts froze.

"We've been too soft," Lattu spat. "Should've used knives, not clubs. You people don't know what's good for you. You need a demonstration." He gave a small, sharp nod to one of the others. Without warning, the man grabbed Chinmay and slit his throat from ear to ear. Chinmay fell to the ground, his scrawny neck a bloody ruin, his eyes wide with surprise. Several people screamed. Irinya cried out and started toward him, but Bholi Masi pulled her back, her grip like iron. Irinya hung on her arms, staring at the sad heap of the storyteller's lifeless body, unable to breathe.

Not Chinmay. Not the sweet old man who'd told them countless stories around the fire, making the world of flowers and magic come alive. Not the council elder who'd considered *her* worthy to be his heir. Fardan would wake to find one of his last remaining relatives gone. A harsh sob escaped her throat.

Vimal and Jai advanced on the killer, their faces tense, their fists clenched, but another man grabbed Saira and held his blade to her throat. "Don't come any closer," he warned. "Not unless you want her dead, too." Saira's eyes went wide with fear.

A keening sound came from the crowd, and an old woman pushed her way to the front. Kaya, Chinmay's older sister and Fardan's grand-mother. She bent over his body, weeping and beating her chest. Shweta, the healer, knelt beside her to check his pulse, then rose and shook her head, her lips pressed in a thin line. She laid gentle hands on Kaya's shoulders, then helped her up.

Irinya's chest felt as if there were knives in it. They'd never hear the elder's stories again. And it was *her* fault. She blinked back tears. "Give me back my blowpipe," she said in a fierce whisper to Bholi Masi.

Her aunt stiffened. "No," she whispered back. "They're watching now."

"He'd still be alive if not for your folly," said Lattu to the crowd. "A death for a death. Do you want more? There might be only five of us, but we'll take dozens of you to the pyre with us."

The man holding Saira tightened his grip on her, and she gave a choked scream.

Irinya's heart jumped at the sound. She had to act now and end this before anyone else died. There was only one solution she could think of. "No, wait, stop," she managed to rasp out. She freed herself from Bholi Masi and took a step forward. "Please."

"Are you offering yourself in her place?" Lattu eyed her.

"I want to speak to Miraben," she said, making her voice stronger. "You'll get the money."

There were horrified gasps from everyone, but Irinya ignored them.

"So there *is* money," said Lattu, his voice heavy with satisfaction. "It had better be enough to make up for Harpal's death, or the baniya will set the law on you."

Irinya went to Miraben and grasped her shoulders. The old matri-arch was hurt, and not just from the knife at her neck. One of her arms hung uselessly at her side, and her mouth was bleeding.

"Please, Miraben, give it to them," she pleaded.

Miraben's eyes snapped like fire. "Never. I'll die first."

"And what good will that do?" Irinya squeezed her shoulders, trying to convey by her touch what she was feeling in her heart. "What good will it do if anyone else dies? If they take our herds?"

"The mohur belongs to us." Miraben's voice cracked.

Irinya's vision blurred. Yes, it did. That mohur was more than just money; it was the symbol of their future prosperity, their gateway to a debt-free life. "We'll get it back," she said. "Somehow. I promise. But for now, give it to these men, and let us heal our injured."

"I like you," Lattu drawled, taking a step toward them. "Want to come back with us?"

She flashed him a look of cold contempt. "No. You won't get anything but the money you came for."

"Are you sure of that?" He gave a suggestive smile. "We could always kill a few more people."

"Won't work," she told him, summoning stone into her face, her voice. It wasn't hard. Beneath the salt, beneath the sand, the Rann was solid rock; she could draw from that when she had to. "Because people aren't things. You'd have to kill all of us, and is that what you want to spend your time and energy on?"

"Get on with it. This place gives me the creeps," said the man who had killed Chinmay, wiping his knife on the grass. *Murderer.*

"Hurry up," said Lattu, losing interest in Irinya.

She turned back to Miraben. "Please. Give it to them. If it was meant to be ours, it will come back to us."

The man gripping Saira gave a great, hacking laugh, but she ignored him. All her focus was on Miraben.

Slowly, hatred burning in her eyes, Miraben withdrew the gold mohur from her bun and threw it on the ground.

Lattu snatched it up, his eyes bulging. "A gold mohur!" He bit into it to make sure.

"Mahajan-ji will be happy," said Chinmay's killer.

"Happy? This means a bonus for all of us," said Lattu. "Poor Harpal; he'll be cursing us from the other side." He twirled the mohur in his fingers. "You all are lucky the old hag was persuaded to part with this. Hope you've learned a lesson for the future. All flowers belong to Mahajan-ji. No other buyers will be tolerated. Oh, and your quota has been increased." He paused, an oily smile on his face, regarding their distressed faces with obvious enjoyment.

Irinya stiffened. They were more than halfway through the season. No way they could meet the baniya's quota, let alone exceed it. They'd given their bluestar to Kavi, and he'd returned the jasmine to her. She couldn't part with it—not now. They needed it.

Lattu held up his hands, his fingers spread out. "You must procure *ten* more flowers this season on account of the expense and stress you have put Mahajan-ji through, not to mention the death of his best man. You won't be compensated for them, either. If you don't deliver, we'll be back. There'll be more of us, and we won't be so nice. For every flower you fail to find, we'll kill one more of you."

Miraben gasped at his words. Coldness filled Irinya's stomach. The baniya was out for blood. They'd never be able to find so many flowers in time.

Lattu gave them a final sneer and swept his eyes over his men. "Load Harpal. Let's go."

Five minutes later, they were gone, horse hooves thundering across the grassland. Silence returned to the camp but for the wind flapping the tents, and the cows lowing in the distance. A child cried and was hushed by an older sibling. Irinya stared at the camp, light-headed. The ground was littered with sticks, pots, ropes, and other household items the kul had used and discarded in the futile fight against the baniya's men. A couple of tents had been smashed, and the grass was stained red where the injured had fallen.

The sound of weeping rose above the wind, eroding Irinya's fraying self-control. Kaya and the others surrounded Chinmay's body, holding each other. Fardan had regained consciousness; he sat propped up against a tent wall, blood trickling down his face, looking dazedly at his great-uncle's body, as if he could not grasp what had happened. Next to him, Jai wheezed, clutching his chest.

Darkness came before Irinya's eyes. *I'm sorry, Fardan. Sorry for what I did.*

Miraben glared at Irinya. "We'll get the mohur back?"

"Yes." Somehow, she would make it happen.

The matriarch narrowed her eyes. "You're the one who shot that dart."

Irinya's face flamed. How had Miraben guessed?

"It was your mother's weapon of choice. I see you inherited her talent." Miraben's face twisted and her voice rose in a scream. "Why didn't you kill *all* of them?"

Irinya forced herself not to flinch at her vehemence. Miraben was grieving; they all were.

"Wouldn't have worked," said Bholi Masi, stepping to Irinya's side. "They were watching. Would have spotted her at once."

"What do you use for the darts?" asked Shweta, her hands on her hips.

"Thorns," said Irinya, staring at the ground, wishing it would swallow her up.

Shweta nodded. "Like your mother. You know the danger, and still you dabble in it."

"I don't *dabble*." Irinya fumbled for words. "I . . . I'm careful."

"Two people are dead. One who deserved it, and one who didn't. And now we must find ten flowers or risk losing more of our people." Shweta tilted her head. "Is that what you call being careful?"

Her words stabbed Irinya. She hadn't thought of the consequences. She'd only wanted to save the kul and its herds.

"See to the injured, Shweta," said Miraben tiredly.

Shweta raised her eyebrows. "I'd better start with you, then. Off you go to your tent."

"I'm barely scratched," argued Miraben. "Take care of the others."

But Shweta chivied Miraben to her tent, despite her protests. Irinya watched them go, the healer's words burning into her.

Bholi Masi laid a hand on her shoulder. "Let's help the others."

Around them, people were checking on the wounded, carrying them to the tents for healing. Someone had covered Chinmay with a white sheet. Irinya dragged her gaze away from his corpse and looked at Fardan instead. Saira was dabbing his bleeding face with a cloth.

Irinya went to him, her feet leaden. His face was drawn in pain, his eyes unfocused.

Saira rose. "I'll ask the men to carry you inside," she told him.

Irinya grabbed her arm. "Are you okay?"

Saira gave a brittle smile. "I am. But many are not." She walked away.

Irinya knelt in front of Fardan and swallowed. "I'm sorry."

"Chinmay?" he said with difficulty.

"I'm sorry," she repeated, her throat burning.

His mouth tightened, and he looked away.

"I'll make it right," she said forcefully. "I promise."

He took a deep, shaky breath, still not looking at her. "What does that even mean?"

A couple of men arrived to help him up and take him to his tent. Irinya rose, her eyes blurring.

She knew what he was saying. She'd broken a promise before. Her words meant nothing to him.

But she was going to fix this. She was going to earn back Fardan's trust and protect the kul. She would find Kavi and get what they were owed for the spider lily, if it was the last thing she did. *Wealth to last your kul for generations,* he'd said. It had to be enough to pay down their debt.

But where was Kavi? What had happened to him? Why had he not sent a message to the sarraf in Junagadh about their debt? Harpal had implied he'd duped them all, but that was unbelievable. Far likelier that he'd run into trouble of some sort. She bit her nails, imagining him beset by bandits, struck by sudden illness, or—worst of all—betrayed to the enemy.

Please be alive, Kavi. Please be safe. You carry the future of my kul in your hands.

CHAPTER 6

You'll need me later, the dream-jasmine had said. It had given no hint it would be so soon.

There was no time to make a proper tincture, and Irinya didn't have the specialized equipment that city apothecaries did. But she knew the basics. That would have to be enough. She stole a gourd of hariya from Gopal Masa's not-so-secret stash, hidden beneath his pallet, and heated it in a pot before keeping it aside. Then she removed her precious jasmine from its box and chopped it with Bholi Masi's sharpest knife, hoping fervently that her aunt and uncle would not return to the tent until she'd finished. She placed the flower bits at the bottom of a clean earthen jar, topped it up with the hariya, and stoppered it. It would be at least twenty-four hours before the flower dissolved and infused the hariya with its magic.

"What are you doing?" Bholi Masi poked her head into the tent, making Irinya jump and bite her tongue. "There are a lot of injuries. We need everyone to help."

"Making a medicinal tincture." Irinya tried not to wince as she wrapped the jar in a rug and stuffed it underneath Gopal Masa's pallet, next to the remaining gourds of hariya. "Be right with you."

Bholi Masi's forehead puckered. "Since when do you know anything about healing or the making of medicinal tinctures?"

Irinya straightened, wiping her hands on her dupatta. "I've watched

Shweta do it many times," she said, putting as much sincerity as she could into her voice. "It won't harm anyone, at least." Praying, as she spoke, that the words were true. Jasmine was the flower of healing; it should be the safest to ingest, even if she made mistakes with the process.

The rest of the day passed in a blur of tense activity. Miraben ordered lookouts to be posted to make sure the baniya's men didn't return. Rishabh led the cleanup, and Gopal Masa organized the retrieval of the herds, tasking the children with counting them all. Four tents were converted into a sick bay for the injured. Bholi and her cousin pitched in to cook the noon meal—not that anyone felt like eating.

Irinya spent the afternoon helping Shweta and the other women tie bandages, prepare salves, set bones, and comfort those in pain. Fardan, Ayush, and Pranal all had head injuries. Jai had several broken ribs. Vimal's shoulder had been dislocated by a club. He bit down on a twig to keep from biting his own tongue as Shweta guided the ball of his arm bone back into its socket. Tears leaked from his eyes, and Irinya wiped his forehead with a damp cloth, trying to distract him with a story of the tiger and the hibiscus while holding back tears herself.

They'd lost so much, and they stood to lose even more. The image of Chinmay's throat being cut flashed before her eyes, and pain stabbed her heart. The elder was gone, taken from them because of *her* meddling. She'd thought she could protect the kul; instead, she had recklessly endangered them all. If only she hadn't used her blowpipe on Harpal, the kul's venerable old storyteller would still be alive.

That evening, they built a funeral pyre for Chinmay. It wasn't easy; there wasn't much in the way of dry wood in the grassland. But a minimum amount was necessary for a dignified burn. Fortunately, one of the children found a desiccated acacia tree some distance away, and the men chopped it for the pyre.

Everyone came except those too injured to walk. Irinya stood beside Bholi, her eyes burning, as Miraben talked of Chinmay's long life in service to the kul. The words of the eulogy washed over her, unreal in their finality. *I still need to listen to your stories,* she wanted to shout. *Please don't leave me and Fardan.* She rubbed her chest, as if that could ease the ache inside her, and swallowed a sob.

"We will not forget him and his stories, and we will not forgive the way he died," Miraben concluded. She nodded to Devesh, and he stepped forward, a torch in his hand.

Fardan should have been the one to light the pyre, but he was ill and feverish, drifting in and out of consciousness. Irinya had checked on him multiple times that afternoon, and each time, he had looked no better, making her nerves thrum with anxiety.

Devesh lit the pyre in Fardan's stead. Flames crackled over the white-clad body, and Tammi recited the last rites, consigning his soul to the sky. Everyone was quiet and still, even the children. Kaya wept continuously, tears streaking down her withered face.

The kul was no stranger to death. The Rann took its toll, and the monsoon brought fevers. One terrible year, their village had been overrun with Black Death. Nearly half of them had died.

But never had anyone been taken from them with such violence. No one had been *murdered*.

People gave Irinya strange looks. No one asked her about the blowpipe; perhaps Miraben had told them not to. But they must know by now that she was responsible for Harpal's death and, as a result, Chinmay's. Kaya did not look at her or speak to her, nor did Irinya have the words to express her guilt and sorrow. What could she say that would make the slightest difference? "Sorry" would not bring him back. She deserved to be blamed and punished. The fact that no one accused her only sharpened her sense of shame and strengthened her resolve to protect the remaining kul members. No one else would die, not while she had breath in her body.

After the funeral, Miraben called a meeting in the communal tent. Less than half the kul showed up; the rest were taking care of the injured, patrolling the camp, or with Kaya. Irinya sat in a corner, feeling small—the youngest person and the only flower hunter present. The air was thick with gloom, faces tight with exhaustion and grief as Rishabh did a grim tally of their losses. One kul elder dead. Eleven people injured, some seriously. Four goats missing. One gold mohur gone. Hope for the future—gone. At least the children were safe—for now.

"How are we going to find ten more flowers in the next few months?" said Rishabh in a hollow voice.

Eyes swiveled to Irinya, and she swallowed. "We won't need to," she said with more confidence than she felt. "Kavi Kampilya will buy our flowers for what they're worth. We'll pay off the baniya."

"Kavi Kampilya lied to us," said Miraben flatly. Her head and neck were bandaged, her face ravaged by loss.

Irinya's heart squeezed. Kavi had not lied. That wasn't the kind of man he was. But how to make the rest of them see this? They were angry and grieving, rightfully so. "Please, Elder, I don't think so," she said, trying to keep her voice calm, her words reasonable. "Why did he give us a gold mohur? Why did he advise us to form a cooperative?"

"He lied about the debt," said Vimal. He leaned against a trunk, his arm in a sling, his face drawn in lines of pain. He had insisted on being present, even though Miraben had tried to persuade him to rest with the other wounded men.

"We don't know that." Irinya's heart constricted at what she was about to say. But it was the only thing that made any sense. "Something must have happened to him, something that prevented him from sending a message to his sarraf."

"We were too happy," said Rishabh in a toneless voice. "*Gloating,* some of us were. This is a lesson not to get too attached to anything, otherwise it gets taken away from you." He gave Miraben a pointed look.

"Are you saying we do not deserve to be happy?" demanded Miraben. "Do not deserve to be debt-free?"

"It is useless to argue about what we deserve," said Shweta. "We must deal with reality, and the reality is bleak."

"I know it looks bleak, but I don't trust anything those men said, and neither should you," said Gopal Masa, surprising Irinya. He hardly ever spoke at kul meetings. "Something may well have delayed Kavi. We can't take their word for it. They were here to steal from us, to take revenge for their master's humiliation." Irinya shot him a grateful look.

"They succeeded in their revenge," said Miraben, her voice bitter.

Bholi patted her arm. "We'll recover. We always do. Let us wait for Kavi Kampilya. He will return, and everything will be all right again."

But that was the one thing Irinya could not believe. Kavi wasn't coming back. Something had happened to him. Something *bad.* That was the only logical explanation for his absence. A knot formed in her stomach as she thought of the myriad ways he might have come to harm. He'd been carrying a silver spider lily, a fortune worth kingdoms. And he'd been all alone. Why hadn't some of them volunteered to see him safely to Ahmedabad? Where was the spider lily now? Had it fallen into the wrong hands?

The thought of the spider lily in Portuguese possession made her nauseous. They'd already won multiple battles against the sultanate and its allies. The spider lily would make them unstoppable. The Dabul massacre would be multiplied many times over across the Indian subcontinent. She pictured corpses piling on the streets of Bhuj and Ahmedabad, and her hands went clammy. She tried to push the horrific visions away—after all, she had no evidence that the worst had happened—but they returned to haunt her dreams that night, and she woke sweating and trembling.

What will you do? whispered the blue petal.

"Find the spider lily," she whispered back. That was the only solution, both to save her kul and to save India.

In the morning, bleary and unrested, she dragged out the earthen jar from underneath Gopal Masa's pallet, removed the stopper, and sniffed.

The fragrance was so strong she nearly keeled over. Thick, sweet, and rich—both like and unlike the flower. No hint remained of the typical fruity aroma of hariya. She hefted the jar in her arms and went to the tents that housed the wounded. One by one, she persuaded them to take a spoonful of her tincture. When they asked, she told them it was an herbal remedy her mother had passed on to her. She didn't want to lie, but none of them would have accepted tincture of jasmine.

Fardan, she kept for the last. He was by himself in his grandmother's tent, his head bandaged, his eyes fever bright. Her heart plummeted as she took in his hollow cheeks, his twitching body. He looked even worse than he had yesterday. She laid her fingers on his pulse, and her throat clogged with fear. It was fast and irregular. "Fardan?" she tried, but he looked at her without recognition. She blinked back tears. The tincture would help him; it had to. She raised his head and managed to pour a spoonful into his mouth.

Now all she had to do was wait and pray she hadn't accidentally poisoned anyone. She threw herself into chores to keep anxiety at bay.

Ayush was the first to recover. He bounded out of his tent that afternoon, looking his usual mischievous self, to the astonishment and delight of his parents. Irinya walked forward, knees weak with relief, and patted his cheeks to reassure herself, to which he responded by pulling her hair. She swatted his hand away, half laughing, half crying.

His brother, Pranal, was the next to emerge. Shortly after, Vimal discarded his sling and announced that his arm was perfectly fine. At first, Miraben refused to believe him, but he demonstrated by picking her up with that arm, making her shriek. One by one, the rest of the wounded walked out of their tents, looking tired but healthy. Irinya watched their reunions with loved ones, her heart full. She hadn't poisoned anyone; she'd *healed* them.

But the one person she'd been waiting for did not come out. She hung around outside Fardan's tent with Pranal and Ayush, letting their chatter wash over her, her stomach roiling with anxiety.

At last, as the sun cast its dying rays over the grassland and the wind picked up, sharp and cold, Fardan emerged from his tent, his face gaunt and puzzled, but his eyes clear. Irinya's hand flew to her mouth, stifling a sob. *You're all right, Fardan. I can leave now.*

"This is a miracle," said Miraben with a tremulous smile, wiping her eyes. "The goddess still watches over us."

Fardan's grandmother embraced him, and Irinya made herself scarce, retreating to her tent, where she'd hidden the tincture. Today, everyone was too happy to think about it, but tomorrow, they would remember her going around with a mysterious medicine, doling it out to all the "miraculous" recovered. The council would question her, and she would be unable to lie to them. They'd stop being happy when they realized that she'd given the wounded a tincture of jasmine. They'd think she'd brought misfortune upon them by using a magic flower. Those who hunted flowers weren't supposed to use them.

But Kavi had given her the jasmine, and the jasmine had spoken to her. If there was a price to be paid, then she would pay it. It was worth it, being able to heal everyone. As for the kul, by the time they realized she'd used jasmine, she'd be long gone.

The thought of leaving made her chest hurt. These were her people, her family, her home. She'd never traveled anywhere without them before. But somewhere, Kavi Kampilya had run into trouble, and she, Irinya Dewa, was going to get him out of it so he could fulfill his promise to her and her kul. If he was ill or injured, she would heal him. If he had been captured by bandits, she would get help from the nearest taluka to free him. But first, she had to *find* him. And she had an idea—wild and improbable though it was—for how she could do that.

That night, the kul celebrated Chinmay's life and the recovery of their wounded with a small feast. Tomorrow, they would face the grim reality of the impossible quota the baniya had imposed on them and the threat Lattu had delivered, but for now, they told Chinmay's stories and sang his songs around the fire. Irinya joined in, telling one of her favorites: the story of the princess locked in a tower who was freed by a black chrysanthemum. Fardan sat opposite her, watching her, his face unreadable. After all the days he'd spent ignoring her, his steadfast gaze made her feel hot and itchy. She couldn't figure out what he was thinking, and she stumbled on her words—something that *never* happened when she was telling stories.

When the tale was done, she made her escape, pleading fatigue. While her aunt and uncle lingered by the fire, she rushed back to the tent to make her preparations. She emptied a jute bag and packed spare clothes, twigs of kharijal to clean her teeth, waterskins, a roll of rotlas, handfuls of berries tied in a cloth, and the dowry bag with her precious blowpipe and darts. The jar with the remaining tincture of jasmine went in a separate bag, encased in her thickest shawl. She pushed both bags under a heap of camel saddles and straightened.

The tent looked cluttered and homely in the sputtering lamplight. The only empty space was in the middle, where she and her aunt spread their rugs to sleep every night. Gopal Masa's pallet was covered by a sheet tucked into the corners, his clothes folded neatly inside an open trunk next to it, as if in defiance of the general mess. The cooking area near the entrance, in contrast, was an exuberant jumble of pots, pans, the black iron kettle, and various jars.

Tears pricked Irinya's eyes, and she dashed them away, annoyed with herself. Now was not the time to get sentimental. Now was the time to finish her preparations. She still had to leave them a message.

Her aunt and uncle couldn't read or write; most of the older people couldn't. But Irinya and others of her generation had learned the basics at their village temple school. Bholi Masi could easily ask someone to decipher the message for her. Irinya opened the wooden trunk where her aunt and uncle stored the papers relating to their debt, livestock, and village property, and stole a bit of precious parchment. She snagged a quill, dipped the end into a mixture of soot and oil, and wrote: *Gone to find Kavi. Taking Veerana. Do not worry.*

That last line was a waste of ink. Bholi Masi would be frantic with worry. But Irinya could not help that. She folded the parchment and placed it under the kettle, where her aunt would find it in the morning when she wanted to brew tea. Then she spread her rug, gathered the clothes she meant to wear during her journey—a white kurta and a dhoti from her uncle's neat stack, as well as a clean square of cloth for a turban—and hid them underneath. She'd barely lain down, pretending to be asleep, when her aunt and uncle returned to the tent, her uncle announcing his presence by tripping over her boots at the entrance.

"Hush," hissed Bholi Masi. "Can't you see she's sleeping?"

"Strange," whispered Gopal Masa, picking himself up. "She usually never sleeps so early."

"Must be exhausted, poor thing. Did you see how she took care of all the injured people today? Made a special medicine for them."

"Miraben was asking what was in it."

Irinya flinched under her quilt. It hadn't taken Miraben long to start getting nosy.

"She can ask Irinya in the morning," said Bholi Masi. "Now do be quiet."

I'll be gone in the morning. Irinya waited, her lips clamped together, as her aunt and uncle turned down the lamp and retired for the night. An hour passed. When she was sure they were asleep, she rose and got ready in the dark. She hoped Gopal Masa wouldn't mind that she was borrowing his clothes. She tied her breast cloth snugly around her chest and retrieved the clothes she'd hidden under her rug. The white kurta, the dhoti around her waist, Kavi's boots on her feet, and all she needed to complete the look of a man—at least from a distance—was a turban. Happily, she'd seen her uncle wrap it around his balding head enough times to know how it was done. She tied her hair in a knot and twisted the large white square of cloth around it.

The pouch with the empty jewelry box remained on her belt. She could barter it for food if things got tough, although she was reluctant to part with it. It had been a gift from Kavi, after all. Perhaps such things were commonplace to him, but to her it was special. She'd show him the empty box when she finally found him, tell him what she'd done, and thank him. If not for the jasmine, the wounded would still be suffering. Fardan might never have recovered.

She wrapped the dupatta with the blue petal around her neck like a scarf and took a deep breath. She was ready now—as ready as she would ever be. It was strange wearing her uncle's clothes. She hoped she'd tied the dhoti properly. It would be awful if it fell off.

Gopal Masa gave a gentle snore, and Bholi Masi mumbled and turned over. Irinya gave their sleeping forms one last look. *Goodbye,* she thought, her heart constricting. *I'll be back with enough wealth to pay the kul's debt. I'll free us from the baniya. See if I don't!*

She dragged her bags out from under the saddles, picked the saddle in best shape, and snuck outside.

It was dark and chilly, the fire tamped, the animals quiet in their enclosures. A slender crescent moon hung like a smile in the sky.

Now for the tricky part. She had no intention of walking hundreds of miles to Ahmedabad. The kul had fifteen camels. She planned to borrow her uncle's.

"Going somewhere?"

Her heart jumped into her mouth, and she whirled around.

Fardan stood a few feet behind her, so still he might have been part of the night itself. Only his eyes gleamed, hazel-bright, in the dark. His gaze traveled over her, making her squirm. "Are those your uncle's clothes?"

"Shh," she hissed, trying not to panic. So much for making a quiet getaway. At least he was by himself. "You'll wake people up."

"Where are you off to?" he asked, crossing his arms, his voice heavy with suspicion.

She gritted her teeth. "None of your business."

He frowned. "It is, actually. We're part of the same kul, in case you've forgotten."

"That doesn't mean you can stop me," she snapped.

He tilted his head and considered. "No, but all I have to do is shout once, and your aunt will come racing to do the job."

The words stopped her cold. Yes, that was all he needed to do. If Bholi Masi caught her in the act of running away, it would be the end of all her plans to find Kavi and get what he'd promised for the kul.

Her mind worked fast, picking and discarding various options. She needed Fardan to back off. There was one way to do that. She hated it, and she didn't know if it would work. But it was worth a try, especially because she couldn't think of anything else. "You're jealous," she said, making her voice cold.

"What?" He dropped his arms and stared at her.

"You're jealous of Kavi Kampilya. You know you can never be like him. And you hate that I . . ." She swallowed and made herself say it: ". . . that I have feelings for him."

It was a shot in the dark; she didn't know whether Fardan liked her or whether he thought of her as more than a friend. Maybe he even hated her after she'd given the spider lily to Kavi. *Good.* Let him hate her even more. Let him hate her so much he wouldn't care whether she stayed or left the kul.

His eyes widened at her words, and he inhaled sharply.

"I'm going to find him," she continued, encouraged by his reaction, keeping her tone flat. "Stay out of my way."

"Don't be a fool," he rasped. "How can you find him? Ahmedabad's a big city."

"I know where to go," she lied, willing her voice not to tremble. She couldn't betray any weakness, not now. "He told me."

"Then take someone with you." He took a step toward her, his face taut.

She held up a warning hand. "I don't need anyone."

"But there are people here who need *you*," he pleaded.

She took a deep breath. "I can't help that. I must go alone."

He threw up his hands. "Why?"

Because I could be wrong. Because it's too dangerous, and I can't risk anyone else. This is my burden to bear, my responsibility, and mine alone. "Because I'm tired of you," she said, the words tasting like poison on her tongue. "*All* of you. I want a new life, and I can't start one with someone dogging my footsteps, holding me back."

"You don't mean it." His voice quivered with uncertainty.

"Yes, I do. I'm sick of this life. Have been, for a long time. Kavi's just the spark that set me free. You didn't see it because you didn't want to." She hardened her tone. "Do you think of anything besides your drawings?"

"I think of you," he said softly.

His words almost undid her. She steeled herself. "Stop, because it's no use. I'm leaving."

"For the sake of the spider lily you stole, and the promise you broke," he said, taking another step toward her, "don't go—not like this."

She gave a scoffing laugh, her throat tight with pain. "It's just a *flower*, Fardan. A valuable one, of course, and the kul must be compensated for it. But you're giving it meaning it never had in the first place. You're wasting my time. Goodbye."

She turned and walked away, her back straight, her head held high, her eyes stinging. She thought he might try to stop her again, but he didn't, and when she looked back, he was gone.

CHAPTER 7

The night was endless, the grassland forever, the stars bright pinpricks of light in the velvet sky. A cold breeze stroked Irinya's cheeks with its chilly fingers, and she shivered, swaying on the camel's back. She'd traveled across Banni in every season, in all hours of the day and night, but never alone. It felt eerie, as if she were the only person in the world, on a journey without end.

Snap out of it, she scolded herself. *You have a plan. Get to Bhuj, join a caravan to Ahmedabad, visit the flower market, and use sunflower to find Kavi.*

Easier said than done. A lot would depend on her own resourcefulness, but a lot would depend on luck as well.

Had she done the right thing? Impossible to tell. Perhaps this was one more terrible mistake to add to her ever-expanding list. Suppose she couldn't find Kavi. What would she do? Return empty-handed?

No, that wasn't an option. *For every flower you fail to find, we'll kill one more of you,* Lattu had said. She would return with the money they were owed for the spider lily, or not at all.

Make sure you return me safe and sound.

She started. "Veerana, did you speak?"

The camel snorted, and she leaned forward to pat his comfortingly broad back. Aloneness did funny things to the mind. Veerana was her uncle's camel. If something happened to him, Gopal Masa would never forgive her. *She* wouldn't forgive herself.

She tried not to think of Bholi Masi. Every single day that Irinya was away, her aunt would imagine the worst that the world could do to her. Irinya should have added *disguised as a man* to her goodbye note. That would have assuaged Bholi Masi's fears.

No—who was she fooling? Bholi Masi's fears would not have been assuaged. *You silly girl,* she would have wailed, *as soon as you open your mouth, people will suspect!*

Well, she would have to use her deepest voice and hope for the best.

Thinking of Fardan was even worse than thinking of Bholi Masi. She'd hurt him, and she'd done it deliberately. He'd never forgive her. First a broken promise and now a broken friendship. Would he tell Bholi Masi about their encounter? She thought not. It would shame him, and the kul would blame him for not stopping her, no matter how unfair that was. She remembered his wounded expression when she'd said all those cruel things, and her heart squeezed. Despite their frequent bickering, he'd always been caring and protective of her. Always packed lunch for her when they hunted flowers together. And this was how she'd repaid him.

I think of you, he'd said. The words gave her goose bumps. For all his silly flirting, Fardan had never given any hint of serious romantic interest in her. If he had, Bholi would have chased him across Banni with her broom. Had he said that just to stop her from leaving?

No, he wasn't like that. Unlike *some* people—Irinya twisted on the saddle—he didn't have a deceptive bone in his body. *What did you mean, Fardan?* she wanted to ask him. *What do you really think of me?* But it was too late for that. And if something happened to her and she couldn't return to the kul, she'd never know. That would be the last conversation they'd ever have.

The thought made her chest ache. *I'm sorry, Fardan. I'll make it up to you. I'll find Kavi and come back; I swear by salt and sun.*

She guided her camel southeast, using the Star of Dhruva as a compass. The wind whistled down the plain, rustling the grass and creaking the boughs of isolated trees. At least she was far enough away from the Rann that Chir Batti was not a danger. Still, it was unnerving traveling by herself in the night with only Veerana for company.

Her first stop would be the city of Bhuj. This part of the journey, at least, was familiar to her. Their own village was on the outskirts of the

Kutch capital. She could reach it in five days. She would have to make her food last until then, although she hoped to find water on the way. There were a couple of large watering holes that lay on her planned route, but she wasn't sure if they'd have any water in them during the peak of summer. Once in Bhuj, she would hop on a caravan to Ahmedabad.

Her eyes closed, and she leaned her head on the wooden pole in front of her. If only she had a charpoy to sleep on rather than just a saddle on the hump. At least the pole reduced the likelihood of falling off.

She woke to stiff muscles, a sore back, and chapped lips. The grass shone dew-bright in the morning sunlight, stretching in every direction as far as the eye could see. Veerana cropped grass, flicking buzzing dragonflies away with his tail. She drank from her waterskin, wincing as she straightened herself on the saddle. Five days of this might kill her, even if nothing else did.

At noon, she made Veerana stop and slid off his back, groaning. While he grazed, she ate a rotla, washing it down with water and a handful of berries. Then she tied him to an acacia tree, knotted the rope around one of her feet, and lay down to rest beneath its shade.

"The ground is softer than your back, Veerana," she said, gazing at the empty blue sky, framed against the branches above.

Veerana did not deign to respond. She fell asleep and woke in the evening to find him nibbling her boots. "Bad boy," she scolded, not that it made the slightest difference to him.

They moved again, skirting a village. She would have liked to stop and replenish her waterskin, but it was too risky. Solo travelers were rare in Banni. She couldn't afford anyone taking special notice of her.

The second night was hard. The first night, excitement had fueled her. But now the moon was bigger by a sliver, shining light upon all the faults in her plan, in *her*.

What was she thinking? That she'd be accepted in a caravan and be able to enter the walled city of Ahmedabad without being stopped and questioned? That she could gain access to the flower market and score a sunflower to locate Kavi? The yellow sunflower could find lost things, but would it work for a person? Her entire plan depended on the answer. But she could barter her tincture of jasmine for a bit of sunflower tea in any flower market.

That is the first idea you have had that is not complete nonsense.

Imagining Veerana's cynical voice cheered her up and made her feel less lonely. And it *was* a good idea. Ahmedabad's fabled Khaas Bazaar hosted the biggest flower market in Gujarat.

The next morning, they came upon a pond, and Veerana drank his fill. She refilled her waterskins, hoping the water was clean. Her back and thighs ached from the long night of riding, and she switched to walking to stretch her legs. It felt odd, walking in a dhoti. She kept thinking it would fall off. The ghagras she normally wore were much more comfortable, although she liked the freedom of the loose kurta as compared to a tight choli. The turban was a pain; it kept unraveling. She had to rewrap it around her head several times.

On the third day, she spied a group of rough-looking horsemen in the distance. Unfortunately, they spotted her at the same time. They turned their horses toward her, and Irinya scrambled up on Veerana, her heart thudding. "*Hiyyup!*" she shouted, and Veerana broke into a half-hearted gallop. The men tried to give chase, but luckily their horses were not used to camels, and they shied away from Veerana.

Her food ran out on the fourth day. On the fifth day, she arrived on the outskirts of Bhuj, footsore and hungry. Her stomach felt like a shriveled berry, all skin and no substance.

She avoided her kul's ancestral village—she was well-known to those who lived there year-round—and stopped at the next settlement, where she managed to get a meal at a temple community kitchen. It was only flatbread with a bowl of dal, but it tasted wonderful. She slept in the temple courtyard with other travelers, taking care to tie her bags and her camel to herself. It was useful being dressed as a man, and a scruffy one, too. Her clothes were shabby after a five-day trek across Kutch, her turban soiled with grass and mud—because she'd stepped on it by mistake—and her face streaked with dust. Her jute bags weren't much to look at, and neither was she. The only thing she had of value was her camel. Gopal Masa was probably missing him much more than he was missing her.

The next morning, she followed a group of travelers to Bhuj. Recently founded by Rao Hamirji, one of the three chiefs of Kutch, the new city was located between a hill on the east and a lake on the west.

Towers and fortifications gleamed white in the sunlight as hundreds of people gathered outside the main gate in the southern wall. Some had animals in tow, others balanced baskets of fruits or vegetables on their heads.

Irinya was glad of the anonymity of the crowd. The guards stopped some people to question them, letting most inside after a cursory check of their goods. She tried to slip in after another camel owner, but a hefty guard held up his hand, stopping her.

"State your business," he rasped.

Her heart jumped in alarm, but she managed to school her expression. "I'd like to join a caravan to Ahmedabad, sir," she said with an ingratiating grin, hoping her turban wouldn't fall off.

He gave her a disparaging up-down look. "What can you do?"

"Do?" she repeated, bewildered.

"Traders don't hire unless you're good for something. Can you hold a sword or wield a mace? I doubt it. Such puny arms. Nah, you're too scrawny. They need muscle to guard the caravan." He flexed his own arm in demonstration.

I could fell you with a single breath of my blowpipe, you overbuilt fool. "I'm good with animals," she said, summoning sincerity. "I can read and write. I can even cook." That wasn't exactly a lie.

He jerked his chin toward a large banyan tree to the left of the gate. Several men sat underneath its spreading branches and aerial roots. "Wait there with the others."

She led Veerana to the tree, trying not to feel dejected. She'd hoped to enter the city itself. She selected a spot near the edge of the tree canopy, away from the men, and sat down. Veerana nibbled her turban, and she pushed him away, annoyed. Unlike her, he'd had plenty to eat during the journey, and yet he wanted to sample her clothing.

"Nice camel," drawled a burly man, leaning toward her. "What do you want for him?"

"He's not for sale," she said flatly.

He narrowed his eyes at her. "Run away from home, have you?"

"Probably stolen the camel, too," said another man with a smirk. "We'd be doing him a favor, taking it off his hands."

Irinya stiffened. She would die before she let them take Veerana.

"Leave him alone," said an older man leaning against the trunk of the tree. "What's your name, kid?"

She panicked and uttered the first name that entered her brain. "Fardan."

A well-dressed merchant strode up to them, and, to her relief, the attention of the group turned away from her. The merchant selected a couple of muscular men and left his clerks to work out the details of their employment. Irinya watched them leave, trying not to feel disappointed that she hadn't been picked. The day was still young; she had plenty of chances. Surely merchants needed more than just brawny men to guard their caravans.

Once they were gone, the conversation turned to the war with the Portuguese.

"They've conquered Goa," said a sad-eyed man with an enormous mustache. "I heard they were helped by a sultanate turncoat."

Irinya's ears pricked up. Kavi had said the Portuguese were poised to take Goa.

Another man snorted. "Why should we care? Poor people like you and me will suffer no matter whether the sultan rules or the foreigners."

"Watch your tongue," warned the burly man who had first spoken to her, glancing toward the guards at the gate. "Or someone will cut it off."

"What news of Calicut?" Irinya asked.

"Taken," said the burly man somberly. "Portuguese ships bombed the city and demolished the Calicut fleet. The palace of the zamorin was destroyed and the city itself is burning. So says my cousin, who escaped with his life but lost his wife and children to the blaze."

Irinya's heart sank. The war was going well for the Portuguese—too well. Was it already too late? Had the silver spider lily come into their possession? And if so, what had they done to Kavi? Was he still alive? Her stomach roiled with anxiety. Once again, horrific visions of streets littered with corpses, and burning ship holds filled with dying men, women, and children did a macabre dance before her eyes. And in her kul, the baniya's men laughed evilly and slashed Miraben's neck, and then Rishabh's, and Shweta's, and Bholi Masi's, and Fardan's. . . .

Stop it, she scolded herself. She took a deep breath and wiped her eyes, turning her face away from the others. Spiraling like this wasn't going to help her or her kul. The war going well for the Portuguese didn't mean that the spider lily had fallen into their hands. If that had happened, the war would already be over. They would have overrun India by now. Besides, Kavi wasn't a fool. He knew the worth of what he was carrying and wouldn't have been deceived into parting with it. A delay had occurred, but it was for a reason she couldn't yet fathom. Only Kavi would be able to tell her the truth. *You'd better be alive, Kavi,* she thought fiercely. *And you'd better still have the spider lily.*

A merchant walked up to them, accompanied by a guard, and the group fell silent. The morning wore on. One by one, the men under the tree found employment in various caravans as guards, porters, or cooks. But no one seemed interested in her. If the *real* Fardan had been around, he'd have been snapped up in minutes. Her prospects were diminishing by the hour.

Veerana settled down next to her to chew his cud. She patted his neck. "Don't worry. We'll go alone if we must."

The camel gave her a soulful glance out of his large, lustrous eyes. If he could have spoken, he'd probably have said, *Are you off your head?*

The routes between Bhuj and Ahmedabad were thickly forested and infested with bandits, to say nothing of lions and tigers. Merchants traveled in large caravans, protected by guards on horseback and camel-back. Even then, it was risky. A quarter of all caravans were attacked by bandits, and someone almost always got carried off by a tiger. Irinya had never seen a tiger, but she'd heard them described and wished fervently never to encounter one. The largest predator in the grasslands was the cheetah, and it was shy of humans.

At last, when only a couple of elderly men were left apart from her, a clerk in an elaborate red-and-white turban and crisp white dhoti strode up to the tree. "Which one of you can read and write?" he asked.

Irinya shot to her feet, her heart leaping. "That's me."

The clerk frowned, taking in her shabby appearance, and thrust a parchment at her. "Read it aloud."

She scanned the parchment. It was Kutchi, written in the Khojki script—a more refined version than she had learned at the temple school, but still comprehensible. "Tribute from Rao Hamirji, chief of Kutch, jurisdiction two thousand and eighty villages, is updated to four thousand horsemen, three thousand foot soldiers, and annual tax equivalent to one-fourth of all land revenue collected from said villages," she recited.

He plucked the parchment from her hand and gave her another. "Now this."

She gazed at the new parchment, and her heart sank. The script bore some resemblance to Khojki but was unfamiliar to her. She licked her lips and tried to focus. She couldn't lose this chance, or who knew how long she'd be stuck in Bhuj. Even a single day wasted was a delay she could not afford. She had to find Kavi as soon as possible.

"You cannot read Devanagari?" said the clerk, disappointed.

"I can almost read it," she said with more confidence than she felt. "It is similar to Khojki." She narrowed her eyes at the parchment and summoned all the gods and goddesses of learning. "Rao Hamirji permission to mine, no—mint—coins? And there's something about the pilgrims of Mecca."

"Rao Hamirji undertakes to provide safe passage to the pilgrims of Mecca," said the clerk. He gave her an appraising look. "Fine, you're hired. My name is Naveen Gupta, and I work for the Department of Revenue."

Triumph welled up in her. She'd been hired, and by the Bhuj administration. That meant the caravan would be safer than most. "Hired for what, Gupta-ji?" She tugged Veerana by his reins, and he rose majestically.

"You will help my assistant with the paperwork generated by his lordship's visit. The task must be completed before the caravan returns to Ahmedabad, so you have a week. The job is temporary, mind. You're only getting it because two of my assistants have come down with marsh fever." He glanced at Veerana. "You can't take the camel. Only the Baluchi cameleers are allowed their personal mounts."

"I can't leave him," she protested. "He's like my brother."

The clerk's eyebrows rose. "You can leave your 'brother' in the care of the royal stable in Bhuj. Of course, it is expensive to feed and house a camel, so this is offered to you in lieu of a salary. If you do not return in a month, the camel will be sold."

Her spirits plummeted. She hated the thought of being parted with Veerana. He was her charge; suppose something happened to her and she didn't return in time?

Don't leave me, said his soulful eyes. *If I am sold, Gopal Masa will kill you.*

"Hurry up," said the clerk, glancing toward the gate, where the flood of people had reduced to a trickle. "I don't have all day."

"Two months," she said.

Veerana gave her a bleak look. *Traitor.*

Shut up, she thought at him. *You'll spend the days eating hay and sleeping in the sun.*

The clerk sighed and rubbed his chin. "One and a half months, and that's my final offer. Come along."

She followed him to the gate, filled with conflicting emotions: relief that she'd gotten employment in a caravan, fear that she might still arrive too late in Ahmedabad, and worry about her kul. Was everyone still in good health? Had the baniya's men returned? *Please be safe,* she prayed. *I'll return as fast as I can.*

It was afternoon, and the heat was at its peak. The crowd had lessened as caravans left one by one for Ahmedabad, Mandvi, Jakhau, Bharuch, and Khambhat. The guards stood under the shade of the stone archway, fanning themselves with palm leaves. Two were eating rolled-up flatbreads. At the sight of the food, her stomach rumbled. She hadn't had anything since last night.

They passed through the archway and entered the city. Irinya stopped and blinked in the bright sunlight reflecting off white domes and colored-glass windows, trying to get her bearings. A jumble of sandstone buildings rose before her, flanked by crowded streets, dusty courtyards, and covered markets. Despite the heat, customers milled around the stalls, which seemed to be selling everything from spices and fabric to goats and fortunes. She'd never seen so many people in one place before. It was noisy and disorienting.

"You can explore the city later," said Naveen Gupta, mopping his forehead with a handkerchief. "Let us house your camel first."

He led her down a quieter street to a large camel enclosure located near the walls. A wrinkled old man in a dusty white turban and dhoti came up to chat with him. As they discussed terms, Irinya stroked Veerana's neck, trying to quell her nervousness. "You'll be fine, I promise," she whispered to him.

Veerana grunted. *Who are you trying to convince?*

Money changed hands, and the elderly camel herder took the reins from her and led Veerana inside the enclosure.

"Here's a chit for him," said Naveen Gupta. "You can collect him when you return."

Numbly, she accepted the chit and pocketed it.

"We'll move at dawn." He wrinkled his nose at her. "You must wash and make yourself presentable before then. His lordship is extremely sensitive to smells."

"Yes, sir." "His lordship" must be a finicky, high-ranking official from the Bhuj palace, perhaps related to the ruling Rao clan. Not that she cared as long as she got to Ahmedabad. She'd do her job, keep her head down, and avoid making waves. She certainly wouldn't go close enough to "his lordship" for him to be aggravated by her odor. "Any chance of a meal, Gupta-ji?" she asked as her stomach rumbled again.

"You can eat and sleep with the rest of the caravan," he said. "I will take you to the barracks now."

They went back down the street and turned into another one crowded with shops and food counters. People stood under the awnings, eating samosas and dhoklas from little leaf plates with obvious enjoyment. Irinya tried not to look at them, but the aroma was impossible to ignore, and her stomach cried out to be fed.

The street opened into a large square with a small garden in the center surrounded by long, low brick buildings. The clerk led her to one of them and introduced her to his assistant, a thin, lugubrious young man called Dayal.

"Dayal will show you the ropes," Naveen Gupta told her. "He's your immediate superior, so do everything he says." He thrust a sheaf of parchments at Dayal and left.

Dayal gazed at the parchments, his mouth turned down, and glanced at her. "You can read and write? I hope you're fast." He pushed open the door to the barracks, revealing a dusty, windowless room, and pointed to a wooden trunk overflowing with documents. "We need to get started right away. They must be sorted, translated, transcribed—"

"If I can please wash and eat first, sir?" interrupted Irinya. "I'm starving."

"Oh, right." He jerked his thumb. "There's a washing area for men on the other side of this building. And you can get a meal in the hall opposite. Tell them you're working for the Revenue Department." He said the last bit with an important air.

Irinya thanked him and went around the building, filled with trepidation. She discovered a wooden enclosure behind the barracks, open to the sky—luckily empty, since it was so late in the day. The stone-flagged floor sloped down to a drain; at the higher end was a water pump with a few tin buckets underneath it.

She pushed the wooden door closed and stacked all the buckets but one against it. At least she'd have notice if someone tried to enter. She pumped water into the remaining bucket until it was full, tore off her grimy clothes, and had the fastest bath in the history of bathing, pumping water directly on her head to wash the dust off her hair.

Clean at last. She wiped herself down with a rag she'd packed along with her clothes, and donned a fresh dhoti and kurta, feeling pleased. She'd better enjoy her cleanliness while it lasted. There would be no opportunity to bathe during the journey, not for her. She washed her clothes—technically, Gopal Masa's clothes—and wrung her hair out. The sun was directly overhead, and her hair was dry in minutes. She combed it, tied it in a knot, and wrapped it in a clean turban, back in manly disguise.

Just in time. The door pushed open, and the buckets toppled and clanged on the stone floor as she was draping her dupatta with the blue-star petal around her neck. "What the hell?" said the would-be bather. "Why'd you keep the buckets *here*?"

"To scare away demons," she said, grabbing her clothes and bags.

The man scratched his head. "What would demons want in a washroom?"

"They dissolve in the water and enter your pores." She rushed out, trying not to laugh. Behind her, she heard buckets being picked up and thoughtfully placed by the door.

She hung her clothes on a line behind the barracks, hoping they wouldn't be stolen, and made her way to the building with the community kitchen. Smells of cooking assailed her nostrils, making her mouth water. Men worked and sweated behind enormous pots and pans, chopping vegetables, stirring curries, and kneading dough.

Most everyone had eaten the noon meal, but she scored a pile of thin rotlas, a bowl of red lentils, sweet and spicy mango pickle, and a heap of bitter green saag. She ate inside, sitting on a bench against the wall, enjoying the simple, filling food despite the heat and smoke emanating from the stoves. No one paid her any attention; the cook and his assistants were busy preparing dinner.

After her meal, she returned to the barracks, hoping for a nap, but Dayal pounced on her and set her to work at once. She spent the next few hours poring over mind-numbingly boring documents that listed how much salt, cotton, sesame, butter, wheat, and wool had been produced, taxed, and traded in the villages of Kutch in the past year. Dayal showed her how to double-check figures and summarize the results on fresh parchment. He also taught her how to distinguish the coat of arms and emblems of the sultanate's major trading partners and rivals, including the Portuguese. Men entered and left; some ribbed her, calling her their "clever new boy." She showed them her teeth in what they probably mistook for a smile.

In the kul, it was Rishabh's job to keep inventory, and Ayush often helped him. But parchment was expensive for the kul, and they wrote much smaller than Dayal did. They were neater than him, too, although she wouldn't dream of telling him that.

When she finally rose to eat the evening meal, it was pitch dark, and she had a pounding headache. She blew out the oil lamp Dayal had lit for her and made her way outside, stretching her cramped limbs.

A cheerful fire blazed in the square, and men danced around it to the beat of the dholak, and the tunes of the sarangi and the flute. Homesickness gripped her. This was how her kul relaxed and celebrated in the evenings when the day's work was done—with one crucial difference. In her kul, men and women ate, sang, and danced together. Gender divisions appeared to be sharper among city dwellers compared to nomads.

She got a plate of food from the kitchen and sat down by the fire to eat. The music was lively, the antics of the dancers amusing. She smiled, tapping her feet to the rhythm.

One of the dancers tried to pull her into the dance; she dug an elbow into his side and pushed him away. He was too drunk to notice.

Bowls of arrack were passed around, and the music became louder, the dancers more boisterous. Someone fell on the man sitting next to her, drenching him with arrack, and everyone laughed. Irinya edged away from the rowdy circle before a similar fate could befall her. She gathered her clothes from the line outside the barracks and went in, collapsing on a grass mat in one corner.

All too soon someone was shaking her awake, telling her to get cracking. Around her, a dozen men sat up, yawning and grumbling. She wrinkled her nose at the odor of multiple human bodies. She must have been extra tired to sleep through all the stench and snoring.

By the time they were all ready, it was light outside. The cook distributed lassi and flatbread, and Irinya ate her fill, leaning against the wall, her bags on her back. Dayal seemed happy to have her around; he talked earnestly of the importance of their dreary task while she scanned the faces in the courtyard.

"Who are they?" She pointed to a group of a dozen lean, tough-looking men in identical white turbans and sand-colored robes.

"Baluchi cameleers," he answered. "They protect the caravan. They go everywhere with his lordship. It's their job to protect us from bandits."

"And who is his lordship?" she asked. Not that she was particularly interested, but she ought to know who the caravan was escorting before it left.

His eyes widened in astonishment. "Are you joking? You truly do not know?"

A commotion sounded from the direction of the street, and a tall, richly dressed, well-built young man stalked into the square, followed by a line of keen-eyed retainers. Among them was Naveen Gupta.

"*Him,*" said Dayal in reverent tones. "Imshan Khan, the wazir of Gujarat and the great-nephew of the sultan."

Goose bumps prickled her skin. She hadn't dreamed "his lordship" would turn out to be one of the most powerful men in Gujarat. She stared at the wazir. He had a haughty, handsome face—clean-shaven, unlike most of the men around him. He wore a long blue kurta embroidered with jewels, loose silk pants, and pointed leather shoes. His white-and-gold turban was simple yet elegant. It suited his smooth bronze skin, his dark, restless eyes, and that sensuous mouth, currently curved in a half smile.

To her horror, she realized the wazir was staring right back at her. She dropped her gaze to the ground, cheeks burning.

"Are we ready, Kafila Bashi?" he drawled, keeping his gaze on her.

That meant the caravan leader. She glanced sideways at the trim elderly man bowing to the wazir. "Yes, huzoor. I have designated one captain for the day, one for the night, one for provisions, and one for security."

"Excellent. And did you find a replacement for your assistant, Gupta-ji?"

"Yes, huzoor." Naveen Gupta pointed at her. "The best we could manage on so little notice, but he seems sharp."

"Bow," whispered Dayal, nudging her.

Irinya gave a clumsy bow, her heart palpitating.

"Your employees get younger every day, Gupta-ji. Soon, you will be snatching them from the cradle," remarked the wazir. There was a sycophantic titter from his retainers.

To Irinya's relief, he switched to discussing provisions and security with the captains of the caravan. She sagged against a wall, trying to breathe. His eyes on her had felt as sharp as a blade, as if he saw through the disguise that had fooled everyone else. She couldn't afford to be discovered, certainly not by *him*. Anyone else might give her the benefit of the doubt, but the wazir was reputed to be a cold and ruthless man. If he realized she was not who she appeared to be, he would interrogate her, perhaps even torture her. How long would she last before she spilled everything about her kul, Kavi, and the silver spider lily? She had no idea what had happened to Kavi, no idea where the flower currently was, but he may not believe her. She bit her nails, then imagined them being extracted one by one, and dropped her hands with a shudder.

"Don't worry," said Dayal, eyeing her. "He never pays any attention to the account keepers, as long as we do our jobs." He paused to think. "Do our jobs *honestly*. Someone or other is executed every couple of years for fudging the accounts."

Before she had time to digest that bit of information, the day captain blew a whistle, signaling them to move out of the square. *Keep your head down,* she reminded herself. *Don't draw his attention. You're beneath his notice.* She squared her shoulders and followed Dayal and the others down the city streets. As soon as they reached Ahmedabad, she would make her escape and go in search of the flower market.

The caravan, consisting of a dozen wagons pulled by horses, was waiting outside the city walls. Irinya's eyes widened as she took in the scene of controlled chaos. Horsemen and soldiers paraded up and down, bristling with swords and spears. The head cook directed the loading of provisions—including goats and chickens—his voice hoarse with shouting. The Baluchis mounted their camels, supercilious expressions on their faces. All told, there must have been over a hundred people milling around. If Fardan had been here, he would have drawn the scene, perfect down to the last detail. She memorized all she was seeing, filing it away in her memory so she could describe it to him later. If there was a "later" for her and Fardan.

No, she wouldn't think like that. She had to believe in a future for herself, for him, and for her kul. As long as she breathed, she would work to secure that future.

The wazir along with his entourage headed for the most opulent carriage in the middle of the caravan. The foot soldiers boarded the first and the last carriages. Dayal and Irinya got into the second-to-last one along with a wizened old clerk who was the designated recordkeeper of the journey, and a small, sleek man with a handlebar mustache who was apparently the treasurer. The carriage had two benches with spaces underneath for the trunks of documents they were carrying, and a shelf overhead for personal items, but it was crowded with all four of them inside. Where would they all sleep?

The carriage jerked ahead, and a frisson of excitement ran through Irinya. She was going farther than anyone in her kul had gone before. Hopefully, she'd return in one piece to tell them about it. If only Fardan could see her now. If only she could see *him,* tell him she was well on her way to finding Kavi and the spider lily. Would he be impressed with her efforts? Would he forgive her for hurting him?

Probably not. She sighed and tried to focus on what Dayal was saying about document classification.

It was impossible to write neatly while the carriage was moving, so they used the time to sort documents by type and place. Windows on either side let in light and air, and Irinya drank in the changing landscape: the bare hills, jutting into the pale blue sky, the occasional acacia or kharijal tree, the patches of scrub munched on by camels, goats, and cows. They passed small villages—wattle-and-daub huts that surrounded a courtyard with a well or a jujube tree. People and animals alike scurried out of their path. Irinya poked her head out to wave at a group of children, and Dayal pulled her back inside.

"Have some dignity," he scolded. "We are employees of the wazir of Gujarat."

The recordkeeper shook his head, and the treasurer sniggered. "Peasants," he said, in the tone in which he might have said "louts."

"Why, what's wrong with peasants?" asked Irinya, nettled.

The treasurer's smile vanished into his mustache.

Dayal dug an elbow into her side. "Forgive him, Sahu-ji; he's new."

"I asked a simple question," said Irinya, pushing away Dayal's bony elbow. "You do realize that without farmers and herders, the entire sultanate would fall? It's their labor that feeds the people and sustains the military. What would the sultan do without his taxes?"

The treasurer purpled. "You insolent boy, I will complain to the wazir about you."

"Please, Sahu-ji, calm down," begged Dayal.

"Go ahead," said Irinya, although a voice inside warned her to be quiet. "I'm sure he'll agree with me."

The wazir did not look like a man who cared about the rural masses. But the treasurer's attitude made her blood boil. Acting all superior because he didn't have to use physical labor to do his job. Hopefully, he was low enough in the hierarchy that he wouldn't dare to voice any petty complaints about her.

She and Dayal went back to work, poring over densely written manuscripts, and she put the unpleasant Sahu out of her mind. The carriage stopped at midday to rest the animals and allow the cooks to prepare a meal. She snuck out while Dayal's back was turned so she could stretch her legs.

The overhead sun was blazing hot, but the path was lined with neem and peepal trees, and there was a watering hole nearby. Already, the land was transitioning from the scrublands of Kutch to the forests of Gujarat.

Men unhitched the horses and led them to the watering hole. The cooks started a fire, and the aroma of freshly baked flatbreads and tea wafted into the air. Irinya walked toward the crowd around the fire, hoping to score a cup of tea.

"You, boy."

She turned, startled. A guard towered above her, resplendent in a dark red-and-gray uniform, bristling with weapons and sweating like a butcher.

"Aren't you hot?" she asked.

"What?" he said with a frown.

She pointed at his uniform. "I would be melting in that getup."

His lips thinned. "Luckily for you, you'll never wear it. The wazir wants you, so hop it."

The breath nearly left her body. Had the nasty treasurer complained about her? She should have kept her mouth shut, after all. She wanted to hit herself. "You must be mistaken," she said, trying not to let her voice shake. "I am too unimportant to bother the wazir."

He grinned, revealing stained yellow teeth. "Even the lowest serf can get into trouble. Make haste, or do I have to drag you?"

He looked quite keen as he said that, so she hurried to the wazir's carriage, her stomach churning with anxiety. There must have been a mistake of some sort. Surely the wazir would not trouble himself over a new recruit, even one who was rude to the treasurer.

The wazir's carriage was large and ornate, lavishly decorated with carvings and led by a team of six horses. The red-and-white sultanate flag fluttered on top, and matching silk curtains hung from the windows. A guard by the door told her to climb up the steps and go in.

It was dark and cool inside the carriage, and she blinked, trying to adjust her eyes after the bright sunlight. The carriage interior was as rich and imposing as the exterior, lined with wooden cabinets, and hung with paintings of lions, tigers, and elephants. A large crimson divan occupied one end of it, and on the divan sprawled Imshan Khan, an amused smile on his face. Two boys, one on each side of the divan, cooled the air with peacock-feather fans.

She bowed, trying to quell the queasiness in her stomach. "You summoned me, huzoor."

He gave a flick of his fingers, and, to her alarm, the two boys bowed themselves out, leaving her alone with the wazir. He studied her with narrowed eyes, his gaze traveling from her boots up to her face.

"I'm sorry," she burst out, unable to bear his silent inspection, as if weighing which method of torture would be most enjoyable to him. "I won't do it again."

He raised his eyebrows. "Do *what* again?"

"Be rude to Sahu-ji," she said. "All I said was, farmers and herders are important. Without them, what would we eat?"

"Indeed," he said. "Your laces are untied."

She looked down. What of it? He seemed to expect her to do something about it, however, so she knelt and began to lace them up, her hands shaking. He hadn't batted an eye at the mention of Sahu, so that wasn't why he had summoned her. The alternatives were horrible to contemplate. Had he guessed she was a girl? She swallowed hard, fumbling with her laces.

"Expensive boots," he remarked. "Where did you get them from?"

"A peddler," she prevaricated, hoping it sounded plausible. "I gave him a goat in exchange."

"And where did you get the goat from?" he persisted.

"I come from a family of herders," she said.

"Ah. Nomads from Banni, yes?" He sounded pleased.

She managed to finish tying her laces and rose. She hadn't meant to reveal that. "Yes, huzoor."

"And does your family engage in flower hunting?" he inquired, his voice casual.

She froze. "No, huzoor, it's too dangerous." Inwardly, she cursed herself. Why wasn't she better at hiding things?

He steepled his fingers. "What brings you to Ahmedabad?"

"I've always wanted to see the capital of Gujarat." Ever since Kavi told her about it, anyway. "I've heard it's beautiful."

He nodded. "And your family gave you permission to leave, did they?"

She hesitated, her nerves thrumming. The more she lied, the easier it would be for him to find her out. And the only possible reason for him to ask her all these questions was to catch her in a lie. She'd best stick to the truth as far as possible. "No, huzoor. I ran away."

His lips twitched. "How old are you? Fifteen?"

"I'm seventeen," she said, indignation overtaking her fear.

He gazed at her with hooded eyes. "Did you see the guard outside my carriage? *He's* seventeen."

"Takes all kinds to make the world, huzoor," she said, wishing she had a deeper voice.

"It certainly does." His eyes gleamed. "You have not tied your turban correctly. Why not unwrap it and let me show you how?"

Panic beat its wings against her chest. He suspected. She didn't know how, but he suspected. "This is the way we tie it in my family," she said, making her voice flat. "My own dead father taught me, and it would be an insult to his memory were I to tie it any other way."

He gave her a faintly admiring look, as if impressed at the audacity of her lie. "I can order you to untie it, you know."

She clasped her hands together. "Please don't, huzoor. I would die of shame."

He gave a cold smile. "You can die of many things. Shame is not one of them. And not, in your case, quite relevant. Come, I am not asking you to take off your clothes. Merely your turban, so I can show you how to do it right. A man's turban is the most important part of his attire. It tells the world who he is. Do not test my patience."

With trembling hands, she unwrapped the white cloth from her head. Her abundant hair fell out of its knot, glad to be free. Lots of men had long hair. It didn't mean anything. Did it? She hastily knotted it up again, keeping her gaze on the floor.

"I have never seen that hairstyle on a man," said the wazir, leaning forward with open-mouthed interest. "Only on women."

"I come from a herding family, huzoor," she said, her face heating. "I know nothing of manly fashions."

"Evidently." He rose and walked toward her. She shrank back from him, but all he said was, "The cloth, please."

She handed it to him wordlessly, wishing the ground would swallow her up. He held it by the edge and gave a disdainful sniff. "This is disgusting. I shall give you one of mine."

"No, huzoor, please," she said in horror, but it was no use. He tossed aside the white cloth and rummaged in one of his cabinets, emerging with a plain blue square of cloth with a texture between silk and cotton.

"Stay still," he ordered and began to wrap the turban around her head in deft strokes. She shut her eyes, trying to slow her pulse. It seemed to take a very long time. She was keenly aware of the light touch of his fingers on her hair, of his terrifying proximity to her. He smelled of rose and saffron, heavy and bittersweet.

At last he stepped back. "Much better."

She opened her eyes and summoned strength into her voice. "May I leave now?"

"You may," he said. "But you will return in the evening. My man has hired you, after all. I must test the full extent of your knowledge. Of *letters*," he added, his mouth quirking.

Her stomach shriveled at his words. He wanted her to *return*? That was like jumping back in the scorpion pit after barely escaping it alive. She left the carriage, biting her knuckles. Could she sneak away at night? She might get caught. Even if she wasn't, this was bandit and big-cat territory. There was a high chance she'd get murdered or eaten by a tiger. She was days away from Bhuj, if her own two feet were all she had to get there. She wasn't sure of the way, either.

Kavi, where are you? Why, oh why, had she caught the attention of one of the most dangerous men in Gujarat? Dozens of caravans went to and fro between Bhuj and the capital, but *she* had to pick the one with Imshan Khan.

"Fardan? Fardan!"

She jerked around. "Yes, that's me." She should have used another name. Every time someone called her that, she was reminded of the real Fardan and his expression when she'd said those cruel things to him. How she wished she could take them back.

It was Dayal. "You want food, line up, or it'll be finished."

She hurried to join him, although her appetite was gone. All through the meal—tea, flatbread, pickles, and dates—she worried about how to deal with the wazir. He'd seen through her disguise; that much was clear. But he hadn't punished her for it. Was he toying with her? Was she going to be his entertainment during the journey and a criminal to be hanged when it was over? She had to time her escape from the caravan perfectly: *after* they entered Ahmedabad and *before* they reached the palace. She should be able to lose herself in the crowds easily enough.

"You changed your turban." Dayal cast a critical eye on her. "It's very high-quality fabric, but a young person in your economic situation should not waste money on such frivolities."

What was he, fifty years old? "Yes, sir," she said meekly, draining her cup.

What would Fardan have made of him? Of the wazir, the treasurer, and all the other characters she'd met? She imagined telling him about them: the dangerous Imshan Khan, the nasty Sahu, the earnest Dayal. She wished he were there to poke fun at them all with her.

No, she didn't mean that. She was *glad* he was safe in Banni, that he wasn't involved in her dangerous mission. Kavi might be anywhere, hurt or imprisoned. He might have hidden the flower or given it to someone for safekeeping. Wherever he was, she would be taking a big risk by following him there. It wasn't a risk she was willing to let Fardan share with her.

They helped clean up, rinsing dishes and cups in the water hole and burying the used leaf plates. The day captain blew his whistle, and they were off again. The forests grew denser, the air heavier, laden with the rich scent of growth and decay. Neem, peepal, tamarind, and mango trees clustered on either side of the path, towering over the caravan, cutting off the sunlight.

Irinya spent the afternoon deciphering reports and ship manifests from the ports of Kutch. She learned that ships sailed from Mandvi, Kandla, Jakhau, and Mundra laden with cotton, silk, indigo, pottery, sugar, glass beads, leather, teak, wheat, precious stones, and incense. They returned with gold, silver, copper, and zinc from Aden; Persian horses, musk, dates, and dried fruits from Ormuz; swords from Egypt; ivory and amber from the east coast of Africa; areca nuts and coconuts from Ceylon; porcelain from China; rice from the Deccan; and mace and nutmeg from the Banda Islands.

Her head swam as a map of the world unfurled before her eyes, ships moving with the magic of wind and water along the trade routes, connecting distant lands with invisible threads.

But the Portuguese were burning those threads, making the Indian Ocean trade both less lucrative and more dangerous. She could see the difference in the numbers from past years—the ships damaged or looted at sea, the plunge in profits, the loss of crew and cargo.

She was so caught up in her work, she clean forgot about the wazir until the caravan stopped and a guard came over to ask for the "new boy."

Dayal's eyes widened in consternation. "Are you in trouble?" He didn't know about her earlier summons, apparently.

Opposite them, the treasurer perked up. "This is what comes of having an insolent tongue," he said sagely. "Sooner or later, it's pulled out."

Irinya stuck her tongue out at him. "I still have mine, thanks." She made her escape, leaving him spluttering. She shouldn't bait the man, but he made it so easy.

"For how much longer?" he shouted, about three seconds too late for it to count.

Outside, the sun had set; the forest was a dark, living wall, whispering in the breeze. Irinya followed the guard, staring at the massive trees, taking in deep breaths of the damp, rich air. Leaves and twigs crunched underfoot, and she nearly tripped on an exposed tree root. She'd never traveled in terrain like this before—no one in her kul had. Kutch was composed of desert and grasslands, beaches and marshes. Trees stood isolated from each other, and you could see for miles on a clear day. Here, the trees crowded in as if they hid secrets in their midst. A tiger could be lurking three feet away from her, and she wouldn't know until it pounced. It was unnerving, to say the least. The cameleers circled the caravan, and Irinya and the guard moved out of their way. Dayal had told her that dusk was when bandits and wild animals were most likely to attack.

A bone-chilling shriek came from the front of the caravan. Irinya started, clutching the guard's sleeve. "What was that?" she managed.

The guard laughed. "Just a goat being slaughtered for the wazir's dinner. There'll be mutton curry tonight, but not for the likes of you, scaredy-cat."

"I'm vegetarian," she said, trying to slow her pulse.

Something crashed in the undergrowth right next to them. This time, the guard jumped, too. A horse whinnied in alarm, and a shout went up among the cameleers.

"And that was a goat, too, was it?" Irinya slipped between the guard and the caravan, her heart thumping.

He cast a wary look at the tangled forest. "Must have smelled the blood. Best not to linger."

They hurried to the wazir's carriage. She climbed inside, sagging with relief. Given a choice between a visible wazir and an invisible tiger, she'd choose the former—at least, for now.

Soft lamplight bathed the interior of the carriage and fell on Imshan Khan's handsome, relaxed face. He was reclining on the divan, a book in his hand. He had removed his turban, and his thick, wavy, shoulder-length hair was carelessly brushed back from his forehead. It made him look undressed somehow, and she found it hard to meet his gaze.

He lowered the book. "Ah, Fardan, is it?"

"Yes, huzoor."

"Come, sit." He patted the divan next to him. "I want you to read this poem aloud."

She froze. Why did he want her to sit next to him? And was he in the habit of asking Revenue Department staff to read him poems? Would he, for instance, have asked Dayal to do this? She thought not.

He leaned toward her, holding the book out, his eyebrows raised. "Fardan? Have you turned to stone? Or were my instructions not clear?"

She took the open book from him, willing her hands not to shake. "I cannot sit next to you, huzoor. May I continue standing?"

His mouth quirked. "You may not. Pull up that chair if you have such scruples."

She pulled up the chair he had indicated and sat, doing her best to project calm. Maybe this was a reading test. She scanned the page. The writing was in Devanagari script, but she recognized a few words. In fact—*wait, no, that can't be right.* Surprise bloomed in her chest, robbing her of breath. Of all the poems he could have asked her to read, this was the last one she'd have expected.

"Something the matter?" Imshan Khan asked, watching her.

She took a deep breath and looked up. "Where did you get this poem, huzoor?"

"My grandfather wrote it. He was, apart from being an excellent administrator, a poet and a reformer. He paid for it with his life." A bitter smile crossed his face. "A lesson for me to be none of those things."

"I'm sorry about your grandfather." She closed the book and handed it back to him, trying to school her expression. Inside, she writhed with indignation. Imshan Khan's grandfather might have been a poet, but he was also a plagiarist if he was trying to pass this poem off as his own. "But he did not compose this poem." And neither, apparently, did her mother.

He frowned. "What do you mean?"

Perhaps it would have been better to say nothing, but she hadn't been able to stop herself. What was she going to tell him—that her mother had learned this poem from the flowers? "It's a common rhyme," she said, knowing that was probably closer to the truth. "Taught to the children of flower-hunting families."

He stared at her, his lips pressed together. "Recite it."

Easy for him to say. She knew the words, but how they hurt. She'd dragged the poem out, line by line, while recovering from the effects of the spider lily thorn, as if the poison had floated the memory to the top. And she could hear it now, rendered in her mother's voice—the mother she barely remembered apart from her stories, the mother who had walked into the Rann one misty night, never to return. What else had she forgotten that only poison would return to her?

Irinya turned her gaze away from the wazir and toward the window. The curtain was half-drawn. Beyond the small circle of light cast by the caravan was the endless night. She spoke the words in a calm voice, keeping her feelings hidden deep inside herself so he would not glimpse them:

> *Sweet white jasmine to cure the ill*
> *Bloodred hibiscus to bend to your will*
> *Blazing sunflower to find and to hold*
> *Priceless pansy for wealth untold.*
>
> *Starry bluestar to counter the red*
> *Gracious green rose to hear what is said*

Silver spider lily to win all wars
Blackhearted chrys to open strange doors.

But as for the flower that rules all the rest
The pretty pink blossom I love the best
That blooms when clouds burst over the ground
The sacred lotus must never be found.

Silence returned to the carriage. Irinya swallowed the lump in her throat and wished she could remember more. There had been another poem, something about the cost of each flower, but the words eluded her.

The wazir stirred. "That's not how it ends," he said, his voice husky.

She shrugged, keeping her gaze fixed on the darkness outside. "It's the version I learned."

He leaned toward her. "Would you like to hear *my* version?" Without waiting for a response, he intoned:

But as for the flower that holds the key
To life, death, immortality
That blooms when clouds burst over the ground
The sacred lotus yearns to be found.

She turned to him, frowning. It was not surprising that multiple versions of a poem existed. This happened to stories as well when they passed from one generation to the next. But they morphed in ways that betrayed the storyteller's own biases. The lotus didn't belong in the human realm. There were no records of anyone having caught a glimpse of it. "The yearning is yours, huzoor," she said. "The lotus is a myth. But if it exists, it certainly must *not* be found. There is such a thing as too much power."

He leaned back, a mask falling on his face. "For someone who doesn't come from a flower-hunting family, you seem rather knowledgeable about floral matters."

Careful, murmured the blue petal.

Her pulse accelerated. She'd gotten carried away and revealed too much. It was the poem's fault. She'd best leave before she betrayed herself. "Everyone in Kutch is," she said, keeping her voice flat. "We raise goats and cows, but we do it next door to magic." She rose. "May I leave, huzoor?"

He looked put out. "You may not. I am bored, *Fardan*. Entertain me."

"Huzoor, soon you will be back at your court," she said, seething, "where, assuredly, much entertainment awaits you."

"Oh yes, it is always entertaining to deduce which one of your nobles is harboring thoughts of assassination and rebellion," he said in a languid voice. "*Executions* are also entertaining." She clamped her lips together and clutched the back of her chair, barely able to stifle a gasp. Was he threatening her?

His mouth quirked at her reaction. "So are dancing girls," he continued. "We have none of those at the moment. We have only you."

"Huzoor ought to travel with dancing girls then," she snapped, hating how her knees trembled.

"Your suggestion is duly noted." His eyes gleamed. "Do you know how to dance?"

She controlled herself with difficulty. "I do not."

"We can try you out at the palace." He crossed his arms behind his head and regarded her. "See how you look in a bright red-and-gold lehenga choli. It would be quite a change from your current getup."

She would be long gone by then. *If* he didn't execute her on the way, or—less extreme but almost as bad—have her restrained and interrogated. "Ha ha ha," she ground out.

He gave her a look of mock concern. "Are you feeling well? You look a little . . . ill."

Inspiration struck. "Yes, huzoor, I do feel ill. I'd better go lie down."

"I can't stop the caravan for you, *Fardan*." His mouth stretched in a smile that would not have been out of place on a tiger. "Feel free to lie down here."

Oh no. She hadn't even noticed the carriage start up again. She pushed aside the window curtains and poked her head out. Didn't the cooks have to serve dinner? Maybe they wanted to put some distance between the undergrowth-crashing animal and themselves. Served them right, slaughtering goats in sniffing distance of predators.

"Are you planning to jump out the window?" said the wazir with interest. "I give you permission to try."

Irinya withdrew from the window and returned to the chair. She was stuck here for the time being, and he was *enjoying* her discomfiture, the horrible man. If not for the urgency of her task, she would have thrown the chair at him. But she had to get to Ahmedabad to find Kavi, and she couldn't afford to antagonize the wazir.

"What shall I do to entertain you, huzoor?" she said sweetly.

"Tell me the truth," he said, all trace of humor gone in a flash. "Who are you, why are you here? Tell me of your own free will. Else I have my own ways of extracting information."

She gulped, fear squeezing her chest. *Whatever happened to keeping your head down?* she berated herself. In truth, she'd probably never had the opportunity to do that. He'd sensed something amiss the first time he laid his razor-sharp gaze on her. At least she wasn't being tortured—yet. "I ran away from home to find a friend," she said. "A friend who might be in trouble." A spasm of pain passed through her at the thought of the kind of trouble Kavi might be in. "I think I may find him in Ahmedabad. He . . . he made a promise to me."

He regarded her with disappointment. "Is that all? A romantic entanglement? I had hoped for something more interesting. Whose clothes did you steal?"

"My uncle's," she said, knotting her hands in her lap.

He tilted his head, eyes boring into her. "And what's your real name? No, don't lie. I will know it if you do."

She took a deep breath. "Irinya." She'd given him her true name; she'd have to be careful not to give him more than that.

"Irinya," he said softly. "You are named after the Rann."

"Yes, huzoor."

"And yet, there are no flower hunters in your family?"

"Not currently, no," she hedged. "But my mother was. I lost her to the desert. She's the one who taught me the poem."

He stared at her in silence, his face unreadable. "I'm sorry," he said at last.

The carriage rolled to a halt. Irinya rose and edged toward the door. "May I go, huzoor? I'm hungry."

"You could join me for dinner," he said, waving an inviting hand. "The cook has promised mutton curry and roasted quails."

She shuddered. "No, thank you. I'm vegetarian."

He studied her. "You can't wait to leave. Do I make you uncomfortable?"

Like a piece of cheese in a mousetrap. "Yes, huzoor," she said. "You are the wazir of Gujarat, and I am . . ." She nearly said *a flower hunter* but caught herself in time. "I am a lowly documentation assistant."

He raised his eyebrows. "Is that the only reason? The difference in our socioeconomic status?"

She groaned mentally. "No, huzoor. It's also because you ask me questions like this."

He broke into a smile and clapped his hands. "Well answered! As a reward, you may go eat with your fellow peasants."

Oh, thank the goddess. She made for the door, giddy with relief, and nearly fell over in her hurry to leave. His low laughter followed her as she stumbled down the steps of his carriage and hurried toward the cook fires.

Dinner was rice and dal with a side of fried bitter gourd that tasted exactly how she felt.

"What did the wazir want with you?" Dayal demanded as they sat on the steps of their carriage, leaf plates balanced on their laps.

"He wanted to test me on my reading skill," she said, making a ball of rice and dal with her fingers and popping it into her mouth. She had zero appetite after her nerve-wracking encounter with Imshan Khan, but she had to keep up her strength.

"Did you pass?" asked Dayal anxiously. "You're not in trouble? Because I can't do all this work by myself."

She licked her fingers. "Of course I'm not in trouble. Everything's fine."

Later, lying sleeplessly on the floor of the carriage while three men snored on the benches above her, she wondered how true that was.

CHAPTER 8

The caravan continued to Ahmedabad, and a tiger followed. It snatched a goat, a sheep, and a brace of rabbits, and reduced one man who had been relieving himself against a tree trunk to a gibbering mass of terror. Irinya caught a glimpse of it one twilit evening, yellow and black stripes moving sinuously in the undergrowth, keeping pace with the caravan. But when the wazir and his soldiers emerged to hunt it down, it melted away into the forest. Irinya was glad of that. It was not the tiger's fault that the caravan had invaded its territory.

She had a bad moment in the middle of the journey when they stopped near a pond to bathe. She refused all invitations to join in, but one of the guards thought it would be funny to drag her kicking and screaming out of the carriage and throw her into the pond. She bit his hand hard, drawing blood and making him yelp.

"Why, you little——" he spluttered, wringing his injured hand and gripping her by the scruff of her neck with the other.

"Problems, Nayak?" came a peremptory voice.

The wazir stood behind them, bare-chested, his muscles rippling in the sunlight.

The soldier dropped her, and she scrambled up from the ground, burning with humiliation and anger. "No, huzoor," he said.

Imshan Khan frowned, taking in her disheveled appearance. "People who do not wish to disrobe should not be forced to. If you try this again, I'll put my sword through your stomach."

The soldier's eyes widened. He bowed, begged forgiveness, and beat a hasty retreat.

"Thank you, huzoor," Irinya murmured, edging away. Of all the people to come to her aid, it had to be *him*. He probably enjoyed being the only one to know her secret. She clutched her slipping turban. She needed to get back to the carriage, adjust her clothing, and make sure her bluestar petal was safe.

He grinned. "The only one allowed to throw you into a pond is *me*. I shall stab anyone else who tries."

She fled before he could demonstrate. To her relief, he did not summon her to his presence again.

As they approached Ahmedabad, she leaned out of the open doorway of the carriage for her first glimpse of the city that Kavi had so eloquently described. Trees dotted the landscape, and herds of goats grazed the lush green grass under the watchful eyes of their herders. Beyond the trees rose the fabled cityscape of Ahmedabad.

Thick walls of brick and stone stretched on both sides, curving away in the distance, topped by semicircular bastion towers. Far to the right, the Sabarmati River gleamed in the sun. Beyond it was the forest, dense and impenetrable. To the left were thick groves of trees. She drank in the scene, wishing Fardan could see it through her eyes.

It had been two weeks since she left the kul. She prayed the baniya's men had not been back to harass them. There were still a couple of months left for the season's end, the baniya's impossible deadline for collecting ten flowers. She had to free the kul from him before then. *Almost there,* she told herself, excitement crackling within her. She would escape from the caravan as soon as they were inside the city walls and make her way to the flower market.

A massive gate loomed before the caravan, twice as tall as a kharijal tree and wider by half than the wazir's carriage. On top of the gate was a roofed platform, paced by guards. She tugged Dayal's sleeve. "Which gate is that?"

Dayal suppressed a yawn. "We are approaching the northern end of the city, so that's the Delhi Darwaza." He glanced at her with amusement. "These are the outer fortifications, built by Sultan Mahmud Begada. The old Bhadra Fort built by his grandfather is to the west, on the banks of the Sabarmati."

The gate was thrown open, and the caravan moved under the thick stone archway. Uniformed guards stood at attention as the wazir's carriage passed by.

"Can I walk beside the carriage when we're inside?" she asked Dayal. "I'd love to look at everything more closely."

"Peasant," muttered Sahu.

Dayal scratched his head. "As long as you keep up with the caravan. I'll need your help unloading the documents when we arrive at the palace."

Poor Dayal had grown to rely on her in the past few days. She had no intention of keeping up with the caravan. She was going to lose herself in this city, which was rumored to be home to over a hundred thousand people. As their carriage passed under the archway and emerged on a broad street lined with trees and buildings, it was easy to believe it. There were more people, palanquins, and carriages crowded in this one street than she had seen in her entire life. The caravan slowed in the traffic, and she took the opportunity to grab her bags and leap out.

"Why are you taking your bags?" shouted Dayal, poking his head out.

"Money," she called back. "I may want to buy something."

That was a laugh. She hadn't a jital to her name. She let the carriage overtake her and fell behind so there was a crowd between her and the caravan. Only then did she allow herself to look around.

Ahead, to her right, a large, imposing sandstone mosque dominated the skyline. To her left was a dispensary and a traveler's lodge. Horses and camels stood patiently near the walls, waiting their turn to be led into enclosures and stables.

Someone bumped into her and scolded, "You're blocking the way."

She moved to the side of the road, clutching her bags. Uniformed soldiers brushed against traders in elegant kurtas and dhotis. Rough-looking mercenaries jostled with foreigners in strange clothes. Fruit sellers with baskets of melons and mangoes balanced on their heads called out their wares in long, lugubrious cries. Palanquin bearers shouted at people to get out of their way.

It was bewildering. She heard a smattering of Kutchi here and there, but mostly people were speaking Gujari, Persian, and other languages she could not identify. *Act like you belong,* she told herself and strode ahead past the mosque.

A triple archway with guards guiding the flow of traffic loomed before her. This must be the famous Teen Darwaza, which led to the plaza that hosted Khaas Bazaar. She quickened her footsteps, passing under the thick stone of the central archway along with a rush of people and palanquins.

At the end of the archway was an enormous square bursting with noise and color. She blinked, trying to take in what she was seeing. *People. Animals. Shouting. Laughter. Smells.*

Chickens squawked in cages and goats bleated in their pens. Men fried samosas and pakoras in huge vats. Crisp roasted khakhras teetered in mouth-watering piles next to thin flatbreads that looked much softer and tastier than the rotlas she was used to having. Mounds of gram-flour fudge and little earthen cups of milky white rice pudding gave off an aroma of sugar and cinnamon. Irinya's stomach rumbled. She would have to figure out a way of earning money, or she'd starve in this city of plenty.

Beyond the food market was a section on books and writing supplies: charcoal for sketching, vegetable dyes for painting, and thick white paper, such as Irinya had never seen before. How Fardan would love this place! She imagined him smoothing the white paper, holding the charcoal firmly in his strong, deft fingers, and bringing a delicate flower to life on the page.

The image brought a lump to her throat. She swallowed it down, surprised at herself. She missed him with an ache that grew sharper with every day that passed. She missed them all.

Between two bookstores with tottering piles of books that hid the booksellers from view was an alleyway with a half-open gate. At first, she passed it without a second glance. But the whiff of a familiar fragrance drew her back. She peered over the gate. It opened onto a narrow path, just wide enough for two people to walk abreast.

A small breeze blew, bringing with it the scent of jasmine. She closed her eyes and inhaled deeply, homesickness tugging at her. She longed to be back in the Rann where flowers grew free and people were few and far between. But here, if her nose wasn't wrong, was her destination: the biggest flower market of Gujarat.

She pushed open the gate and stepped through, nerves thrumming with anticipation. Near the end of the alleyway, the fragrance grew stronger, more complex, the sweetness of jasmine overlaid by the heaviness of rose and undercut by the acrid whiff of bluestar.

The alleyway opened onto another, smaller square. On the right was an open-air workshop where large fires crackled under bulbous copper stills. The heat from the fires vibrated the air, softening the edges of the day.

The left side was lined with over a dozen stalls. Vendors sat crosslegged on carpets, surrounded by glass vials, camel-skin bottles, and earthen jars. Well-dressed customers bent to examine their wares. Everyone spoke in hushed tones, as if they were in a temple or a mosque. Irinya made a beeline for the shops, clutching her bag with the precious tincture.

"You, boy. What are you doing here?"

Irinya started. A hulking guard loomed over her.

"The gate was open, and I walked through," she said, bewildered.

"Acting innocent?" The guard glared at her. "Only buyers and sellers are allowed in the flower market. That's the rule, and everyone in the city knows it."

"I'm sorry. I just arrived, so I didn't know. But I do belong here. See?" She withdrew the earthen jar from her bag. "Tincture of jasmine. I prepared it myself."

His face swelled. "You know what we do with fraudsters? Chop off their heads and nail them to the gates."

"What, all the gates?" she asked, nettled. "You have over a dozen, don't you? Do the gates get turns to host my head?"

"We'll see how insolent you are after a night in jail." He grabbed her shoulder with his thick hand. She twisted away from him, her pulse racing. Why couldn't she control her tongue sometimes?

"Stop." The voice was soft yet authoritative. The guard backed away and saluted.

A thin, sharp-eyed elderly man dressed in a white dhoti and simple blue kurta stood behind them. "Forgive the guard," he said with a smile. "He tends to get overenthusiastic in the performance of his duties. You would hardly walk in here with fake tincture of jasmine, would you? Because there's a straightforward test for it, and the penalty for forging is death. Especially now, when the sultan is ill and jasmine is dearer than diamonds."

This gentle, well-spoken man was way more frightening than the guard, and the fact that he was the guard's boss was the least of it. It was his eyes, perhaps, that seemed to see through her disguise the way Imshan Khan had. "It's not fake," she said, forcing calmness into her voice. "I prepared it myself. I have healed people with it, and I've come here to barter it."

"You're not allowed—" began the guard, but once again, the sharp-eyed man stopped him. He beckoned to her. "Come with me."

Irinya followed him across the square, the jar held carefully in her hands, hope and anxiety warring within her. She was so close to her goal; she could almost taste the sunflower tea.

"What's your name?" asked the man, glancing over his shoulder.

"Fardan," she said. "May I know who you are, sir?"

"I'm Rampal, the overseer of this flower market." He ushered her into an empty stall and opened a door at the back. "Let us test this tincture of yours."

The room behind the stall was small and claustrophobic. The air was saturated with rose vapor, sandalwood oil, and incense. A small window let in some light, but it was still too warm, too close for comfort. A babble of undefined voices rose around her, and she nearly dropped her jar in fright.

Oh, hush, said the bluestar petal, and the voices subsided. She took a deep breath, trying to slow her pulse. Had those been the remnants of flowers stored in glass jars and vials? She sent a wave of gratitude to her petal for quieting them.

"Sit." Rampal indicated a chair behind an ornate desk piled with papers. "Tell me about yourself."

"Nothing much to tell." She perched on the edge of the chair, trying to control her nervousness as the overseer removed the stopper from her jar and delicately sniffed the contents. "I come from a family of herders in Kutch. One of my cousins found a jasmine. A little later, people in our kul fell ill, and I made this tincture to help them. Then I thought, *I can make money in Ahmedabad; why not go there?*"

"Why not indeed." Rampal dipped the end of a reed into the jar and placed it on a white parchment. The drop of tincture at the end of the reed seeped into the paper and spread in concentric yellow-gold circles. He nodded in satisfaction. "The tincture appears to be genuine. I will need to run a couple more tests to determine safety and efficacy, if that's all right with you?"

"Of course, sir." She hesitated, torn between politeness and hunger. Hunger won. "I've had nothing to eat since yesterday."

He smiled—a more genuine one this time. "I will get my assistant to fetch you some food." He rose and left the room, and she heard him talking to someone outside.

He returned a short while later and continued to test the tincture. Irinya watched in fascination as he added drops into various vials, studying them through an oval glass he held up against his eye.

The door pushed open, and a slender young woman appeared, bearing a wooden tray with a steaming earthen cup and a leaf plate full of food. She set it down in front of Irinya and bowed.

"Thank you," said Irinya, both to the woman and the overseer.

"My pleasure," said Rampal. "Don't mind me; please eat."

Irinya didn't need another invitation. The smell of freshly brewed chai wafted into her nostrils, displacing the odor of treated flowers. She took a sip of the hot, sweet, milky tea. It slid down her throat like nectar. The food looked as wonderful as the tea. There was a small pile of fried twisted dough, crispy lentil kebabs, a bowl of spiced yogurt, and soft, round flatbreads with pickles. She ate with gusto, washing down her food with the tea. When she finished, she realized that Rampal had stopped what he was doing and was observing her, his expression unreadable.

"I'm sorry," she said. "I was so hungry, I ate it all." Her words slurred. She felt terribly sleepy.

"It was for you to eat," he said. "Are you feeling tired? You can lie down on that mat if you wish."

She tried to thank him, to say she wouldn't dream of lying down in his presence, that it would be rude. But no words emerged from her mouth. A wave of exhaustion washed over her, and she barely made it to the mat before passing out.

CHAPTER 9

Irinya surfaced from sleep layer by layer, like a diver swimming slowly to the surface. Something was wrong. *Many* things were wrong, but her brain could only grasp them one by one.

She was lying on a vast bed with an ornate wooden canopy and translucent white hangings. Her hair was no longer in a turban, but scattered around her head, which was resting on a soft pillow. The dupatta with the hidden petal, thankfully, was still wrapped around her neck. It was dark and cool, a lamp burning fitfully on a table to her right. A breeze blew in through latticed windows, bringing the scent of roses past their bloom.

Her head was pounding as if someone were beating a drum inside it. Her mouth was dry, her stomach a roiling pit. Was it the tea that had been drugged or the food? It had been afternoon when she collapsed in the overseer's office, and it was dusk now. She'd lost several hours. She wanted to cry in frustration. She'd been so close to getting a sunflower and finding Kavi.

But the worst, the very worst thing, was the man sitting in a chair opposite the bed, chin resting on steepled fingers, eyes glittering in the darkness. His face was in shadow, but she had no doubt, even in her bleary condition, who he was: Imshan Khan, the wazir of Gujarat. Dread laid icy hands on her chest and squeezed, making it hard to breathe.

"We meet again, my duplicitous little clerk," he rasped.

She tried to swallow and coughed instead. "I'm not—not that thing you're calling me."

"You're no clerk, that is certain. Dayal is quite heartbroken at the loss." He rose and began to pace. "You dressed as a boy to get into my caravan. I thought that was amusing—and understandable, if dangerous. But you lied about who you are. You hid the deadly weapon you carried. And *that* is unforgivable. Because you could be anyone. A spy, even."

Some of the fog lifted from her brain. "I'm not a spy, I swear."

He stopped pacing and faced her. "I will need more reliable proof than your words." His voice was grim. "What kind of poison do you tip your darts with?"

Her stomach clenched. He'd found her blowpipe. She pushed herself up, anger overriding her fear. "You've been going through my things."

"You have more to worry about than your *things,*" he said coldly. "Answer my question."

Lie and hope for the best? No, he would have the darts tested and know she'd lied. A sour taste flooded her mouth. "I make my darts from thorns."

His eyes widened. "*Thorns?* From the flowers of the Rann?"

"Yes." She wished her head would stop reeling. She needed to figure out her next move.

He whistled softly. "I never heard of such a thing. What an interestingly vicious choice to make. I loathe all poisons, but this is almost elegant. A spy's weapon, if ever there was one."

"I'm not a spy!" she tried to shout, but it came out as a hoarse whisper.

"No? We will see." He flicked aside the bed curtain, and she flinched. "I hate to waste this on the likes of you, but I have no choice."

Confusion swirled through her mind. "Waste what?"

He leaned forward, holding a tiny crimson object between his thumb and forefinger. "Look at it," he commanded, "and tell me your name."

A hibiscus petal. It grew before her eyes, unfurling until it took up her entire field of vision. Red, the world was red, and the voice a deeper, darker shade of it. It hurt to look, and it hurt to listen. "My name is Irinya Dewa," she said, her eyes burning.

The blue petal hidden in her dupatta stirred and stretched itself.

It is time, it whispered. And at last, she understood why the petal had spoken to her from the dead man's hand, demanding to be taken. *Thank you,* she thought.

"Who are you?" the voice continued. "Where do you come from?"

The edges of the world began turning sky blue. She wanted to weep with relief. "I'm a flower hunter from the Rann."

"A flower hunter?" His voice roughened. "What are you doing in my city?"

The truth rose within her, demanding to be spilled. *Kavi Kampilya. Silver spider lily.*

But blue was overtaking the red before her eyes. If she looked at the blue, she didn't have to obey the red any longer. "Exactly what I told the overseer. I had tincture of jasmine; I wanted to sell it and make some money. Was I wrong?"

He exhaled. "Then you're not a spy?"

"Of course not," she said. Some of the tension seeped away from her body; she had the blue petal to thank for that. Perhaps she could still work the situation to her advantage. "Who could I be a spy for?"

"The Portuguese," he said, his tone bitter. "They're sniffing at our secrets, buying up our people, infiltrating our court. That's why they've been so successful in their attacks."

She thought of Kavi, and her heart constricted. Had he been betrayed after all? She had to find him and the spider lily at any cost. Her plan to barter jasmine tincture for sunflower tea had failed, thanks to the wazir, but the palace was the best place to get leads on Kavi's whereabouts. And this, if she was not mistaken, was the royal palace at Bhadra Fort. Kavi's patron was the famous Malik Ayyaz, the governor of Junagadh and Diu. Surely there were people here who knew Kavi, who could tell her if he'd gone missing and where he'd last been seen. She just had to make sure the wazir didn't suspect her of harboring secrets from him.

The blue dissipated; she could see again, although the world seemed out of focus.

The wazir leaned too close to her, his face taut, his eyes wary. But the petal in his hand had no more power over her. She blinked, hoping she wasn't going to be sick. "Why do you carry a miniature blowpipe?" he asked.

The truth would not hurt her here. "I inherited it from my mother," she said, making sure not to meet his eyes. Instead, she gazed over his shoulder at the mahogany cupboard on the opposite side of the room. "It is a way for me to remember her."

"And the thorns?" he demanded.

She shrugged. "The thorns are magical. Nothing else will work on a blowpipe of this size. My mother taught me how to handle them safely, although I was only five when she passed."

"Hmm." There was a pause as the wazir studied her. "Have you ever killed anyone with it?"

She swallowed. She could lie if she wanted to, make herself appear harmless to the wazir.

But she couldn't bring herself to utter the lie. "One man," she said finally. "He had his blade at our kul leader's throat. I did it to protect her."

"Did it work?" he asked, sounding curious.

Her shoulders slumped. "No. They killed one of our elders in revenge. And they took our money. That's why I'm here." This was mostly true, although she'd left out a good bit.

He straightened, some of the tension leaving his shoulders. "Thank your lucky stars you ended up with me and not with your throat slit in a dark alleyway. I'll tell my assistant to pay you for the tincture. Don't try to bypass the flower supply lines again. The rules are there for a reason."

She said nothing. As long as the moneylenders controlled the market, flower hunters would never get a fair wage for their labor. They'd live and die mired in debt. It had always been her dream to free her kul from the talons of the baniya, but until Kavi came along, she'd never heard the term "cooperative." He'd shaken them all out of their fatalistic attitude and made them see another way.

"The visual effects of the hibiscus should have worn off by now," said the wazir. "The true impact can last weeks or months. I plan to make full use of you until then." He tilted his head, regarding her. "Tell me what you are thinking."

Horrible man. She focused her gaze on him, summoning a look of wide-eyed innocence. She'd have to pretend to be under the influence of the hibiscus for the time being. That meant she would have to obey him and answer every question. "I'm thinking that my tincture of jasmine is effective. Why not try it on the sultan?"

He gave a harsh laugh. "You think I'll waste it on that greedy old goat? He's been guzzling tincture of jasmine every day for months. Meanwhile, people who could benefit from it are dying for lack of supply. No, this will go straight to pharmacies across Gujarat. I told Rampal last month to divert jasmine from the palace apothecaries to my own people."

His words jolted her. She'd never heard the sultan spoken of in any but reverent tones. And this was his own great-nephew. "People will think you do not want him to recover, huzoor," she said.

"I don't," he said plainly. "He's an old man who's lived too much and sinned even more. Jasmine cannot help him."

"It won't help those who need it most," she murmured, remembering one of Chinmay's stories in which Black Death tore through a village, killing dozens. Among the dead were the wife and children of a poor farmer. A beautiful jasmine grew from the tears he shed on the ground and healed the remaining people of the village. But because his own family could not be saved, the man cursed the jasmine, saying it would never be able to help those who needed it most.

"What?" Imshan Khan gazed at her, his eyebrows furrowed.

"Nothing, huzoor," she said, her face blank. "Why don't you want your great-uncle to recover?"

His mouth twisted. "He's ruled for fifty years—isn't that enough? He's eaten mountains of food, bedded innumerable women, conquered dozens of kingdoms, and killed his own family members. It's time he went to the place in hell especially reserved for him."

"Killed family members?" The words chilled her.

"They call him the Poison Sultan for a reason," the wazir grated. "He poisoned his brother so he could gain the throne. His brother—my grandfather."

"I'm sorry." No wonder the wazir hated poisons.

He gave a mirthless smile. "Killing off siblings is not uncommon in our family. Nor is imprisoning the sons of those you've killed so they cannot take revenge. No, I'll tell you what's really horrifying. Mahmud Begada poisoned *his own son*. My uncle, Apa Khan."

Her mind reeled. "Why?"

His face set in austere lines. "Apa was caught trespassing in a noble's harem. For that offense, Mahmud Begada killed his son and declared his daughter to be his heir. Zahra, a woman!" That last word said in a tone of outrage, as one might say "criminal."

"A woman can rule as well as a man," said Irinya, her tone neutral. Inside, she stewed at his patriarchal attitude. Even the Delhi Sultanate had been ruled by a sultana—briefly, it was true, but at least there was precedent.

He narrowed his eyes. "And you know such things, do you, flower hunter? The nobles will never accept her. They will rebel as soon as my great-uncle dies. The sultanate will be torn apart."

Irinya attempted to summon her look of wide-eyed innocence. "Not if you support her."

His expression hardened. "I am the next male heir. By rights, the throne should be mine. Just as it should have been my father's, may he rest in peace. He died in prison; my great-uncle as good as murdered him, too."

There was no talking to him. The longer this conversation continued, the greater the danger that she'd blurt out something to make him suspect her. "Why are you telling me all this, huzoor?" she asked in a humble tone. "It's none of my business."

His eyes gleamed. "Because you will never repeat a single word of this to anyone. You are mine now, to do with as I wish. Open your mouth."

Her body tensed. Briefly, she fantasized about grabbing the lamp and braining him with it. But he was probably faster than her, and certainly much heavier. Better to let him believe she was under the influence of his hibiscus. She still had the bluestar petal for protection; it would continue to work against the red flower if she ate it within the next few minutes. She opened her mouth in a show of obedience. He placed the red petal on her tongue, and it dissolved, leaving a bitter aftertaste. She coughed and swallowed.

"Water?" He passed her a glass from a table.

She hesitated only a moment before accepting it. If he wanted her dead, she would already be dead by now. He wouldn't have wasted a hibiscus petal on her. She drank without stopping until she'd drained it dry.

He locked his hands behind his back and gave her an appraising look. "Make yourself presentable. This is the court of the sultan of Gujarat. You will dress appropriately. You may eat if you wish, and then you will report to me. I want your insights on the dwindling flower situation in the Rann."

"Yes, huzoor." She would seize the first opportunity to snoop around and ask after Kavi. Once she had some clues on his whereabouts, she'd slip out of the palace. "If anyone asks, how am I to introduce myself?"

He raised his eyebrows. "As my secretary."

She stared at him, flabbergasted. *Secretary?* Surely he had others, more qualified and far more interested in such a job. But it made sense from his point of view. He wanted to keep an eye on her and extract as much information as possible while she was under the influence—he thought—of his hibiscus petal. But she stood to gain, too. As the wazir's new secretary, she would be able to ask questions of palace personnel without raising suspicions.

He cast a glance toward the door. "I must go now. Someone will be here shortly to guide you through the palace." He strode out of the room before she could ask any more questions.

Now, whispered the bluestar petal.

She tore it out from the edge of her dupatta and gazed at it, her eyes blurring. *I don't want to.* The petal had been with her so long, it had become like a friend.

You must. I'll still be with you.

She closed her eyes and placed the petal on her tongue. It dissolved in a mixture of sweetness and pain, obliterating the last of the hibiscus-induced heaviness in her head.

A girl of around her own age dressed in a red-and-saffron lehenga choli entered the room and bowed to Irinya. "My lady, if you will please follow me to the zenana." Her voice was soft and pleasant, her face round and good-natured.

"Who are you?" asked Irinya, scrambling off the bed and pulling on her boots.

The girl darted a glance up at her through long eyelashes and gave a dimpled smile. "A lowly palace maid. You can call me Tarana. My mistress has given me a set of robes for you that will be more appropriate for the palace."

"Your mistress?" Was the wazir married?

"One of the wazir's relatives," said Tarana. "He requested help from the zenana, and I was sent to take care of you." She hesitated. "My lady, I'm sorry. This is the wazir's guest room, and we should not linger here."

"Just a minute." Irinya grabbed her jute bag from the floor and checked it. To her dismay, her mother's dowry bag with the blowpipe was gone. The tincture was nowhere to be seen, either. She cursed the wazir inwardly. "Why can't we linger here?"

"The women of the palace stay in the zenana," murmured Tarana, ushering her out of the room. "It's not suitable for you to be here."

"I'm not a woman of the palace." She remembered what the wazir had said about the sultan bedding innumerable women. "The sultan's harem lives in the zenana?"

"Yes, my lady. And all his female relatives as well."

"I suppose the wazir has a harem too somewhere?" she hazarded.

Tarana laughed. "No. He is only twenty-one and has not made any marriages, although there are suitable alliances in place."

Twenty-one? He looked years older. It was the way he carried himself and the way he spoke, as if born to command.

They walked the length of a torchlit corridor, down a winding stone staircase, and across an open courtyard patrolled by guards. Irinya took deep breaths of the fresh air and glanced up at the inky sky, glad to be outside. The stars were beginning to peep out, though the stones underfoot still retained the heat of day.

Tarana knocked on a narrow wooden door at the far end of the courtyard. It creaked open to reveal an ancient woman in black robes. She waved them inside, and they emerged into another firelit courtyard, paved with smooth stones and lined with flowering plants. The air was fragrant with night-blooming jasmine and humid from water splashed on the ground to cool it.

Two guards—both women—paced the courtyard. Tarana called out a greeting to them, and they nodded to her.

As they walked across the courtyard, Irinya asked, "Do you know a man named Kavi Kampilya?"

Tarana whipped her head around to stare at her and said, after a beat, "The name sounds familiar, but I don't know most people who work in the fort. Only in the zenana, because that's where I live. Why do you ask, my lady?"

Why had her question startled the maid? "I have a message for him from a merchant in Bhuj," said Irinya, having made up this excuse beforehand.

"What's the message about?" asked Tarana, her eyes wide and innocent.

Irinya suppressed her annoyance. She should have thought up a more detailed lie. "It's a personal matter."

"And yet, he entrusted it to you rather than relying on a messenger pigeon?" Irinya flushed. The maid knew she was lying. Tarana smiled to take the sting out of her words. "You can ask someone who works in other parts of the palace if they know this man. Like these guards, for instance."

Irinya glanced at the guards. She would question them as soon as she'd finished her bath and eaten something—but not right away, or her urgency would betray itself to Tarana and she might report the matter to the wazir. If that happened, Irinya would have to think up a different, more plausible excuse. The wazir was harder to fool than anyone she'd met, and she didn't want him hindering her search for Kavi.

They climbed the steps to a columned portico and entered a passage through a trellis door. "I assume you wish to wash before changing?" said Tarana, taking down a torch from the wall.

Irinya assured her she was deeply interested in a wash, and Tarana gave her a dimpled smile before leading her down the passage. A fruity, flowery fragrance assailed Irinya's nostrils, and she quickened her steps, curious. Tarana flicked aside a curtain at the end of the passage, revealing a cavernous room. "The bathhouse," she announced with a flourish.

Irinya stared, awestruck. The light from the torch danced over blue-and-white tiled walls, a marble floor, and a large oval pool in the center of the room. All around were wooden tables and benches, laden with towels, oils, soaps, and perfumes. Royal ladies sure had luxurious bathing facilities.

Tarana fixed the torch in a bracket on the wall. "In the morning, this place is full. The ladies have a lot of fun, splashing and soaping each other. In the olden days, the sultan used to join in."

"I did *not* need to know that," she muttered.

The maid laughed. "Would you like my help?"

"No, thank you," she said, startled. "I can bathe myself."

"Then I'll leave you to it. I'll return in a while to do your hair." She indicated a pile of robes on a table. "Please wear these when you are done and leave your dirty clothes on the floor. I'll have them laundered."

She bowed and left. Irinya crouched by the pool and dipped her hand into the water. It was neither hot nor cold, perfect for bathing. A current indicated that it was being drained and replenished constantly through some unseen mechanism. Irinya had never seen such a bath before.

She stripped off her grimy clothes and sank into the warm, scented water. The pool was only waist-high, but she could bend her knees and submerge herself completely. All the dirt and dust of her journey sloughed away. She grabbed a bottle of jasmine-scented soap essence and rubbed some on her skin, delighting in the fragrance and the bubbles. What luxury! If only Fardan could see her like this.

Her face heated. No, she didn't mean that. What she meant was, if only he had an inkling of her lavish surroundings. He'd be sorry he'd ever fought with her, and he'd wish he were there, too.

No, she didn't quite mean that either, she meant—

"*Irinya?*" came Fardan's voice in her ear, nearly stopping her heart. "*Can you hear me?*"

She flailed in the water, swallowing some of it. Had she imagined his voice? It had sounded so real. She glared at the shadowy corners of the bathhouse, but there was no one. Had her brain melted into the bathwater?

"*Is it working?*" Incredibly, that was Bholi Masi's voice. "*I don't think it's working.*"

I'm haunted, thought Irinya, breaking out in goose bumps. *I missed them so much, I summoned their ghosts.*

"*Please, Bholi, back off a little. You're breathing down my neck.*"

"I can't hear her! Can you hear her?"

"How can I hear her when you're screaming in my ear?"

Some of the fog lifted from Irinya's brain. There was nothing remotely ghostly in the way those two were arguing. "Fardan?" she croaked. "What—how is this possible?"

"She heard me! No, Bholi, please let me speak. Irinya, how are you? Are you alive? I mean, are you okay?"

"I'm okay," she managed, still stunned. "How are you doing this?"

"We found a green rose," said Fardan triumphantly.

Gracious green rose to hear what is said. Irinya remembered the line from the poem. "And you're wasting it on me?" She was aghast. "Have you forgotten the baniya's threat? If we don't give him ten flowers by the end of the season, he's going to kill more people! I'm trying to find—"

"Irinya," he interrupted, his voice calm. *"Listen. We won't find ten more flowers. You know that. Even if we do, it's no good. He'll increase the quota next year, make more threats against us. The kul has decided not to give him any more flowers at all."*

Her stomach heaved. "No! Fardan, that's too dangerous." If they gave the baniya a few flowers, there was a chance he might opt to be merciful. If they gave him none, he'd take it as a challenge to his authority and let loose his mercenaries on them. Her heart shrank at the thought of the carnage that would follow. Her task of finding Kavi and the spider lily was now more urgent than ever.

"The entire kul decided this," Bholi cut in. *"No good saying anything about it.* You *tell me why you ran away from home. How could you do this to me? Do you know how worried we've been? Your uncle can barely sleep at night. Did you steal his clothes?"*

"Where are you?" asked Fardan, interrupting Bholi's onslaught.

"In Ahmedabad," said Irinya, trying to fill her voice with strength and confidence. "Don't worry about me. I'll find Kavi, and I'll return home, I promise."

"I should never have let you go." Fardan's voice wavered. *"I should have known what you were trying to do that night."*

Irinya swallowed. He'd seen through her facade. At least he didn't sound mad at her anymore. She wished the green rose would let her do more than talk to Fardan and Bholi Masi. After so long away from them, she ached to see their faces. Even more, she ached to hug Bholi Masi, to watch Fardan draw, to play pachisi with Gopal Masa, to sit with the kul around the fire, to join in the music and dancing. Her eyes blurred, and she suppressed a sob. She couldn't let them sense how homesick she was.

"*What are you talking about?*" demanded Bholi. "*What was she trying to do?*"

Fardan ignored her. "*Tell us exactly where you are. We can help.*"

"No, you cannot," said Irinya. "I'm in no danger. You should stop now; conserve the green rose."

"*You will tell us where you are,*" said Fardan flatly. "*And you will tell us how you plan to find Kavi.*"

She took a deep breath. "I'm in the royal palace at Bhadra Fort." Bholi Masi gave a squeak of surprise. "I found a job here," Irinya continued, "but it's only so I can ask people about Kavi. His patron is the governor of Junagadh and Diu. Someone here must know where he is or what happened to him. As soon as I find out, I'm going to leave."

There was a brief silence. "*Why didn't you take me with you?*" asked Fardan. Did she imagine the break in his voice?

"*Why didn't you take* anyone *with you?*" countered Bholi Masi. Irinya could imagine her glaring at Fardan.

"I'm sorry," said Irinya, her heart constricting. "We can talk about this later. Let's not waste the green rose."

"*I'll call again in a few days,*" said Fardan, his voice heavy. "*Please try to stay alive until then.*"

"*What? Are we stopping already? But there's so much I have to say!*" wailed Bholi. "*Are you getting enough to eat?*"

"Yes, the food here is delicious," Irinya assured her.

"*Be careful of everything!*"

"I know. Bye now."

"*Take care, Irinya,*" said Fardan. Silence returned to the bathhouse.

Irinya finished washing herself, the repetitive movements calming her until her pulse had returned to normal. She still couldn't wrap her head around it: they'd found a green rose and used it to speak with *her*. Only the richest noblemen could afford magical messaging. A lump came into her throat. She missed them even more now that she'd heard their voices.

She tried to picture the two of them together. Had they been in the council tent or by the fire outside? Had the others been gathered around them, listening intently? Who had found the green rose? Was Fardan completely well now? Had his grandmother recovered from Chinmay's death? And Gopal Masa—how was his health? So many things she longed to know, but there had been no time to ask.

At least she'd heard their voices. At least they'd *talked,* even if it had been brief. She would have to be satisfied with that much. When they talked next, she should have a clear lead on Kavi. They must pay off their debt before summer's end; there was no other option. The kul had burned its bridges with the baniya by deciding not to deal with him, but she couldn't fault them for it. It would have taken great courage to arrive at that decision, especially after they'd seen what the baniya's men were capable of.

She dried herself and reached for the clothes Tarana had indicated. There was a snug embroidered blouse and a long skirt embellished with bits of sparkly glass—like the lehenga choli Tarana wore, but more decorative. She slipped on the blouse and tied the skirt around her waist. She wasn't going to wear the flimsy sandals Tarana had left for her, though. Perhaps it was silly to roam around the palace in boots, but she wasn't going to relinquish them.

Tarana returned to do Irinya's hair, detangling it with coconut oil and tying it into a thick plait, which she twisted into a knot. "The ladies of the zenana have already eaten," she said, patting the knot with satisfaction. "If you are hungry, we can go to the kitchen and ask for a plate of food."

"Yes, please," said Irinya gratefully. She would question the guards once she'd eaten. As she followed Tarana out of the bathhouse, she asked, "Do you ever go outside the palace?"

Tarana nodded. "I accompany the royal ladies sometimes, but we go in palanquins, protected by guards."

The luxurious life of the palace came with heavy restrictions, at least for the women. The bath had been lovely, but it wasn't worth being cooped up like an expensive songbird. Nostalgia gripped her as she thought of the Banni grasslands. She longed for the wide-open spaces, the endless blue skies, the gazelles leaping out of the long grass, the tartness of newly plucked berries, and the sweetness of freshly churned yogurt. *Patience,* she told herself. *Fortitude.* She'd left for a reason. It was no good weakening now.

The kitchen turned out to be a huge space, open to the courtyard and staffed by over a dozen women. Irinya was given a brass plate full of rice, dal, pickled cabbage and onions, and a glass of sugarcane juice. There were also—treat of treats!—samosas left over from the ladies' teatime. Irinya ate in the courtyard, savoring each bite.

As she ate, she listened to the chattering of the kitchen staff.

"I'm putting my money on the sultana," said a woman, crouching over the massive stove and fanning its flames. "Have you seen the Royal Women's Guards? Been training them for years, she has. Each one is a match for three of the wazir's men."

Irinya sucked in a quick breath. The *sultana* had been training guards? She was obviously no expensive songbird, but a military leader in her own right. And yet the wazir had talked of her in such disparaging tones.

Another woman snorted as she kneaded an enormous mound of dough. "You'd lose your money. There are twenty male soldiers for every one of those women, worse luck."

"But some of the men might be loyal to the sultana, too," argued the first.

"It's the nobles who'll decide," said a third woman, carrying a pile of dishes to the courtyard pump to wash. "And they're leaning toward the wazir, aren't they? Typical."

The second woman lowered her voice, so Irinya had to strain her ears to hear. "I haven't seen her in weeks. He's confined her to her rooms, except for court appearances."

Had he? Irinya's stomach plummeted. She hadn't thought the wazir capable of imprisoning his own aunt. She would underestimate him to her peril.

The rest of the conversation was carried out in more muted tones, and she couldn't catch it. She glanced at Tarana, who was sipping a cup of tea, perched on a ledge outside the kitchen. What did the maid make of all the palace intrigue? Where did her loyalties lie? But Tarana's face betrayed nothing.

When she had finished, Tarana walked over to her and gestured to the women pacing the courtyard, swords at their belts and staffs in their hands. "Ask them about your friend, my lady. They won't bite."

"Ha ha." Irinya returned her empty plate to the kitchen and girded herself. She had thought up a different excuse for asking about Kavi. The one about passing on a message was paper-thin, as Tarana's reaction had demonstrated. *Be confident, as if you have every right to make such inquiries,* she told herself as she walked up to the nearest guard—a tall, statuesque woman with long hair coiled in a topknot. She bowed, heart palpitating. "Greetings. I am looking for someone by the name of Kavi Kampilya. Do you know where I can find him?"

The guard gave her a piercing stare. "Who wants to know?"

The guard's first reaction had not been to deny any knowledge of him. Irinya's pulse sped up. "Irinya Dewa." She hesitated before adding, "New in the service of the wazir of Gujarat." Surely dropping the wazir's name would help her.

"Does the wazir know you are making such inquiries?" asked the guard, hefting her staff.

"No," she admitted, quailing. Should she not have mentioned the wazir at all? She didn't want her inquiries getting back to him. At least they were at the far end of the courtyard from the kitchen, so the kitchen staff could not overhear them.

The guard's lips thinned. "A matter of the heart, is it?"

"No, nothing like that," said Irinya, squashing her indignation and offering a shy smile. It might be better for them to think it *was* a matter of the heart. They'd be less likely to report it. "I just need to talk with him for five minutes."

"These girls." A second guard wandered up to them, shorter and rounder than the first but no less imposing. "Khawaja Daulat tells us to be strict, but I was fifteen once myself."

"I'm seventeen!" said Irinya sharply. Why did everyone assume she was a child?

"And you are in the zenana, where you will remain until the wazir decides otherwise," said the first guard in a voice like granite.

"I'm not part of the sultan's harem," Irinya pointed out.

The guard gave her an up-down look. "No, you're not the type. What are you here for, then?"

"I'm the wazir's new secretary," she said, stifling her frustration. They obviously knew of Kavi, and she needed their cooperation. "*Please,* can you tell me about Kavi Kampilya? When is the last time you saw him? He's gone missing, and some people I know are worried about him."

The two women exchanged a glance. "Sorry to break your heart, but Kavi Kampilya isn't *missing*. Not missing you, either. Just missing *to* you," said the first guard.

The breath caught in her throat. "What do you mean?"

The guard shrugged. "He's been in Junagadh all this time. I know, because I delivered a message from the governor to the sultan a few days ago and it mentioned him. Anyway, he's on his way to the palace, accompanying Malik Ayyaz. Should be here in a day or two. You can have it out with him then."

"Didn't figure him for a heartbreaker," said the second guard. "Isn't he married? And, like, all stiff and sober?"

"Eh. All men are the same below the belt."

They both gave dirty laughs.

Dark clouds of confusion roiled through Irinya's mind. Kavi had been safely in Junagadh all this time. Why hadn't he told the sarraf to buy the kul's debt? She thought of Chinmay, and her stomach clenched. "You must be mistaken," she said, hating the tremble in her voice. "The person I'm thinking about can't be the same as the one you are talking of. Maybe there is more than one Kavi."

"Sure, sure," said the second guard. "Must be dozens of Kavi Kampilyas floating around the sultanate. It's not like it's an unusual name, right?"

"Enough," said the first guard, hilarity gone. "Stay in the zenana; it's the safest place for you."

Like hell she would. If the guard was right, Kavi would be here soon. She'd have it out with him, all right. She'd tell him he'd put her kul in danger and demand the flower back or enough wealth to last her kul generations, as he'd promised. Her eyes burned as conflicting emotions rocked her. She was relieved that he was all right, but how could he have forgotten her and her kul? Where was the silver spider lily? Had he sold it already? To whom? He certainly hadn't given it to the sultan. If he had, the wazir would have known about it. But it couldn't be with the Portuguese, either; they were still fighting along the Malabar Coast.

Had the flower been stolen from him? Had shame prevented him from returning to the Rann and confessing he'd lost it? That was the only explanation that made any sense.

And he was *married*. Not that it mattered, but he certainly hadn't given any hint of it when he was with her. Her fists clenched; she couldn't wait to confront him.

The gate at the end of the courtyard creaked open, and the elderly woman poked her head in. "Irinya Dewa?"

Irinya's heart jumped. "That's me."

"Khawaja Daulat is here to take you to the wazir," she said.

The guards turned incredulous eyes on her. "Newly arrived and already a favorite?" said the first. "The wazir has never asked for a girl before."

"I'm his *secretary*. It's to discuss flowers," said Irinya, controlling herself with difficulty. The guards had been helpful, but their attitude was annoying.

"And perhaps to pluck them?" The second guard dug her elbow into the first one's side, grinning.

Irinya's face burned at the insinuation. "Some flowers have thorns," she retorted. "*Poisonous* ones."

"Ooh, *spiky*. No wonder she's a favorite," cackled the second guard.

Tarana came up to them. "Don't tease her, please. My lady, Khawaja Daulat will escort you back to the zenana. When you return, I will show you to your room."

Irinya thanked her and made her escape from the sniggering guards. The old woman stood aside to let her pass and bolted the gate shut.

Beyond the gate stood a slim, elegant eunuch, dressed in brocade and silk robes. "Irinya Dewa?" he said in a smooth, cultured voice. "Please follow me."

He led her across another stone-flagged courtyard with a peepal tree in the middle and potted plants arrayed on all four sides. A tiny breeze blew, making the leaves tremble and bringing the scent of summer flowers to her nostrils. Ordinary flowers, without any magic, but the fragrance still reminded her of the Rann and its special blooms. "The sultan likes greenery," she said, inhaling deeply.

Khawaja Daulat glanced at her. "Indeed, he does. He has built a magnificent garden east of the city, Bagh-i-Firdaus."

"Garden of Paradise?" she hazarded.

He gave her an approving smile. "That is what the name means in Persian, yes. Nine hundred thousand mango and khirni trees have been planted there. You should visit if you get the opportunity. But watch out for the tigers."

"There are tigers in the *gardens?*" The thought made her stomach curdle. In Kutch, cultivated gardens were few and far between and harbored nothing more dangerous than the odd peacock or monkey.

"They have even been known to enter the city. Soldiers bang drums to chase them away." He pushed open a door in the courtyard, nodded to the guard on duty, and led her up a flight of steep stone steps. Torches flamed in brackets, their light falling on small paintings of illustrated Persian texts. At the top of the staircase was another guard blocking the corridor. He bowed and moved out of their way.

"Does the sultan live in this part of the palace, too?" Irinya craned her neck to gaze at the geometric red and blue designs painted on the corridor ceiling.

He laughed. "No. The palace is huge, and there are many wings."

"Where does the governor of Junagadh stay when he arrives?" she asked in a casual tone, as if it was trivial. If she knew that, she would know where to find Kavi when Malik Ayyaz showed up with his entourage.

His eyebrows shot up. "How do you know him?"

"I don't *know* him. I've just heard a lot about him," she prevaricated. "Didn't he fight the Portuguese in Diu?"

His face relaxed. "Yes, the governor is a famous person, widely admired all over Gujarat. He usually stays in the eastern wing of the palace when he is here. He divides his time between Junagadh and Ahmedabad, and you're fortunate he will be arriving soon. Maybe you will get a distant glimpse of him."

Oh, I'll get a lot more than that, she thought, tingling with anticipation. She imagined grabbing Kavi by the scruff of his neck and shouting: *Why didn't you return to Banni? Why didn't you tell the sarraf to buy our debt? Where's the silver spider lily? Where's our money?* Then she would tell him about poor Chinmay and the baniya's threat to kill more of them if they didn't make his quota. She would make him feel the guilt that poured like molten lava through her own veins.

They stopped before an ornately carved door at the end of the corridor. Khawaja Daulat rapped on the door, and the wazir's deep voice barked, "Come in."

Khawaja Daulat pushed open the door, ushered Irinya in, and bowed himself out.

Several lamps placed on tables scattered throughout the room revealed a spacious study, made cozy with carpets and walls lined with bookshelves. Imshan Khan sat behind a huge wooden desk piled with parchments, ink, quills, scrolls, and books. There was an ink stain on his cheek, making him look a bit more human. He stared at her, a slow smile curving his lips. "You are almost pretty when you dress appropriately. Although I note you have retained the boots out of some misplaced sense of independence. Tomorrow, I expect you to wear footwear more suitable for a palace than a jungle."

She said nothing, though she longed to throw one of her boots at him.

"Sit." He indicated a chair opposite. "How long have you been a flower hunter?"

"Five years, huzoor," she said, sitting down. "Since I was twelve."

He leaned forward. "What flowers have you collected? How many per season? Tell me everything you know about them." The hunger in his eyes and voice made her squirm.

"Do you not have flower hunters of your own to give you this kind of information?" she asked, although they hadn't heard tell of any hunters employed directly by the court of the sultan. Middlemen held the flower supply lines in a tight grip. Kavi was the first person she knew of who'd tried to surmount that barrier. Her lips thinned. She would make him keep his end of the bargain, no matter what it took.

The wazir shook his head, the corners of his mouth turning down.

"The court has sent people to the Rann from time to time—the best of our soldiers and trackers. But none of them ever returned, and the court stopped authorizing such expeditions. It is safer to rely on the existing network."

The one that keeps flower hunters sunk in debt all their lives, she managed not to say. "Still, you must have experts in your court that you can consult, right?" she asked instead. Not that she would trust any information from an outsider, no matter how well educated, but she wondered how they viewed the magical flowers of the Rann.

"*Experts.*" He snorted. "They know nothing. One tells me the flowers are not magical at all. They work because we think they must. All the stories of how Zafar Khan used a silver spider lily to gain independence from the Delhi Sultanate are myth. Yet another so-called expert claims that the flowers come into existence in the moment they are found. When we stop looking for them, they cease to exist. A third says the flowers feed on the bones of dead men; they are evil spirits that hold us in their thrall."

"It is not flowers that are evil, huzoor," she said. Warmth filled her as she thought of the blue petal that had saved her. "It is humans who use them for evil ends."

"You think I do not know that?" He drummed his fingers on the table. "I did not call you here to debate ethics. Come, answer my questions."

It would not hurt her to tell the truth here. "We find between five to eight flowers every year, huzoor. Last year, we harvested four jasmines, a sunflower, and a rose. We give them to our baniya, to whom we owe money, and he sells them to the big flower markets in Gujarat. Flowers were more common in my mother's time. She told me they have become rarer, not just from overharvesting, but because we have killed most of the wasps that feed on the flowers' pollen."

"Yes!" The wazir snapped his fingers. "The ecological balance was destroyed. That is my theory, too. What fools they were to burn the hives."

Although she agreed with him, she protested: "Many died from wasp attacks. Have you ever seen a wasp, huzoor? They are nearly as big as your palm. A single sting can kill you. People were trying to protect their families."

"They were greedy," he stated. "I don't just mean the flower hunters.

I mean the nobles who lusted after the wealth promised by the pansy, the power promised by the hibiscus. I mean all the sultans after Zafar Khan who used the silver spider lily to annex neighboring kingdoms until our forces were stretched too thin to repel foreign invaders. If not for their greed, I wouldn't be in the situation I am today. A single spider lily, and I could bring the entire court to heel. No one would dare oppose my bid for the throne."

"Doesn't that make you as greedy as all the rest?" she blurted out, then bit her tongue.

His face darkened. "I could throw you into the dungeons for your impertinence."

If he did that, she wouldn't be able to confront Kavi and get what the kul was owed for the spider lily. They would be at the mercy of the baniya—not a man who had shown himself to be merciful. She swallowed, wishing she had not spoken. She couldn't afford to make the wazir angry with her. "I wouldn't be much use to you there," she pointed out, her voice even. "I only meant: Wouldn't you use the spider lily to defeat the Portuguese rather than to take the throne?"

He rubbed his cheek, spreading the ink. She resisted the urge to laugh. The wazir was not a man one laughed at—not twice, anyway. "Only when I am in power can I rally our forces against the invaders. I would use the spider lily to defeat my internal enemies before taking on external ones."

She stared at him in dismay. If he used up the spider lily for personal gain, what would that leave for the war? How would they get rid of the foreign invaders? Did he not care about the people who had died in Dabul, Diu, and other places? Perhaps it was a good thing that the spider lily was *not* in the palace. If Imshan Khan got his hands on it, he would use it only to increase his own power.

The wazir got up and began to pace. "This is a moot point. I do not, in fact, possess a spider lily. When the sultan dies, there will be a period of turmoil that may destabilize all of Gujarat. The nobles are already sniffing for blood, choosing factions. In the west, the Portuguese have chased Malik Ayyaz out of Diu. Farther south, they've captured Goa and Kochi and destroyed Calicut. They will no doubt take advantage of the upheaval."

What are you going to do about it? she wanted to scream. She held her-self in, clenching her fists. Her task was to save her kul. If she could *also* manage to ensure that the spider lily was used to defeat the Portuguese, that would be the best outcome. But first she needed to know where the flower was. *Kavi, wait till I get my hands on you.*

Imshan Khan turned back to her. "Have you seen the rarest flowers? The black chrysanthemum? The sacred lotus?"

She started. "No, huzoor. Those have not been seen in living mem-ory. They are rumored to be mythical."

"I don't believe that. There is a written account of how a Gujarati trader used the petal of a black chrysanthemum to travel to the Maluku Islands. He bought up available stocks of mace and nutmeg before rival ships could arrive and made a huge profit selling his stock to them." The wazir gave a savage smile. "He was murdered shortly after."

Surprise pooled in her stomach. That was the first official account she'd heard of the black chrysanthemum. Chinmay had told many sto-ries of the flower, of course—stories she remembered by heart—but there'd never been any reports of actual usage. She stored away the precious information, to be shared with the kul later. "But there are no reports of the sacred lotus ever being seen by anyone, let alone used," she said, hoping to prod him into revealing more.

Unbidden, a memory surfaced from the depths of the past. Her mother, smiling her secret smile, saying, *I have seen the flower that must not be seen. And I have lost it on purpose. But I will find it again.*

She rubbed her forehead. Where had that memory come from? Was it real? What flower had her mother been talking about? There was only *one* that must not be seen—the sacred lotus.

The wazir laid a hand on his desk and leaned toward her, his eyes sparkling. "All the other flowers exist; why should this one be mythical? Just because it hasn't been found yet?"

"Should *not* be found," Irinya muttered, wishing he would move a bit farther away from her. The wazir smelled of soap, sandalwood, sweat, and something sharp she could not name but which put her in mind of a blade.

His eyes narrowed. "Superstition. The sacred lotus is the most pow-erful flower. Imagine having the ability to manipulate time. No, I don't think you can. Have you ever thought about what time *is*?"

Something that is passing rather slowly right now. "I haven't had the time," she said, her voice flat.

He didn't appear to hear her or notice her tone. He perched on the edge of his desk, gazing into the distance. "There are philosophers who believe that time is not linear but cyclical. Or, if it is linear, it goes *both* ways, past and future. Others claim that all time has already passed, and what we are experiencing is but an error-filled memory. Still others believe that time does not exist. We live in an endless stream of present moments."

The way we experience time is linear because we are human, Irinya wanted to say. *Anything else would make us other than human.* "What do *you* believe?" she asked instead.

He refocused his gaze on her. "I don't know. But if I had the lotus, I'd turn back time and prevent my grandfather's murder."

Was he a child? "I don't think it works like that, huzoor."

His lip curled. "Why, what else is the lotus for, if not to right past wrongs? My grandfather Daud Khan was sultan for just twenty-seven days. He was a forward-thinking ruler, curtailing courtly expenses and appointing the lowborn to high office based solely on merit. *Too* forward thinking, according to his courtiers. They liked the Poison Sultan better. You know where you are with poison, but a progressive might ruin them all. If I had my way, Daud Khan would reign for many peaceful years, and after him, my father, who would *not* die in a dungeon, regretting the spark of rebellion against his uncle that led him there."

Her throat constricted. What kind of person would Imshan Khan have been without such a painful past? A nicer, more trusting one, perhaps. "I'm sorry about your family, huzoor. But things that have happened stay happened. Even if you could change them, you cannot change yourself, and you cannot change how those things made you feel. That is why we should only go forward."

He tilted his head. "If you had a chance to go back, wouldn't you take it? If you had a chance to save your mother, wouldn't you save her?"

She stared at him, unable to answer. Of course she would save her mother if she could. But sometimes people didn't want to be saved. Sometimes they walked into the night and never returned, not because they'd lost their way, but because they'd found it.

If she could turn back time, wouldn't she avoid showing Kavi the

silver spider lily? Wouldn't she request of the kul that a few men accompany Kavi back to Junagadh to make sure he bought their debt?
And wouldn't she persuade Fardan to take the spider lily directly to the
sultan himself?

It was pointless dreaming of such things. Regret choked her throat,
making it difficult to swallow. In hindsight, it was easy to see what she
should have done. But could she have done any differently with the
knowledge she had then?

"Time; time is key," said Imshan Khan. "My desire to find the sacred
lotus is second only to my desire to find a silver spider lily, which is a
shade more realistic. Maybe one day you will take me to the Rann, and
we will find it together." He gave her a lopsided smile.

Her stomach seized at the thought of taking the wazir to the Rann. *It
won't come to that.* She would escape as soon as she got what she needed
from Kavi.

The wazir rose from his desk. "You should return to the zenana now.
You will find Khawaja Daulat in his office at the end of this corridor.
Tomorrow morning, I expect you attend court and take notes for me."

He was serious about using her as a secretary, although she wasn't
sure why. This was all to the good. She would find out more about the
different court factions, besides knowing exactly when Malik Ayyaz—
and Kavi—returned. "Must I stay in the zenana?" she asked. "I am not
part of the harem."

He gave her a penetrating stare. "Do you wish to be? It would
be most unsuitable. The sultan's concubines are all princesses from
neighboring kingdoms. Besides, he's nearly dead. Unless"—his lips
twitched—"you wish to be part of *someone else's* harem?"

Was he deliberately misunderstanding her? "I have no wish to be
part of anyone's harem, huzoor," she said, keeping her voice even. "I
meant, perhaps I could stay elsewhere in the palace."

"Certainly not." He reached for a manuscript on his desk, dismissing
her. "The zenana is not just for the wives and concubines of the sultan.
It's for all the women of his extended household, including my aunts
and cousins. It's the safest place for you."

A place she would find it difficult to escape from, he did not need to
add. She gave a perfunctory bow and stepped out of his room. Khawaja

Daulat escorted her back to the zenana and left her with the elderly woman in the courtyard.

The guards had changed during the past hour, but one of them told her to wait and sent for Tarana. The maid arrived shortly after and took her inside, up the stairs to a gallery on the second floor. As they walked past doors hung with white muslin curtains, Irinya heard a peal of feminine laughter. It had been ages since she'd laughed like that, and she longed to join in. She imagined barging into a room full of elegant, richly dressed ladies and bit back a giggle. She'd stick out like a frog among flamingos.

Tarana ushered her into a room and lit an oil lamp for her. The light revealed a small but well-furnished space with a bed, a carpet, a wardrobe with a mirror, and narrow lattice windows that looked out into the courtyard.

When she was gone, Irinya turned down the lamp and lay on the too-large, too-soft bed. She twisted and turned, trying to get comfortable. Finally, she took the pillow and sheet and lay on the carpet instead. That was better. Closer to the earth, closer to home.

"I miss you, Fardan," she whispered. "I miss you, Bholi Masi. I miss you, Veerana."

Then come and get me, said Veerana's aggrieved voice in her head.

Soon, she thought to him. *Hang in there.*

Kavi would be here within a day or two. All the questions she was burning to ask him would be answered, and the mystery of the missing spider lily would be solved.

CHAPTER 10

Tarana woke Irinya the next morning, laden with a bundle of fresh clothes, a tray of fruit, and a leather bag packed with writing implements. She made no comment on the fact that Irinya had chosen to sleep on the carpet instead of the bed, something Irinya was grateful for.

"The wazir says you are his secretary." The maid placed the fruit on a table next to the bed and opened the bag, showing Irinya the parchment, ink, and quills. "That means you must have all the tools for writing."

Irinya thought with a pang of how Fardan scrounged for materials to draw with. If she could, she'd sneak one or two quills and paper for him as souvenirs.

"You must hurry, my lady," continued the maid, laying out the clothes she'd brought on the bed. "The court meets in half an hour, and the wazir dislikes tardiness."

Half an hour? Irinya leaped up from her makeshift bed, gulped down a bit of fruit and tea, and changed into the clothes Tarana had brought: loose trousers, kurta, and a dupatta wrapped around her head and shoulders. Tarana finished off by draping her in a shapeless garment of fine blue muslin with long sleeves and a translucent veil. "I'm going to be hot in this," Irinya muttered, flapping her arms.

Tarana laughed. "It's quite thin. You must be veiled if you are to be in court. Even the sultana speaks from behind a screen."

Anticipation coiled within Irinya as she followed Tarana out of the room and down the corridor, armed with her new leather bag. She was going to attend the court and see the sultana, the official heir to the throne. Well, not *see* her, but at least hear her voice. "What kind of person is the sultana?" she asked as Tarana pushed open the door to the courtyard and led her out. Early-morning sunlight sparkled on the freshly watered plants that lined the courtyard, and the air vibrated with birdsong. At the opposite end, Khawaja Daulat waited for her, the picture of patience.

Tarana gave her a sideways glance. "A very different person from the wazir."

What did she mean? Irinya would have asked more, but Khawaja Daulat called out, "Ten minutes until the court is in session," and she flew across the courtyard to him.

Khawaja Daulat took her through multiple courtyards—a shorter route, he explained, as compared to going from inside the palace—until they arrived at an imposing red sandstone building with a wide, plant-lined terrace and an ornately carved wooden door. "The public entrance to the audience hall," he said, opening the door and ushering her in. "Although today is a private meeting of the ministers and courtiers of the sultan."

Irinya walked into a pillared hall, eyes nearly starting from her head. It was the largest room she'd ever seen, with a high, intricately carved ceiling, mural-covered walls, and a black-and-white marble floor. In the center were two parallel rows of cushioned seats—most already occupied by richly dressed courtiers, who turned to look at her askance. A wooden screen with lacelike jali work stood at the head of the rows, guards stationed on either side of it. Was the sultana behind the screen? Irinya's nerves thrummed with excitement. What would the kul say when she told them she'd attended the sultan's court? She was glad of the anonymity of the veil, that no one could see her avid expression beneath it.

"You may sit behind the wazir," murmured Khawaja Daulat before edging to a door at the rear of the hall.

She scanned the seats and spied the wazir's handsome face, intent as he listened to the elderly, turbaned courtier next to him. He glanced up and frowned as she walked over.

"Farah, you are late. Sit; I expect you to take notes."

Farah? Was that her alias in the court? She was relieved he wasn't using her real name, but he should at least have asked her preference. She settled on a mat behind him and opened her leather bag, hoping she wouldn't spill any ink.

"A new secretary again, huzoor?" said the elderly courtier, casting a quizzical look at her.

"I doubt she will last long," said the wazir with a sigh. "None of them do."

I can't think why, she thought, jabbing a quill into an ink bottle with unnecessary force. She studied the people sitting on the cushioned seats, talking with each other in low voices. Most were older than the wazir; all were men.

A couple of late arrivals hurried in, and a calm feminine voice from behind the screen said, "Let us begin."

A ripple went through the assembly, and everyone fell silent. Irinya stared at the screen, barely able to sit still. That must be the sultana.

A middle-aged man with a sleek mustache and elaborate pink turban rose and cleared his throat. "We have four items to bring before the court today: the health of the sultan, the confinement of the sultana to her rooms, the progress of the war with the Portuguese, and the petition by his lordship, the wazir of Gujarat, Imshan Khan, to be declared by this court the heir apparent of the sultan."

Hubbub broke out across the hall. Nobles seated on the opposite side rose and began to shout, shaking their fists. But those in the wazir's row remained seated, smiling at each other. Had they divided themselves into two rows depending on where their loyalties lay? Irinya counted—around a dozen on each side. An even split. She peered at the wazir to gauge his reaction, but he sat with his back erect, his face expressionless.

"Silence!" came the voice from behind the screen, and the noise subsided. "Let us deal with the items one by one. Hakim-ji, what news of my father's health?

The nobles sat down, murmuring in dissatisfaction, and a plump man in a white turban rose from the end of the opposite row. "There is some deterioration from the week before," he said, his tone somber.

"Sometimes His Highness recognizes me, and sometimes he doesn't. His appetite, too, is not what it was."

Imshan Khan gave a quiet snort. The hakim cleared his throat and went on, "I believe we must all be prepared for the worst."

The wazir leaned back and whispered, "He's been saying that for weeks." Irinya suppressed the urge to push him away from her and tell him to behave. The wazir would not take kindly to that suggestion.

Courtiers discussed the sultan's failing health and uttered empty platitudes before moving on to the next item on the agenda: the sultana's confinement.

A slim man, younger than the rest, rose and said in a passionate voice, "Zahra Sultana is one of the most capable and beloved members of the royal family. She is also the heir to the throne. Why has she been confined to her rooms? Why is she only allowed to attend court when there is no public audience? Why can she not continue her military exercises? This is a grave injustice, perpetrated by her own nephew, the wazir of Gujarat." He pointed a quivering finger at Imshan Khan. "If the sultan were healthy and strong enough to walk in here, he would throw you into the dungeons!"

"Watch your words," snarled a noble a few seats down from the wazir, "or they'll be the last you utter."

The wazir raised his hand. "Please, let us be civil. I will respond to each of the culture minister's points one by one. You say the sultana is capable. For a woman, yes. But you need more than individual capacity to unite the sultanate. You say she is beloved. By whom? Yourself, clearly." The men in the wazir's row tittered, and the culture minister's face went beetroot red. Irinya transcribed in a quiet fury, stabbing the quill on the parchment until it ran with ink.

"You say she is the heir to the throne," continued Imshan Khan. "I dispute that statement. I am the legitimate male heir of the sultan. He no longer has his wits, or, knowing how close he is to death and how close the sultanate is to chaos, he would recant the decree he signed declaring my aunt to be his heir. As to why she has been confined, it is for her own safety. You know how people speak against her in the palace."

"Imshan," said the quiet voice from behind the screen. "I know whose voice speaks the loudest against me. But come, we have a more important item to discuss."

"What can be more important than deciding the rightful successor to the throne?" demanded the wazir.

"Defeating the Portuguese" was the answer. Irinya's heart soared at the words. "If we don't get rid of the foreign invaders, we may not have a throne to fight over—not for long, anyway."

There were murmurs of agreement. *You tell him,* thought Irinya.

"The sultanate was born of blood. It has survived worse," snapped Imshan Khan. "Besides, the Portuguese are a *naval* power. Their interest is limited to the coastal cities. They have made no move inland."

"The ports are the lifeblood of India," said the sultana. "If commerce is choked off, people will starve. And once they've taken the coast, there's nothing to stop them getting more troops and moving farther inland."

"Malik Gopi, the governor of Surat, advises taking the diplomatic route with the Portuguese," came an oily voice from the middle of the opposite row. A thin, sharp-featured man in a white turban rose and bowed in the direction of the screen. "As you know, Sultana, your father greatly respected Malik Gopi's opinion on the matter."

There were murmurs of agreement from some and disparaging snorts from others.

"We all know Malik Gopi's views," said the wazir, his voice like granite. "He persuaded my great-uncle to release the Portuguese prisoners captured from Diu last year. And what did we get in return? *Nothing.* We lost an important bargaining chip. I wonder what they promised Malik Gopi in return for his cooperation."

"Imshan Khan!" The oily-voiced man's face darkened. "How dare you slander Malik Gopi in this court?"

"As a result of the prisoner transfer, the Portuguese held off on attacking Surat," said the sultana, her voice cutting through the mutters of the court assembly. "Malik Gopi did the right thing for his own constituency. But was it the right thing for the sultanate? I have my doubts."

The debate continued, with first one side arguing and then the other. Irinya bent over her parchment and scribbled fast, her mind working. The court was not evenly divided after all. On the matter of the Portuguese, the wazir and the sultana were more closely aligned than the Malik Gopi faction. Her head swam as she tried to piece the different faces, names, and alliances together.

A guard came running up as the debate wound down with no clear victor on either side. "Malik Ayyaz, the governor of Junagadh and Diu, has arrived at Bhadra Fort," he announced with a bow.

Irinya's heart jumped. Malik Ayyaz had arrived. That meant Kavi was here. She itched to leap up and look for him right away but managed to control herself.

"Excellent," said the sultana. "Let us adjourn for the day. Tomorrow morning, we will ask Malik Ayyaz for his insight into the situation."

The wazir rose. "Escort the sultana back to her rooms," he ordered.

Irinya craned her neck to catch a glimpse of the sultana, but the guards on either side of the screen formed a shield around her, blocking her from sight as they marched her down the hall to a door at the back. Was this truly for her safety, or had Imshan Khan manipulated events so she was a prisoner in her own palace? It made sense, and it fit what she knew of his character. The sultana was his rival for the throne, and the throne mattered more to him than anything else.

Courtiers rose and left the hall, talking to each other in low voices. Irinya blew on her parchment to dry the ink and followed the wazir out the door at the back of the hall, skin tingling with anticipation. She was finally going to get hold of Kavi.

"Farah? Farah!"

She started. The wazir was frowning at her, leaning against the wall of the corridor outside the hall. Most of the nobles had left. Khawaja Daulat stood at the end of the corridor, waiting. "This is the third time I have tried to get your attention," said the wazir. "Where is it?"

On the man who promised to deliver my kul from debt in exchange for the dearest item in the world. "Still thinking about the meeting," she said, her voice even.

"You may have lunch in the zenana," he said. "Then meet me in my office with your notes. Khawaja Daulat will escort you as usual."

"Yes, huzoor," she said meekly. He stalked off, and Khawaja Daulat beckoned her with a smile. "How was your first assignment?" he asked. "Did you manage to take notes?"

"Yes," she said, following him out the door into a courtyard and blinking in the sunshine. How was she going to give him the slip? Could she double back once he'd left her? No, the ancient woman who stood guard at the zenana courtyard door would report her, and the walls were too high for her to scale. She would have to take a risk and take it now.

"Oh no." She came to a halt and slapped her forehead. "I forgot to ask the wazir an important question. Could you please let me know where he's gone?"

Khawaja Daulat raised his eyebrows. "Can't it wait till afternoon? He's probably at lunch with some of the ministers."

She summoned penitence into her tone. "I am sorry, but it's urgent. I will wait in his office until he returns."

His mouth thinned. "Very well. Please make sure you stay in the office. I have multiple errands to complete for the zenana, so I must be elsewhere."

She assured him she would wait for the wazir, her stomach fluttering. The wazir being out of his office was a bit of luck; she wouldn't waste it.

Khawaja Daulat left her in the corridor outside the wazir's office and hurried away. She stepped inside, counted to sixty, and stepped out again, her heart pounding.

The corridor was empty but for the usual guard blocking the entrance. She walked toward him, head held high and back straight.

The guard moved out of her way and frowned, glancing behind her.

"I have an urgent message to carry from the wazir to Malik Ayyaz in the east wing," she told him. "Can you tell me where it is located?"

His face cleared. "Go down the stairs, walk along the corridor till the end, and turn right. Climb the stairs to the first landing, walk past the sword hall, and ask the guard for His Excellency the Governor of Junagadh and Diu."

She thanked him. Amazing what assumed confidence could do for you. She didn't feel the slightest bit confident inside, of course. Her stomach churned as she thought of what the wazir might do if he found out she was wandering around the palace without permission, searching for Malik Ayyaz. He would question her, and if her answers didn't satisfy him, he would imprison her. He may even decide she was a spy after all, guessing she'd been armed with a bluestar petal against his hibiscus. Then she could bid goodbye to seeing daylight ever again. She swallowed her nausea and hurried down the stairs. She had very little time to find Kavi and discover what had happened.

She strode past the guards at the bottom of the stairs and down a stone-flagged corridor parallel to the courtyard. A few people passed her, but no one gave her a second glance. Mentally, she thanked Tarana for the clothes and veil, which allowed her to blend in and pass for a palace retainer. She climbed the stairs at the end of the corridor and arrived at a torchlit landing. A wide doorway opened onto a high-ceilinged, carpeted room with walls hung with swords and shields. This must be the sword hall the guard had mentioned. At the rear of the hall, she spied a narrow passage and made a beeline for it. She was lucky she had a good sense of direction, or she'd have been thoroughly lost by now.

Four men stood guard before a closed door at the end of the passage. They didn't have the same uniforms as the palace guard; perhaps they worked for Malik Ayyaz. She could hear voices within the room, but they were too faint for her to make out what was being said.

She walked up to the guards and announced, "I have a message for His Excellency the Governor Malik Ayyaz from the wazir."

Surprise crossed their faces. "Why is the wazir using the girls of the zenana to deliver messages?" asked one.

"Perhaps she *is* the message," suggested another, and they all sniggered.

"Why don't you share the message with us, pretty one," said a third, winking. "We'll make good use of it."

"Sure," she said, seething. "The message is, anyone who messes with me will find their head on a pike at dawn."

They drew back from her, as if a butterfly had grown teeth and bitten them.

"We were only joking," said the third man, scowling.

She grinned underneath her veil. "I am also only joking. Where's the governor?"

"His Excellency is in a meeting right now," said the first guard. "You'll have to wait."

"I don't mind waiting," she said. "Is Kavi Kampilya around?"

"He's with His Excellency," said the guard.

Her heart leaped. She was finally going to see Kavi. "Please don't bother His Excellency. The wazir said I can deliver the message to Kavi Kampilya."

One of the guards showed her to a small waiting room with a divan. She sat on the edge of the divan, trying not to shake. Now that the moment was upon her, all the words she'd intended to say to Kavi had vanished. Nothing could express the depth of the loss that the kul experienced and what they still stood to lose. *Where's the silver spider lily?* she would scream. That would do for a start.

The door pushed open, and a stranger entered—a plump, middle-aged man dressed in rich courtly robes, pearl necklaces wrapped around his silk turban. Was this the governor Malik Ayyaz himself? Irinya shot to her feet and bowed, her palms sweaty. "Your Excellency, I am sorry for disturbing you. I told the guards I could easily give my message to Kavi Kampilya."

The man's forehead creased. "I *am* Kavi Kampilya. What message does the wazir have for us?"

Irinya froze. Her mouth opened, but no words emerged.

"Well?" said the man impatiently.

Her mind blanked. This. This man was. Not Kavi. Not the person who'd given her his boots. Not the person who'd gone to the Rann with her. Not the person who'd shared how he lost his father and mother.

A scowl spread on the man's face. "Speak up. I haven't got all night."

"I'm sorry," she said with difficulty. Coldness rose within her, numbing her lips. "Is there another Kavi Kampilya who works for Malik Ayyaz?"

His brows drew together in outrage. "Is this your idea of a joke? I shall complain to the wazir."

"I'm sorry," she said again. *I met a man who said he was you, and I gave him the most precious thing in the world, and now how will I face my kul?*

She turned away, leaving the real Kavi Kampilya spluttering with annoyance. She walked in a daze down the passage, across the sword hall, down the stairs, and into the sunny courtyard. Her eyes burned, and her chest felt like she was carrying live coals within it. She leaned against the peepal tree in the middle of the courtyard, trying to breathe.

But there didn't seem enough air left in the world for her to breathe easy ever again.

He'd lied about who he was. Lied about everything. And she'd fallen for it like a naive fool.

Fardan, I'm so sorry.

A sob rose inside her, but she suppressed it. She would not cry. She would find the man who'd deceived her and make him pay for what he'd done.

CHAPTER 11

Irinya made her way back to the wazir's office, her mind picking and discarding various options, even as her insides quivered with anxiety. She needed help to discover fake Kavi's identity, for there was still a chance that the silver spider lily had not fallen into enemy hands. The best person, in ideal circumstances, would have been the sultana. She was the official heir, and it was clear from the argumentative court assembly that she had her priorities right: defeating the Portuguese. Irinya had liked the sound of her voice, calm and self-assured, even as Imshan Khan challenged her right to the throne.

But if the sultana could not even leave her rooms except under guard, she could not help Irinya retrieve the spider lily. That left *one* person Irinya could approach: the wazir. She didn't trust him, but time was of the essence, and perhaps he could be bargained with to do the right thing, both by her kul and by the sultanate.

And perhaps he would throw her into the dungeons for fooling him and withholding critical information. She broke into a sweat. If she was imprisoned or killed, that would be the end, not just of her, but of any hopes the kul had to be free of the baniya and his threats.

She arrived at the door leading to the wazir's office and gulped. She was barely able to lift her hand to knock.

"Come in," snapped the wazir, and her heart jumped.

Focus. Everything depended on how she framed the situation; she would tell it as a story, and her words would convince the wazir. Had Chinmay not thought her worthy to be his heir? She would not let him down.

She pushed open the door and entered, her feet leaden, her face blank. Her stomach knotted at what she was about to do.

The wazir tapped a quill on his desk, regarding her with a frown. "Where have you been wandering around? Khawaja Daulat sent word that you had an urgent question for me."

She raised the veil over her head and bowed to him. "Huzoor, I am here to tell you a story."

"Do I look like I have nothing better to do than listen to stories?" demanded the wazir.

Irinya straightened, her heart thumping. Her voice fell into the cadence of a storyteller of its own accord. "It is a story about a stolen silver spider lily. The fate of kingdoms hangs in the balance. Will you listen?"

The wazir went still, his eyes narrowed. He gestured with his hand. "Speak."

"Once, there was a girl who broke a promise by salt and sun," she began. She shifted her gaze away from him. *I am in the kul,* she thought. *I am telling a story to the children.*

Her heart rate slowed, and the words flowed out of her. She walked around the room as she told the tale, imitating the wicked baniya who had threatened the poor kul, and enacting the death of the venerable storyteller. The quill dropped from the wazir's hand, and he leaned forward, rapt. When she reached the part where the hapless protagonist realizes she has been betrayed, he swore.

She came to a halt in front of him and bowed once more, her throat raw, her eyes stinging. "Thank you for listening, huzoor," she said, wiping her face with the edge of her veil.

The wazir pinned her with his gaze. "Is that it? What happens afterward?"

She swallowed the lump in her throat. "That depends on you, huzoor. Shall we find the stolen spider lily together?"

"I see," he said, his voice as cold as a winter's night in the Rann. He picked up the quill and broke it, the *snap* loud in the quiet study. His lips pressed together, and his eyes glittered as if he was suppressing great emotion. She crossed her arms, trying to hold herself in. Would he call for guards to throw her into the dungeons?

"Sit," he said at last, sounding calm. She perched on the edge of the chair opposite him, feeling light-headed. She wasn't being imprisoned—yet.

"That was quite the performance," he said, raising an eyebrow. "You had me fooled until the very end. Why didn't you tell me about the spider lily earlier?"

She wet her lips and willed herself to continue speaking in a strong, confident voice. "This is the pivotal moment, when the protagonist must take the help of a morally gray character to save the world. I had to reach this point alone, huzoor, or it would not be a story worth telling."

He gave a dry laugh. "You are clever with words; I'll grant you that. Am I the protagonist or the morally gray character? No, don't bother to answer. I'm not sure my ego could take it." He poured water from a carafe into a cup and pushed it toward her. "Drink."

She drank, holding the cup with both hands, afraid it would fall and break like everything else around her.

"Describe the man," Imshan Khan commanded.

She knotted her hands on her lap. "Huzoor, there are conditions for the two characters to cooperate with each other. May I list them?"

"This is not a story, and you are in no position to make conditions," rasped the wazir.

"Requests, then," she said, trying not to let her desperation leak into her voice. "It is a matter of life and death, and it would be so easy for you to grant the first one."

He leaned back and crossed his arms, regarding her with hooded eyes. "I already know what it is. You wish to save your kul, yes? *If* I gain the spider lily with your help, and *if* you remain loyal to me, I will send word to your baniya to back off. I might even decide not to punish you. You have until the season's end, so there's still plenty of time."

Relief flooded her, cold and sweet. He had said nothing of their debt, but as long as they all stayed alive, stayed together, they could get through this. The baniya would still demand his quota, but he would not be able to threaten them again, much less send his men to kill them.

"Where is your kul?" continued Imshan Khan, his voice a shade too casual. "What is the name of your baniya?"

She froze. Of course, he needed to know this to fulfill her "request," but once she gave this information to him, he would hold the lives of her entire kul in his hands. Suppose he turned on her in the future? He was way more dangerous and powerful than the baniya. She cursed herself for not thinking far enough ahead.

But she didn't have to tell him everything right now. "The kul moves often during the summer," she said, choosing her words with care. "When you are ready to grant my request, I will give you their most likely position as well as the name of our baniya."

"I see." His lips twisted. "And the second request?"

"To use the spider lily to drive the Portuguese out of India," she said. "If you use it for personal gain, it will cost you." The words of the spider lily came back to her, and she shivered. *Are you sure?* it had said. *The price will be more than you can bear.* She was beginning to understand what it had meant.

The wazir gave a short, grim laugh. "I will use the spider lily well; do not presume to tell me what my priorities should be. Describe the man; we need to find out who he is and go after him. There's a chance we might still find the flower, especially as it has not yet made an appearance on the battlefield."

It was probably the best she'd wring out of him. In truth, she was lucky he'd given her this much instead of clapping her in irons or ordering her execution. If—*when*—they found the spider lily, she would remind him of her requests and of his own duty to his people.

She tried to describe Kavi. What to say about him? He was slim and elegant, around twenty years old, well-dressed, and well-spoken, fluent in Kutchi. He appeared to be kindhearted, generous, passionate, and, like her, the child of a flower hunter.

Except none of that might be true. It could all have been an act to impress her.

His voice when he spoke of his mother—had that been an act, too? Her stomach roiled to think of it.

"You have been well and truly had," said the wazir at last, leaning back and sounding remarkably calm.

She stared at him. "You're not angry?"

"I am *furious*," he said in the same even tone. "But my objective right now is to recover the spider lily. Once the flower is safe, I shall indulge myself with thoughts of how to vent my anger. Let us look at this logically. This personable young man whom you have fallen for—"

"I have *not*," she said, her face heating.

"—pretended to be Kavi Kampilya, who is the right-hand man of Malik Ayyaz," he continued, ignoring her. "If word of the spider lily got out, rumors would lead to Malik Ayyaz. Let us then eliminate Malik Ayyaz as a suspect. He is not a careless man. Moreover, he loathes the Portuguese and would never conspire with them. He fought in the Battle of Diu, and the loss hit him hard. He had to retreat with his forces to Junagadh after the defeat."

Her throat was still dry despite the glass of water. "It could be an enemy of Malik Ayyaz."

He pursed his lips. "There are no *enemies* among the nobles. Alliances shift and flow like water. But there are rivals, as you would have guessed from the meeting today. You haven't given me much to go on. The kind of man you describe is common in noble households. Think, Irinya. Did he have any mark or feature out of the ordinary?"

She tried to focus. Kavi's handsome face swam before her eyes, making her nauseous. "Not a feature, as such, but he had an unusual ornament: a blue enamel locket that hung on a gold chain around his neck."

"Hmm." The wazir's eyes turned inward. "I have seen such a locket. But where?"

"Name the prominent nobles of the sultanate," she suggested. "Perhaps you will remember."

"Let me see. Malik Kiwam-ul-Mulk. Nizam Khan. Ahmed Khan. Malik Usman. Malik Gopi." His gaze sharpened. "*Malik Gopi,* the merchant governor of Surat. He visited the court last winter. In his entourage was a young man wearing such a locket." He slammed the desk in triumph.

Her pulse quickened. Malik Gopi's name had been brought up in today's meeting. "And Malik Gopi is a rival of Malik Ayyaz?"

He nodded. "He's also my great-uncle's favorite noble."

"But not yours," she said, catching the inflection in his voice.

"No," he said flatly. "He pushed for compromising with the Portuguese, giving in to their demands and letting them build a fortress in Diu. He even persuaded the sultan to release Portuguese hostages. After our defeat in Diu, his voice has gained power in the court. Not everyone has the appetite to keep fighting. His talk of commerce and trade sounds sweet to noblemen's ears. His ships sail unmolested on the trade routes; apparently, he has no problem getting Portuguese cartazes. People think it's his diplomatic skill. They don't see that he has not an ounce of loyalty to anyone or anything—except wealth."

If the spider lily had fallen into his hands, all was lost. He sounded like the kind of man who would sell it to the highest bidder, even if that was the sultanate's worst enemy. She bit her nails, trying not to think of the carnage wreaked in Dabul. "How is the spider lily used?" she asked. "Jasmine is a tincture, sunflower is made into tea, hibiscus and bluestar petals are consumed whole, and rose attar is heated to create magical vapors. But I haven't learned how the spider lily is processed. The enemy may not know, either."

He gave her a flat stare. "There are no records of how the rarest flowers were used. Perhaps this lack is a safety feature. But a flower hunter should know. What would you do if you wanted to access the power of a spider lily?"

Have my head examined. She wrinkled her nose and considered. "The flower must be consumed in some way. The method differs, depending on the flower, but making a tincture seems the safest bet. It's more concentrated than tea and more readily absorbed than simply eating it."

He nodded. "That is what I would do. But would our enemies do the same? I'd give anything to know the extent of their knowledge of magic flowers."

She thought back to the dead body they'd found in the Rann, and coldness crept through her limbs. Had the Portuguese sent more trackers to the Rann? Was her kul in danger, not just from the baniya's men, but from foreign flower hunters? "Huzoor, the day before the fake Kavi showed up in our kul, we found a dead foreigner in the desert." She described the dead man and his clothing, leaving out all mention of the bluestar.

He heard her out, a frown on his face. "They're already venturing

into the Rann. I will alert our allies in Bhuj. Rao Hamirji can post lookouts on the borders." He drummed his fingers on the desk. "We'll leave
for Surat at dawn. Meet me in the courtyard."

Some of the tightness in her chest dissipated. They had a plan, and
they were acting on it. "You will miss the court assembly with Malik
Ayyaz tomorrow," she pointed out. "You'll need a good excuse for your
absence."

"I will tell the palace I am going to Bharuch to do a surprise inspection." He gave a mirthless smile. "We'll take the turncoat by surprise."

"Should I dress as a man again?" Irinya asked.

"No," he said. "Too many people in my employ have seen you in that
guise. Veil yourself each time you step out of the carriage, and you can
continue being my secretary." He waved a hand. "Go. I have much to
prepare."

She stood, trying not to let her relief show on her face. The meeting
had gone as well as could be hoped, but her nerves still thrummed with
tension in the wazir's presence. "Can I have my bag with the blowpipe
back?"

He knitted his brows. "Why do you want it?"

"It belonged to my mother," she reminded him. "It is one of the few
keepsakes I have of her."

He leaned back, fixing her with a hard stare. "I mean, why do you
want it *now*? Do you intend to use it?"

She bit her lip. No point trying to lie to him. "This will be a dangerous mission. It might come in useful."

He gave a short laugh. "My dear girl, I will be well armed, and we
will have bodyguards. I have no intention of letting you have a weapon
you might decide to direct toward *me*."

"But—" she began.

He held up a hand, stopping her. "If our mission is successful, I will
return your precious blowpipe to you, minus your nasty little thorns.
Now leave."

She left, curbing her irritation. She'd get back her blowpipe once
they'd retrieved the spider lily.

Khawaja Daulat was waiting for her outside the wazir's office. "You
have been wandering unaccompanied in the palace," he said, his voice

heavy with disapproval. "I have had a complaint from Malik Ayyaz's entourage. Kavi Kampilya said you were acting most strange."

"I'm sorry," she said, her mind elsewhere. Would they find fake Kavi
in Surat? Would he still have the flower, or was it already too late?

"It is not seemly," he insisted. "Ladies must be chaperoned."

She focused on him. "Why?"

He spluttered. "What a question!"

"In my kul, men and women live and work together," she said.

"This is the palace," he snapped. "Not the uncivilized land of Kutch."

Oh, how I wish it were. Homesickness grabbed hold of her. She was
no closer to her objective than before. She was, in fact, *further.* At least
she'd still believed in Kavi when she started out. Her eyes blurred.

"Forgive me," said Khawaja Daulat in alarm. "I did not mean to distress you."

"I want to go back home," she said, her voice wobbling. "And I can't."

"Ahmedabad is beautiful," he said earnestly. "I shall arrange for you
to accompany the ladies the next time they go to the markets or the
gardens."

"Thank you," she said, because he meant it kindly, and he would not
have understood if she talked of the wide-open spaces and skies of her
homeland. They arrived at the zenana, and he left her with the ancient
woman stationed at the courtyard door.

Tarana met Irinya in the zenana courtyard and took her to the
kitchen for an early-evening meal since she'd missed lunch. "Did you
find the person you were looking for, my lady?" she asked as they sat
together on a stone bench some distance away from the kitchen, so they
were out of earshot of the staff.

Irinya stared at the food on her plate, exhaustion creeping up her
limbs. "No, he's not in the palace at all."

"Isn't Kavi Kampilya in the entourage of Malik Ayyaz?" asked Tarana.
"I heard one of the guards say so."

Irinya pursed her lips, wishing she hadn't mentioned his name. "The
man I was looking for wasn't Kavi Kampilya at all. He lied to me about
his name."

"What?" Tarana's normally placid face puckered. "Why would someone do that?"

"So I cannot find him. So I cannot make him keep his promises." She dashed a hand against her eyes, ashamed and angry.

Tarana squeezed her shoulder. "I am sorry, my lady. Men are untrustworthy, their affections as fleeting as clouds in a desert. So says my mistress. I hope you can remind him of the meaning of love and honor."

Assuming she could even find him after he gave her a false name and dropped off the face of the earth. Irinya tried to smile. "I hope so, too. I'm leaving with the wazir at dawn tomorrow. Maybe we'll find him."

Tarana tilted her head, puzzled. "Why is the wazir helping you search for your boyfriend?"

He's not my boyfriend, she wanted to scream. But better if Tarana believed that. "The wazir is interested in him for different reasons," she improvised. "Don't tell anyone, please. This is our secret."

Tarana placed a finger on her lips. "I can keep secrets. I haven't told anyone about you except my mistress. And my mistress is the best lady in the world."

"I am happy for you," said Irinya, wondering who Tarana's mistress was. One of the ladies in the sultan's harem, most likely.

Tarana rose. "Please finish your meal, my lady. I'll make sure you wake up in time and are ready before dawn."

Irinya gave her a grateful smile. "Thank you. I would be lost here without you."

Tarana gave a pleased smile. "Just doing my job."

Irinya finished eating and returned to her room, tired but too tense to sleep. She lay on her makeshift bed on the floor of her room, trying to relax but failing. How were Fardan, Bholi Masi, and the others doing? Fardan had said he would contact her again in a few days. She would have a bleak update to share with him this time. Her heart squeezed as she thought of what she would say and how he would feel. He hadn't trusted Kavi from the start. Like a fool, she'd put it down to jealousy. She should have trusted his instincts—trusted *him* instead of trusting a stranger. Her eyes burned in the darkness. *I'm going to find you, stranger, and the spider lily, too. I'm going to make you wish you'd never deceived me and my kul.*

_*_

Early the next morning, Tarana helped Irinya pack and get ready, then led her to the courtyard where Khawaja Daulat was waiting to escort her outside the zenana. "Well in time," he said approvingly, taking her bags from Tarana.

Irinya gave Tarana a quick hug. "Thank you for everything."

"Good luck," whispered Tarana. "I hope you find the person in your heart."

An interesting way of putting it. But she didn't know who he was, and the name was the least of it. The person in her heart did not exist. There was a dagger in her heart instead, one that she could pull out only when she found the man who'd put it there.

Khawaja Daulat took her through a series of courtyards filled with trees, fountains, flowers, and sculptures. If not for her nerves, she would have enjoyed the beautiful carvings, the fragrance of the flowers, and the twittering of the sparrows, buntings, and finches that filled the morning air. But she was stretched as tight as a drum.

The wazir was waiting for her in the outermost courtyard of the fort. It was a far smaller company than the one that had set off from Bhuj all those days ago—four carriages for the wazir, his bodyguards, a couple of cooks, and the provisions. The wazir ushered her into his carriage, and they set off, trundling toward the gates.

She sat on a chair opposite the wazir's divan and shrugged off her veil, giving him a covert glance. She hadn't expected to be in *his* carriage. Would he continue questioning her throughout their journey? She wouldn't be able to relax her guard at all. She had hoped to use this time to calm herself and mentally prepare for the confrontation with fake Kavi.

Imshan Khan eyed the veil and gave her an amused smile. "Not something you are used to, flower hunter."

"No, huzoor." She folded the veil and laid it on one of the small side tables. It made her feel like an imposter.

"Purdah is common among both Hindu and Muslim women," he remarked. "But not, perhaps, among the nomads of Banni."

"No," she said again, irritated. She had no desire to make idle chit-chat with him. "Huzoor, what if we do not find the man we are looking for in Surat?"

"Then you shall go back to the Rann and find another silver spider lily for me," he said, all trace of amusement vanishing from his face. "You obviously have special skills. Put them to good use, and you shall not find me ungrateful. I will protect your kul—but remember, I must get what I want."

Her throat went dry. She wasn't special. It was Fardan who had found the spider lily. If fake Kavi and his patron had already sold off the flower, there was no way she could find another one. Then how would she save her kul? She crossed her arms and took a deep breath. "The spider lily is extremely rare, huzoor. I got lucky."

He gave a flat smile. "Please, no false modesty. It has been over twenty years since the last spider lily was found. Skill or luck, whatever it was, consider yourself hired by the wazir of Gujarat."

I can't think of a worse employer, she nearly said, but managed not to. All spider lilies belonged to the sultan, and by rights, the one Fardan found should have been handed over to the baniya for delivery to the palace. The wazir would have been well within the law to imprison her, even execute her. He must think she would be useful to him in the future. She would only be hurting herself if she tried to correct him. "Why have you never hired a flower hunter before, huzoor?" she asked.

He gave a lopsided grin. "None ever barged into my caravan, poorly disguised as a boy, piquing my curiosity."

Her face warmed. "That disguise fooled everyone else."

"Ah, but I am difficult to fool." He tilted his head, regarding her with an expression she could not parse. "Remember that the next time you wish to deceive me."

She knotted her hands in her lap. "I do not wish to deceive you," she said, her voice even. "I wish to save my kul. And I wish that when you gain the spider lily, you use it wisely."

"What did *you* do when you had the spider lily?" he countered. "Gave it to the first young man who wormed himself into your heart."

His words stung. That wasn't why she'd plucked the flower, and it wasn't why she'd given it away. "I thought it was for the sultan, to help him defeat the Portuguese."

He gave a dry laugh. "Before we can do that, we need to unite India under one flag. I will need the spider lily to ensure my accession to the throne and get the support and submission of all the other kingdoms of the subcontinent, including the Delhi Sultanate. *Then* I will rally our combined forces to fight the Portuguese."

Her heart sank. "Your priorities are clear, huzoor," she said, matching his tone. "But the foreigners have warships. Their naval power is far more advanced than ours. If you do not use the entire spider lily against them, I am afraid you will lose much more than Diu."

He leaned back and regarded her, his brow furrowed. "What do you know of their naval power?"

She shrugged, uncomfortable, not wanting to bring up fake Kavi again. "How many days to Surat?" she asked instead.

"Five days at our current pace." He tapped his foot, frowning. "And each day is precious. But I take heart from the fact that the spider lily has not yet made an appearance in public. Perhaps the turncoats are still weighing offers from rival buyers."

Or perhaps the spider lily has left the subcontinent. But there was no point agonizing over that. At least they were on their way.

She pushed aside the window curtain and peered out. They had already left the city behind. The carriage rolled through cultivated fields, passing bullock carts laden with sugarcane and wheat. After a while, the fields gave way to dense jungle. The movement of the carriage was soporific, the air warm with sunlight and heavy with the scent of vegetation. Her head fell forward, and her eyes closed.

She woke sometime later, her neck and shoulders stiff, her mouth dry. Dusk had fallen. On her lap, someone had draped an embroidered pashmina shawl that probably cost more than her entire kul earned in a year. Had the *wazir* done that? Lamplight flickered on the walls and softened the planes of his face, bent over a book. She carefully folded the shawl and placed it on a stool, out of harm's way.

He looked up, his lips twitching. "You snore in a most unladylike way."

"Everyone snores," she retorted, her cheeks heating. "You should hear my uncle."

He gave a slight shudder. "Happily, that will never happen. Shall we eat?"

She acquiesced, and they dined together, the wazir on lamb curry and rice, and Irinya on lentils and gram-flour fritters. She watched him covertly as she ate. When had the barriers between them eroded? He was the wazir of Gujarat, the sultan's great-nephew. She was a flower hunter and a nomad. They should never have met, let alone be dining together. She couldn't figure him out. He'd used the red hibiscus on her; maybe that was what had allowed him to lower his guard. As for herself, she felt like a mouse playing with a cat.

She slept that night in a smaller carriage that was emptied specifically for her, and the wazir's men slept out in the open. She was grateful for the consideration and hoped, for their sakes, there weren't any tigers about. At least they weren't carrying live animals this time.

She'd thought he'd designated her his secretary solely as a disguise, but he appeared serious about getting work out of her. The next morning, he dictated notes, disparaged her writing, and made her practice the Devanagari script until her wrist ached.

"Not like that," he said irritably, plucking the quill from her hand. "You aren't holding it correctly. You have a human hand, not a paw. Let the quill rest between your thumb and forefinger. Like this, see?"

She glared at him. "I am not actually your secretary, huzoor."

"You're all I have right now," he retorted. "Earn your keep."

She bent her head to the parchment, fuming. Little as she enjoyed it, the forced writing did improve her Devanagari. It also gave her another window into the wazir's life. He dictated a courteous letter to an aunt; a brief, stilted one to the sultan; a thinly veiled threat to one of the nobles; and a series of romantic, bittersweet couplets addressed to "Anonymous."

That last one caught her by surprise, and she couldn't help darting a gaze up at him. Did he have a secret lover back in the palace?

He raised his eyebrows. "Why have you stopped? Do you not approve of my verse?"

"I am no judge of poetry," she said. "But I do know that letters addressed to 'Anonymous' are unlikely to reach their destination."

He gave a lazy smile. "I have my ways and means. Now write. 'Heart of my heart, breath of my breath . . .'"

She went back to transcribing his words. His couplets were full of a yearning passion that seeped into his voice when he recited them. It felt as if he were saying them to *her,* making her hot and uncomfortable. He seemed to know this and derived great amusement from her discomfort. In fact, he discarded his other letters and devoted himself to increasingly explicit poetry until she longed to throw the ink on his face. She didn't let what she was feeling show, however. That would just encourage him.

What would Fardan think of what she was doing? Of the wazir and his passionate love poems? Her face flamed at the thought of Fardan's clear-eyed gaze, and the wazir gave a gleeful chuckle. *It's not because of you,* she wanted to shout. *You don't affect me in the least.*

But that wasn't quite true. It was odd; she had started by being afraid of him. She was still afraid, but his presence didn't make her jittery anymore. He had so many facets to his personality: some shone bright and clear, others were dark and clouded, but she didn't want to look at them too closely. If they could deal with each other fairly, she wouldn't have to.

Four days later, they arrived on the outskirts of Surat. Irinya poked her head out of the window, adrenaline coursing through her veins. She was so close to finding the spider lily again, she could almost smell it.

"Surat was developed by Malik Gopi fifteen years ago," the wazir lectured, pointing out the minarets and temple domes rising in the hazy distance. "He persuaded many other merchants to settle here as well. But it has been a port for longer than that. And it's rich; don't be fooled by its looks."

She understood what he meant as the caravan rolled into the city. In sharp contrast to Ahmedabad, the streets were narrow and crowded on both sides with mud-and-bamboo tenements. Taller, statelier buildings rose from among them like herons among toads. In the distance, water glittered in the noonday sun. Ships and boats of all types were moored at the docks, and men scurried to and fro, loading and unloading cargo. The air smelled of salt and dried fish.

"Is that the sea?" She craned her neck out of the window. She'd never seen the actual sea, even though the Rann was flooded by seawater in the rainy season every year.

"It's the Tapti River, my ignorant flower girl," said Imshan Khan, making her want to hit him. "It drains into the Arabian Sea, fifteen miles from here. In the monsoon, when large ships can enter the port without danger, the population of Surat doubles."

It was already too crowded. The wazir's men got out of their carriage and shouted at people to make way. But it still took them an hour to reach their destination: a large white house with triple domes, set in a walled garden near the waterfront.

"This area is called Gopipura in honor of its dear founder," said the wazir as the carriage rolled to a stop. "Keep your veil on."

"I know." She wriggled into the shapeless garment. The wazir dismounted, and she followed suit, nearly tripping on the steps in her excitement. Her stomach clenched with anticipation. This was the home of Malik Gopi. That meant fake Kavi might be here, in this very house. She would have to be careful not to betray herself in front of other people, no matter how much she wanted to shout at him: *What did you do with the flower? Why did you lie to me?*

The gate was guarded by six men armed with swords and maces. A messenger went running inside to inform the master of the arrival of unexpected guests. A short while later, the gates were opened, and the caravan allowed through.

The governor's servants ushered them down a garden path lined with camellias and poppies. A breeze sighed through a grove of orange trees on their right. A pond covered with white lilies glittered on their left. The lush, quiet greenery was a stark contrast to the squalor and bustle outside the gates.

"The governor of Surat does himself well," murmured Imshan Khan as they walked down the path toward the opulent house.

She glanced through her veil at the high walls topped by broken glass that glinted in the sun. "He certainly doesn't take his power and wealth for granted."

The house had a large covered porch that boasted a carved wooden swing and what seemed like hundreds of potted plants. At the bottom of the steps leading to the porch was a plump, smiling man dressed in a white dhoti and kurta. He joined his hands and bowed, the single lock of hair on the crown of his shaven head falling on his face—a comical effect that was surely unintended. "Welcome, huzoor, welcome! What a wonderful surprise." His voice had an inflection to it, as if the surprise was not as wonderful as his words indicated.

Irinya raised her gaze to the man standing behind their host, and her breath caught.

It was Kavi, as handsome and elegant as ever, regarding them with a polite smile on his face, as if he were not a snake in human skin whose empty promises had caused the death of her favorite elder, put her entire kul in danger, and cheated them out of a treasure worth kingdoms. If not for him, the silver spider lily would still be safely in the Rann, and so would she. Chinmay would still be alive, and the kul would not be under an impossible deadline to find ten more flowers by season's end. She choked back a sob as she followed the wazir to the porch, but every step she took, the dagger embedded itself deeper in her heart until she could scarcely breathe from the pain.

CHAPTER 12

They entered the house and were ushered into a large sitting room with doors that opened onto a plant-filled courtyard. The sitting room was filled with sumptuous paintings and expensive furniture, but Irinya barely noticed. She seethed beneath her veil, dying to tear it off and confront the man who had betrayed her and her kul.

"Please sit," said Malik Gopi, beaming at them.

She perched on the edge of a carved teak chair, nails digging into her palms, while the wazir and the governor exchanged barbed courtesies. A serving boy came around with bowls of iced lemon tea and damp towels. She glugged her tea down, lifting the veil away from her mouth, trying to calm herself.

But she couldn't. Kavi—*fake* Kavi—stood beside his master's chair, debonair in silk and brocade, that phony smile plastered on his lying face. *You ruined my life,* she wanted to scream. *You killed Chinmay.* If she'd had her blowpipe in her hands, she would have shot him.

"Huzoor, I have never known you to take a *lady* secretary before," said Malik Gopi, casting a dubious glance at her.

"She is a distant cousin," said Imshan Khan, sliding with ease onto a divan. He looked supremely at home, far more so than the home's actual owner. "She was widowed at fifteen, the unlucky creature. By giving her work, I hope to make her life meaningful."

"You are the soul of generosity, huzoor," murmured the governor without a trace of irony.

Irinya barely heard them. Her entire being was focused on the slender young man standing beside Malik Gopi, his eyes lowered, the picture of unassuming grace.

"And who is this personable young man?" asked the wazir, turning his interested gaze on fake Kavi.

"My assistant, Deven," said Malik Gopi. "Please feel free to speak in front of him. I would trust him with my life."

Irinya clenched her fists. *Deven.* At last, his real name.

Deven bowed to the wazir, placing his hand on his heart. "It is an honor, huzoor," he murmured, his tone warm.

That voice. It sent a shudder through her. With that same voice, he had coaxed her to wear his boots. With that same voice, he had persuaded her to pluck the spider lily and give it to him. With that same voice, he had promised to return with enough wealth to last her kul generations. She remembered how he'd laced the boots up for her, making her pulse race, and she burned with rage and humiliation.

"How wonderful to be able to trust someone like that," said Imshan Khan, his words dripping with sincerity. "Truly, a gift that cannot be bought. You are fortunate."

"Indeed." Malik Gopi gave her a puzzled look. "Your secretary seems to be having trouble with her footwear."

Irinya was unlacing her boots, one by one. She couldn't stop herself. They bit into her skin, poisoning her with shame and regret.

"Surely you can do that later," said the wazir in his most quelling tone of voice. "There must be pebbles in them," he explained to Malik Gopi.

Irinya tugged the boots off and stood, hefting one in each hand.

Deven's expression changed from confusion to alarm to the shock of recognition. She savored the moment, making it last. Then she threw the boots at him, one by one. The first hit his chest, the second his jaw. He didn't even hold his hands up to protect himself, just kept staring at her with the same slack-jawed expression. The governor leaped to his feet, outrage on his face.

"Farah, I demand an explanation," snapped the wazir, sitting up.

Oh, do you? "I would rather walk barefoot on broken glass than wear those boots again," she said, keeping her voice calm even as she quivered with anger.

"But was it necessary to throw them at that nice young man?" said the wazir. "You barely missed the governor of Surat! What will he think of us?" He turned to Malik Gopi. "I apologize. My secretary is prone to fits of unreason."

Malik Gopi recovered his voice. "Not the best quality in a secretary." He sat down again, eyeing her as one would a cobra. She bared her teeth at him from beneath her veil, wishing she had something else to throw at both him and his jackal of a lackey. Deven moved behind his patron's chair, as if for protection, still staring wide-eyed at her.

"On the contrary," said Imshan Khan, lounging back on the divan with a wolfish grin, "it makes for interesting conversation. For instance, it allows me to ask your assistant if he has ever seen those boots before. Do sit, Farah. And do not attempt to throw anything else, or I shall be most displeased."

Deven tore his gaze away from Irinya. "I have not, huzoor," he said, his voice filled with the warm conviction she knew so well. It had fooled her and her entire kul. Nausea rose in a sick green wave inside her as she remembered how earnestly he'd talked to them of setting up a cooperative.

"But they fit you, do they not? Go on, try them out. You may as well keep them. Farah would rather—what was it you said?—'walk barefoot on broken glass than wear those boots again.'" The wazir shook his head. "So dramatic. Would it be a good method of torture, do you think, Governor?"

Malik Gopi started, as if waking from a bad dream. "What, huzoor?"

"Walking barefoot on broken glass," said the wazir, leaning toward him with raised eyebrows. "Method of torture—yes or no?"

"I don't know." The governor dabbed his forehead with a scrap of silk. "I tend not to think of such things. That is your domain, huzoor. I am just an ordinary merchant."

"Dear Malik Gopi, humble as always," said the wazir with a smile like a knife. "What would Surat be without you? A provincial little back-water, rather than the bustling hub of trade and commerce it is today. No wonder my great-uncle is so fond of you."

Irinya forced her attention away from Deven and on the conversation, which had entered dangerous waters. She needed her wits about her, especially because she'd shown her hand by throwing those boots. Deven knew who she was, and the wazir knew who *he* was: the man who'd cheated her kul out of the silver spider lily. Which of them would survive the night? And where was the spider lily now? She clenched and unclenched her hands, wishing she could demand the truth from Deven right now. *Patience,* she told herself. She'd caught the swindler by surprise; now to see if he or his patron would make a mistake and reveal more than they intended.

The governor gave a self-deprecating wave of his hand. "You do me too much honor, huzoor. How is our beloved sultan's health?"

"Failing," said Imshan Khan. "There will be a new sultan soon."

"Or a sultana," said Malik Gopi with a guileless air that did not fool Irinya.

"My dear Governor," said Imshan Khan in a cold voice, "you know quite well the chaos that would ensue should a woman attempt to take the throne."

"Chaos caused by *who* exactly, huzoor?" asked Malik Gopi, a slight smile playing on his lips.

The gloves had come off. It was like watching two fencers battle it out, except Irinya was in the ring with them and was just as likely to get stabbed instead.

Imshan Khan bared his teeth. "Let us talk in the language of self-interest, which you can understand. Chaos would not be to your advantage. Do not think that if the sultanate disintegrates, Surat will be spared. Have not the Portuguese already burned this city once? Why should they stop at Diu?"

Irinya started. It was news to her that the Portuguese had already targeted Surat in the past. Of course, it was an important port of Gujarat. She was far from home and close to the war here—closer than she'd ever been before. Her stomach churned at the thought.

"Their envoys have assured me—" began Malik Gopi, but the wazir cut him off.

"I am aware of your cozy relationship with them. Most people would characterize such fraternity with the enemy as treason."

Malik Gopi purpled. "Your great-uncle does not think so. He knows the value of diplomacy."

Imshan Khan snorted. "He is *dying*. He scarcely touches the samosas that are left for him every night by his bedside. Soon he will stop eating altogether. Your staunchest and most powerful supporter in the palace will be gone to the hell he deserves. Then you will have me to deal with. And the likes of Malik Ayyaz, who hates your guts and would enjoy removing them from your body and strangling you with them."

Deven flinched at the wazir's words—the first honest reaction he'd shown—and bent to whisper in his patron's ear. Malik Gopi took a deep breath. "Come, huzoor, we are men of the world, above the petty rivalries of minor nobles. Tell me how I can help you. Surely you did not come all this way merely to threaten me."

Imshan Khan steepled his fingers. "Of course not. I came for a flower."

Beside the governor, Deven stiffened. He gave Irinya a tiny shake of his head, as if to say *No*.

Irinya's skin prickled. What did he mean? Don't talk about flowers?

No, he meant don't talk about *the* flower—the silver spider lily. But why? Irinya stared at him, wishing she knew what was going on in his devious brain.

"As a merchant," continued the wazir, "you know that the magic flower trade is highly regulated. All authentic flowers are sold via a network of baniyas to a list of preapproved apothecaries and flower markets. The rarest flowers belong to the sultan, and the penalty for stealing them is death, the manner of death depending on the type of flower."

Deven gasped, and Malik Gopi's mouth fell open. "I am aware of this, huzoor," he said in a voice full of reproach. "There is no illegal trade in flowers in *my* city. Smugglers are executed."

He hadn't faked that reaction, which meant he didn't know about the spider lily. Irinya clutched the edge of her chair, her mind working furiously. Had Deven sold it without the knowledge of his master? No wonder he wanted them to keep quiet about it.

Imshan Khan leaned back and gazed at Malik Gopi with hooded eyes. "Has no one in your employ recently visited the Rann to source magic flowers directly from the flower hunters?"

Malik Gopi froze, looking like a trapped rabbit. Irinya leaned toward the wazir and whispered, "Enough, huzoor." They needed to question Deven without alerting his master.

The wazir frowned at her but gave a grudging nod.

Opposite them, Deven bent to whisper in his patron's ear again, no doubt advising him the way Irinya was advising the wazir. "Huzoor," said Malik Gopi in a sincere voice, "you must be mistaken. Someone is trying to set me up. I have many enemies in court. Can we continue this discussion tomorrow? The hour grows late. You are my guest, and I would be remiss in my duties if I did not offer you rest and refreshment. We shall talk of serious floral matters tomorrow morning, yes? For now, please accept my humble hospitality."

"Very well," said the wazir. "I accept. Farah here is probably starving."

She shot him a glare from under her veil.

Malik Gopi gave a polite laugh and rose, clapping his hands. Servants entered to escort them to their rooms. Deven picked up the boots to examine them, as if the story of how they got there were written on their tongues.

"So that was your young man," murmured Imshan Khan as they walked down a latticed passage parallel to the central courtyard, his voice low so that the servants walking in front could not hear him. "Smooth as an eel and just as slippery."

"He's not *my* young man," she hissed.

He gave her an appraising glance. "Not anymore, I can see. Why did you stop me?"

She slowed down to put more distance between the servants and themselves, and the wazir followed suit. "I don't think Deven gave him the spider lily," she whispered. "We have to get Deven alone to question him."

The wazir gave a sharp nod. "I'll have someone follow him," he whispered back. "And you—be careful. Two of my guards will stand watch outside your room tonight. Make sure you keep the windows closed."

She swallowed. "Why? What do you think will happen?"

His mouth twisted. "Our host will try to kill us."

Her stomach clenched. "Are you serious?"

"Never underestimate the power of greed," he murmured, picking up his pace. "I would do anything for a spider lily. I bet the governor is willing to do even more." He added, in a louder voice, "Do hurry, Farah. Let us not keep the staff waiting."

They parted at the foot of a broad staircase, and a maid led Irinya up the stairs while another escorted the wazir down a different corridor. Fatigue flooded Irinya as she climbed—not the kind that came from the honest labor of hunting flowers or herding goats, but the kind that came from having to watch and weigh every word in a tense conversation with those who were planning how to kill you.

The power of greed. Didn't the spider lily exploit this very weakness in humans?

It was the humans who were at fault—people like Imshan Khan and Malik Gopi who had everything that anyone could possibly desire and yet wanted more, more, *more*. If they were forced to live as peasants for a while, their priorities would get straightened out quite fast.

The maid ushered Irinya to a small room on the second floor. It was well furnished with a large mahogany cupboard, windows that opened onto the courtyard, and a soft bed with an embroidered quilt that she knew she wouldn't get any sleep on. She would be too busy worrying about getting murdered.

A boy brought in her bags, and the maid asked if she would like a bath. After five days' travel, she jumped at the chance to wash. If she was going to die tonight, at least she'd die clean.

Stop being morbid, she told herself as the maid escorted her to the women's bathhouse. *You'll have guards outside your room.* But would that be enough? They were in the enemy's lair, and she'd betrayed herself by throwing those boots in Deven's face. At least it had given her a momentary satisfaction. *Snake.*

The bathhouse turned out to be a rock-lined pond in the orchard behind the house, surrounded by a high wall covered with ivy. It was late evening, starting to get cool, and Irinya had the pond to herself. It was a relief to wash off the grime and sweat of the last five days. She was rinsing her hair, luxuriating in the feel of water against her skin, when a voice spoke in her ear.

"*Irinya?*" said Fardan. "*Are you well?*"

At least this time she recovered faster. "Why do you always inter-rupt me when I'm bathing?" she snapped.

There was a heavy silence, and she cursed herself. She clambered out of the water and grabbed a towel. "I was joking. I'm not bathing. How is everyone?"

"*Still worried about you,*" said Fardan. "*Wishing you would return home. By the way, it's just me this time. Everyone wanted to talk to you, but Miraben put her foot down. Tell me where you are. We don't have much time left on the rose, and we need to make it count.*"

"I'm in Surat," she said. "I found Kavi. He works for Malik Gopi, the governor."

"*Surat?*" She pictured him frowning. "*He said he worked for Malik Ayyaz.*"

"He lied," she said, keeping her voice even. "He even lied about his name. His real name is Deven."

"*The despicable fraud,*" he ground out. "*Where's the spider lily?*"

She took a deep breath. "I don't know, but I'm going to find out."

"*Can you wait?*" he asked. "*A bunch of us could be there in a week.*"

"No, that'll be too late." It might already be too late. They didn't know where the flower was or who had it. How much to tell him? She didn't want them even more stressed than they already were, and she certainly didn't want them here. Malik Gopi might well be colluding with the Portuguese, and Surat was too close to the front lines of the war. "I'm not alone. I'm with the wazir of Gujarat."

"*The wazir?*" Amazement crept into Fardan's voice. "*What are you do-ing with* him?"

"He made me his secretary," she said. "It's a long story. Fardan, is everyone okay? Have the baniya's men been back?"

There was a pause during which she could picture him calculating how much to tell her, just the way she had been. "Please, Fardan," she said, trying not to let her voice break. "I need to know."

He sighed. "*They came by three days ago to remind us of the baniya's quota and their threat to kill more people. Miraben lied and groveled in front of them, and they left without hurting anyone this time. She hated to do it, and she's been bad-tempered ever since. I don't think it will work again. We have until season's end to get the ten flowers, but they're bound to get suspicious if we don't give them something soon.*"

"Keep aside a jasmine for them the next time they come around," she said. "Just to buy us time."

Fardan made a noncommittal sound, and her heart sank. If the kul had decided not to deal with the baniya, that was that. She would speak to the wazir about him as soon as she had the opportunity. "Look, I better go back to the house. Don't worry about me. We have bodyguards. Give Bholi my love."

"*Wait, Irinya.*" His voice took on urgency. "*Don't do anything dangerous. Stay safe. I'll speak again soon.*"

"Don't worry," she repeated, hollowness growing inside her chest at the distance between them, the impossibility of what she asked. Of course he would worry. They all would. The fate of the kul rested in her hands.

She donned a fresh salwar kameez and struggled into the veil. Luckily, Tarana had packed a pair of embroidered leather slippers for her, so she didn't have to go barefoot. She stepped out and walked down the path to the house, meeting the maid halfway. The girl escorted her to a lamplit room off the vast kitchen, where she was served a delicious meal. Apparently, the governor's household was not sure of her status. Was she an employee, a servant, or an exalted guest? Ultimately, the wazir's claim that she was a distant relative was enough for them to err on the side of caution, and she was served before the women of the family ate. The meal consisted of sweet and spicy dal, fluffy rice, fresh yogurt, stuffed taro leaves, and a local specialty of mixed vegetables and chickpea fritters called undhiyu. She ate her fill, relishing every bite.

Would the wazir's twelve guards be enough to protect them from Malik Gopi's homicidal schemes? Had the wazir been exaggerating the level of danger? It was difficult to believe, while eating his scrumptious food, that their host was capable of cold-blooded murder.

Irinya didn't meet Imshan Khan again that night, but two of his guards were waiting outside her room when she went upstairs after dinner, just as he had promised. She shut and bolted the door and leaned out of the window, enjoying the cool jasmine-scented night air. In the courtyard below, a group had gathered around a small fire to sing and play the dholak and the sarangi. Was Deven there, too? More than anything, she longed to confront him herself. She couldn't spot him anywhere in the courtyard; perhaps the wazir's guard was trailing him at this very moment. The wazir and the governor were sitting side by side, clapping and encouraging the performers. Behind them stood five of the wazir's guards, armed and alert.

She withdrew and slid the shutters down, bolting them. It was a pity to deprive herself of fresh air, but now there was no way to enter her room, unless someone overpowered the guards and broke down the door. That seemed too obvious and violent a move for a man like Malik Gopi. Poison in the food or drink—that would be more his style. She ought to have thought of that before eating so much. But she wasn't dead yet, or even a little sick, so poison could be ruled out.

What about Deven; did he want her dead, too? She thought of that tiny shake of his head when the talk turned to flowers, and her stomach squeezed. Of course he wanted her dead. If he had betrayed not just her but also his own patron, then he needed to silence her. She was the only one who could tell Malik Gopi he'd come into possession of a silver spider lily.

She turned up the oil lamp and threw the cover off the bed to inspect it. No knives, snakes, or poisoned pins to prick her flesh. But she wasn't about to risk sleeping on it. She spread her veil on the cool marble floor and lay down. The smell of the oil lamp pervaded the room, but she didn't dare tamp it down. The minutes ticked past. The muffled sounds of music and singing from the courtyard died away. Her eyes watered from staring at the painted ceiling. She couldn't sleep, even though she was bone tired. The situation was too strange, too far removed from her usual reality. She wished she were back in Banni with the rest of her kul. She wished she were asleep in her own tent with Bholi Masi and Gopal Masa snoring next to her.

Briefly, she toyed with the idea of leaving her room, making an excuse to the guards that she needed the outhouse, and going in search of Deven by herself.

Of course, she might find him. And he would have the perfect opportunity to kill her. She imagined his graceful hands strangling her neck and she grimaced. If only she had her blowpipe, she would have taken the risk.

She closed her eyes, hoping for rest but saw flowers instead. One by one, they drifted across her closed eyelids: jasmine, hibiscus, sunflower, pansy, bluestar, spider lily. And, so black she could scarcely see it in the dark behind her eyes, the dense, richly furled chrysanthemum. All the stories about this strange flower were half myth, half wish fulfillment. The wazir's account was the only one she'd heard that was remotely historical. As for the queen of flowers, the pink lotus, even the stories shied away from it.

Something creaked. Her eyes flew open. Had she fallen asleep? Dreamed that sound? The lamp burned low, the oil almost gone. Her back and shoulders ached. She should have lain on the bed after all.

Another creak, and she sat up, her heart thumping. She hadn't imagined that. The sound had come from behind her. She twisted her head back, trying not to breathe too loudly.

The wardrobe door was opening, inch by inch.

She stared at it, petrified. Her limbs unfroze, and she shot to her feet. Should she throw open the door and scream for the guards? If they'd already been neutralized, she would be trapped on both sides.

What did she have for a weapon? She scoured the room, trying not to shake, and spied an earthen pot of water that had been placed for her on a table. She grabbed it and crept forward.

The wardrobe door opened, and a slim, elegant figure stepped out. *Deven*. Her hands trembled, and water sloshed inside the pot.

Deven put a finger to his lips. With the air of a conjurer producing a mango from a seedling, he opened a carved wooden box and held it up. Inside, on blue velvet, nestled the silver spider lily.

CHAPTER 13

The pot shook in Irinya's hands. Emotions roiled within her: shock, anger, suspicion, and, overwhelming them all, relief—*the spider lily was safe*. And so was the sultanate—for now, at least. The flower had evaded Portuguese hands.

Deven gave her a tentative smile. "I'm sorry," he whispered. "Did I startle you? The wardrobe has a secret door to the next room."

Do you think I care about the wardrobe? she wanted to scream.

It hit her then, how much he'd hurt her. Her chest squeezed, and she blinked back tears. "You lied," she said, speaking with difficulty. "Lied about everything."

"Not *everything*," he said humbly. "I didn't lie about my parents. And I kept the spider lily safe. I didn't show it to anyone." He closed the box and offered it to her.

She put down the pot—as a weapon it left a lot to be desired—and reached for the box, unable to believe the precious flower was back in her hands. "*Why?*" she asked. A thousand questions burned behind that one word, but if she spoke them aloud, she might break down. *Why did you tell our kul you'd buy our debt? Why did you take the spider lily? And why are you returning it to me now?*

He lowered his gaze. "My life belongs to Malik Gopi. I am his to command. I was only able to keep the spider lily from him because he didn't dream I would find such a treasure, didn't think to ask for it. He was happy with the bluestar I brought him."

Realization sank into her with a sick twist of the gut. "He used the hibiscus on you."

"Many times over the years," he said in a monotone, staring at his empty hands. "Ever since I was a child. But he hasn't needed to in a while. I do everything he wants. And I no longer know whether it is the flower at work or whether it is myself."

She shivered. One dose of the hibiscus tore one's willpower to shreds. It took weeks to recover. If she hadn't been armed with a blue-star petal, she would be the wazir's creature with no volition of her own. Two doses could take months or years to wear off. Three doses were rumored to be permanent. What would repeated doses do? "You should leave," she managed.

He looked back at her, his mouth twisted in a bitter smile. "Where would I go? He'd find me. No, Irinya, *you* go. Take the flower and return it to the Rann."

She took a deep, shaky breath. "Why make me pluck it in the first place? I thought you meant to give it to the sultan to defend India from the Portuguese."

"So did I. I even went to Ahmedabad." He gave a hopeless shrug. "But I couldn't make myself do it. My feet refused to enter the palace. I broke out in a sweat, and the whole world came crashing down around me. It would have been a betrayal of the man who raised me."

"What about *his* betrayals?" she demanded. "Hasn't he been colluding with the Portuguese? By working for him, aren't you a traitor, too?"

"Yes, yes, and yes." He placed his hands on hers and pressed them around the box. "That's why I hid this flower. I never should have taken it in the first place. I overestimated my ability to act independently."

"You even lied about your *name*." Her stomach heaved, remembering how she'd felt when she met the real Kavi Kampilya.

"I am sorry," he repeated, his voice close to breaking. "I was following my patron's orders. He thought it would be *amusing,* trying to trap his rival while circumventing the regulated market himself."

"Our kul's debt . . ." She stopped, unable to go on. Chinmay's murder flashed before her eyes, and her heart squeezed.

He gave her a wistful look. "I meant those things when I said them, even though part of me knew it was impossible. I wanted to free you and your kul from that greedy moneylender. I wanted you all to form a cooperative and set your own terms."

She stepped back from him, aching inside. "The price of your wanting, your pretense, must be borne by my kul. The baniya's men killed Elder Chinmay. We'll never hear his stories again." Deven's face crumpled. "The baniya is demanding ten more flowers as compensation before the season's end," she continued, swallowing the lump in her throat. "And for every flower we fail to find, he's threatened to kill another one of us."

Deven wiped his eyes with a sleeve. "I deserve to die," he choked out.

If not for Chinmay, she could have found it in her heart to pity him. "Your death will help nothing," she bit out. "The silver spider lily has been taken from the Rann, and it cannot be returned. If we had left it alone, at least it would be safe from enemy hands. You haven't just endangered my kul, you've endangered all of India."

He leaned forward, clasping his hands. "Take the flower and run away from here. I can arrange a carriage for you."

Easy for him to say. The wazir would hunt her to the ends of the earth if she ran off with the spider lily. And then what would happen to her kul?

A black thought struck her. "The day you arrived, we found a dead body in the Rann. A foreigner, perhaps Portuguese. Know him?"

He frowned. "Not sure, but he could have been a scout in the employ of the Portuguese envoy assigned to Surat."

Her stomach dropped. "How did they find out about the flowers?"

He lowered his gaze, unable to meet hers. "Malik Gopi told the envoy about them in exchange for trade favors. I was tasked to accompany the scout to the Rann, but we got separated in Bhuj. I warned him not to venture into the Rann by himself, but I guess he didn't listen, for he never returned."

She stared at him, coldness creeping up her limbs. The worst she'd imagined had turned out to be true. "They'll send more men," she whispered, her throat raw, her hands itching to shake him till his teeth rattled. Perhaps they already had. Hopefully, the palace in Bhuj had received the wazir's message and dispatched soldiers to guard the borders of the Rann. But the border was more than a hundred miles long, and forces were already stretched thin because of the war. The invaders were both better armed and more numerous in number than the Kutchi soldiers.

"They won't find anything," Deven said with breezy, misplaced confidence. "The flowers are so rare. It takes a skilled flower hunter to find one."

They could force us to find flowers for them, she wanted to scream. But what good would that have done? No, she had to make sure those men never returned to the Rann. And the only way to do that was by winning the war against the Portuguese.

"You should leave now while it's dark," Deven continued. "A carriage will take you to Ahmedabad. From there, you must make your way back to Kutch."

"I'm here with the wazir," she said, finding her voice. "He'd think it suspicious if I vanished in the middle of the night. He'd be sure to track me down. Besides, I plucked this flower to save the sultanate." *And my kul,* she added silently to herself.

Deven knitted his brows. "Surely you do not trust the wazir? He will use the spider lily to gain the throne and subjugate the rest of India. He has only his own self-interest at heart. In that, he is no better than Malik Gopi."

"The wazir isn't colluding with the Portuguese," she reminded him dryly. *Or hiding the spider lily despite the atrocities committed by the foreign invaders.* Deven had held on to the one weapon that could drive the Portuguese from India, while knowing full well how many people they'd already killed.

"But he would use the spider lily to cement his own power," argued Deven.

Yes, I know. She clenched her jaw. The only reason she'd gone to the wazir instead of the sultana for help in finding the spider lily had been because the sultana was confined to her rooms, and Irinya didn't know how to approach her. But now that Irinya had the flower, she could deliver it to the sultana, asking for her kul to be freed from the baniya in return. The sultana would surely use the spider lily to defeat the Portuguese. The only problem was hiding it from the wazir.

Deven cast an anxious glance at the wardrobe. "You need to hurry." He turned back to her. "What about giving the flower to Malik Ayyaz?

He hates the Portuguese and is revered across the sultanate. He's more trustworthy than the wazir."

She gave him a scornful glance. "Aren't you forgetting the sultana? The sultan's chosen heir?"

His jaw dropped. "You'll give it to *her?*"

Somebody clapped. "An excellent plan, with one minor problem."

Deven whirled around. Irinya stumbled back, heart thudding.

Malik Gopi stepped out of the wardrobe, pristine in his white clothes, a thin-lipped smile on his face. Two beefy guards armed with swords followed him into the room, crowding it. Coldness flooded Irinya's stomach. How much had Malik Gopi overheard? She backed away another step and bumped into the bed. She glared at the governor, trying to hide her fear. If only she had her blowpipe in her hands. Curse Imshan Khan for confiscating it! He'd said he would have Deven followed; where was he when they needed him?

"Huzoor," said Deven, hanging his head. "I'm sorry."

"No, *I'm* sorry," hissed Malik Gopi, his smile vanishing. "I'm sorry I trusted you, treated you like a *son,* you backstabbing—"

"Are you in the habit of using the hibiscus to control your children?" inquired Irinya, even as her knees shook. "That's not very fatherly of you."

"Do not speak unless spoken to," said Malik Gopi coldly. "You are less than a servant in my eyes. Give me the spider lily if you wish to keep your worthless little life."

"Huzoor, please!" Deven cast an agonized glance at her.

Irinya put the box behind her back, her mind racing. Of all possible situations, this was the worst she could have imagined. She needed to stall for time. "Traitor," she spat. "Aren't you afraid of what the wazir is going to do to you?"

Malik Gopi laughed—a flat, humorless sound. "The wazir is my prisoner. By the time I release him, this flower will have changed the map of Gujarat—no, the map of all India!—and I will be the most powerful man in the sultanate. The Portuguese will reward me richly."

Her heart plummeted to her feet. If the wazir had been captured, no help was on its way. And just as she suspected, this man wanted to sell the spider lily to the foreign invaders. But she wouldn't trust his words. There was still a chance they could get out of this with the flower intact. If the worse came to worst, she'd jump out the window. If she was lucky, she might not break any bones. "You will be nothing but a lackey," she told the governor, summoning contempt into her voice. "Once the flower is in their hands, you think the Portuguese will care what happens to you?"

His face swelled. "Get the box from her," he ordered one of his guards. "Kill her if she resists." The guard advanced, his sword out, his face menacing.

Deven stepped before her, shielding her with his body. "Please, huzoor, wait. I'll persuade her to give it to you."

She'd die before she gave up the flower to his master, and he knew it. She stared at his back, her stomach roiling. *What are you thinking, Deven? What are you planning?*

Malik Gopi gave an imperious wave of his hand. "Get out of the way, boy, unless you wish to share her fate."

"Just a few minutes," Deven begged. "Let me talk to her." He turned to face her, gripping her shoulders, his eyes pleading. "I'm sorry about everything, Irinya. I'm not the man you thought I was. But I swear, I didn't mean for any of this to happen. I thought I could change things for the better." He took a deep breath. "It's up to you now."

"Hurry up," snapped Malik Gopi.

"What do you mean?" she asked, confused.

"I'm trying to buy us time," he whispered. "Give it up," he continued in a louder voice. "Return home to the Rann where you belong."

Something heavy thudded against the door. "Irinya?" came a commanding voice. "Open up!"

Imshan. He'd managed to escape. Malik Gopi's men froze at the sound of his voice, and in that instant, Irinya flung herself on the door and slid back the bolt. One of the guards sprang at her with a snarl, but Deven threw a stool at him, making him stumble and fall.

"Turncoat!" screamed Malik Gopi, shaking his fist. "This is how you repay me?"

The door slammed open, pushing Irinya aside. A sword entered, gleaming in the lamplight, followed by the man holding it: Imshan Khan, the wazir of Gujarat, his eyes glittering with fury. "You dare try to hold *me* captive?" he rasped.

Malik Gopi made a cutting gesture with his hand, and the guards attacked. Irinya crouched behind the door, her heart in her mouth as the wazir fought back, parrying their blows. Deven pulled Malik Gopi against the wall, out of harm's way. Even now, he cared about the safety of his patron. Not that Malik Gopi was the slightest bit grateful. He pushed Deven away and shouted, "Get the spider lily!"

The wazir kicked over a table, sending it flying across the room. It struck Malik Gopi in the stomach. He bent over, groaning. Deven grasped his shoulders and helped him up. "We should leave, huzoor," he urged.

"Not without the flower," wheezed Malik Gopi, casting a hate-filled glance at Irinya. She glared back at him, torn. Should she try to run away while they were all fighting? She wouldn't get very far before the victor of the fight tracked her down.

The wazir knocked the sword out of the hands of one of the guards and stabbed him in the chest, splattering blood everywhere. The guard's face crumpled in shock, and Irinya flinched away from the sight. Imshan Khan wrenched his blade out, kicking the wounded guard back with one foot, then whirled around to block the thrust of the other guard's sword.

As the wazir fought the second guard, Malik Gopi slunk around the edges of the room and sidled up to the door. Irinya drew in a sharp breath. So what if she didn't have her blowpipe? She had her teeth and her desperation, as sharp as the wazir's blade. She placed the box with the precious flower on the floor behind her and dropped into a defensive stance, her fists clenched.

She waited until he was almost upon her, then launched herself on him, kneeing him in the groin and tackling him to the ground. He hissed and clutched her neck in both hands, squeezing. She twisted away, managing to free herself, and bit his hand as hard as she could, drawing blood. He squealed and kicked, dislodging her.

"Enough," said the wazir in a cold, authoritative voice. "Get up."

Irinya scrambled to her feet, retreating to her post between the door and the wall, her throat on fire. Malik Gopi rose as well, his face unrecognizable in its snarl. Imshan Khan stood against one wall, his sword aimed at the governor. His face was bruised, and one of his sleeves was in bloody ribbons, but he had no other injures Irinya could see. *Good.* He needed to defeat Malik Gopi and whatever remained of the turncoat's forces.

Both guards lay inert on the floor, blood seeping from their chests and throats into crimson pools. Irinya averted her gaze from them and looked at Deven instead. He came over and stood next to Malik Gopi, his face taut. Malik Gopi glanced through the open door to the corridor outside, his forehead creasing.

Imshan Khan thrust his sword at him, making him stumble back. "Are you wondering where your minions are?" he growled. "My guards have killed or captured most. The rest ran away. Your household is under arrest. You have a poor opinion of my intelligence. I knew what you were plotting before I entered the room where you thought to trap me."

"How . . . how did you escape?" Malik Gopi stammered.

"I may have brought only twelve men, but each one of them is a match for three of yours. Did you think your poorly trained guards could overpower mine?" He gave a bleak smile. "True, three of them lost their lives trying to free me. You will pay for that."

Malik Gopi swallowed. "Huzoor. This is all a misunderstanding."

"Feel free to explain it to a court of law when we return to Ahmedabad," said Imshan Khan, his eyes narrowing. "Personally, I have little doubt of the outcome. Courtiers have begun to speak up against you. The sultan is dying. You don't have the support you once did. After this latest proof of your treasonous tendencies, you can look forward to being blown from a gun."

Malik Gopi ran for the door. The wazir shouted and thrust his sword toward the governor's back. To Irinya's horror, Deven threw himself in front of his patron, just in time to catch the sword point in his chest. "Deven!" she screamed. He gasped and crumpled to the floor.

The wazir swore. "You fool." He withdrew his sword and cut his eyes to Irinya. "The spider lily. *Now.*"

Irinya crouched beside Deven's body, her heart plummeting at the sight of the gaping wound in his chest, the savage rip in the flesh revealing red muscle and white bone. "We need to save his life, stop the flow of blood," she choked.

"You can help him once you deliver the flower to me," said the wazir, his eyes snapping cold fire. "Hurry up. He doesn't have much time left, and I have a traitor to catch."

Coldhearted brute. Irinya set her jaw. "Do you remember your promises, huzoor?"

"I promised nothing," he said coldly. "The rarest flowers belong to the sultan. Have you forgotten?"

"You are not the sultan. Have *you* forgotten?" she shot back.

He stared at her. "Have you taken leave of your senses? Remember why we are here."

"*You're* here for yourself. *I'm* here to save my kul. But my kul won't be safe for long if the Portuguese overrun the subcontinent," she said. "They're already sending people into the Rann. You must use the spider lily to defeat them, huzoor. Promise me, or I won't give it to you." In truth, she had no idea how to keep the spider lily from him. He held his sword with terrifying competence, he was about twice her size, and Deven . . . Deven was dying before her eyes.

The wazir's face darkened. "You deceived me from the start, didn't you? I knew it the moment you told me the story about the spider lily. You had a bluestar, or you would have spilled the truth of why you were in Ahmedabad."

Why was this relevant *now*? "You should not have tried to compel me with the hibiscus," she snapped. "If that is the only way you can trust someone, you do not deserve true loyalty. Tell me, did you ever mean to help my kul?"

He gave a brittle smile. "*You* tell me, Irinya, if I cannot compel you with the hibiscus, what else is left?"

My kul. Her gut twisted. She'd been right to suspect his intentions. He was the one who'd deceived her all along. Had any of the moments between them been real? The silly poetry, the shawl laid on her lap, the meals they'd shared. Anger burned like a blue flame inside her. "I'll never tell you where my people are," she ground out.

He raised his eyebrows. "You don't have to. Give me the baniya's name, and I'll have a message sent to him. No one in your kul will be killed—*if* you remain loyal to me. Understood?"

She understood all right. He would help her kul, but the cost was both the silver spider lily and her own freedom. She dug her nails into her palms, trying desperately to think of a way out.

"The flower, please," he said with iron calm. "Do you not wish to save the life of the man who betrayed you?"

Deven coughed blood, and Irinya's eyes blurred. She reached behind, grabbed the box, and threw it at the wazir. "Take it. You don't care for anything else."

Imshan Khan caught the box and opened it, his eyes avid. A silver glow emanated from the box and fell on his face, making it seem, for a moment, inhuman. He rocked back on his heels, smiling. "At last," he murmured, closing the box and tucking it into his breast pocket. "Bind his chest. I will send for a physician once I've caught Malik Gopi."

He leaped over Deven's body and dashed outside, leaving Irinya alone with the dying man.

She tore her dupatta into strips and began to bind Deven's chest, willing her hands not to shake. The blood soaked through the thin cloth, and he moaned. She laid her palm on his clammy forehead, smoothing his hair back. "Hang in there," she said, making her voice calm. "You'll make it."

"I won't," he whispered, his eyes full of pain.

"Don't say that. Don't give up," she said fiercely, wrapping another strip around his chest.

He flinched and shivered. "It's time . . . I met Ma."

Irinya gulped back a sob. "I can't believe you risked your life for *his*. He's not worth it."

"I could not . . . help it." He trembled. "Please . . ."

"What? What should I do?" she asked, eager to help.

"Take . . . locket."

Her gaze went to the fine blue enamel locket that hung on a chain around his neck. Did it hold a keepsake from his mother? A picture? Or some secret medicine? Carefully, she undid the clasp of the chain and slid the locket out. It was small and beautiful, with tiny gold flowers patterned on the enamel surface. She held it up between her thumb and forefinger so he could see it. "What do you want me to do with it?"

"Open it." Blood trickled out of his mouth. She dabbed it with the edge of her ripped dupatta, feeling useless. "Open," he insisted, his voice breaking.

"Yes, all right, I'm opening it." She felt around for a catch and found it on the top right of the locket. She inserted her fingernail into the catch and pried it apart.

Inside was a thin, translucent black petal. She stared at it, trying to process what she was seeing. *Black chrysanthemum.* Goose bumps prickled her skin.

"Legacy," he whispered. "Now . . . yours."

"What do you want me to do with it?" Keeping her voice calm and reasonable, as if she didn't hold the impossible in her hands. As if the man dying before her eyes were a patient to be soothed, not someone she had known and trusted and been betrayed by.

He closed his eyes. "Use it."

"To do what?"

But he did not speak again. She caressed his forehead, waiting, hope refusing to die until his breath hitched and stopped. Then, at last, she allowed her tears to fall.

"Goodbye, Deven." She rose, cold and shaky. Her hands were red with his blood. She wiped them on her kameez, feeling sick.

Just a body, she told herself. This wasn't the man she'd taken to the Rann, the man who'd laced his boots on her feet, the man she'd broken a promise for. That man was gone, released from his earthly bondage. This was just the part he'd left behind, the part he longer needed.

Irinya, came a thin, papery voice. *Where do you want to go?*

The hair on the back of her neck rose, and her gaze darted back to the ancient petal. She didn't want to use it. All her instincts as a flower hunter rebelled against it.

But it had spoken to her. And flowers never spoke without a reason.

Swords clashed and a shout came from outside, snapping her back to the present. She shut and bolted the door, then hurried to the window, opened it, and peered down. The courtyard was awash in blood, littered with bodies. Men fought with swords, axes, and clubs. The wazir dueled with his back to a wall, holding off two swordsmen with ease. Malik Gopi lay in an unmoving heap, ropes around his feet and hands, surrounded by the wazir's men.

She turned away from the window, shivering. She had moments to decide what to do. The wazir could return anytime. She gazed at the black petal. She could snap the locket closed, wear it around her neck, and try to keep Deven's legacy safe.

But she wouldn't be able to protect it from the wazir. And the thought of this petal falling into the hands of the man whose sword had pierced Deven's chest was abhorrent to her. There was only one sure way to prevent that.

Use it.

There was no alcohol, no time to make a tincture or even a tea. All she had was plain water. She crossed the room to where she'd left the earthen pot, stepping around the bodies and the pools of blood, and poured some out into a cup. She dropped the dried petal into the cup, trying not to think about the generations who had kept it safe, how it had been handed down from parent to child until, at last, it ended up in her unworthy hands.

The petal dissolved with a whiff of smoke. A musky, earthy odor flooded her nostrils, so strong she nearly gagged. The water darkened to an unappetizing gray. Was she really going to drink that?

A crash came from the corridor, and she didn't hesitate any longer. She put the cup to her lips, took a sip, and almost spat it out.

It was the most awful thing she'd ever tasted. *Drink,* she told herself fiercely. But with every swallow, it got progressively worse, like something sick, dead, and rotting. A buzzing sensation enveloped her, and she wanted to throw up. With enormous effort, she managed not to. The words of an old poem bubbled up from the depths, as if thrown up by the poisonous taste of the black chrysanthemum.

> *Sweet white jasmine will betray you in the end*
> *Bloodred hibiscus, you'll never trust again*
> *Blazing sunflower will misplace something else*
> *Silver spider lily, to lose to yourself.*

> *Priceless pansy to break the stoutest heart*
> *Gracious green rose to keep you apart*
> *Starry bluestar will fail to keep you safe*
> *Blackhearted chrys will rob you of your days.*

Her vision blurred. Was she crying because of Deven, the black chrysanthemum, or the poem her mother had taught her, which had chosen to make its appearance *now*? Now, when she had no time to examine the words or consider the cost of what she was about to do.

She wiped her eyes and glared at the cup. There was a single sip left. She couldn't drink any more or she'd throw up. Neither could she waste it. As a compromise, she poured it into the locket and snapped it closed. Then she retrieved the chain from Deven's neck, trying not to look at him, and slid the locket back onto it. She didn't want to wear it, but it was the safest way to keep it. She clasped it around her neck and hid the locket beneath her kameez.

Where do you want to go?

Imshan Khan had told her the story of a trader who used the black chrysanthemum to travel to the Maluku Islands. That meant it was possible to *will* yourself to your destination.

She took a deep breath and closed her eyes. She *wanted* to go home. But she *needed* to go to the royal palace of Bhadra Fort and tell the sultan and his heir what had happened. She could sell this information in return for protection for her kul. She would frame her request in such a way that she didn't have to give any details of her kul to anyone. It was worth trying; she had nothing to lose.

Blackhearted chrys to open strange doors.

She opened her eyes and stared at the wardrobe. The wardrobe stared back at her. It had a secret door at the back that led to the next room.

But a secret door could lead anywhere. You just had to believe in it. She closed her eyes and smelled salt and sea, sand and sun—all things that reminded her of the Rann.

No. That's not where I should go. Her thoughts skittered like nervous kittens, even as the petal hummed within her. *Ahmedabad. The palace. The sultan. The spider lily. The invaders.*

The door thudded, and her heart jumped. *Run,* came the thin, papery voice, and Irinya ran to the wardrobe and burst through to the other side.

CHAPTER 14

Bright sunlight stabbed her eyes. A sharp, salty wind tugged her clothes and tossed her hair. Cold spray lashed her face. A dull, continuous roar sounded in the background, punctuated by human voices and the flapping of canvas. The ground beneath her feet rose and plummeted, taking her stomach with it. She clutched a wet railing and bit back a scream.

She was on a *ship.* She'd never been on one before—not even a boat or a raft. She twisted her head back. No trace remained of the wardrobe or her room. The door behind her led to a small, cluttered cabin filled with charts, brass tubes, globes, and hourglasses. Below her, steep wooden steps led down to the main deck. Fair-skinned, rough-looking men in long tunics and tight pants were scrubbing the deck boards, hauling ropes, and working with the rigging. Masts towered above her, fitted with huge triangular and square sails that flapped against the sunlit sky. A white flag with a golden crown and red shield fluttered in the wind.

The Portuguese coat of arms. Her stomach dropped. She was on a Portuguese ship. *This is not where I wanted to go,* she shouted silently at the black chrysanthemum.

The ship rose and fell. All around were the endlessly crashing waves of the ocean. She clung to the railing, the only solid thing in a world that had turned inside out, upside down. It had been the middle of the night back in Surat. She was displaced, not just in space but in time. Why had the flower brought her here, to the worst possible place in the world?

One of the sailors pointed at her, shouting in a strange tongue. She shrank back against the railing, her heart thudding. All the sailors stopped work to stare at her, their sunburned faces tight with suspicion. An imperious-looking man with a blue cape, red cap, and gray beard barked out a command, and a sailor rushed across the deck and bounded up the steps to her.

Irinya's gut clenched. She turned and fled through the cabin door, her only thought to get as far away from these men as possible.

The cabin *vanished*. In its place, a shadowy corridor stretched before her. She ran down the corridor, risking a quick glance back. Would they follow her?

But behind her was only darkness. Fear clogged her throat.

Ahead of her, *another* sunlit door beckoned.

Not Surat nor anywhere in Gujarat nor, for that matter, the entire subcontinent. Not if it was daylight there. But it had to be safer than what she was leaving behind.

She stepped through the door and into the sunshine, more cautious this time, and found herself on a noisy, stone-paved street crowded with carts and people.

A sluggish breeze blew, bringing with it the smell of the sea and the cries of gulls. In the distance was a green hill topped by a half-ruined palace. A fortress of whitewashed brick and stone sprawled at its base, the likes of which she'd never seen before. A river wound around the fort and emptied into the sea, far to her right. A massive stone gatehouse reared before her, guarded by fair-skinned soldiers. On top of the gatehouse fluttered the dreaded Portuguese flag.

Her heart sank. What did it mean that two separate doors had led her to the invaders? That they controlled both the seas and the land, to the west and to the east?

She glanced behind, but the door had vanished, and there was nothing but a brick wall. She regarded the boats bobbing in the river, a cold pit opening in her stomach.

She'd drunk nearly an entire petal's worth of the black chrysanthemum. How many doors would that open for her? Her insides still buzzed, as if the petal were vibrating inside her. She fingered the locket around her neck. In the worst case, she still had a sip of that horrible liquid left. *The palace at Bhadra Fort,* she told herself fiercely. That was where she needed to go.

She turned left and walked down the street, following the crowd to the river market. Despite the heat and humidity, the sun was not yet high in the sky, which meant it was early morning. Vendors had set up stalls of porcelain, silk, and spices on a deck of wooden planks stretching over the river. Merchants of every hue and garb milled about, fingering fabrics and haggling over prices in a multitude of tongues.

To Irinya's relief, she caught a few words of Gujari from the direction of a stall stacked with bales of vibrant cotton fabric. It was manned by a merchant dressed in the typical white dhoti and kurta favored by wealthy Gujarati traders. He was chatting with a couple of fellow merchants who were similarly attired, and normally, she would never have approached them. But in this sea of strangeness, his words struck the first familiar note. She went up to him and bowed, pressing her palms together, and asked, in broken Gujari, which town this was.

"What kind of question is that?" he said, frowning. "How can you not know this is Malacca?"

Her head reeled. She was thousands of miles from Gujarat. Malacca was the strategically located port that controlled the Strait of Malacca, on the shortest trade route between India and China. Deven had told her it had fallen to the Portuguese.

The merchant peered at her more closely and gasped. "Is that *blood*? What happened? Who are you?"

She glanced down at her clothes and cringed. Her kameez was streaked red. *Deven's blood.* She retreated into the crowd before the merchant could ask her any more questions, cursing herself for not grabbing her veil before running through the wardrobe. She needed to find a place to make a door to Ahmedabad, and she needed to do it fast.

"Young woman, listen!"

She twisted back in alarm. The merchant had followed her, his companions close behind him. He gave her a peremptory wave. "Wait."

Did they think she'd committed a crime? She had no intention of waiting to find out. She ran, dodging carts and people and nearly tripping on a beggar sitting by the roadside. Behind her, she heard running footsteps and shouts. Adrenaline coursed through her veins. She couldn't get caught. She didn't know how long the effects of the black chrysanthemum would last, and she had to keep moving until she reached her goal.

A tent loomed before her; without pausing to think, she pushed open the flap and dived in. A corridor of darkness stretched before her, ending in a door shaped of light. She ran toward it, filled with relief.

She emerged on a sunlit terrace on a green hill, overlooking a sapphire sea. She rocked back on her heels, her throat constricting. *Still not Ahmedabad.*

Sailing ships dotted the harbor, and men worked on the distant docks. White minarets and domed palaces sparkled at the base of the hill—a beautiful, prosperous city, if ever there was one. She leaned over the railing, marveling at the view, and caught sight of a Portuguese flag flying over a large white building. A whiff of garbage and rotting corpses assaulted her nostrils, and she shuddered and backed away from the railing. *Home. I want to go home.*

But she couldn't. Had her conflicting desire to go home and her stated goal of going to the palace messed up her destinations? Or had the petal deliberately done this to show her the extent of Portuguese power?

She turned around to take stock and was confronted by a row of wooden doors, painted blue. A wave of disorientation washed over her. They were just doors to the interior of this palace or fort, whatever it was. But they posed a challenge. Which door was the right one? Did the right door in fact exist? Or were all doors the same, and the only difference lay in the person traveling through them? *Deven, I wish you were here to tell me.*

She took a deep breath and closed her eyes. She summoned images of Ahmedabad into her mind: the mosques, the gates, the tree-lined streets, the whitewashed houses, the tumultuous markets, and Bhadra Fort, brooding over the Sabarmati River. She opened her eyes. Nothing had changed.

Pick a door—any door—and make it yours. She chose the one in the center and pushed it open. A shadowy corridor stretched beyond it, beckoning her. The wood was sun-warmed and rough to the touch, real in a way the corridor was not, and she had to force herself to step inside. The door closed, and she was engulfed in darkness with not even a pinprick of light to guide her.

She walked down the corridor, remembering her first glimpse of the Ahmedabad city walls, the thick grove of trees on the city's eastern side, and the imposing Delhi Darwaza. The space around her shifted, and she blinked.

The thick, musky scent of blooming mango trees invaded her nostrils. Leaves crunched under her feet, and a sliver of moonlight filtered through the branches above, bright after the pitch dark of the corridor. Irinya leaned against the trunk of a tree, trying to breathe. She'd ended up in a forest instead of the palace. But the trees had a familiar scent and feel to them. The air was warm and still. She was likely quite close to Ahmedabad. She was debating whether to try to make another door or walk out of the forest on her own two feet, when an odd *pook* sound thrummed the air.

Her heart jumped, and she pressed herself into the tree as if it could swallow her.

A pair of golden yellow eyes gleamed at her from between the trees, and a rank smell overlaid the scent of mango. *Tiger.* She nearly retched in fear.

The eyes came closer, dropping lower to the ground. She sensed the enormous striped animal crouch, bunching up its powerful legs. She pressed herself harder into the tree trunk, chest tight with panic.

The tiger leaped and she screamed. The tree gave way to empty air. She fell hard, banging her head on a marble floor. Lamplight flickered on a painted ceiling above her. The walls around were hung with rich tapestries. Most important, nothing was trying to kill her or chase her. She lay still, trying to get her breath back.

"Who is it?" came a querulous, elderly male voice.

She sat up carefully, rubbing her head. When she was sure she wasn't going to pass out, she stood and turned around.

A huge, intricately carved wooden bed draped with crimson covers stood before her. On the bed, propped by numerous satin pillows, was an old, fat man with sagging jowls and a wispy gray beard. Beside the bed was a table with a large platter of samosas. Realization sank into her with a mixture of relief and triumph.

"I am a flower hunter, and you are the sultan of Gujarat," she said, her voice even, as if she was not in the presence of the man who had ruled Gujarat for over fifty years.

He coughed weakly. "Not for much longer. What is a flower hunter doing in my bedroom, and how did she get past my guards?"

She bowed. "I used a petal of the black chrysanthemum to make a door." Saying it aloud didn't make it any more believable.

He nodded, as if she'd said the most normal thing in the world, and his eyes filmed over. "I always knew you'd come back to me, darling."

Her brain processed what he'd said. "Excuse me?"

"Roopba, my beloved." A tear slid down his ravaged cheek. "Why did you throw yourself in the well? Did you not know how much I loved you?"

"You are mistaken, huzoor. I am not her," said Irinya, backing away a step.

Rani Roopba had been famous for her beauty. She'd also been Rana Veer Singh's wife. Sultan Mahmud Begada had defeated and killed her husband in a battle and asked her to marry him instead. *Certainly,* Roopba had said, *but first, you must complete this stepwell my husband was building.* The sultan had complied. When the stepwell was complete, Roopba descended its steps and drowned herself rather than marry the man who'd killed her husband.

"Don't leave," begged the sultan. "I dream of you every night. I sink in a sea of regret."

Irinya stared at him, her spirits plummeting. The sultan was too ill to distinguish between past and present. It was no good telling him what had happened in Surat. Still, she tried. "I'm here to warn you that Malik Gopi is a traitor," she said. "Also, Imshan Khan has a silver spider lily and plans to use it to take the throne."

"What?" He attempted to throw off his coverlet. "Assist me," he commanded. "We must mobilize the army. I will have Roopba, if I have to destroy Veer Singh's entire kingdom for it."

Irinya squelched her frustration. It was his daughter, Zahra, that she needed to speak with. She wasn't sure what the sultana could do about

it, but it was better to be forewarned. Perhaps Zahra could mobilize
her own troops to protect herself from Imshan Khan.

Irinya turned away from the sultan and walked toward the ornately
carved bedroom door. Had the effects of the black petal worn off? No,
she could still feel a faint hum within. It ought to be enough for one
more door.

"Imshan killed his uncle, you know. My son, Apa," said the sultan.

The words jolted her to a halt, and she turned back to him. "I heard
that you yourself had your son poisoned for trespassing in some noble's
harem."

His face twisted. "What kind of father would kill his own son?"

"I don't know," she said. "Not a very forgiving one, I imagine."

"It wasn't just the harem incident." He plucked his coverlet, restless.
"He was bad to the bone. Pushed his nursemaid into a well when he was
eight. I had the sole witness imprisoned. He said he'd only been playing,
and I chose to believe him."

Then you created a monster, she did not say. "You admit you had Apa
Khan killed?"

He twitched. "It was Imshan who saw him sneak into the harem,
Imshan who reported it. If I had sat back and done nothing, the nobles
would have rebelled. They would have killed Apa themselves. I cannot
rule if I am not seen to be impartial. But I never forgave Imshan for it.
Apa was unsuitable to be sultan, but so is Imshan. He will always put
his own self-interest before that of the sultanate."

Exactly what Irinya had herself concluded about the wazir, but it
made her flesh crawl to hear it from Imshan's great-uncle, who had
imprisoned Imshan's father and was at least indirectly responsible for
his death.

"That's why you made Zahra your heir," she said. "But the nobles—"

"—will rejoice when I die. And so must you." He gave her a watery
smile. "I'm going to join you, Roopba. Very soon."

"I look forward to it," she told him. "Good night, huzoor."

She laid her hand on the door, focused her thoughts on the sultana,
and pushed it open, hoping she wasn't going to be confronted with a
corridor bristling with armed guards.

The door swung open into a large, lamplit bedchamber similar to the sultan's. Irinya stepped through, let the door shut behind her, and glanced back. The door had vanished; in its place was a tapestry-covered wall. She gave a long, slow exhale. The petal had worked. But where was the sultana? Was Irinya in the right room? It appeared empty.

She was about to cross the room to the door when a shadowy figure dressed in black leaped out of a corner and thrust the edge of a sword toward her neck.

CHAPTER 15

Irinya froze. The sword stopped a scant inch away from her throat. She gulped and gazed into a pair of large, dark eyes that were the most arresting feature in an otherwise plain face.

"Who are you? How did you get here? Who sent you?" demanded the woman. She was robed and hooded like an assassin, although her voice was cultured and oddly familiar. Perhaps she was a royal bodyguard. "Speak the truth, and quickly, before I spray your blood all over the room."

Irinya tried to still the hammering in her chest. "I am a flower hunter. No one sent me. I used a petal of the black chrysanthemum to arrive here."

The woman inhaled sharply. "*Liar.* The black chrysanthemum is a myth."

"I'm not a liar," snapped Irinya, outrage pushing fear aside. "How do you think I got here if not by magic? Just because *you* haven't seen it doesn't mean the black chrysanthemum isn't real."

The woman tilted her head, considering. "Prove it. Make a door."

"I can't," said Irinya. She could no longer sense the hum of the petal within her. "The effects seem to have worn off."

"How convenient," said the woman, the sword held steady in her hand. "But you did just appear out of nowhere into what must be the most secure room in the palace, so I'll give you a minute to explain yourself. Start with your name."

Irinya debated whether to use the alias the wazir had given her and decided against it. Most people she'd met in the palace knew her real name anyway. "Irinya Dewa," she said, trying to figure out where she'd heard the woman's voice before. Had she met her in the palace? "I'm looking for . . ." Her words trailed away at the wide-eyed expression on the woman's face.

"You're *her*," said the woman, shrugging off her hood.

"Who?" said Irinya, confused. Did the woman know her?

"Never mind." The sword drew back. "Go on. Who are you looking for?"

It hit her, then, where she'd heard the smooth, calm voice. It had been in the court assembly, and the voice had come from behind a screen.

"*You*," Irinya stammered. "The sultana. I mean, are you? Zahra Sultana?" The woman didn't look like royalty in those plain black robes without jewelry, makeup, or adornments of any kind. Her hair was tied back in a simple bun, and her face was that of an ordinary young woman, except for those flashing eyes. But there was that voice, soft yet commanding, identical to the one Irinya had heard in court.

"Perhaps." The woman raised an eyebrow. "What did you want with the sultana?"

"To give valuable information," said Irinya. Exhaustion welled up in her. All the doors she'd opened and the places she'd been swam before her eyes, blurring into each other. She blinked and swallowed, mustering strength into her voice. "I have a favor to ask in return. It will not cost the sultana much but will mean the difference between life and death for my kul."

The woman gave a grim smile. "Yes, everything has a cost, does it not? What favor do you wish to ask for?"

"There are only a few weeks left before the end of the flower-hunting season in the Rann of Kutch," said Irinya, summoning all her powers of persuasion. "This is the time when baniyas ramp up pressure on flower hunters to meet their unreasonable quotas, and the time when flower-hunting families across Banni have the most fatalities. Please issue instructions to the baniyas to leave all flower hunters alone for the rest of this season. It will not make a big difference to the number of flowers collected, and it will reduce the likelihood of accidents."

The woman—the *sultana*—stared at her with knitted brows. "You're from Banni. A flower hunter yourself?" Irinya nodded, and the sultana lowered her sword. "It is a complicated ask, but not impossible."

Relief flooded Irinya at the words, loosening the knot in her stomach. "Thank you, Your Highness."

"Do not thank me yet. What valuable information do you have to share in return?" demanded the sultana. "It had better be worth my while."

"Malik Gopi is a traitor," Irinya blurted out.

The sultana gave a dismissive wave of her hand. "I already know that."

"He may not survive long," said Irinya, twisting her hands together. "Last I saw, Imshan Khan had overpowered him." She took a deep breath. "The wazir has a silver spider lily. He means to use it to secure the throne."

"Ah. Now *that* I did not know." The sultana gave a bleak laugh. "You gave him the flower, did you not?"

Irinya's shoulders slumped. "I'm the one who harvested it, so I am to blame. But I gave it to someone to deliver to the sultan to help him defeat the Portuguese. Except that person simply kept the flower. And I thought he'd betrayed me, so I told the wazir about him."

The sultana frowned. "If Imshan has a silver spider lily, there is little I can do about it."

"You have guards of your own," Irinya pointed out. "You could escape the palace, leave Ahmedabad. The spider lily will not last forever. When its effects wear off, you can safely challenge him for the throne." If there was a throne left by that time to fight over.

The sultana narrowed her eyes. "What has happened between you and him? We thought you were his creature."

We? Irinya swayed as fatigue seeped into every pore of her body. "It's a long story, Your Highness."

The sultana sheathed her sword. "Start at the beginning, flower hunter. I am paying for this information, am I not? And sit down; you look like you might collapse any moment."

Irinya sat on a divan, and the sultana poured a cup of water for her from a copper jug. The drink revived Irinya, and she began her story.

She started with Deven, backtracked to the dead body and the bluestar, leaped ahead to the baniya's men killing Chinmay, then backtracked again to her mother and the poem she'd taught Irinya. By the time she reached the part where Deven had thrown himself on Imshan's sword, her voice was hoarse, her throat parched once more. Her eyes burned as she remembered Deven's last words. He'd kept the spider lily hidden from his master, and he'd given her the black chrysanthemum petal. In his own way, he'd tried to atone for his sins. She would not withhold forgiveness from him.

Zahra made her drink another cup of water. "Tell me where you've been," she said, a note of longing in her voice. "Where did the doors take you?"

Irinya grimaced. "First, a Portuguese ship. Then all the way east to Malacca. Then back west to a port by the sea that looked beautiful but smelled of death. Then—I *think*—to Bagh-i-Firdaus, where I met a tiger. Though it could have been a jungle anywhere in Gujarat. Then to the palace."

The sultana sighed. "I envy you. I have not seen the outside of this palace in months. Do you have any more petals?"

"Sorry, Your Highness." She wasn't about to part with the last drop of Deven's legacy to satisfy the sultana's curiosity. It might come in useful someday—perhaps as a last-ditch defense against the wazir himself.

"How much time has passed since you were in Surat?" Zahra asked. "How long do I have before my nephew shows up?"

"It's just been a few hours, Your Highness," said Irinya.

"Are you certain?" The sultana's brow knitted. "One of the myths of the black chrysanthemum is that it has a time price. For every door you take, you lose a bit of your life."

Irinya quailed. The words of the second poem came back to her: *Blackhearted chrys will rob you of your days.*

"It is the sixth day of the dark half of the eighth lunar month," said Zahra, watching her.

Irinya's head reeled. No wonder she felt all hollow and disoriented. "It was the first day when I left Surat."

The sultana's face set in grim lines. "Five days ago. He will be here any moment. I have no time to prepare. Else I could have sent a message to my guards to break me out of here." She rubbed her chin. "Why has he not used the flower yet?"

"Because he does not mean to use it against the Portuguese," said Irinya. "Not right away. He means to use it *here* to gain the throne. And he's on his way." Her stomach roiled at the thought.

"Then there is only one thing to do." Zahra reached forward and placed a hand on Irinya's shoulder. "Find another spider lily."

Irinya controlled her exasperation. No one except a flower hunter understood just how impossible that was. "Silver spider lilies are one of the rarest flowers. This is the first to be found in over two decades. I could hunt for years and not see another. No, Highness, that is not an option."

Zahra dropped her hand and regarded her out of those large, lovely eyes that seemed to see much more than most people did. "Yet you found one. *And* a black chrysanthemum."

Irinya took a deep breath. "I didn't *find* a black chrysanthemum; a petal was given to me. I didn't find the silver spider lily, either; that was a . . . friend."

"Regardless of how they came into your possession, the fact remains that you have drawn rare flowers to yourself," said Zahra, her expression somber. "It is a gift. Do not let others misuse it."

She wanted to tell the sultana that it was Fardan who had found the spider lily, that it was *his* gift, not hers. All she'd done was break a promise and hurt her friend. But the sultana would not understand, and she didn't want to bring up Fardan. "Are you still not allowed to leave your rooms except for court meetings, Your Highness?" she asked instead.

"Yes." Zahra gave a bitter smile. "For my 'safety.' I have my own bodyguards outside the door, but Imshan's men guard the corridors and staircase. I have a bit of leeway, but that will doubtless vanish when Imshan returns. Half the court wants to kill me, apparently. It is a good excuse for Imshan to lock me away. If he'd been on my side, it would have tilted the court in my favor. But my nephew has his own ambitions."

"You are very close in age to be his aunt," ventured Irinya.

"I am three years older than him," said Zahra, leaning back on the divan with a sigh. "Apa—my brother—was five years older than me. Our father did not have more children, despite his numerous concubines."

Her mouth twisted. "There are some that whisper we are not his, that we are the offspring of the queen's lovers. Poor mama. Such slander would kill her if she were not already dead."

It struck Irinya how alone Zahra was. Mother—dead. Brother—dead. Father—dying. Nephew—plotting. Her heart ached for the sultana. No matter Irinya's own losses, she'd never felt lonely until she had to leave her kul. "Do you not have anyone left?" she asked. "Someone you can trust?"

"Trust?" Zahra raised her eyebrows. "Oh, yes, I do." She clapped her hands.

The curtains twitched, and a demure, familiar figure stepped out.

Irinya gasped. "Tarana? What are you doing here?"

"She works for me," said Zahra with her first genuine smile. "My eyes and ears in the zenana." Tarana bowed to the sultana and gave Irinya a sly wink.

"So that's how you recognized my name," said Irinya, smiling.

Zahra nodded. "She had only good things to say about you—except that you were working for the wazir."

"Not anymore," said Irinya. Anger coiled within her as she remembered how he had manipulated her. He would help her kul, but only if she remained loyal and useful to him. Still, she would have paid that price if she hadn't had any other choice. "I didn't choose to work for him in the first place. It was only to retrieve the spider lily. I didn't think beyond the fact that I needed to save my kul, and that the flower shouldn't fall into Portuguese hands."

"He's a good administrator," said the sultana. "If not for the fact that he has turned half the court against me, I might wish for him to remain at his post." She leaned toward Irinya. "Do not worry; I will send a message through Tarana to one of our Revenue Department staff tonight itself. Imshan won't come to know—not anytime soon. He'll be too busy gloating over the spider lily."

Gratitude flooded Irinya. If the baniya got the order from the palace to ease off, he wouldn't dare kill any of her kul members using the quota as an excuse. She'd won a temporary reprieve for her kul as well as all the other kuls that toiled under their baniyas' unfair demands. "Thank you, Your Highness." At last, a bit of good news to share with

Fardan the next time he contacted her. Then she wondered if Fardan had already tried to reach her using the green rose and failed because she'd been traveling through doors, losing bits of time. The thought made her stomach roil.

"Has Imshan confided in you at all?" asked the sultana, reaching for a glass of water. "Is it just the throne he craves?"

"Revenge, too, I think. He's angry about the fate of his grandfather, Daud Khan," said Irinya, remembering what he had told her. "Your father poisoned him? His own brother?"

Zahra gave a short laugh. "My father is nicknamed the Poison Sultan, but he was only thirteen at the time. Daud Khan was poisoned by nobles. Years later, Daud Khan's son tried to raise an army against my father and ended up in the dungeons, where he later died. My father raised Imshan, educated him, made him the wazir. He should have foreseen this. Perhaps he was trying to assuage his guilt. In a way, Daud Khan was killed because of him. The nobles thought a thirteen-year-old boy made for a better, more malleable alternative."

"What will happen now?" asked Tarana, who had been listening quietly.

"If Imshan has the spider lily, he will have me executed," said the sultana in a calm voice, as if she were discussing the menu for dinner.

Tarana uttered an inarticulate cry and flung herself at the sultana's feet. Zahra grasped her shoulders and pulled her up to sit beside them.

"Surely not." Irinya stared at the sultana, coldness spreading in her limbs. They'd only just met, and Irinya had spent the first few minutes of their meeting with the sultana's sword at her throat, but already, she liked her. She would be a good ruler: unruffled, unpretentious, and efficient. "Why would he kill you if he can simply take the throne?"

"It is the only way to ensure I do not challenge his rule in the future," said Zahra, squeezing Tarana's hands in her own.

"There is another way, my lady," said Tarana, speaking fast, as if she were afraid of her own words. "If you marry one of the nobles, you will gain some protection, and the wazir will feel less threatened by you."

Zahra frowned at her. "Leaving aside the fact that I have no desire to marry any man, let alone one of the greedy nobles of this court, my nephew will not feel *less* threatened if I marry. He will feel *more* threatened, because then I will have a husband eyeing the throne as well."

Irinya listened in silence, her heart hurting for them both. It was cruelly unfair that a woman's right to rule could be called into question by any male noble of the sultanate. In her kul, it was always a woman who was the leader, a woman who inherited her parents' property and debt, a woman who chose whether and which man to marry.

Tarana's face fell. "If you were cousins, you could have married the wazir."

"I am his *aunt*," snapped Zahra. "And I would rather die. You, of all people, should know how I feel."

"I just want you to be safe," said Tarana, her eyes brimming with tears.

"Sometimes safety is not in our hands," said Zahra in a gentle tone. "Sometimes all we can do is die with honor."

"Then I will die with you, my lady," said Tarana, sniffing.

"Silly girl." A tender look passed between the two of them—a look of mingled love, hope, and fear. Irinya averted her eyes, not wanting to intrude in this deeply private conversation. She rubbed her chest, as if that could ease the ache inside it. Was this the way Fardan had looked at her when she abandoned him? *I miss you. I want to talk to you.* She wished she could send that thought to him.

Boots thudded outside the door, and someone shouted. Irinya's heart jumped. Was the wazir already here?

"Hide," commanded Zahra, rising from the divan, her hand going to her sword.

"But my lady—" began Tarana, her eyes huge with distress.

"Do it," said Zahra harshly. "You are the one good thing in my life. Why do you want them to take it away?"

Tarana gave a sob and slipped back into her hiding place behind the damask curtains that covered half a wall. Irinya rose and stood behind the sultana, facing the door, trying to summon strength and calm. She wasn't going to run or hide from Imshan Khan again. The sultana's message to the baniya network would be enough to stave off the worst for her kul. What mattered now was the spider lily. Perhaps there was still something she could do to make sure it was used for the right cause.

Swords clashed, and someone screamed. "Hurry," snapped the sultana, her body held in taut readiness, her eyes on the door. "My bodyguards are loyal, but they won't be able to hold off the wazir for more than a few minutes."

"I'll stay with you," said Irinya, swallowing. "I'll talk to him." As if her *talking* might be enough to not get them killed.

The sultana cut her gaze to Irinya, frowning. "What use will that be? Do you have some hold on him?"

"No, but he values my flower-hunting skills." She bit her lip and added, hoping she was right, "He might be ambitious, but I don't think he's wicked enough to kill you."

The sultana snorted. "You *child*. You will be sadly surprised."

The door slammed open. Imshan Khan stalked in, sword in hand, flanked by his men. Irinya's stomach clenched at the sight of his blood-soaked blade and the bodies that lay near the entrance of the door. A few groaned and twitched, but some were still, awash in blood. Imshan Khan drew closer, his face grim, the box with the spider lily peeking out of his breast pocket. Irinya's muscles tensed as he approached. She eyed the box, wishing she could knock him out and snatch it away.

"Hello, dear Aunt, it's time we had a chat," he began, and then he spotted Irinya, standing behind the sultana. His jaw dropped and his eyes widened. It would have been funny, if Irinya hadn't been so nervous. He strode toward them. "*What the hell are you doing here?*" he yelped.

Irinya lifted her chin up, trying to slow her heart rate, glad that the sultana stood between her and the wazir. "Chatting."

"How did you get here?" he demanded, the sultana forgotten, the blood-stained sword hanging loosely from his hand. "How did you vanish from Malik Gopi's house? I searched for you everywhere! Do you know how worried I was? I thought his henchmen had captured you. My men are turning out every house in Surat even as we speak."

Worried I had escaped your clutches, more like. The worst thing was that she had allowed herself to believe that she had for a few minutes. But while he held the spider lily, he held the fate of India in his hands. There was no escaping him. "I jumped out of the window," she improvised. "As to how I got here, I had five days, same as you."

"I don't believe it," he said, his eyes narrowing. "You're a flower hunter, not a warrior, and certainly no horsewoman. You had help, didn't you?" His gaze went to Zahra and hardened. "Did my aunt get to you, as she has gotten to so many of my people?"

"Of course not," said Irinya, indignation chasing away her fear. How dare he assume she was *his people*?

"Paranoid as ever, dear Nephew," said Zahra, her voice icy. "I never met this girl until twenty minutes ago."

"Then I'm surprised at you, Aunt," he said, matching her tone. "You could have taken her hostage and extracted some concessions from me."

Irinya's skin tingled. What did he mean? Did he value her skills that much? Could she leverage that in some way?

Zahra's gaze darted to Irinya, her eyes speculative. Then she pressed her lips together and turned back to Imshan Khan. "I would never stoop that low. But I suppose you wouldn't understand that."

"No, I wouldn't. After all, like father, like daughter." His mouth twisted. "The ends justify the means, no matter how bloody, correct?"

"That is *your* philosophy, not mine." Zahra's hand hovered above her hilt, and her stance was that of a fighter, waiting for the right time to strike.

Imshan Khan did not fail to notice. "Do you mean to say you are not visualizing my death right now?" His face darkened. "Take out your blade. Give me the pleasure of driving mine into your heart."

The sword was in Zahra's hand before he had finished speaking. She leaped at him, her attack sudden and vicious. He parried her blows, dancing out of her reach. His men fanned out around the room, watchful and tense. Irinya stumbled back to the wall, her heart thumping. She could hardly bear to watch. Why had Zahra attacked him? The sultana was a skillful fighter, but the wazir was bigger and stronger. Even if she won this round, she would still be the loser.

"Stop," Irinya shouted. Neither of them listened. They whirled around the room, their swords a blur. She followed their moves, her heart in her mouth. Zahra slid her blade on Imshan's, right up to his chest, nearly stabbing him. Imshan folded himself back with fluid grace and struck Zahra's sword; it slipped from her hand and clattered across the floor. He bore down on her, a savage smile on his face, and Irinya's gut clenched.

"Stop, huzoor!" she screamed with all the power of her lungs.

The wazir paused midstrike to cast a glare at her. "A fair fight, flower hunter, which is more than my father or grandfather ever got," he grated.

At least he'd listened to her. "It's not a fair fight." Irinya hurried up to them, determined to stop him before he wounded the sultana. Poor Tarana, hiding behind the curtain, was probably dying inside. "You're twice her weight. Please let her be."

"*Let her be?*" The wazir shook his head. "She'd never stop plotting my murder."

"The way you plotted my brother's?" said Zahra, panting.

"I didn't plot anything," he bit out. "I happened to see him where he shouldn't have been, that's all."

"*You* shouldn't have been there, either," Zahra shot back. "What excuse did you give for your presence?"

"I was *twelve,*" he said coldly. "The ladies used me to carry messages to palace officials. It was no secret. Why are you bringing this up now? There was no love lost between you and Apa. A cruel, greedy man who would have been a cruel, greedy sultan."

"You are becoming him," said the sultana. They stared at each other, and Irinya saw the flame of self-knowledge flare in the wazir's eyes. For a moment, she allowed herself to hope that it would be enough to change him, change his course.

But the flame died, and Imshan Khan's handsome face twisted in a grim smile. "It's you or me, dear Aunt, and I know which I prefer."

Disappointment tightened Irinya's chest. Why had she expected more from the man who had strung her along with the promise to help her kul? All he cared about was himself and the throne. "Why can you both not govern?" she asked, knowing even as she spoke that it was useless.

"There can only be one sultan," said the wazir in a patient voice, as if speaking to a child. "And the nobles will never accept a woman. It would break the sultanate apart and leave us easy pickings for the foreign vultures. If she were not my aunt, I would marry her, but as it is, it's forbidden. Not to mention, the thought makes me nauseous."

Zahra showed him her teeth. "Not as nauseous as it makes me."

"Enough," said the wazir, making a cutting gesture with his hand. "Tomorrow, at dawn, the traitor Malik Gopi will be tied to the mouth of a cannon and blown into oblivion. You may join him. Or you may kneel before me now and request the mercy of my sword."

The words struck Irinya cold. If he killed the sultana, all was lost. There would no longer be an official heir to the throne. Imshan would use the spider lily to quell the chaos and uprisings that would follow the sultana's execution. And the Portuguese would move in for the kill.

"Please, huzoor, spare her life," she begged, seizing the wazir's sword arm. He gave her an incredulous look, outraged, no doubt, at her temerity, but made no move to shake off her hand. "She's a prisoner here; what trouble can she make for you?"

Zahra narrowed her eyes. "Do not plead on my behalf, flower hunter. If I must die, then I must. I only regret that I leave the sultanate in my nephew's grasping hands."

"I will be a far better ruler than you or your dead brother could have been," said Imshan Khan, tearing his gaze away from Irinya. "Choose the manner of your end; it is the last favor I grant you."

"Huzoor, if you will spare the sultana's life," said Irinya in desperation, "I will go back to the Rann. I will find the rarest flowers for you." This would not only buy her time, but also might delay the wazir's use of the spider lily.

"You will do that anyway, flower hunter," he said, raising his eyebrows, a question mark in his voice.

"I will not, huzoor," she said, although she was quaking inside. "You could tie me to the mouth of a cannon, and I will not. If you want my loyalty, you must purchase it with the sultana's life as well as a promise not to let my kul come to harm. Did you not want a hold on me?"

"*No*." Zahra glared at her. "What did I tell you? Don't let anyone misuse your gift."

"I could simply use the hibiscus on you," said the wazir, a frown creasing his forehead.

"It doesn't work on me," lied Irinya, summoning the confidence of the storyteller into her voice even as her stomach churned with fear. "You already tried it once. You thought I had bluestar on me. The truth is, I must be immune to its effects because of all the hibiscus I've harvested in my lifetime."

"Hmm." The wazir glanced down at her hand, still clutching his arm, and said, his lips quirking, "You can let go now. Unless you have designs on my person? I can feel your pulse racing."

She released him at once, her face heating.

He sheathed his sword and stepped back, his eyes speculative. "All right, flower hunter. I have a proposal for you. Find me another spider lily. I give you one month. I will keep Zahra alive until then. If you are successful, you can use that flower to buy her life."

"I accept," said Irinya, relief flooding her. She'd succeeded in buying time for the sultana.

He gave a crooked smile. "Be ready to leave tomorrow morning after the execution. I expect you both to watch."

Her stomach curdled at the thought of having to witness such a horrific method of execution. Malik Gopi was a traitor and deserved to die, but even the worst criminals had the right to due process. "Will he not have a judicial trial?" she asked. "How can you execute him without one?" It was important for the public to witness such a trial, to have faith in the law. Not to mention, by the time the trial was over, she would be nowhere in the vicinity.

"I questioned him during our journey." Imshan Khan's lip curled. "I have proof of his treason. What need have I for a trial?"

"That's not what you said earlier," said Irinya. "You said he would go before a court of law. And it's not what you need; it's what your people need that matters. What has changed in you, huzoor?" She knew the answer—it was the spider lily. But did he know it?

Uncertainty flickered in his eyes. Then his face hardened. "Do not presume to question me." He whipped around, barked orders to his men to guard the room and pick up the wounded, and strode toward the door. At the entrance, he paused and cast a glance back at her. "Hurry up. Don't you need a room to sleep in? Food? A *bath*?"

Irinya's eyes met the sultana's. Zahra gave a slight nod, and Irinya hurried after the wazir, wishing she could stay with the sultana but knowing it was not possible.

In the corridor, men were carrying away the dead and wounded on stretchers. The floor was slick with blood, and Irinya nearly slipped as she ran to catch up with the wazir. The wazir whirled around and caught her arm, frowning. "Steady now. Don't want you to break your bones, not when you might still prove useful to me."

She tugged her arm out of his grip, trying to breathe evenly. But it was hard, with him standing right beside her while all around was the evidence of his bloodlust.

As they walked down the corridor, followed by two of his guards, Imshan Khan glanced at her, his face unreadable. "I sent a message through our sarraf to the Kutchi baniya network the night we left Surat," he said, "telling them all to ease off on their flower quotas for the rest of the season. That should work, right?"

She gaped at him, her thoughts reeling. Had he read her mind? He'd sent the exact message she had requested the sultana to do—and he'd done it without her begging him for it. "Thank . . . thank you, huzoor," she managed.

His mouth quirked. "I didn't know where you were or what had happened to you or which kul you belonged to. But I kept my word. Try to keep yours."

They arrived at the landing where Khawaja Daulat was waiting to escort her to the zenana, and the wazir turned to talk with his guards. She followed Khawaja Daulat down the stairs, twisting around to stare at Imshan Khan's back, as if that would give her some clues into his convoluted mind. Just when she thought she had him figured out, he proved her wrong. *So you are not a complete villain, huzoor.*

And yet he had been ready to kill the sultana—his own aunt. And yet he was going to execute a man without a trial. The spider lily was already affecting him. It would be his undoing if he had not the heart to resist it.

CHAPTER 16

Soldiers arrived at dawn to escort Irinya to the exterior courtyard where Malik Gopi was to be executed. Irinya followed
them out into the marble corridor, across multiple halls, and
down endless steps, too jittery to pay attention to her surroundings.
She hadn't been able to sleep much last night or eat anything apart
from a bit of porridge Tarana had coaxed into her. She didn't know if
it was nerves or the delayed effects from all her magical traveling, but
watching a man being blown to bits was *not* the way she wanted to
spend her morning.

The exterior courtyard was a large, circular space paved with rough
stones and crowded with noisy spectators. People stood against the
brick walls, chattering excitedly, balancing children on their shoulders
and arms. Some were even eating. Beyond the walls, minarets pierced
the pale blue sky.

In the middle of the courtyard was a large black cannon on wheels.
Tied to the mouth of the muzzle was Malik Gopi. His clothes were
grimy, his face distorted with terror. He shook and struggled uselessly
against his bonds. Irinya's stomach clenched at the sight. She wished
with all her heart that Deven had not thrown away his life for him. A
sword would have been a cleaner end than this, and Deven would still
be alive.

Guards stood behind the cannon, ready to fire on the wazir's command. Raptors circled overhead, instinct alerting them to the presence of a ready-made meal. The wazir paced a few feet away from the guards, his hands behind his back, a grim smile on his face. Zahra stood next to him, her arms crossed, her face expressionless. The wazir came to a halt as he spotted Irinya and beckoned her over.

"People occasionally need a lesson on how traitors are punished," he said, surveying the eager crowd with satisfaction. "No one will forget what they see today."

"Huzoor, please reconsider. Malik Gopi is the governor of Surat," said Irinya, trying to summon calmness in her face and voice. "Won't his subjects rebel at his fate?"

He gave an indifferent shrug. "They can rebel all they like; I will crush them like ants under my bootheel. He is a traitor and a coward. We found him hiding in the women's quarters of his household. I could have killed him then, but I wanted to make an example of him."

"He colluded with the Portuguese," said Zahra, her expression somber as she took in the scene. "He deserves to be punished, but this . . . His relatives will swear revenge. They'll never accept your leadership now."

His lip curled. "I have the silver spider lily; did you forget?"

"It does not make you immortal; did *you* forget?" she snapped back.

Before the wazir could respond, one of the guards hurried up to him. "Huzoor, the crowd is getting restless."

Imshan Khan waved his hand. "Make them stand farther back. Only blanks have been loaded in the cannon, but still. We must make sure no one gets hurt by flying bits of flesh and bone."

Irinya shuddered. She was directly behind the cannon and had an unfortunately good view. She would close her eyes when it was fired.

Guards went around, ordering the onlookers to move back. Malik Gopi stopped struggling. He hung limp on the ropes that tied him to the cannon, his head lolling. The small of his back was pressed against the muzzle. Irinya hoped he'd passed out. It would make the last minute of his life more bearable.

Someone squeezed her shoulder. "Close your ears," whispered the sultana.

"Fire!" shouted Imshan Khan, startling Irinya so that she jumped and forgot to close her eyes *or* her ears.

A deafening crack split the air. Malik Gopi's head shot upward forty feet into the air. His arms flew left and right, landing amid the excited crowd. His torso vanished in a spray of blood. Raptors swooped down, snatching bits of flesh from the air.

Cheers broke out. Irinya's head swam. She gripped the sultana's arm for support. Zahra stood straight-backed, her eyes flinty, her mouth a thin, disapproving line.

The wazir glanced at Irinya, a frown creasing his forehead. "Are you all right?"

No, she wasn't. She would never be able to unsee this horrific sight. Where had the head gone? Had it been grabbed by a large eagle?

Irinya let go of Zahra and tottered away. She managed to make it through the crowds and into the next courtyard before she was violently sick into a potted plant, the porridge causing a great deal more distress on its way out than it had on its way in. *I'm sorry,* she thought, but whether she was addressing the plant or the dead man, she didn't know.

A warm hand massaged her back, and she flinched. "You have a weak disposition for someone of peasant stock," the wazir remarked, his tone mild. *Not* the voice of someone who had just had a man blown from a cannon.

Irinya wiped her mouth with the edge of her dupatta and made herself stand straight. Thankfully, the courtyard was empty; no one else had witnessed her puking—apart from the wazir. "I'm fine," she said, her voice flat. "Shouldn't you be back there, celebrating the end of a traitor?"

"Fun part's over. Now it's the cleanup and ensuring no one makes off with a gory souvenir." He narrowed his gaze at her. "Why did you run away from Surat?"

The abrupt change of topic threw her, and she didn't have the energy to think of a plausible lie. "Deven died. There was nothing I could do for him. I left because I wanted to tell the sultana what had happened. But I arrived too late for it to make any difference." She'd lost five days to the black chrysanthemum—days that the sultana could have used to make her getaway. In the end, the petal had not helped her much. But she still had a sip left. She would make that one count; she didn't yet know how, but Deven's legacy had to be worth something more.

"Ah." Imshan Khan crossed his arms, a stony expression on his face. "Since when have you been her creature?"

"I am no one's creature," she snapped. "My only loyalty is to my kul." Of course, the wazir was not someone who would understand feelings that could not be bought or controlled with a flower.

He raised his eyebrows. "And yet, you made a long and hazardous journey to warn her the spider lily was in my possession."

You have no idea how hazardous. "I did what I thought was right," she said, exhaustion welling up in her. "I wanted her to have the chance to escape the palace, but I never met her before yesterday."

He gave a tight smile. "And yet you are willing to give me *another* spider lily to save her life."

It was not a question, and she didn't have to answer. There was no way she was going to find another spider lily in the next month. She shouldn't have made such a bargain with him, but it had been all she could think of to stop him from killing the sultana. She would return empty-handed after a month and beg for more time—unless a better idea presented itself before then. She stared at the ground, wishing she could erase the memory of the execution she'd been forced to witness.

"Are you even fit to travel?" he continued, studying her with a skeptical frown. "You look like you'll keel over any moment."

"Give her a day or two," said Zahra, walking up to them. "Let her rest and recover."

"No!" Irinya calmed herself with difficulty. The prospect of spending even one more day in this place made her stomach heave. "I will leave today. I can be ready in an hour."

"Excellent," said the wazir, his face expressionless, his tone matter-of-fact. "Now you have seen what I will do to the sultana if you don't return in a month, so I hope you are properly motivated."

Was he serious? Irinya could not be sure. Zahra sneered and turned away from him. She didn't seem afraid of him at all, even though she had just witnessed what he was capable of.

The next hour was a blur of preparation. Irinya didn't get a chance to speak privately with the sultana again. Tarana packed sensible clothes and shoes for her in a leather bag, as well as a basket of dates, figs, dry-roasted chickpeas, jaggery, and flatbreads. Irinya thought with a pang of the boots she had thrown at Deven and wished she had them back. At least she was going to see Veerana again soon. She hoped he was still safely in the stable in Bhuj where she'd left him.

The one bright spot was that the wazir summoned her to his office and returned her mother's dowry bag with the blowpipe, minus the thorns. The thorns represented many hours of labor, but she didn't care. She could always pick more. But the bag and the blowpipe were irreplaceable.

"Try not to kill any of my guards," Imshan Khan said with a mirthless smile as she clutched the bag to her heart.

"What guards?" she said, confused.

He leaned back and steepled his fingers. "Four of my best will accompany you to the Rann. Think of them as your bodyguards."

"I don't need bodyguards," she protested.

He gave an exasperated sigh. "Any flower that you find will certainly need protection. And I plan to guard my investment, even though she seems more interested in my rival than in me." He waved a dismissive hand. "I wish you good hunting."

She left his office, fuming. She was an *investment,* was she? Power-mad, paranoid creature! She wished she could tell him exactly what she thought of him, although it would probably be the last thing she ever did.

Outside the sultana's chamber, the four guards who would be escorting her to the Rann had already arrived—all tough, capable-looking men with swords and daggers hanging from their belts. Zahra and Tarana were waiting at the door to bid her goodbye. Tarana pressed the basket of food and the leather bag into her hands. "Stay safe," she said, her eyes wide with anxiety. Irinya tried to give her a reassuring smile.

One of the guards took the bag and the basket from her, and she turned back to say farewell to the sultana. Zahra squeezed her shoulders. "Good luck." She leaned forward and whispered, "Don't give him any more power over you."

Irinya nodded, her eyes stinging. It was too late for that. He didn't even need the hibiscus; he held Zahra's and Tarana's lives in his hands. That meant she would do as he asked, or at least try to. She didn't owe them her loyalty the way she owed her kul. But she liked them and how their relationship was not that of a sultana and a servant at all, but something quite different. Perhaps if the wazir had that kind of relationship in his own life, he could have forgiven the wrongs that had supposedly been done to him. But she doubted he had a single trust-worthy friend in the world, let alone a special someone to love. It must have warped him.

The guards led her out of the palace. She had been dreading walk-ing through the exterior courtyard and witnessing the "cleanup" but, to her relief, they exited from a different gate in a smaller courtyard. Her carriage was waiting outside: a small, nondescript affair pulled by two horses and driven by a coachman. She had the carriage to herself; the guards rode beside her on horseback. As they clattered down the broad, tree-lined streets of Ahmedabad, she tried to unclench herself and relax.

But she couldn't. Again and again, she heard the burst of cannon fire and saw Malik Gopi's head shoot up into the sky. Had the wazir always been so ruthless? Or was the silver spider lily unleashing a monster inside him? She thought of how he had been on their journey to Surat: tolerant, teasing, even considerate. When she'd gone missing in Su-rat, he had tried to find her. He hadn't forgotten her kul, either. There were aspects of him that were likable. And then there was the part that wanted to control her, kill all competition, and gain the throne, no matter how much blood was shed in the process. If he'd truly had the makings of a good ruler, he would have used the spider lily against the Portuguese by now.

Silver spider lily, to lose to yourself.

You could win the whole world and it mattered not a jot if you lost the most important battle of all—the one against yourself. All the sto-ries of the spider lily made it seem more of a curse than a gift. Was it the reason the sultanate had such a violent history? Every sultan had come to power in a bloodbath. Every sultan had killed his father or brother or uncle to gain the throne. Every sultan had invaded neighboring king-doms and killed the rulers who refused to convert to their faith.

And she'd promised the wazir another. She leaned back against the carriage seat and closed her eyes, sick and exhausted. If—*when*—she re-turned empty-handed, would the wazir listen to her excuses and grant her more time? Or would he execute the sultana? How long could she delay the inevitable? She imagined Zahra tied to the mouth of a cannon, and her stomach seized.

"Irinya? Can you hear me?"

Her heart leaped into her mouth. "Fardan?" she whispered when she had calmed down enough to speak. "How are you? How is everyone?"

He gave a shaky laugh. *"They'll be okay now that I've managed to contact you. I tried a couple of days ago and couldn't. Bholi was beside herself. I managed to quiet her, told her I must have made a mistake."*

That would have been when she was traveling through doors. *Gracious green rose to keep you apart.* It had been because of the black chrysanthemum, but still. The rose had not worked when they'd needed it. It couldn't be trusted—no flower could, not wholly. "Sorry," she said. "But I have news, both good and bad. First tell me yours."

"Miraben told me to tell you that the kul has moved again, near the village of Khavda. We'll be here for ten days. When are you coming back?"

She calculated. "Seven or eight days. I must stop in Bhuj first. But I won't go to Khavda. I won't risk the kul. Listen, Fardan, *without speaking,* because I have a lot to tell you."

As quickly and concisely as possible, she filled him in on what had happened since the last time they'd spoken, ending with her bargain with the wazir and the message that had been sent out to the baniyas. She skipped nonessential details; he didn't need to know about the black chrysanthemum or Malik Gopi's gory end, for instance. She expected him to yell at her, to get worked up at the dangerous situation she had brought upon herself, but instead he reacted with surprising calm.

"What have you gotten us involved in?" he said in a mild voice.

"Not *us*. Me. I have no intention of taking these guards anywhere near the kul," she said.

"I agree," he said, surprising her again. *"By 'us,' I meant you and me."*

She frowned. "What do you mean?"

"I'll meet you at our campsite near the village of Bhitiara," he said. *"That's where we found the bluestar and the silver spider lily."*

She sat up, her stomach clenching. "Don't interfere," she warned. "I can't have anyone else—"

"*Stop,*" he said sharply, cutting her off. "*You don't get to do this again. You don't get to dictate what I do or manipulate how I feel.*"

She swallowed, her chest tight with guilt. "I'm sorry," she managed. "I didn't want to risk anyone else." She couldn't bear to risk *him*.

"*I know,*" he said. "*But you can't decide the level of risk for someone else. You've trusted me with the truth of what happened. Now trust me again. Let me help. Tell those guards I'm your flower-hunting partner. We'll find a spider lily together. Nothing bad will happen to us.*"

She bit her nails, his voice calming her. She didn't want him involved in any of this, but she couldn't help the hope surging inside her at his words. "How can you be so sure?"

"*All this time, I've been worried sick about you,*" he said. "*Not knowing was the worst. And now that I know, it's not so bad.*"

Not so bad? She didn't know whether to laugh or cry. She settled for saying, "I've been worried sick about you all, too."

"*I know,*" he said. "*That was why you left. But we haven't heard a peep from the baniya in days. Everyone's tense about it, wondering what he's planned. They'll be happy to hear about the message. That was clever, Irinya.*"

Warmth flooded her at his words. "If he or his men return, remind them there's an order from the palace to ease off on quotas," she said.

"*Will do. See you in a week or so,*" he said. "*I'll use the rose every evening until we meet.*"

"No, don't," she said, remembering the words of the poem. "Not unless it's an emergency."

"*Why?*" he asked, sounding surprised.

"Just save it, please? Tell Bholi I love her."

"*I'm not telling her anything. She hates that I get to talk to you and she doesn't. She hit me with a broom yesterday and pretended it was a mistake. She didn't even bother to pretend very hard.*"

Irinya laughed, but her eyes stung. Homesickness clogged her throat, making it difficult to breathe. After he'd said goodbye, she stared out the window, missing his voice. Missing *him*. She'd always taken his presence for granted. It was only when she had to leave him that she realized how much he meant to her. In a little more than a week, she would see him again. Despite her anxiety, her heart lifted at the thought.

They made good time, moving at a quick pace through the dense forests between Ahmedabad and Bhuj, unmolested by tigers or bandits. The lone carriage must have seemed like poor pickings to any self-respecting bandit, and the absence of fresh meat meant they didn't attract any wild animals. They ate dry food that had been packed in Ahmedabad, and it got boring fast. The only thing the guards made fresh was tea, and she was grateful to get a cup of that now and then to supplement what was in her basket. The guards were a taciturn lot, but that suited her, and they didn't bother her in any way. They never stopped for long, and they reached the gates of Bhuj four days later.

The guards went into the city to change the horses, replenish their food and water, and deliver messages to the palace. Irinya handed the chit Naveen Gupta had given her for Veerana to one of the guards. No point venturing inside the city herself. No one would recognize her in her current getup, and the camel herder might refuse to hand Veerana over. She waited on tenterhooks in the carriage outside the gates. It had been over a month since she'd left him there. Suppose he'd already been sold?

But to her relief and delight, the guards emerged with Veerana in tow, looking his usual grumpy self. She had to restrain herself from jumping out and embracing him. But once they were some distance from Bhuj—slower now, because Veerana refused to go faster than a sedate walk, and the horses didn't like to be near him—she asked the coachman to stop the carriage and went out to greet him.

Veerana gave a snort of delight—she *assumed* it was delight—and nibbled her hair. *I thought you'd left me in that hellhole to die.*

"It's not a hellhole; you were perfectly well taken care of," she said, patting his flank. "Look at all the weight you've gained! How nice and firm your hump looks. Even your coat is clean and shiny."

The guards gave her strange looks, and she retreated into her carriage after giving Veerana a flatbread to munch on. As the carriage bumped and rolled through the familiar arid landscape of Kutch, peace settled on her. She was back in the place of her birth, the home of her people. It was a small window of tranquility, all the more precious because she knew how transitory it was.

That night, while the guards took turns standing watch under the crescent moon, she stepped out of the carriage for a walk. The stars burned bright in the cloudless sky, and a tiny breeze tugged her hair. She inhaled the warm air, rich with the scent of the desiccated earth, the spiky grass, the sweet berries. Monsoon was still a couple of weeks away. Rain would change the landscape, flooding the low-lying areas and bringing flocks of migratory birds from faraway lands. If you were lucky, you could see pink flamingos.

A guard coughed behind her, breaking the spell. "Don't go too far," he warned. "There might be leopards."

He was probably more concerned that she'd try to escape, but he had a point. Leopards were as dangerous as tigers if they developed a taste for human flesh. Reluctantly, she returned to the carriage. She lay on a bench, huddled under her shawl, wondering if Zahra and Tarana were all right. Fardan would be at their old campsite by now. Did he really think they would be able to find another spider lily? Even if they did, the wazir was the worst possible person to give it to. Except that was the only way she could buy the sultana's life. But if the Portuguese overran India, none of this would matter. Her home would be destroyed, millions of people displaced. Her mind jumped from one nightmarish scenario to another, and she twisted on the bench, unable to sleep.

The next morning, she gave the guards directions to the village of Bhitiara. There was a rough track the carriage could follow to the village; after that, they would have to leave the carriage and the coachman and ride the rest of the way to the kul's old campsite. She mentioned that one of her fellow flower hunters might be around at the campsite. They didn't seem concerned about it, and why would they be? They were some of the best fighters in the sultanate army: grizzled veterans of multiple conflicts, handpicked by the wazir himself.

"What instructions did the wazir give you about me?" she asked them that night as they sat around a small fire, sipping tea.

The leader, a scarred, silver-haired man named Tej, gave her a wary glance. "To protect you and to ensure your safe return."

"What would you do if I tried to run away?" she asked. "Throw your spear at me?"

Tej raised his bushy eyebrows. "Are you going to run away?"

She thought about it. "No, there would be no point."

"Then the question does not arise," he said calmly, and that was that.

They arrived in Bhitiara the next day, generating great excitement in the little village. She kept her veil on so no one would recognize her, and people stared as if she were nobility, banished to this remote region for some terrible transgression.

They watered and rested the horses and set off, Irinya riding on Veerana, the familiar sway of the camel's back lulling her with a false sense of peace.

But there was no peace now; that brief interlude was over. Ahead of her lay the Rann, beautiful and dangerous—far more so than the men who rode beside her, thinking they had any control over the situation.

CHAPTER 17

I t had been more than two months since the kul moved from this spot, and the grass had begun to recover. Green blades pushed out of the ground, and the brush grew thick, erasing marks of the kul's passage. The sun beat down, relentless, and the air shimmered with heat. The only unnatural thing for miles around was a small canvas tent under a kharijal tree. *Fardan*. Irinya's heart leaped in anticipation.

"You told us your kul moved away from this site," said Tej, halting before the tent, his voice heavy with suspicion.

"Didn't I mention Fardan?" she said with an impatient click of her tongue. "This is our lucky place. We found the silver spider lily a few miles from here. It's good he decided to return; he can help me find another."

"Call him out," ordered Tej.

She cupped her hands to her mouth and shouted, "Fardan! Come out; it's me."

Fardan emerged, scratching his head and yawning, as if he'd been napping. His hair was longer; it fell in unruly curls on his forehead, and she had the absurd desire to push it out of his eyes. She had the even more absurd desire to rush into his arms and cry, but she curbed herself. Had it only been a month and a half since she last saw him? It felt like years. So much had happened, but the worst had been being away from her kul—away from *him*.

"Irinya, you're back." He gave her a sunny smile that lit up his face and made her heart flutter. He jerked a thumb at the guards, his smile fading. "Who are your friends?" he asked in a casual tone.

"Not friends, *minders*." She waved a scornful hand in their direction. "They're the wazir's men, here to keep an eye on me."

He did a double take, his eyes widening. "You're working for the wazir now?" he asked in an awed tone. "The wazir of Gujarat?"

Such excellent acting skills. "Yes. And he wants another spider lily." She dismounted from Veerana and tied him loosely to a tree so he could graze. Beside her, the guards did the same with their horses.

"Will there be money in it for us?" demanded Fardan.

"Of course," said Tej. "The wazir will reward you richly."

"What about the first spider lily, has he rewarded us for that?" asked Fardan with wide-eyed innocence. Irinya gave him a warning glance.

Tej's voice hardened. "The wazir recovered that spider lily from a traitor. Your friend is lucky she wasn't punished for her role in the affair."

Fardan knitted his brows, and she said, for the benefit of the guards, "I'll tell you what happened later. Can we eat? I'm starving. It's too late to go anywhere today."

"Sure," said Fardan. "But I hope you're carrying water."

Tej dumped his pack and sword belt on the ground. "We replenished our waterskins in Bhitiara."

Fardan started a fire to boil water for tea, and the guards unpacked what remained of their rations. Irinya wandered into the bushes, searching for her favorite berries. It was late in the season, and pickings were slim, but she found enough to supplement their meager repast.

It was a strange meal, sitting by the firepit with Fardan on one side, the guards on the other. Even aside from the guards' presence, she felt awkward around him. Had he changed in some way, or had she? She'd thought of him so often during their separation, and now that they were reunited, she couldn't speak freely. She longed to unburden herself to him, to describe in detail everything that had happened, but she could only give him the briefest, most sanitized version in the guards' hearing. She left out all mention of the black chrysanthemum or the sultana. He seemed to understand; he didn't ask any but the most innocent questions: What was Ahmedabad like? Did she see ships in Surat? Was the food delicious? What kind of clothes did people wear?

After eating, the guards sprawled under the shade of a tree and slept, taking turns, as usual, to keep watch. It was all the privacy Irinya was going to get with Fardan, and when he leaned forward to talk to her, she scooted closer to him, eager to hear what he had to say.

"You smell awful," he whispered. "When was your last bath?"

She glared at him, even as her insides writhed in embarrassment. She wished he could have smelled her after her scented bath in the palace. No, no, she didn't mean that. "Fardan Hajani, it is none of your business. Since when have you been so interested in my baths?"

"Since I had to smell you." He sniggered.

She threw a berry at him—too sour to eat, so it wasn't a waste. He ducked, laughing. Then he sobered up. "I'm sorry about Kavi—I mean, Deven. That must have been painful."

She tried to smile. "At least I found him. At least he didn't betray me all the way. In the end, he wanted to do the right thing. And he died for it."

He gave her a sideways glance and lowered his gaze. "I know how you felt about him. I'm sorry I wasn't there to help."

Her face heated and she bit her lip. She'd made Fardan think she liked Deven and accused him of being jealous so he would let her leave the kul without raising an alarm. "Not your fault. I didn't even tell you where I was going."

Fardan didn't really know how she felt about Deven. It was both more and less than he imagined, but she didn't have the words to correct him. It was too messy and complicated. She'd been attracted to Deven, but that flame had been doused by his betrayal. What she felt now was mostly sadness at the way he'd died, and shame at the way she'd hurt Fardan. She needed to talk to him about it, but the thought of it gave her butterflies in the stomach. What was she going to say—*I have feelings for you, too*? He'd think her shallow-hearted, and she wouldn't blame him.

No, safer to stick to the topic of flowers. Her hand went to the locket hidden beneath her blouse. "Deven gave me a gift before dying," she said. She told Fardan about the black chrysanthemum petal and where it had taken her, keeping her voice low. Fardan listened with open-mouthed amazement, but—unlike in the past—he did not interrupt her, nor did he show any disbelief. When she revealed the locket containing the last few drops of the infusion, his eyes widened. He raised his hand as if to touch the locket, and, with obvious effort, withdrew it.

"That is a rare treasure," he murmured, his gaze shifting from the locket back to her. "I would say I envy you, but what would be the point? The flowers choose who they choose. You've beaten me good and proper."

She shifted, uncomfortable with this opinion. She preferred it when he was being combative because she didn't have to feel bad about what she'd done. "*You* were the one who found the silver spider lily, not me. I stole it. And Deven gave me the petal; I didn't find it on my own."

"Yet the flowers somehow ended up with you," he said, rubbing his chin, a thoughtful look on his face.

The sultana had said the same. *Had* the flowers chosen her? She was the only person, as far as she knew, who could hear them—a gift her mother had possessed as well.

"Why did you tell me to stop using the rose?" asked Fardan.

She hesitated. It seemed an overreaction now when she thought of it. But he deserved an answer. "Because every flower has a cost. When I consumed the black chrysanthemum, I remembered a poem my mother had taught me." She recited it to him.

He tilted his head, absorbing the words. When she was done, he gave a mischievous smile. "*Gracious green rose to keep you apart.* What were you afraid of?"

That I'd never see you again. She made a face. "Maybe it's only superstition, but I thought I'd never be reunited with Bholi Masi or the rest of the kul. How much have you told them?"

He shrugged. "Not much, or they'd all have come rushing back here to see you. I said I wanted to hunt flowers in this area for a while. The elders weren't happy about it, especially since I told them about the message sent by the palace to the baniya network. They know we don't have to worry about the quota for the rest of this season. Finally, Miraben said I could go if I returned before the monsoon."

"How are they all doing?" she asked, both needing and dreading the answer.

"Everyone's fine," he said, rubbing his nose and speaking fast. "Don't worry about them."

Fardan always rubbed his nose when he wasn't telling the truth. She narrowed her gaze at him. "You're a terrible liar."

He gazed at her with wide, unblinking eyes. "What do you mean?"

"You have a tell," she said, ruthless. "Now speak. What's going on?"

He sighed, his shoulders slumping. "Your uncle's not too well. He's been coughing a fair bit."

Coldness spread in her stomach. "Old injuries acting up?" Gopal Masa's lungs had been damaged by the years he spent working on his family's salt farm as a child.

Fardan shook his head. "I don't know. Even Bholi is worried this time."

"Tincture of jasmine would help him." She bit her nails, thinking of her precious tincture, confiscated by Imshan Khan. Could she find another jasmine? Could she make a tincture for Gopal Masa and give it to Fardan to take back to the kul?

Fardan studied her. "Tincture of jasmine. That's what you gave us, right? When we were injured from the fight with the baniya's men?"

She took a deep breath and squared her shoulders. "Yes. I think the stories about ill luck befalling hunters who use the flowers are meant to be a deterrent, so flower hunters don't bear the cost of using the flowers. But the costs are unequal. Remember what the poem says about the jasmine?"

"*Sweet white jasmine will betray you in the end,*" he recited.

She nodded. "I think it means that sometimes the jasmine will not work—not when you most need it to. The way it doesn't work for the sultan, for instance. But the benefits of trying far outweigh the costs." She didn't tell him the jasmine had spoken to her, telling her she would need it.

He jerked his chin at the guards. "What's the deal with them? Have they troubled you in any way?"

"Not at all. The wazir said they're my bodyguards." Irinya grimaced. "I think they're here to ensure I don't try to run away."

He gave her a flat stare. "But you're not even going to try, are you?"

She shook her head. "No. The sultana's life is at stake, and Tarana's, too." She leaned against the tree, fatigue creeping up her limbs. "Listen, Fardan, I don't think we can find another spider lily—not this fast. Here's what's going to happen: I'll return empty-handed to the wazir, or maybe we'll get lucky and find a couple of other flowers to assuage him—like a sunflower or a hibiscus. He has a thing for hibiscus. Anyway, I'll beg for more time, and maybe he'll grant it. It will be the end of the season by then, and we'll have to wait until next year. I'll be able to postpone the sultana's execution, buy us more time."

"That's a terrible plan, and you know it," said Fardan, frowning. "The wazir may not grant your request. He might punish you for returning empty-handed. Besides, he already has a spider lily. No telling when he will decide to use it to kill the sultan and his heir and take over the throne. There'll be chaos and bloodshed, and you'll be stranded in the middle of it all. You cannot allow yourself to be in the power of this man."

True words, but what choice did she have? "You have a better plan?" she demanded. "Something that saves me and the sultana *and* the kul?"

He eyed her. "Maybe. Let's try our luck in the Rann first and see what the desert decides to give us. And now, since you look so gloomy, let me lift your spirits with a melody." He withdrew a battered old flute from his pocket.

"Don't you dare!" She sat up, fatigue forgotten. "I'll ask Veerana to bite you."

"I promise I've improved," he said earnestly. He put the flute to his lips and blew, emitting a mournful, discordant sound. Irinya clapped her hands to her ears and Veerana bellowed in alarm. The guards woke up and shouted at Fardan to shut up.

He put away the flute, grinning. "Can I at least draw you?"

"As long as you don't wake me up." She curled up on the grass, tucking her bag underneath her head as a pillow. Fardan ducked inside his tent and returned with a bit of parchment and a lump of charcoal. She remembered all the fine paper and quills she'd seen in Ahmedabad and felt a pang of regret. She hadn't managed to get any for him. He bent over the paper, concentrating, his face absorbed and serious in a way it never was when he was doing anything else. She fell asleep watching him draw, intent on his art, oblivious of the fact that Veerana had shifted closer and was nibbling his hair.

—※—

They left at dawn the next day. Irinya tried to dissuade the guards from accompanying them. They could not help with the flower hunting and would be four more humans she had to watch out for. "The salt desert is a dangerous place," she said. "Fardan and I are used to it, but you are not."

Tej gave her a condescending smile. "We know the true meaning of danger. Sand and sun do not scare us."

"Carry enough water," warned Fardan. "Stay close to us, no matter what happens."

"We have two full waterskins each," said Balbir, Tej's second-in-command. "When we return, we'll have to replenish them in Bhitiara." He cast a dour glance around. "You should have picked a place with water."

"Sometimes there's a pond or a ditch here the animals can use," said Fardan. "But it's late in the hot season, and everything's dry."

"Let's go," said Sameem, the youngest guard, with an impatient flick of his hand.

Irinya led the way to the edge of the grassland and toward the salt desert. The sun had not yet risen, and the air was sharp and cool. The Rann stretched before them, glowing pink in the twilight, looking as beautiful as it always did at this hour. Her heart gave a swoop of gladness mixed with apprehension. The last time she was here, she'd broken a promise by salt and sun. Fardan had forgiven her; would the Rann do the same?

Fardan glanced at her and gave her a reassuring smile, as if he knew what she was thinking. She smiled back at him, her unease dissipating as salt crystals crunched under her feet. If not for him, she would have found it harder venturing back into the Rann. His presence made all the difference.

They didn't find anything that first day, nor did anything of note happen. They returned a few hours later, hot and dusty, and ate a skimpy

meal. Two of the guards rode to Bhitiara and returned at dusk laden
with water and provisions, including a freshly slaughtered chicken. As
they roasted the bird over the fire, Irinya wondered if they had paid
the villagers for all the food they'd brought back. It was unlikely. They
would have shown their weapons and bullied the villagers into parting
with food and water. The poor villagers could not afford to give away
their meager resources for free, but if she tried to tell them that, the
guards would laugh at her.

Tej was in a good mood after eating the chicken. "Let's hope you
have better luck in the coming days," he told her. "I want to go back to
the wazir with positive news at the end of the month."

To Irinya's surprise, they *did* have better luck the next day. Fardan
found a jasmine—a gift from the Rann, just when she'd been thinking
about making a tincture for Gopal Masa. The guards crowded around
Fardan as he warned them about the jasmine thorns. It wasn't a silver
spider lily, but it was something. And Irinya was able to harvest several
thorns.

That night, the guards relaxed by the firepit and drank the arrack
they'd taken from the villagers. They offered some to Fardan, but he
refused and went to sit with Irinya some distance away under a tree. "If
they misbehave," he whispered to her, "run into the wilderness and hide
in the shadows. I'll keep them busy."

Irinya shook her head. "They won't misbehave. They were handpicked by the wazir and won't risk his wrath. They know I'm valuable
to him because he thinks I can find rare flowers."

Fardan glanced at her. "Is that all?" he asked, his voice quiet. "You're
sure he doesn't want anything else from you?"

Surprise pooled in her stomach. "What else could he want?"

Fardan's gaze lingered on her. "Maybe he wants *you*."

She gave a snort of laughter, putting a hand over her mouth to stifle
the sound. "Don't be silly, Fardan. The wazir can have his pick of beautiful ladies from across India. He doesn't see me in that light."

Fardan didn't laugh. "You're beautiful," he said. "Have I ever told
you that?"

Her face heated. "No, you've mostly talked about how beautiful *you*
are," she retorted. He opened his mouth to speak, and she held up

a hand, shushing him. "No, stop. The wazir wants another spider lily, that's all."

Wasn't it? A tiny seed of doubt entered her mind, and she cursed Fardan for planting it. The wazir had sent a message to the baniya network even when he knew it was the one thing he held over her. If he'd wanted to control her, he would have withheld his help. Did he want her to feel indebted to him?

"With or without the flower, you're not going back to Ahmedabad alone," said Fardan, his face set.

She said nothing. She wasn't going to expose Fardan to danger, but there was no point arguing with him right now.

Around the fire, the men laughed and slapped each other's backs, sharing lewd jokes. Their loud, drunken voices were an aberration, a disturbance in the quiet night. She glanced in the direction of the Rann, and her skin tingled.

"A night for Chir Batti," she murmured, leaning toward Fardan.

His forehead creased. "Are you sure? It's a clear night."

She shrugged. "Just don't wander around."

"Wouldn't dream of it." He got up and fetched blankets from his tent. Irinya huddled into one of them and nodded off, her back to a tree trunk, Fardan on one side of her and Veerana's comforting bulk on the other.

She woke a while later to find Fardan crouching beside her, shaking her shoulder. She sat up, bleary and disoriented. It was pitch dark—a new moon night, although the stars shone like beacons in the sky. Close to the ground, however, a mist hung over the grass, obscuring Fardan's face.

Alarm bells rang in her mind, chasing away sleep. The mist was always perilous. "What's going on?"

"One of the guards has vanished," said Fardan, his voice urgent, his face pinched with anxiety. "The leader wants to organize a search."

She woke all the way up, coldness seeping into her bones. If they lost their way in the mist, they might end up in the Rann, and Chir Batti would not leave them alive. "The fools." She scrambled to her feet and walked toward the blurry silhouettes of the three remaining guards, Fardan close behind her.

The guards were talking to each other in low tones. Tej turned to her when she approached, the whites of his eyes shining through the mist. "Balbir is gone," he rasped.

Irinya hugged herself, trying not to shiver. Every sense screamed danger. She wanted to be safely asleep with Bholi Masi and Gopal Masa in their tent, not exposed to the mist this close to the Rann. "When was the last time you saw him?" she asked.

"He had the first watch, so two hours ago," said Tej. His gaze bounced from one mist-shrouded spot to another. "Then it was Sameem's turn, but Balbir didn't wake him up. Luckily, Sameem has the skill of waking whenever he needs to, so he was up in time for his watch. When he didn't see Balbir, he alerted the rest of us."

"You should wait for him to return on his own," said Fardan, stepping beside Irinya. "He could have gone to relieve himself."

"For half an hour?" Tej shook his head. "That's just how long we've been awake. He could have been gone a lot longer than that."

"You must wait till morning." Fardan put a hand on Tej's arm, his voice persuasive. "Night is a dangerous time to roam around here, and the mist makes it a hundred times more so. Suppose you stumble into the Rann by mistake?"

Tej made an impatient noise and shook off Fardan's hand. "You called the Rann dangerous, but I didn't see anything to be concerned about. It's the same now, except there isn't any light. We'll carry torches." He gestured to the other two guards, and they went off to look for suitable branches.

"If you end up in the Rann, you might never make your way out," warned Irinya, trying to control her frustration. "Out on the salt flats, the mist creates phantoms that can break your mind. Even if your mind survives intact, Chir Batti will lure you to your deaths."

"Superstition," said Tej with a dismissive wave as the guards returned with a few spindly branches. "Is that the best you can do?" he barked.

"It's a grassland, sir," said Sameem, sounding peeved.

They lit the ends of the branches from the embers of their fire. The light only served to enhance the ghostly quality of the mist. Irinya glanced in the direction of the Rann, and her gut clenched. She couldn't see anything because of the mist, but somewhere out there, Chir Batti danced, waiting for its next victim. Had it already taken Balbir? She shuddered, and Fardan squeezed her shoulder. She inched closer to him, glad of his presence.

"You need to come with us," said Tej to Irinya.

She cut her gaze back to him, her muscles tensing. "No," she said flatly. "It's not safe. I can't stop you, but I won't risk myself or Fardan. We need to be fit to hunt flowers again tomorrow, remember?"

He seemed about to argue with her, then changed his mind. "Fine. Stay here. We should be back soon."

"Don't follow the ghost light, no matter what you see!" Irinya called as the three guards walked away.

Tej raised a hand in farewell, and the men moved farther into the grassland, dissolving into the mist. Their torches flickered in the thick dark, and they shouted the missing man's name. After a while, their voices grew fainter, and silence returned to the night.

Don't go, Irinya thought, her throat aching. But it was her mother who stood before her, waving goodbye before vanishing forever into the mist.

Snap out of it; that was years ago. Irinya collapsed before the embers, rubbing her arms. Perhaps the guards would get lucky and survive the night. And perhaps they would end up dead or missing, like Urmila. Why was she thinking of her mother right now?

Fardan fetched one of his blankets and offered it to her. She accepted with gratitude, stretching part of it over his legs as he sprawled next to her. The light from the dying fire fell on his face, calm and unruffled as always. She exhaled, some of the tension seeping out of her limbs. His solid, familiar presence would keep the strangeness of the night at bay; she just had to stay close to him.

"What do you think happened to the missing guard?" he asked, lacing his hands beneath his head.

"I don't know," said Irinya, biting her nails. *The same thing that happened to my mother,* she did not say.

"Balbir!" came a faint voice, and Irinya jumped. It had come from the *other* side, between them and the Rann.

"The fools," she repeated. She knotted her hands in her lap, her throat tight, wishing the men had listened to her and Fardan.

"You can't help them." Fardan propped himself up on one elbow and fixed his gaze on her. "Maybe they'll get lucky and return safely."

Although this was what she was hoping, Irinya shook her head, thinking of the jasmine they'd found and the lack of nasty surprises the Rann had thrown at them in the last couple of days. "They've used up all their luck already."

"*Now* you're being superstitious," said Fardan in a reproving tone.

There was a sudden scream, abruptly choked off. Irinya's stomach seized. She must have started to get up, for she found Fardan's hand clamped around her elbow, pulling her back down. "Don't move," he grated. "Don't even think of going anywhere."

The scream was followed by a long, drawn-out wail. It sounded like an animal being tortured. Irinya covered her face with her hands and tried to still the trembling of her body. Was that one of the guards? What could make someone cry like that?

Fardan placed his hand on her back, his touch warm and sure. "It will be okay," he whispered. "Trust me."

But the wail still reverberated in her ears, and Urmila stroked her head, telling her that the things you saw in the mist became real. And she left, walking into the night from which she would never return. Irinya could not move, could not call out and beg her to come back before it was too late. She drew a shaky breath, and Fardan sat up and slipped an arm around her, anchoring her to the present.

She dropped her hands and faced him—the one person in the world who could understand what she was feeling. "My mother," she said, barely able to get the words out. "My mother went like this."

He shook his head. "Not like this. She loved the Rann. She went of her own free will. Whatever she saw, it was far different from what these men are seeing."

A distant howl split the night, sending tremors up her spine. She twisted her neck to scan their surroundings, her heart thumping, but the mist still obscured the grasslands. Had it been a cheetah? A jackal? Or something else? "Do you think it will come here?" she said, her voice wavering.

"Look at me, Irinya." She turned to face him, and he lay back on the grass, gently pulling her down next to him and tugging the blanket over them. She rested on her side, gazing into his hazel eyes, feeling his warm breath on her cheeks. "There is no *it*. They have wandered into the Rann and are seeing things in the mist and are scared. That is all." His voice was so calm, so sure, that some of the tightness left her chest, and her breath evened out.

"My mother said that what you see in the mist becomes real. Or you become less real, I don't know which. And when Chir Batti beckons, you run after it, because it's the one bright, true thing left in a world of darkness." Was she remembering bits and pieces of her mother because of what was happening to the guards? If that was the cost, it was too high, and she wanted no more of it.

"*We* are not seeing anything in the mist," said Fardan firmly. "And we are certainly not following Chir Batti. We are in the old campsite, you and I, and we are staying put."

As he spoke, an awful desire came over her to get up and walk into the desert, to confront the worst of what was out there. Hadn't her mother done the same?

As if he read her thoughts, Fardan put an arm around her and scooted closer. "You'll have to walk over my corpse to go anywhere tonight."

She gave a shaky laugh. Why was her heart beating so fast? Was it his nearness, or was it the night? His face was mere inches away from hers. "If Bholi could see you, she'd beat you senseless," she said, keeping her tone light.

His mouth quirked. "Lucky for me she's not here then."

She stared at him, her hands itching to smooth the hair away from his forehead, stroke his stubbled cheeks, and trace the outline of his jaw. Her breath hitched, and she closed her eyes, biting her lips. *What's wrong with me?*

Another scream. Irinya flinched at the terror and agony embedded in that sound—like someone begging for the release of death.

"Hush," said Fardan, and she realized she was babbling about the guards, about no one deserving that kind of end. He drew her closer, and she laid her head on his chest, the steady beat of his heart slowing her own frantically racing one.

He stroked her head. "Do you remember the story of the moon and the sunflower?"

"Of course," said Irinya, her voice muffled, knowing he was trying to distract her. "I remember all of Elder Chinmay's stories. It's one of my favorites."

He kissed the top of her head, and warmth pooled in her stomach. "Tell it to me, Irinya. Tell it just the way Chinmay did."

Irinya drew back a little so she could look at his face. How would telling a story help right now? But Fardan had asked for Chinmay's story, and she would not deny him. "Then listen." Her voice took on the cadence of a storyteller. "Once, the moon lost her favorite jewel, a white pearl the ocean had gifted her. She was really upset about it."

Fardan smiled and brushed her cheek with the back of his hand, making her skin tingle. "Did she find it?"

"Not right away." Irinya sat up and took a deep breath, trying to focus on the words so she didn't have to think about anything else. "Each night, she searched the earth, shining her light on deserts and mountains, cities and seas, but she had no luck. One day, she spied it around the neck of an ordinary peasant girl. The moon took her maiden-shape and went to the girl to demand its return. The girl refused. The sun had given it to her, she said, and it belonged to her."

A sobbing shriek split the air, much closer than before. Irinya jerked around, clutching Fardan's shirt in her fist, her heart pounding.

"That can't have made her happy," said Fardan, his voice calm, as if they sat around the kul campfire and not by themselves in a misty night pierced by the screams of lost men.

She turned back to him, swallowing, and let go of his shirt. "The moon was furious," she said, but her voice trembled, and she stopped.

"Go on," said Fardan gently, his eyes glowing in the light of the embers.

She counted to ten, forcing blankness in her mind, and continued, "She asked the sun what business he had giving her pearl to a human. The sun protested that all he'd done was shine his light on it; the girl had picked it up herself. To appease the moon, the sun gave her a special flower that would find anything she lost in the future."

"Did that appease her?" Fardan asked with wide-eyed interest.

She shook her head. "Not a bit." She felt calmer now, as if the story had loosened the knots in her chest. "She threw the sunflower to the earth and never spoke to the sun again. That's why we don't see them together in the sky. And that's where our magic sunflower comes from."

"Ah." Fardan gave a happy sigh. "I like this version. It's not dark like most of the other stories." He pulled her back down next to him and resumed stroking her head, his hand gentle, as if she were a child. His touch soothed her, just as telling the story had.

"I wish Elder Chinmay was still around," she murmured. "He would have told me if I was good enough to replace you as his heir."

Fardan chuckled. "You're the storyteller, I'm the artist. He always knew that. We should make a book of the flower stories. You write them down, and I'll do the illustrations. Deal?"

She smiled. "Deal."

There was another scream, but distant this time, distorted, as if they were hearing it through a wall. She shivered, and Fardan drew the blanket up on top of them. "Sleep," he said, putting his arms around her. "I'll wake you at first light."

She thought she wouldn't be able to. But she felt safe in his arms, cocooned under the blanket, as if the terrors of the night could not reach her there. She closed her eyes and breathed in his rugged, familiar scent, and sleep overwhelmed her.

Moments later, it seemed, a cheerful voice rudely interrupted her dreams. "Hey, sleepyhead. Time for tea."

She sat up groggily, the blanket falling away from her. The mist had dissipated, and the eastern sky was rose-pink. Fardan was crouched by the firepit, boiling water.

Had she fallen asleep in his arms? Fantasized about caressing his face and hair? Her cheeks went hot with embarrassment. Her entire being must have been desperate for a distraction from the terrors of the night. Bholi Masi would have a fit. Thankfully, Bholi Masi need never know.

Shameless hussy, came Veerana's dour voice. *You better make an honest man of him.*

She twisted back and glared at the camel, sitting beneath a tree and chewing his cud with a judgmental look on his face. *Nothing happened,* she wanted to shout.

Not between her and Fardan, at any rate. She rubbed her arms and watched him brew tea. Had the guards survived? What was she going to tell the wazir if they went missing? The kul had no records of people making it out after nights spent in the Rann, not when mist hung like a miasma over the land. Irinya's mother had been the only one in years to even make the attempt. Perhaps Urmila had believed she would be the exception—or perhaps she had *chosen* to leave Irinya. But that thought made her throat ache, and Irinya pushed it away.

Fardan glanced at her and gave her a sunny smile. She smiled back, her shoulders relaxing. Thank the goddess she had him by her side. This would have been much harder on her own. Of all the people in the world to be with on a misty night at the edge of the Rann, none was better than Fardan—solid, unflappable, and a decent cook to boot. She remembered his wounded expression when she'd deliberately hurt him, and her heart squeezed.

"I'm sorry," she blurted out.

He glanced at her with raised eyebrows, then turned his attention back to pouring the tea into two earthen cups. He passed one to her and blew on the other to cool it down. She wrapped her hands around her cup, reveling in the warmth and fragrance.

"You didn't ask me what I'm sorry for," she said.

He ducked his head and sipped his tea, rubbing the back of his neck. Then he raised his head and gave a familiar grin. "'Sorry' won't save you from Bholi's wrath, and neither will I. How much are you going to tell them?"

He'd deflected that neatly. She wanted to apologize properly, to tell him he was more important to her than all the Kavis of this world, real and fake. But the thought made her toes curl, especially after last night. He'd only been comforting her, so why had she felt a spark of something other than friendship from him? And after all this time, all that she'd done, how did he feel about her? Later, when the fate of the sultanate no longer hung on the stem of a single flower, she would ask him.

He threw a grass stalk at her. "What're you thinking?"

She brushed it away. "I'm going into the Rann to look for the guards."

"*We* are going," Fardan corrected her. "But you know we may not find them." *Or find them alive,* he did not need to add.

She gave a slow exhale. "We'll try." If only they'd listened to her. If only she'd warned them about not venturing into the Rann at night *before* they arrived here, perhaps they would have taken her seriously.

He unrolled the last of his rotlas. "For one day, we will try. We'll retrace our route from yesterday and circle back using a different path. And now, I think, some food will do us both good."

Silence returned, but it was a comfortable silence, punctuated by slurps of tea. They dipped pieces of rotla in the tea to soften them before eating. As the sun peeked over the horizon, chasing away the shadows, she could not understand why she'd been so afraid last night. This was where she'd lived most of her life. She knew the rules, and she'd never broken them—except that one time she broke her promise. The guards were strangers to this land and had not understood. Still, they were men of courage and experience. Perhaps they had survived the ordeal.

No, she didn't quite believe that. She shivered as she remembered the screams she'd heard last night.

They got ready, packing extra waterskins in case they found the missing guards. Fardan carried the jasmine in a small wooden box for "luck." He didn't say more, but she knew what he meant. Jasmine was the flower of hope and healing, after all.

In the golden yellow light of the early-morning sun, they walked to the edge of the grassland, salt crystals crackling under their feet.

Irinya was overwhelmed with a sense that she'd done this before. Not flower hunting in the Rann with Fardan; of course she'd done that umpteen times. This was different, a memory of a similar situation. She'd gone into the Rann to find someone who shouldn't have been there. But that didn't make any sense. She would have remembered it if she had.

They entered the salt desert, not speaking, preserving their strength for the hike ahead. The Rann stretched before them, beautiful and empty, glowing in the morning light. A moving meditation, to traverse the desert at that hour. Irinya knew she should be grateful for it, but she couldn't calm herself enough to enjoy it. Her thoughts kept jumping from the missing guards to the mystery person she'd once gone looking for. Where had that memory come from? Was it a story she'd heard from someone else? She walked at an even pace, trying not to anticipate the worst.

In half an hour, the sun was high enough that they had to stop to drink water and shield their eyes. Fardan wrapped a white headcloth around himself, and Irinya did the same with her dupatta. But when she resumed walking, he did not follow.

"What's the matter?" she asked, but she already knew, had already sensed it from his tense posture.

He pointed. "See that?"

Around fifty yards to the west, a dark heap lay unmoving on the ground, looking out of place and faintly menacing.

Her heart sank. It could only be one thing—a human body. But whose? She stared at it, rubbing her arms with her hands, cold despite the glaring sun. Was it a foreign scout or one of the missing guards?

Fardan glanced at her. "I can go check, if you'd rather not."

She shook her head, pressing her lips together. "The least I can do is be a witness."

In silence, they made their way toward the unmoving object. As they drew closer, the heap resolved into the shape of a human body. Irinya squared her shoulders. She'd seen dead bodies before. The body was only a skin people left behind when they went elsewhere.

But nothing could have prepared her for the expression on the poor man's face, frozen in a rictus of terror. She flinched away from it. His mouth was open in a soundless scream, and his sightless eyes stared up into the sky, a world of horror within them. What had he seen in the moment of his death? His turban was loose, his clothes torn, although she saw no obvious wounds. Perhaps he had torn the clothes himself.

"Sam . . . Sameem," she managed. The youngest of the four guards.

Fardan woke from a daze. "What?"

"That was his name." She gripped Fardan's arm. "Are you okay?"

He shook his head. "No. Are you?"

She couldn't lie. "No." It had only been a small chance that any of the guards would still be alive, but even so, the reality of the body and the expression on Sameem's face had shaken her. She'd known this person, even though it had only been for a few days. Somewhere he must have a family who depended on him and waited for him to come home. And now he never would. Her vision blurred.

Fardan took a deep breath. "We'll have to leave him here."

"I know. His body will be washed to sea when the rains arrive." She knelt and tugged Sameem's turban over his face. There was little else she could do for him. She stood and swallowed the lump in her throat. "May you find water and rest in the garden of death."

Fardan repeated her words. "Should we go on?" he asked.

"We must." There wasn't much point to it, but they had to make the effort.

They found Balbir an hour later, lying spread-eagled on the ground, his face swollen red like a watermelon.

Fardan made to move closer, but Irinya clutched his arm. She'd spotted a black-and-orange wasp as big as her palm crawling up the dead man's equally swollen chest.

"Flower eater," she whispered. The man had been stung in multiple places. He would have died in slow agony from the poison. That explained some of the screaming. Had Chir Batti lured him to a hive?

The two-inch-long stinger at the tip of the wasp's abdomen quivered, as if sensing their approach. Fardan swallowed visibly, and they backed away, not relaxing until they'd put more than a hundred yards between themselves and the unfortunate Balbir.

"That was the missing man," said Irinya, her voice uneven.

"He's likely to be the farthest out," said Fardan. "Even if he isn't, we need to head back now."

Irinya nodded, fighting down her nausea. "We'll circle back."

They turned east, making a large circle so they could cover more ground. But they didn't find the two remaining guards: Tej, the leader, or the nameless guard who had been the fourth. It bothered her that she didn't remember his name. The guards had not been her friends, but neither had they been bad or cruel men. They'd followed the wazir's orders, that was all. They'd been sent here to protect her; instead, they'd become victims themselves. Guilt settled into her stomach, as heavy as salt. She should have tried harder to stop them from going into the Rann at night. How would she explain what had happened to the wazir? Would he believe her, or would he blame her for their deaths? She was no closer to finding another silver spider lily; returning empty-handed without the guards might get her executed along with the sultana.

Late that afternoon, as they made their exhausted way back to the campsite, Fardan finally echoed her thoughts. "That first body we found—what must he have seen to make him look like that?"

"His worst imaginings brought to life." She collapsed under a tree next to Veerana, who nuzzled her shoulder. "That's what the mist does. And Chir Batti takes you deeper into it."

He sat next to her and passed her a fresh gourd of water. "His worst imaginings or his best."

"Yes, that's how it lures you." She tilted the gourd to her lips and drank deeply, trying to drown the memory of those dead faces. But they drifted before her eyes, accusing her, in pained silence, of having abandoned them. She set the gourd down, her shoulders slumping under the weight of the knowledge that she hadn't done enough to prevent this tragedy.

Fardan glanced at her. "It's not your fault. We tried to stop them. Men like that—they don't listen. Chir Batti is the guardian of the Rann. It does what it does for a reason."

She stiffened. "You think it took my mother for a reason?"

He held her gaze. "We don't know what happened to your mother," he said, his voice gentle. "She was a flower hunter of great skill. You cannot compare the two situations."

She bit her lip. He was right. "Well, we can guess what happened last night. Chir Batti used the mist to make phantoms, horrific enough that it killed Sameem just to see them. Balbir was lured to a hive. The other two most likely met similar ends."

"The Rann gave us a jasmine and took the four guards," said Fardan slowly, his eyes unfocused. "There is an opportunity in this."

She nodded, grasping at the silver lining in their current situation. "You could take the jasmine back to the kul. Make a tincture for my uncle."

His gaze went back to her. "And you?"

She took a deep breath. "I'll continue looking for another spider lily. He gave me a month, so I still have more than two weeks left." Not that it was enough. Even two years might not be enough to find another spider lily. She shuddered at the thought of the wazir's reaction to her failure and to the death of his guards. Would he turn his wrath on her kul? It wasn't just the sultana who was in danger; it was *all* of them.

"You're not going to find another spider lily, and you know it." Fardan crossed his arms, his face set. "And you're not going anywhere without me this time."

She looked at him, his curly hair, his hazel eyes, his serious expression, and something hot and painful tugged at her heart. "There's nothing you can do to help. You'd be one more person he can use against me, don't you see? Just like he's using the sultana." Only this would be infinitely worse. She liked and admired the sultana, but Fardan meant much more to her. The thought of him falling into the wazir's blood-stained hands made her nauseous.

Fardan got up abruptly and went over to where the soldiers had left their packs.

"What are you doing?" said Irinya, puzzled.

He emptied the packs on the ground, his face intent. A flash of unease went through her. Of course, they would take the food and water; it made no sense to waste those. But Fardan was picking through the dead men's clothes, examining and discarding them.

"I have an idea," he said with a grin, holding a tunic up to his waist.

Her stomach dropped. So *that* was what he was thinking of doing. The fool. "No. *Never.*" She got up, her throat dry, her fists clenched as if she could knock some sense into him.

"You haven't even heard me out," he protested.

"I don't need to," she shouted.

"They left most of their weapons here." He waved a hand at the swords and spears laid against a tree trunk. "And we have their horses. It's the best disguise."

"No," she repeated, forcing her voice down. "Fardan, that is the most ridiculous and audacious idea you've ever had."

"Thanks," he said, looking pleased.

"It was not a compliment," she snapped. "I've already seen one man being blown from a cannon. I do *not* want to watch it happen to my friends." Even just saying it aloud made her gut clench.

He dropped the tunic on the ground, came over to her, and grasped her shoulders, levity gone. "Listen, Irinya. What choice do we have? What are you going to tell him when you go back to the palace? That the Rann took all four of his men? You think he'll believe you? Even if he does, you won't find another spider lily. We could spend the rest of our lives looking and never find another. He has the only one. That makes him utterly powerful."

"*I know*." She narrowed her eyes at him. "What are you planning to do to make him less powerful?"

"Walk in and grab the spider lily," he said with a gleeful smile.

Her heart plummeted to her feet. "Have you taken leave of your senses?" She pushed his hands away and stepped back, crossing her arms, trying to breathe. Fardan would get cut down the moment he reached for the flower.

"I know it won't be easy," he said, in his most persuasive tone. "But dressed like those guards, on their horses, people won't give us a second look. And when we enter the fort, his eyes will be on you. Didn't you say he carries the flower with him in his breast pocket? We just need the right moment to snatch it from him. We take him unawares; we take the flower."

This was all nonsense, but she couldn't help asking, "Even if you managed that, how many seconds do you think you'll live after snatching it?"

"We need a way to get out fast." His gaze went meaningfully to her chest.

"What are you staring at?" she demanded, wanting to box his ears.

He summoned an injured look. "The locket you hide beneath your kameez. Why—what did you think?"

A flush rose from her neck to her face, and her desire to box his ears increased severalfold. Couldn't he have just *said* what he wanted instead of making her think he was staring at her chest? She withdrew the locket from underneath her kameez and glared at him. "What about it?"

"Do you think you could spare the remaining infusion?" he asked. "I know it's all you have left from what Deven gave you."

"Of course I can *spare* it." Did he think she needed a memento from Deven? She'd remember him just as well without it. "But I may not have time to use it. Your plan is too risky."

He rubbed his chin. "How much do you have?"

"A few drops," she said. "Enough for one door, I think."

"One door is all we need." He stared at the locket, his eyes full of yearning. Was it the fast escape he coveted or the door itself? She wouldn't blame him for the latter. And to think she'd wasted so much of the petal trying to reach the sultana!

"Here." She unclasped the locket from the chain and held it out.

His face went slack with surprise. "Why are you giving it to me?"

To test you. "To make a door," she said, watching him. Would he take the bait? "Isn't that what you want? This foolhardy plan won't work. One of us will end up dead for sure. Isn't it better if you simply take the infusion? Doors aren't exactly safe, either. You never know where you'll end up. But at least you won't be riding to certain death."

For a moment, he wavered, his eyes fixed on the locket.

Take it, she thought. *Make a door and step through it. No matter what happens, at least you'll be safe from the wazir.* Her heart squeezed at the thought that he might leave her alone, but still, she had to offer him the choice.

He cut his gaze to her and frowned. "I know what you're doing, and it won't work."

She sighed, half-relieved, half-disappointed, and slipped the locket back onto the chain around her neck. "Even if I go along with this dangerous plan of yours, there were four guards, and there is only one of you. Are you planning to magically copy yourself?"

He grinned. "Way ahead of you there. Jai, Pranal, and Ayush should be in Bhitiara by now, waiting for me."

"Are you out of your mind?" She stared at him, aghast. "Ayush is a baby!" How could Fardan think of exposing the youngest of them all to danger? Suppose something happened to him or Pranal; how would she tell their mother? How would she live with herself?

"He's nearly sixteen," countered Fardan. "And he's grown a bit taller. We'll bulk him up with clothes."

"No." She shook her head, closing her ears with her hands, as if she could unhear his reckless, madcap plan. "You'll all be killed."

He pried her hands away, his expression serious. "It's the only way out—the only way we can get back the spider lily. If your sultana is as honorable as you seem to think, she'll use that flower against the Portuguese invaders, and she'll give us enough money to pay off our debt. We'll never need to worry about the baniya again. Otherwise, it's the end of flower hunting for us. The end of a lot of things."

Horribly, it made sense. It offered a slice of hope, however thin. But the thought of walking into Bhadra Fort with her childhood friends disguised as the wazir's dead guards made her insides roil. The wazir would see through their disguises the moment he looked at them. He would be doubly, triply angry with her; she'd returned without a second spider lily, without his guards, and she'd had the temerity to try to deceive him. He might kill them all on the spot. She chewed her lip, her mind working. "There must be another way. A way that doesn't involve your stomach being ripped by a sword."

"No sword will dare enter my stomach," Fardan assured her. "It's made of iron."

She glared at him. Was that supposed to make her feel better? *No, Fardan,* she wanted to shout. *You're made of flesh and blood, weak and vulnerable. If the wazir pierces you with his blade, you will die. I'm dying just thinking of it.* "I can't go along with this. I just can't."

"Look, how about this," he said in a cajoling tone. "At the first sign of danger, you open a door and take us through it. *Anywhere.*"

"It doesn't work like that." She pressed a knuckle against her mouth. "I don't know how I opened those doors in the first place."

"You just have to drink the remaining drops of chrysanthemum, right? It worked once; it'll work again."

"You don't *know* that."

He caught her hand and squeezed it. "I know this is the best chance we'll have of recovering the spider lily. Of saving your sultana. Of saving ourselves. If you think of something better, tell me."

He went back to the soldiers' stuff and began sorting it, food and water on one side, clothes on the other. After a while, she got up and helped him. Not because she'd accepted his plan, but because she couldn't think of anything better, and she couldn't go back to the kul. Lives depended on her: Zahra, Tarana, the kul, Fardan, the other flower hunters. And not just individual lives, but the fate of the sultanate—of all of India—rested on her. The weight of it pressed down on her shoulders, and she longed to set it aside. To have no one be dependent on her. To walk into the Rann and never return.

The last thought unsettled her. Perhaps it was what her mother had thought when she left Irinya and walked into the night.

But Irinya was not her mother. She might long for freedom, but she'd never desert those who needed her. She sorted the clothes, food, and weapons, weaving different scenarios in her mind, each more terrible than the last. At least she had her blowpipe and a new set of jasmine thorns. She would convert the thorns to darts before sunset today. She didn't know if she could shoot the wazir in cold blood, but the blowpipe was her only weapon apart from the door. She would use it if she had to.

CHAPTER 18

They rode to Bhitiara the next morning, Irinya on Veerana and Fardan on one of the horses, holding the reins of the rest.

She'd spent a wakeful night in his tent while he slept outside it, right at the entrance, as if guarding her from monsters. She couldn't stop thinking about the previous night: the ghostly mist, the bone-chilling screams, the distant howl. Finally, she'd risen and poked her head out of the tent. It was cold and quiet but for Fardan's snores and snuffles. *That boy* was noisy even while asleep. She'd gazed at him, her lips twitching, and the strangeness of the previous night had fallen away. He'd held her and put her to sleep like a child—like her own mother might have done once. She'd fit in his arms like she belonged there. The thought heated her insides. When had her feelings for him changed? Had it been during their separation? Or earlier still when she'd deliberately hurt him and realized that he liked her? *Do you still like me, Fardan?* she wanted to ask. *Do you still think of me?* She tossed and turned on her blanket, wishing she were back in his arms, and it was a long time before sleep finally took her.

Half a mile from Bhitiara, they dismounted and tied the horses to a tree. It wouldn't do to raise the villagers' curiosity about their original riders. Fardan went ahead on Veerana while Irinya stayed with the horses. They cropped grass, indifferent to the fates of their owners, and Irinya picked berries to supplement their food and to calm herself.

How much had Fardan told the other flower hunters? They must blame her for both the loss of Chinmay and the loss of the spider lily, and rightly so. She wished, for the hundredth time, that she'd left the flower alone, that she had not been dazzled by Deven into parting with such a priceless treasure. She wished even more fervently that she had never met the wazir and become entangled in his schemes. She was walking a tightrope over an abyss; if she looked too hard and long at their so-called plan, she'd plunge into darkness, taking her entire kul along with her.

Fardan returned an hour later, Ayush perched behind him on Veerana while Jai and Pranal followed on foot. She crossed her arms as they approached, her gladness at seeing them tempered by the tension churning her stomach. Ayush seemed slightly taller, but he was as slender as ever, putting Irinya in mind of a weed. In what world did Fardan think they could make him look like a soldier? Pranal wasn't much better. Only Fardan and Jai were well-built, and even they knew nothing of the fighting arts.

As Fardan and Ayush dismounted, she blurted out, "None of you should agree to his pigeon-brained scheme. I'll think of something else." Not that she'd been able to think of anything else yet, but there had to be another way. Even if there wasn't, and this was their best chance to get back the spider lily, how could she let her friends walk into the wazir's lair? It was akin to walking into a hungry tiger's cage.

"Hello, Irinya, nice to see you, too," said Ayush, grinning.

Jai frowned. "What pigeon-brained scheme? He told us we're going to get a better price for our flowers."

Irinya cut her eyes to Fardan. "You haven't told them?" she accused.

"Let's get away from here first," said Fardan with an airy wave of his hand. "We can talk when we stop later in the evening."

"Nice, expensive horses," said Pranal, patting the nose of the nearest one. "Where did you steal them? Wait—" He turned to Fardan, his eyes wide. "They belong to those soldiers, don't they?"

"Later." Fardan glanced behind his shoulder as if he expected the dead men to chase after him. "Let's go."

They untied the horses and each of the boys mounted one. Irinya rode on Veerana along with all their provisions. The guards' bags hung on either side of her, concealing their clothes and weapons. It felt wrong somehow—worse than taking their horses. Nothing good would come of stealing from the dead and trying to pass yourself off as one of them. It dishonored them. But if she said that aloud, Fardan would say she was being superstitious.

"Where are we going?" asked Pranal.

"Ahmedabad," said Fardan with a grin.

Irinya shot him a glare. "*I'm* going to Ahmedabad. You all return to the kul."

But no one listened to her. Ayush pumped a fist in the air. "I've always wanted to go to the sultanate capital. Ma would have a fit if she knew. Do you think we'll see the sultan?"

"Don't be silly," said Jai. "You'll be lucky to see the sultan's servant."

"It has the biggest flower market in Gujarat," said Pranal with a satisfied smile.

"It has soldiers with swords and a power-mad wazir who likes to tie people to the mouths of cannons and blow them to pieces," Irinya shouted. "I know, because I saw it happen!"

They finally looked at her, their smiles fading. Fardan reached over and squeezed her hand. "We'll be fine, Irinya. This is the only way. I'm sure they'll agree."

"We'll decide what to do once we've heard you both out," said Jai in a tone of finality.

Irinya fell silent. If they had any more sense than Fardan did, they'd go right back home once they heard the dangerous scheme he'd cooked up.

When dusk fell, they stopped for the night near the ropy roots of a large, spreading banyan tree. Pranal dug a hole and built a small fire away from its branches. They sat cross-legged around the fire while Fardan produced food from the soldiers' packs: flatbreads, pickles, dried lentil kebabs, and the berries Irinya had picked earlier that day. The boys had brought more provisions from Bhitiara, but they decided to save those for later.

"What happened to the soldiers?" asked Ayush, popping a kebab in his mouth and chewing with obvious enjoyment. "This is their stuff, right? Everyone in Bhitiara was complaining about how they grabbed food and water without paying for it."

"The Rann took them," said Fardan flatly. "Why don't you make tea, and I'll tell you everything once we finish eating."

Jai, Pranal, and Ayush exchanged wary glances. "I get the feeling I'm not going to like what you have to say," said Jai, leaning back with his palms on the ground.

"You never like anything I have to say," retorted Fardan with a grin. "But I'm always one hundred percent right."

Irinya rolled her eyes. Pranal said, "Not even ten percent, but we forgive you because you're entertaining."

"Only when he isn't playing the flute," Jai pointed out.

"True, true," said Pranal. "Little brother, make the tea strong and sweet. I think we'll need it."

Ayush put a pot of water on to boil. "They have nice tea and sugar," he said, sniffing the contents of a couple of small sachets. "We missed our vocation."

"What? To steal stuff?" said Irinya.

He gave her a reproving look. "To *redistribute* stuff in our favor. We should have been soldiers."

"You'd be dead in the training ground before your first battle," said Pranal in a caustic tone.

The boys continued to rib each other. Irinya held her hands out to the fire, glad of the little circle of light and companionship against the oncoming night. Fardan doled out the food, and Ayush poured tea into five earthen cups, one for each of them. Ayush was right; the soldiers' food was good, but she preferred Fardan's cooking. It was a surprising thought to have. It must be all the lunches he'd packed for her over the years they'd hunted flowers together—not that she'd dream of telling him. He already had a high opinion of his skills.

"All right," said Jai after they'd eaten, wiping his hands on the grass. "Now that my stomach is full, I am ready to hear about your pigeon-brained scheme."

Fardan set down his cup and laced his hands together. "It all started when I found a silver spider lily—"

"You found a *what*?" interrupted Ayush.

"Liar," said Jai, shaking his head.

"Where is it?" demanded Pranal.

Fardan spread his hands, a tragic look on his face. "I don't have it anymore. I gave the flower to Kavi because I thought he would give it to the sultan to save us all from foreign invaders."

Irinya stared at him, surprise robbing her of breath. That wasn't what had happened. Why was he lying to their friends? Was he trying to shield her from their criticism?

"You donkey!" cried Jai. "You *gave it away*? That flower could have freed our entire kul from debt."

"I know. I'm sorry I was so foolish." Fardan hung his head, and Pranal smacked his shoulder with a twig.

Warmth flooded her. He wanted to spare her feelings, but she wasn't going to let him take the blame for her mistake. She deserved their criticism, and they deserved the truth, no matter how painful it was for her to admit it. "I'm the one who stole the flower and gave it to Kavi," she said in a calm voice. "I'm the foolish one."

Jai gave her a thoughtful glance and transferred his gaze back to Fardan. "Tell us everything. And no more lies."

Fardan sighed and gestured to Irinya. "It's your story more than mine. Do you want to tell it?"

She nodded. "When you've heard my story, you can decide what to do. I should never have broken my promise to Fardan." She started with the spider lily, her journey to Bhuj, her encounter with the wazir, and her employment in his caravan. She went on to describe her meeting with the real Kavi, her confession to the wazir, and their journey to Surat. The words stuck in her throat when she told them how Deven had died. Fardan passed her a gourd of water. After a few sips, she was able to continue. Her listeners' eyes got bigger and rounder as she recounted her travels with the black chrysanthemum.

"I don't believe it," burst out Pranal, thumping the ground with his fist. "Why do *you* get to have all the adventures?"

"It wasn't an *adventure*," she rasped, her stomach shriveling as she remembered how the first door had landed her on a Portuguese ship. "I was scared all the time."

"The flowers choose who they choose," said Fardan softly, echoing his own words.

The four of them stared at Irinya as if she'd grown wings. It made her hot and uncomfortable. "Don't look at me like that. I made the wrong decision, and it's gotten us into trouble. Nothing to do with being chosen."

Jai leaned forward, his face intent. "Can we see it? The bit that's left?"

She lifted the locket and showed it to him. "I don't want to open it. Suppose it evaporates? But I think there's enough for one door."

Jai sighed, a familiar longing on his face. They all felt it—the pull of a rare flower, the one that everyone thought was myth. "I'd give anything to be able to go through a door like you did."

"You may have a chance to do just that," said Fardan brightly. "My plan is that the four of us dress up like soldiers and ride into Ahmedabad. We pretend to be the guards who accompanied Irinya. When the wazir approaches, we wait for the right moment and snatch the spider lily from him. Irinya says he keeps it in a box in his breast pocket. Irinya makes a door, and we escape."

Three heads swiveled to stare at him. "By salt and sun," said Pranal in a voice torn between admiration and disbelief. "That's a pigeon-brained scheme, all right."

"One of your worst," added Jai, shaking his head.

"Walking into the lion's den, begging to be eaten," put in Ayush.

"Glad you all share my viewpoint," said Irinya in relief. Fardan's plan was leakier than a sieve. Even if they managed to snatch the spider lily from the wazir and escape through a door, he would hunt them down. He might kill the sultana to eliminate the possibility of the spider lily falling into her hands. "Go back to the kul with the jasmine we found. I'll return to Ahmedabad on my own."

"I'm going with you even if they decide not to," said Fardan in a tone that brooked no argument.

"I'm going, too," said Jai unexpectedly. "I may never get another chance to see a silver spider lily or use a black chrysanthemum."

"You can't rely on it." Irinya fingered the locket, nerves thrumming with anxiety. "I don't know if it will work. Even if it does, it might not save you. All the wazir has to do is take one look at you and he'll know you're not the men he sent with me. He's excellent with a sword."

"I'm not too bad at wrestling myself," said Fardan, waggling his eyebrows.

She gritted her teeth. "You won't be wrestling with a foot of cold steel inside your chest. Give it up. We'll think of something else. I'll find a way to steal the spider lily back from him." Knowing, even as she spoke, how empty her words were.

Fardan's mouth set in a stubborn line. "You'd be returning empty-handed to him without his guards. You think he'll let you live? Let the sultana live? You don't have a better idea; admit it."

"It'll be a story to tell my children and grandchildren," murmured Jai, his eyes distant.

"You'd have to live long enough to have children," Irinya pointed out, but no one listened to her. Ayush and Pranal could barely sit still from excitement. They went over Fardan's minimal plan, discussing all the ways it could go wrong—which were nearly endless—and what they would do with the spider lily.

"Sell it to the sultana, of course," said Fardan. "We'll never be in debt again."

"Try to open a door back to Banni," Jai told her. "We can hide until it's safe. Then a couple of us can circle back to Ahmedabad to find the sultana."

"It will never be safe." Irinya glared at them. "Even if we pull this off, the wazir might kill the sultana in revenge. He might even try to track down our kul."

"He won't be able to," said Fardan. "You didn't give him any details, did you? There are dozens of kuls scattered across hundreds of miles of grassland, and they move all the time. And we won't endanger our kul by staying with them. We can give tincture of jasmine to your uncle and move on. As for the sultana, the wazir is more likely to keep her alive as a bargaining tool."

Irinya bit her nails. What he said made sense, but the thought of walking back into Bhadra Fort with her friends in a disguise that would fall apart at the wazir's first glance made her stomach heave.

"We should plan our arrival for after dark, right?" said Pranal, his eyes sparkling.

Fardan nodded. "Irinya will tell us the best gate to use. We'll say who we are, and the wazir will come out to meet us in the courtyard. Irinya will hold out the jasmine and say it's a spider lily—he won't notice the difference in the dark—and as soon as he reaches for the jasmine, I'll snatch the spider lily from his pocket. Irinya will make a door, and we'll run through it."

Irinya massaged her forehead, feeling the beginnings of a headache. "He won't meet us in the courtyard. We'll be taken to wherever he is in the palace. Even if we meet him outside, there will be torches. It won't be dark enough to fool him."

"Yes, you're making a whole lot of assumptions," said Jai, frowning.

Fardan shrugged. "This is the best-case scenario. But even if he spots us, Irinya can make a door. And if she can't, we have the horses. We'll make a run for it."

Irinya clasped her knees, her insides fluttering between fear and hope. The wazir would see through their disguise and kill them instantly. No, his attention would be on her and the flower in her hand. Fardan would attempt to snatch the spider lily, and the wazir would cut him down. No, Fardan was quick, he would succeed in stealing the flower. But she wouldn't be able to make a door in time. And if she did, the wazir might follow them through it. No, why would he? He would be too stunned, too apprehensive of the magic. Even if he did, they could fight him. Her thoughts whirled from one possibility to the next, unable to predict the outcome of Fardan's wild scheme.

A small chance of success and a huge probability of failure. But the chance for success gleamed in their eyes. And wasn't it possible that her luck would turn?

The jasmine nestled in Fardan's box stretched its petals. *There are three I will heal,* it murmured.

Irinya's breath caught, and she looked at the boys, but they chattered, oblivious of the jasmine's words. Of course, she was the only one who could hear it. But which three did it mean? There were five of them. And the jasmine could have been speaking of different people altogether. *Curse you and your riddles,* she thought.

"Let me show you how the fort is built," she said at last, and they gathered around her. She spent the next hour drawing lines in the dirt with a twig, explaining the layout of the city and its defenses, answering their questions as best she could. Although she hadn't spent much time in Ahmedabad, she'd seen documents and maps of the city during her brief time working for the Revenue Department.

They took turns keeping watch at night and woke early the next morning for a quick breakfast of tea and dried fruits. The boys donned the soldiers' uniforms, buckling swords to their belts and wrapping turbans around their heads. Irinya stared at them, unable to recognize the boys she'd grown up with. Was that muscular young guard with the rugged good looks *Fardan*?

He preened under her scrutiny. "Don't I look handsome?"

Yes. Yes, you do. Irinya swallowed. "Don't get carried away. This is just a disguise."

"It's really uncomfortable," said Ayush, his voice muffled as he struggled to pull a second tunic over his head. "Why do I have to wear two layers?"

"Stop complaining." Fardan cast a critical eye on him. "It's your fault for being so thin. You need to eat more."

Ayush made a face. "You sound like Ma."

"We didn't tell them we were going," said Pranal. "Just left a note. Like *you*, Irinya. Ma's going to beat us up when we get back home."

If they got back home, Irinya couldn't help thinking. *There are three I will heal,* the jasmine had said. Assuming it was referring to them, what would happen to the remaining two? Perhaps they would not need healing? Putting herself in danger was one thing, but she couldn't bear it if anything happened to the others.

Fardan glanced at her. "You'd better disguise yourself, too. Less questions that way. Got any of your uncle's clothes handy?"

She didn't, but she managed to fit into Ayush's clothes and wrap a turban around her hair.

They traveled all day, breaking off at noon to eat and to practice stabbing the innocent vegetation with their new swords. "Stop," said Irinya, unable to bear the sight. "You'll hurt yourselves."

"I hope we don't have to use these." Fardan eyed the sword in his hand with distaste before sheathing it. "I don't enjoy shedding blood, especially my own."

Irinya pursed her lips. "The swords are a *disguise*. All you have to do is wear them and pretend to be soldiers. If something goes wrong, *run*. Don't try to fight, because you will certainly lose."

They couldn't argue with that. They might be fit and healthy, but they were no match for trained soldiers.

Their disguise turned out to be good for one thing: no one bothered them. In fact, people went out of their way to avoid them. When they stopped to water their horses at a pond and replenish their gourds at a village well, no one scolded them or asked them to pay. And when their food ran out, they didn't have any trouble buying more. Irinya didn't let them take anything for free, although they had very little money.

"Others have even less," she told Ayush when he showed her the few jital they had left. "Think of it this way: if we succeed, we'll never want for money again."

They stopped briefly in Bhuj to rest the horses and buy provisions. The boys wanted to stay longer to see the sights and wander through the marketplace, but Irinya didn't let them. "Your disguise only works as long as you don't talk much," she warned. "Anyone of authority in Bhuj can stop and question you. You might wear the uniform of the wazir's guards, but this is not Ahmedabad." Reluctantly, they agreed. Ayush waited with Irinya beyond the city walls, bemoaning his fate at being left behind while the others ventured in to buy food and replenish their water.

A couple of hours later, Fardan returned by himself. "We got work guarding a merchant caravan," he reported with a grin. "We'll earn money and get free food."

Irinya's mouth fell open in horror. "You four? Guard a caravan? Do you know how dangerous the route is? There are *tigers*. And bandits!"

"Better to go in a caravan then, isn't it?" he countered. "At least the target will be diffused." She couldn't argue with that logic.

The caravan turned out to be six carriages laden with silk, spices, cotton, and ceramic, owned by three merchant families. They had a couple of cooks and assistants, but no guards, apart from Fardan and his cohort. Irinya felt bad for them as she listened to the instructions from the caravan leader. Suppose they were attacked by bandits or tigers? Fardan and the rest would be utterly useless. The only one who had a working weapon was *her*. And how effective would her blowpipe be against a tiger? At least they looked the part with their unshaven cheeks, swaggering gait, rumpled uniforms, and wooden scabbards.

To her surprise, the caravan leader seemed to think she was their boss, maybe because she was sitting on the sole camel and not deigning to speak with anyone. In truth, she was afraid to say anything and be recognized as a girl. Fardan did most of the talking. He told the caravan leader they were ex-soldiers, honorably discharged from the sultanate army after the last skirmish with Malwa. She listened to him, torn between admiration and annoyance at his cheerful lies.

The first day and night were uneventful. She made the boys take turns circling the caravan and keeping watch during the night. "It's the least you can do," she snapped when Pranal complained at being woken up. "If someone attacks, we'll have advance notice."

On the second night, she and Fardan took the first watch. Fardan was on horseback, and she was on Veerana, as usual. It was the first time they'd been alone together since meeting up with Jai, Pranal, and Ayush, and it felt weirdly intimate to be the only two people awake in a jungle in the middle of the night. She remembered how it had felt to spend the night in his arms, and heat flushed through her body. They circled the caravan, passing each other every so often, and each time, Fardan smiled at her as if they were at a feast or a wedding.

Odd, she'd known him all her life, and she'd never noticed what a beautiful smile he had, like a lamp in the dark. *Fardan, I've wasted so much time. I should have realized how much you meant years ago.* She smiled back at him, lulled by the quiet breeze, the half-moon sailing high in the inky sky, and the soft thud of Veerana's hooves on the grassy earth.

She was nearly half-asleep when a rustling sounded in the undergrowth, followed by a rattling of stones. She jerked upright on the saddle, fully awake. Veerana went stock still and flicked his ears.

Fardan trotted up next to her. "Tiger?" he whispered.

She shook her head, putting a finger to her lips. Tigers were heavier. This was a smaller animal or a human. Should she give the alarm? She clutched her blowpipe, scouring the undergrowth, straining to see in the dark.

For a minute, nothing happened. She'd begun to think it was a small animal, when over a dozen horsemen burst through the trees. Moonlight glinted on steel, and her heart leaped into her mouth. *Bandits.*

Fardan yelled out a warning in a voice that would have woken the dead. The lead horseman raised his mace and charged toward him.

Fardan fumbled to unsheathe his sword. By the time he got it out, it would be too late.

There was no time to think, to aim, or to ask herself whether she wanted the burden of another dead man on her conscience. Irinya put the blowpipe to her lips and blew. The thorn-tipped dart *whoosh*ed out. She loaded another dart, trying to make out if she had managed to hit her target. The horseman was almost upon Fardan, his face split in a snarl, his mace raised to cleave Fardan's skull.

Suddenly, the mace dropped from the horseman's hand. He scrabbled at his face, and a current of triumph went through her. She hadn't missed. The bandit frothed at the mouth and slumped forward on his saddle. Fardan managed to unsheathe his sword, and held it protectively in front of him. He cut his eyes to Irinya and dipped his head in acknowledgment.

Men emerged from the carriages, bearing stout sticks in their hands, shouting curses at the bandits. At least Fardan had managed to rouse the caravan. She scanned the crowd for Jai, Pranal, and Ayush, hoping they were all right.

The bandits raced up to their fallen leader. A couple tried to haul the unconscious man up on the saddle, but the others went for the caravanners. Steel clanged as Fardan blocked a nasty looking curving sword with his own. But one of the bandits came at him from behind with his mace. Irinya bit down her panic and summoned cold calmness. *I can do this. I can take them all.* She shot her dart into the back of the bandit's neck. He slid off his horse and fell to the ground in a twitching heap, the whites of his eyes staring up at the moonlit sky.

More riders cantered up—far too many for Irinya to deal with all at once. She couldn't afford to fumble in the darkness and waste any of her darts. How many did she have left?

"Come on, Veerana, help me here," she shouted, urging him forward.

Seriously? This is below my dignity, grumbled Veerana. But, to her surprise, he broke into a growling, snorting gallop, charging into the riders' midst.

Horses whinnied in alarm and broke away. Veerana gnashed his teeth and bit a couple of exposed flanks. They bucked, dislodging their riders.

Jai thundered up on his horse and unseated a rider by grabbing him and throwing him to the ground. Ayush and Pranal followed, uttering war cries as they stabbed the air with their useless swords.

In the melee, no one noticed as Irinya continued to shoot her darts silently into the bandits' flesh. One by one, her darts found their targets and the men dropped. Outnumbered and vanquished, the remaining few fell back into the forest, whistling for their horses. The caravanners stamped out a fire that had started from a torch dropped by one of the attackers. On the ground, the wounded bandits groaned and shuddered. Some did not move at all. Irinya hoped they were merely unconscious and not dead. She'd never know. She swallowed her nausea at the sight and turned to address the caravan.

"Let's move," she barked in her deepest voice. "They may return with reinforcements."

The caravan leader snapped his orders. Everyone sprang into action. They carried their wounded into the carriages—thankfully, not too many, and the injuries seemed light. The horses were hitched, and in minutes, they'd left the scene of carnage behind. Fardan gazed at her with awe on his face, and Jai gave her a mock salute. Pranal trotted by on his horse to whisper, "You're amazing, Poison Princess."

She leaned forward and patted her camel's neck. "Veerana's the real hero here," she said, keeping her tone light.

At last, you recognize my true worth, he said in a smug tone.

In truth, she felt sick at what she'd been forced to do to save the caravan. The worst part? Her darts were gone. She had nothing now to protect Fardan and the others from the wazir, except the door. She squeezed her locket and prayed the chrysanthemum would work one last time to save her friends.

CHAPTER 19

They arrived at the fabled Delhi Darwaza of Ahmedabad four days later without further incident. The boys stared with open-mouthed wonder at the imposing gate and fortified walls, mirroring what Irinya had felt when she first beheld the city. She watched them, her throat tight. Now that the confrontation with the wazir was upon them, she could scarcely breathe from anxiety.

The price will be more than you can bear, the spider lily had said. Had she paid in full, or was she still in debt? How much more could she afford to lose? *Not them,* she thought, as the boys pointed out the sights to each other. *Please, not them.*

"Try to look less like awestruck tourists," she said as they waited in line outside the gate, her tone clipped. "You're supposed to be hard-bitten warriors."

Fardan snapped his mouth closed, and Jai summoned a look of so-phisticated boredom. But their gazes kept returning to the cityscape that rose beyond the walls.

"If only Ma could see us," murmured Pranal. The many days of riding had accustomed them to being on horseback, and they sat easily on their mounts, resembling the soldiers they were supposed to be.

"She wouldn't recognize us," said Ayush with a grin. "Good thing, too, or she'd beat us with her sandal for leaving home."

"Ma won't beat us again," said Pranal, twirling an imaginary mustache. "We're *men* now."

Fardan snorted with laughter. "Try telling your mother that."

"Hush," hissed Irinya. It was their turn at the gate, and the guards were checking the caravan leader's documents. Fardan and the rest had taken the precaution of changing their shirts and removing their turbans so their uniforms wouldn't be recognized. No one gave them a second glance, and the caravan was allowed through a few minutes later.

"We're in the capital of the sultanate," said Jai as they entered the broad, crowded streets of Ahmedabad, staring at the imposing mosque that rose before them. "I can't believe it."

"And we got the caravan safely here, thanks to Irinya and the excellent Veerana." Fardan gave her a salute. "That means wages!"

"And that means food," crowed Ayush. "I'm starving."

Irinya's lips twitched. They'd eaten breakfast a mere three hours ago, but Ayush's appetite was bigger than him.

The caravan came to a halt in front of the traveler's lodge opposite the mosque, and they dismounted. The head of the merchant families handed Irinya a small purse of coins with a bonus, he said, for dispatching the bandits so effectively. "Anytime you want a job, please come and see me," he told her.

She bowed her thanks to him and led her cohort away from the caravan, down a side street that wound along the city walls. The other side was crowded with stalls and food counters and vendors shouting their wares and holding up tempting samples on tiny leaf plates.

"Can we eat?" Ayush cast a longing eye at a stall where a man was frying a fresh batch of samosas in an enormous wok.

"Soon. We need to stable the animals and find a place to spend the night." Irinya patted her camel's flank. "The wazir mustn't see Veerana. He'd know something was amiss. I left Ahmedabad in a carriage."

The carriage. Coldness flooded her. "I forgot the carriage and the coachman in Bhitiara!" she blurted out.

Ayush whistled. "So he's still there, waiting for you to return?"

Fardan frowned. "He would have realized something's wrong by now."

Irinya took a deep breath. "Nothing to be done about it. He won't move for another few days. He'll be too afraid of the guards. By the time he returns to Ahmedabad, we'll be long gone." She *hoped.*

"We can take a day or two to explore, right?" said Ayush with a winning smile. "Who knows if we'll ever come back here, and you have all that money we earned."

"Money *she* earned," Jai corrected. "If not for her blowpipe, we'd have been overpowered."

"It's *our* money," said Irinya. "I'll divide it, but we need to work out how much to save for food and lodging. I think we should approach the wazir tomorrow night." Saying the words aloud made her heart palpitate. Was there only a day of safety left for them all? She wished she had been able to save a few darts. Only the thorns of magical flowers worked on the blowpipe, or she'd have tried to find a substitute.

Ayush whooped. "We have the rest of today and tomorrow."

"We'll need to go over our plan, practice a few more scenarios." Jai swung his scabbard like a walking stick and nearly hit Pranal.

"Practice not killing me," said Pranal, ducking away from him.

Fardan caught Irinya's eye and smiled at her. She tried to smile back at him. The afternoon sunlight fell on his hair, and she wanted to reach out and ruffle it. He had such gorgeous curly hair—not like hers, straight and long like a thick, sober curtain. Fardan's hair was exuberant, just like him. *Nothing bad can happen to you,* she thought, her fists clenching. *No flower is worth that much.*

"Why do you look as if you're going to hit someone?" asked Ayush, glancing at her. "It's not me, is it?"

She shook her head and smoothed her expression. "Just worried about tomorrow. I don't have any more thorns for my blowpipe." Her best—her *only* weapon—and she was out of ammunition.

"Oh no." Pranal's face fell. "You wasted them all on those bandits?"

Jai punched his shoulder, making him stumble. "She had no choice. It was them or us."

"We still have the door," said Fardan. "And in the worst case, our horses."

She threw him a grateful look. The street widened and divided into two, and they chose the one that led to the city. As soon as they turned into it, they found a rest house with stalls for animals. Fardan took a few coins from Irinya and went inside to check if they could afford to stay there.

You're abandoning me again? came Veerana's accusing voice as Fardan returned with a stabler a few minutes later.

"Not for long," she assured him, handing his reins to the stabler, a competent-looking man in a white turban and dhoti.

"We can stay here," Fardan told them as a couple of small boys led the horses away. "It's expensive, but it's only for one night. I don't know what the room is like, but we got one."

"Now can we explore?" wheedled Ayush. "I want to go to the market and try the food."

Fardan looked at Irinya, and she nodded. "I'll take you through Teen Darwaza to Khaas Bazaar. But you can't buy anything on the way, or we won't have enough to spend."

It was hard enforcing that rule, because they passed dozens of enticing stalls on their way to Teen Darwaza. She chivied them along, not letting them stop, although they wanted to stare and sniff at everything. It was exhausting but worth it to see their expressions when they finally passed under the gateway and laid eyes on Khaas Bazaar.

She took them to the area of the market specializing in prepared foods and bought leaf plates of soft, savory dhokla, crunchy chakri, crisp fried pakoras, a large round handvo stuffed with bottle gourd and crushed peanuts, and earthen cups of sweet tea. They stood under the awning of the tea stall, sharing the leaf plates.

"What a feast." Ayush popped the last chakri in his mouth and chewed, his expression ecstatic. "I'll never be able to eat plain rotla and pickles again."

Irinya laughed. "This is a treat. You can't have such rich, spicy food every day, or your stomach will rebel."

"My stomach says it wants to live in Ahmedabad forever," said Fardan, draining his cup.

Did he? Ahmedabad was exciting and glamorous, but she'd never want to live here. It was too crowded, too noisy, too intense. She'd miss the wide-open spaces of the grassland, the star-speckled bowl of the night sky, and the brilliant white salt flats glittering under the sun.

He caught her staring at him and grinned. "Admiring my handsome face?"

She rolled her eyes. "I was thinking you'd get tired of the city pretty fast."

"Not me. Imagine owning one of these shops," said Pranal wistfully. "Selling snacks all day, sleeping in an actual house at night."

"You'd eat all the snacks," said Jai with a snort. "There'd be nothing to sell. I don't like the idea of being hemmed in by brick walls. I'd rather sleep in a tent or out in the open."

"That's what you'll do all your boring life," said Ayush, "while me and Pranal live it up in the capital."

"You wouldn't be able to afford it," scoffed Fardan.

"If we can get the spider lily and sell it to the sultana," said Ayush, lowering his voice, "we'll use our share to open a . . . a sweet shop."

"No, savory snacks are better," said Pranal.

The two brothers began to argue about the kind of food they'd stock in their hypothetical shop. Irinya's lips twitched, even as a wave of unease washed over her.

"You're counting your petals before finding the flower," she said in her driest voice, but they didn't seem to hear her. Perhaps this was their way of finding courage for tomorrow's encounter. She glanced at Fardan. If it was okay to dream, then she wanted him to have one, too. "There's a shop I want to show you."

"Don't tell me you want to open one, too?" he said, raising his eyebrows. "You'd make an awful shopkeeper, Irinya. You'd scowl at the customers—yes, just like that—scaring them all away."

She thwacked his shoulder, making him wince. "Very funny. You want to see it or not?"

"Go on, you two," said Jai, waving them away. "I want another cup of tea."

She led Fardan across the square toward the stationery shop, leaving Pranal and Ayush still arguing about their dream establishment.

Fardan kept turning and twisting his head at some new delight. "This market is amazing. You could live here for a year and not see everything."

"Well, here's one of the most interesting stalls." She tugged his arm and pointed at the stationery shop. "I thought of you when I saw it."

He gasped at the sight of the beautiful paper, pens, inks, and scrolls on display, and went still. Her throat ached as she watched him examining the wares, his eyes wide, his mouth parted. It wasn't fair that all he had to draw with were bits of charcoal and used parchment that no one else wanted.

"You should buy something from here," she said, poking him. He didn't move.

"Want to touch the paper?" said the proprietor, a small, plump man with an oiled mustache. "It's very smooth."

Fardan recovered his poise. "No, thanks. Some other time." He turned and marched away.

Irinya hurried after him. "What's the matter?" she called. Was he angry with her for bringing him here?

He wheeled around, his face taut. "Their paper is nice—too nice. Too expensive. I'd be worried the whole time I was drawing on paper like that. That it was wasted on me."

"It wouldn't be a waste," she argued. "You're a good artist."

He broke into a familiar grin. "By salt and sun, you're complimenting me? That's a first. Let me remember this day forever."

She waved her hand. "Whatever. Just buy something for yourself."

He shook his head. "It wouldn't be right. We have so little money. We need to eat tomorrow and set aside something for emergencies. When this is over, and you decide to write down your stories, we'll buy their paper."

She sighed. "Fine." She'd wanted so much for him to have a nice quill or parchment from this shop. But he was right. They couldn't afford it, not now.

They rejoined the others and wandered through the market until evening. Irinya made them all eat a cheap and simple dinner of khichdi with yogurt before they returned to their lodgings. Their room was small but clean, with an oil lamp, earthen pitchers of water, and five grass mats and cotton sheets for them to sleep on. The boys dragged their mats to one side of the room, leaving her with the other. Fardan even made a dividing line of swords. An illusion of space and privacy was better than nothing. She turned her face to the wall and tried to sleep while they snored a few feet away from her. But sleep refused to come. She thought of the thousand ways tomorrow could go wrong, and it was all she could do not to wake everyone up and get them the hell out of there.

They spent the next day practicing with their swords and trying on different combinations of the soldiers' clothing until Irinya decided they looked as close to the dead men as possible. She assigned each of them a name and a personality, except Ayush. He would have to be the guard whose name she didn't remember. Jai was the biggest, so he was Tej. He was also the best at speaking Gujari. Fardan was Balbir, and Pranal was Sameem. She herself discarded Ayush's clothes and returned to her usual salwar kameez, tying her hair in a knot and draping a dupatta over herself.

As the day drew on, and the time for them to leave for the palace approached, her nerves increased to a fever pitch. "Don't speak," she said for the tenth time as they gathered around for a final run-through in their room. "Let me do the talking. I'll distract him."

Pranal rolled his eyes. "We know, Irinya. You'll show him the jasmine, and Fardan will snatch the spider lily. Then you'll make the door. If it doesn't work, we gallop away on our horses, leaving you the wazir's prisoner."

"He won't hurt me," she said, trying to sound as if she meant it.

"You don't know that." Fardan's forehead creased. "We can't leave you with him."

"If there's no other choice, that is what you must do," she insisted. "Promise me, Fardan. Or I can't go through with this."

He pursed his lips. "You jump on my horse, and we run away together."

She wanted to tear her hair. "No. No. There's a chance you might get away, but it'll never work if I try to go with you. The wazir will send his men after us. He prizes my flower-hunting skills. He'll never let me escape. In fact"—she unhooked the chain from around her neck and held it out to Fardan—"take the locket. If I get stuck, you can use it to make a door."

But Fardan frowned and clasped his hands behind his back. "No, Irinya. You're the only one among us who has any experience of it. *You* need to be the one to make the door."

"I agree," said Jai. He narrowed his eyes at Irinya. "We'll adapt as the situation demands. But we aren't going to leave you behind if we can help it."

Irinya slipped the chain back around her neck, squashing her frustration. Jai was right; they would have to adapt depending on how the wazir reacted.

As evening fell, they went down and saddled the horses. They were as ready as it was possible to be. They headed toward the palace, the four boys riding at a walking pace, with Irinya a few steps ahead. The jasmine was tucked into a cloth bag tied to her waist. She would produce it for the wazir with the air of a magician, and Fardan would pluck the box with the spider lily from his pocket. She could picture it so clearly. She could also picture the wazir unsheathing his sword and chopping Fardan's hand off. Or his head. Sweat beaded her forehead and trickled down her face. She shivered despite the warmth of the evening. *Please let them be safe,* she prayed.

The boys fell quiet as they approached the imposing walls of the citadel. Jai urged his horse ahead of them. As "Tej," he was the one designated to talk to the guards on duty at the gate.

"All the best," Irinya murmured as he rode past. He gave her a tight smile. He'd smeared charcoal on his upper lip and chin and was unrecognizable as the boy she'd grown up with. But he still looked too young to be the grizzled leader of the guards.

Then they were at Bhadra Gate, and Jai was dismounting, the guards barking sharp questions at him. Irinya's hands went cold, her lips numb. Jai spoke up, identifying himself.

"Move," said Fardan from behind her in a low voice, and she started. The guards were already waving them through. They must not know Tej personally.

They went through the archway, Irinya keeping her head down, her eyes on the paved stones below. She didn't realize until they'd passed through the gate that she'd been holding her breath. The boys dismounted, walking the horses down the carriage drive, passing guards, gardeners, and servants. The evening pressed down on her, both familiar and strange. She'd been here before, but nothing was the same. She was no longer the wazir's make-believe secretary, but a thief—the kind whose head got sliced off and nailed to the gate as a warning. She swallowed, trying to unsee the gory image of her severed head.

"That was easy," said Jai.

She threw him a sharp glance. "That was only the exterior gate."

"What are you going to tell the wazir about the carriage?" asked Fardan.

She shrugged. "That the horses have been stabled, now that we're back. I don't think we'll have time to talk about the carriage."

They arrived at the next gate. Jai had to spend longer at this one, explaining that they had been on a personal mission to the Rann at the behest of the wazir and needed to report back to him.

"And who's *she?*" The captain of the gate jerked his thumb at her.

"The wazir's secretary," said Irinya, summoning an authoritative tone. "He will want to see me right away. Do not delay us, Captain."

The captain sent a runner to the palace and allowed them in. Dusk had fallen, and lamps were being lit at the gate and in the courtyard. Irinya was glad of the dark. Fardan could not see her expression.

But he sensed it anyway. "It will be fine," he whispered, leaning toward her. She tried to smile at him.

At the gates that led to the interior courtyard, they were told to proceed on foot. They exchanged glances of dismay. They should have anticipated this. Irinya wanted to scream. So much for making a quick getaway on horseback. They left their horses tied to a mango tree, and one of the guards escorted them in.

The plant-filled courtyards were as lovely as ever, filled with the scent of wet earth and blooming flowers. But today Irinya did not find them in the least soothing. Her nerves thrummed. Where would the wazir meet them? Could they take him by surprise?

The guard led them up the steps of a porch and down a corridor. Irinya wiped her sweaty palms on her kameez and tried to stay calm. Fardan was walking beside her, Jai was ahead with the guard, and Pranal and Ayush were behind her. Too late to turn back, too late to tell them to stay out of it.

The melancholic notes of a sitar punctuated by the beats of a tabla drifted toward them. Was the wazir listening to music? Her stomach knotted. For their ridiculous plan to have any hope of working, they needed to meet the wazir alone.

The guard opened a door and jerked his thumb. "Huzoor is waiting for you."

Irinya pushed herself ahead of Jai. "I'm the only one he needs to see," she blurted out. If the wazir was in a crowd, they had no chance of grabbing the spider lily from him. They would be risking themselves for nothing. "Why don't the rest of you wait outside? He's listening to music, and it would be rude to disturb him."

The guard frowned. "He said to bring all of you in. He said it would be more entertaining."

Entertaining? Irinya's gut clenched. Something was wrong. But before she could speak, Jai said, "Of course," and practically pushed her inside.

They entered a large, lamplit hall filled with an alarming number of people. The wazir was sprawled on a divan to the left, a ruby-red glass in his hand. Behind him were a couple of burly bodyguards. On the right was a stage with an elegant dancing girl and half a dozen musicians.

The guard bowed, waiting for the wazir to notice them, but the wazir appeared to be completely absorbed by the performance.

Fardan bent toward her and whispered, "Does he have the spider lily?"

She leaned forward and strained her eyes, trying to make out if the box was peeking out of his breast pocket.

That was the moment the wazir raised his head and locked eyes with her. She flinched at the heat of his gaze.

His mouth twisted, and he set down his glass and clapped his hands. The music stopped. The girl and the musicians bowed low and backed away, leaving the hall from a door at the rear of the stage.

He rose from the divan and walked toward her with easy strides. Irinya's heart beat so fast, she thought it would jump out of her chest. The box with the spider lily was in his breast pocket. But there were three armed guards to deal with, to say nothing of the wazir himself. If only she hadn't used up all her darts.

"The flower hunter returns," he drawled, stopping a few feet away from her. "What have you brought for me?"

Irinya untied the cloth bag from her waist with shaking hands. "Another silver spider lily, huzoor, just as you wished."

"Is that so? Did you really bring me a spider lily?" His eyes glittered. "Or did you bring me death?"

She inhaled sharply. *He knew.* Fardan stepped forward until he was right behind her. She wanted to push him out of the room, to get them all to safety, far from the wazir's searing gaze.

Imshan Khan's smile widened. "Why have you stopped? Come, I wish to see what you have harvested from the Rann. Is it a flower, or is it a thorn?"

"Huzoor," she said, summoning all her sincerity into her voice even as her insides quivered, "I don't know what you mean. I have brought you a flower."

"Have you?" He took a step forward and held out his hand. "Let me see it."

She opened the cloth bag and held up the jasmine, concealing it in her palm so he could only glimpse the top of the petals. His eyes widened, his gaze losing some of its sharp focus, and he moved his hand to hers.

Jai threw himself on the guard who had escorted them, wrestling him to the floor. Fardan leaped for the spider lily.

The wazir moved with incredible speed, blocking Fardan's hand and twisting it behind his back. On the floor, the guard shouted for help as Jai clobbered his face. The two bodyguards raced up to them, unsheathing their swords.

Irinya retied her jasmine in the cloth bag and backed away, her heart in her mouth. Ayush and Pranal attacked the bodyguards to buy Fardan and Jai time. To her horror, one of the men plunged his sword into Pranal's shoulder. Pranal gasped and staggered back. Ayush leaped on the man from behind and locked his arms around his neck. But the second bodyguard grabbed him and hauled him off, throwing him across the floor. Fardan and the wazir fought on, evenly matched in strength.

Irinya cast her eyes about, desperate for a weapon. She ran to the divan and grabbed an ornately carved wooden stool beside it. The bodyguard who had thrown Ayush was bearing down on him with his sword. She rushed forward and hit him on the head from behind, as hard as she could. He stumbled and fell.

"Run," she screamed to Ayush. But Ayush looked at her, dazed, blood trickling down his forehead.

"Too late to run," said the wazir in a calm voice.

She spun around. Pranal lay unconscious on the floor, blood seeping from his chest and shoulder. The bodyguard who had stabbed Pranal tackled Jai, knifing his back with a small, wicked-looking dagger. Jai's grip went slack, and the man underneath him rolled away, sobbing, his face a bloody mess. The bodyguard repeatedly stabbed Jai, as if once was not enough, as if the wounds would magically heal themselves. *Stop!* she tried to scream. *Stop!* But no words emerged from her mouth.

Because Fardan . . . Fardan leaned against the wall, gasping, a sword through his chest, the hilt in the wazir's hand.

Imshan Khan withdrew his blade, and Fardan slithered to the ground, leaving a trail of blood on the wall, his chest a ruin, his head lolling forward.

Darkness came before Irinya's eyes, and she thought she would faint.

Soldiers poured into the hall and surrounded them. The wazir dropped his sword and turned to her, his mouth twisted in a bitter smile. "*Traitor.* Everyone betrays me in the end."

"Fardan." Her voice sounded like a stranger's, weak and thready. She stumbled toward him, her hand reaching for his, desperate to feel a pulse.

The wazir caught her arm in a viselike grip. "You lied to me," he hissed. "I would have given you the entire world."

Blood trickled out of Fardan's mouth. If he didn't get help soon, he'd die. They'd *all* die. And she'd get no quarter from the wazir.

She freed herself from his grip and gave him a flat smile that felt like a cut on her face. Each breath was a wound in her chest, but she forced herself to speak calmly. "I have the entire world already, huzoor. There is nothing you can give me that I want. But I still have magic beyond your reach. I am making a door. Would you like to walk through it?"

"You what?" He narrowed his eyes at her.

She snapped open the locket and drank the remaining infusion, trying not to gag at the disgusting taste. She had one slim chance to save Fardan and her friends. But for it to work, she had to remove the wazir from here.

"That locket." His gaze sharpened. "It belonged to Deven."

"Who died by your sword, yes." She closed the locket and tucked it back under her kameez. "Come with me," she said in her most compelling voice. "And I will show you something most people can only dream of." She took a step toward the stage exit and glanced back, summoning stone into her soul.

Jai and Pranal both lay unmoving, bleeding from multiple wounds. Ayush was bleeding profusely but was still conscious, his eyes wide and scared. Fardan's chest rose and fell with his labored breathing. Still alive—but only just. Her eyes burned with unshed tears. They would survive. They had to. "See that they get medical attention right away," Irinya commanded the guards. "The wazir and I are going for a little walk. I'm sure he'll want to question them when we get back." She was betting all their lives that the guards would err on the side of safety and obey her; after all, criminals could always be executed later. And Imshan Khan would not be there to disabuse them.

His forehead creased. "Your games will not work, flower hunter."

She walked away from him toward the stage exit. The door lay beyond it, she was certain.

Where do you want to go, Irinya? came the ghost of a paper-thin voice.

You know where I want to go. The one place where I have power and he doesn't.

"No games, huzoor," she said. "Only magic. Are you coming?"

She pushed open the door, and he followed.

CHAPTER 20

The door swung closed behind them, and Irinya found herself once more in the corridor between the known and the unknown. She took a deep, shuddering breath. Luck had failed her, and to every flower there was a cost. But the infusion had worked.

"The black chrysanthemum?" The wazir sounded stunned. "You found the *black chrysanthemum*?"

"It found me." Her voice so calm, so strong. As if Fardan were not on the brink of death. As if her friends did not lie in pools of blood, their bodies still and bent at awkward angles. A sob rose in her throat. Fiercely, she swallowed it down. They would get the aid she had asked for. They would survive until she returned with the jasmine to heal them. She had to believe that.

"Is there anything you cannot do, flower hunter?" There was a rough yearning in his voice as he gazed at her—the yearning of a man for something that forever slipped his grasp. He caught her hand in his, stopping her.

I cannot raise the dead. I cannot even protect the living. Her eyes blurred, and she freed her hand from his. "We must not linger here."

"What will happen if we do?" His face held no trace of fear as he examined the shadowy corridor.

She walked toward the door of darkness at the other end. "Stay here if you wish to find out. I suspect you won't last very long."

He gave a brief, savage laugh and strode up to her. "You won't get rid of me that easily."

"I never wanted to get rid of you, huzoor," she said evenly. "I just wanted to be free of you."

He was silent for a moment. "Do you dislike me that much?" he said at last, his voice wavering. "Most women find me irresistible."

She dug her nails into her palms. Arrogant, selfish man. Did he think good looks and inherited wealth and power could buy him true love or loyalty? *Just a few more steps,* she told herself.

The door of darkness resolved into a brilliant, starry night and pale, salt-cracked ground that stretched as far as the eye could see. The wind sang sharp and cold, filled with the smell of salt and sea. Crystals crackled beneath their feet as they stepped into the desert. She could have cried with relief. She was in the Rann where she belonged. Where it all began, where it would all end.

The wazir spun around, disbelief etched on his handsome face. "You've brought us to the Rann of Kutch. Why, flower hunter?"

Because in his absence, the sultana would fill the power void in the palace, and Fardan and the others would have a chance to be saved. She needed to buy time for the sultana and her friends, and the Rann was the one place she was deeply familiar with that was also isolated from the rest of the world. It would take at least a week to return to Ahmedabad, even if the wazir commandeered the fastest horses in Bhuj. Enough time for the sultana to consolidate herself in the palace, and enough time for Irinya to figure out a way to get the spider lily from him.

She took a deep breath of the fresh air. "It is my home."

"I thought you would take me to the Rann one day," he said softly. "I didn't dream it would be through a door."

She gave him a sidelong glance. She hadn't dreamed it would come to this, either. *Wait for me,* she thought to Fardan. *Wait for the jasmine.*

The wazir eyed her. "Can you take us back to Bhadra Fort?"

She shook her head. "The infusion is finished." There were a few drops left, but she had no intention of revealing that. If she could make another door back to the palace, she would do it without him.

"Show me," he commanded.

"No." She stepped back from him, her voice cold. "You will not touch this locket. It is Deven's legacy."

He tilted his head, puzzled. "I could simply take it from you," he said, a question mark in his voice, as if he was not quite sure.

"You will have to fight me for it, and is that how you want to waste your time?" She turned away. "Come, huzoor. There is no guarantee we will survive the night. Stay with me." At least there was no mist. There was a chance they could make it out. The wind whipped her hair, and she pushed it away from her face, scanning the horizon. The Rann glimmered in the starlight, looking like a frozen lake. Had it looked like this the night her mother vanished?

"What do you mean?" he asked, falling in step beside her. "Why shouldn't we survive?"

"Chir Batti," she answered. "The ghost light that guards the Rann." She could not sense it—not yet. A distant howl sounded over the wind, and her heart jumped. *Just a jackal.*

The wazir gave a derisive laugh. "There's a scientific explanation for so-called ghost lights. They arise because certain gaseous compounds that emanate from the earth ignite on contact with air."

"And yet that is how your guards died." She should have been more anxious about her current situation, but the worst that could have happened had already happened. Her friends were wounded, possibly dying. She'd left Fardan battling for his life, struggling for each breath. And *she* was to blame. The Rann could not hurt her any more than she was already hurting.

The wazir narrowed his gaze at her. "Somehow, you overpowered and killed four of my best fighters. Don't pass the blame for your crime to harmless natural phenomena."

She gave him a flat stare. The wazir found it easier to pin the crime of murder on her rather than admit there were things he knew nothing about. "Huzoor, you give me way too much credit. I did nothing but warn them not to venture into the Rann after dark, especially not on a misty night. But one of the men went missing, and the rest insisted on searching for him that very night. None of them returned. In the morning, Fardan and I went into the salt flats to look for them. We found two bodies. By then, we had been out for hours, and we were forced to turn back ourselves."

"Wounds or marks on the bodies?" he asked, frowning. "It could have been a predator."

She shook her head. "Their clothes were torn, and one of them had been attacked by killer wasps. But the other's face was frozen in terror, and there were no marks that I could see."

They walked in silence, the wazir mulling over her words. An owl hooted from the skeletal branch of a desiccated tree that stood like a lone sentinel in the starlight. Irinya filed the marker away in her mind. If she'd been by herself—or, best of all, with Fardan—she would have paused to check it for flowers first.

No, Fardan would have grabbed her hand and hurried her along to safety, all while maintaining a cheerful monologue to keep the darkness at bay. Her eyes burned. Did he still breathe? Had someone bandaged his chest, stopped the blood flow? *Hang in there, Fardan. I'll come back for you.*

The wazir studied the sky. "You are taking us southeast."

"Toward the Banni grasslands," said Irinya, forcing herself to focus. "But I don't know how deep in the Rann we are. I don't recognize this place. We could be days away from water or food." Strange, she felt no fear at the prospect of dying of hunger or thirst. It wouldn't come to that. She had opened a door into the Rann and brought an outsider with her. The Rann would pass its judgment on her actions tonight itself.

"Why are you guiding me?" asked the wazir. "I doubt I could make my own way out of here. If I am lost, the sultana will reign over Gujarat. Isn't that what you want?"

"What I want is for my friends to live," she said, her voice flat. "You don't matter to me one way or the other."

He gave a cold, unhappy laugh. "You know how to break a man's heart, flower hunter. But if you wanted your friends to live, you should never have betrayed me."

"*Bloodred hibiscus, you'll never trust again,*" she murmured.

"What did you say?" He leaned toward her, his face intent.

She spared him a single glance. "Every flower has a cost. You have used the hibiscus to bend people to your will. Not once, not twice, but countless times—isn't that right? You never considered the price you'd have to pay."

"And the price is betrayal?" He sneered. "You blame me for your disloyalty?"

"Loyalty cannot be commanded, huzoor; it has to be earned."

"What has my aunt done to earn it?" he demanded.

She didn't answer; she couldn't. Ahead of them, barely twenty steps away, a ball of blue fire hung a few feet above the ground. She came to a halt, her pulse accelerating. Red and yellow sparks danced within its heart, the crackling edges making it seem alive.

"Ah, the infamous ghost light," came the wazir's amused voice. "Where will it lead us?"

She clutched his sleeve as he took a step toward it, her stomach shriveling. The ball of fire rose higher, as if beckoning. "No, huzoor, do not follow it, or you will be in its thrall."

He turned to face her, raising his eyebrows. "I thought I didn't matter to you."

She let go of his sleeve. "I took you through the door. It's only right that I warn you."

"Keep a few steps behind me," he said, his teeth glinting in the moonlight. "That way, when the monsters attack, you'll have time to run away."

She suppressed her frustration. "We must head southeast to get out of the Rann."

"We can always change direction," he said impatiently. "You people are so superstitious. This is a natural phenomenon, and I have no intention of letting it go unobserved." He strode toward the ball of blue fire, his kurta flapping.

The ghost light darted away from him, heading west—in the *opposite* direction from where they needed to go. "Interesting," said Imshan Khan in a thoughtful voice. "I'd heard that locals claim the lights like to play hide-and-seek. I always thought that was a delusion."

The light zipped away like an arrow. The wazir chuckled and ran after it, salt crunching underneath his boots.

"Huzoor," called Irinya in a panic. "Stop."

The wazir did not respond. The ball of blue fire changed shape, becoming humanlike. It ran ahead of the wazir like a child.

Irinya gritted her teeth and followed him. She wished she could abandon him to Chir Batti. He didn't deserve her help or guidance. But having brought him here, she couldn't leave him to die—or else how was she any different from him? Besides, he still carried the silver spider lily in his pocket.

She tried not to look at the light herself. She kept her eyes on the wazir, checking the sky to orient herself. But she was soon confused and lost. Where was the Star of Dhruva? Why had the stars changed position in the sky? Around them was the same featureless white desert, glittering in the starlight, although she spied a rocky outcrop a short distance to the north. But above, nothing was the same. A thick black storm cloud covered the western horizon, moving rapidly across the sky, sending tendrils of darkness toward the crescent moon. Her stomach clenched at the sight.

She managed to catch up with the wazir. "Huzoor! Look at the sky."

He turned to face her, panting, his hair in disarray, his eyes wide with excitement. "Flower hunter, you'll never believe what I just saw."

"It's not real," she said, gripping his arm. "You're hallucinating."

"I saw myself," he said, ignoring her. "I saw myself as a child *with my father*. And my father wore a crown." He took a deep, shuddering breath. "Reality as it should have been."

The moon vanished behind the cloud, plunging them in near total darkness. She repeated, "*Look at the sky.*"

He looked up, frowning. "It is cloudy. What of it? The monsoon is imminent."

"We have lost the guiding light of the stars," said Irinya, forcing calmness in her voice. "The safest thing to do is climb a hill or a rock; I saw one five minutes' walk to the north. The rain turns the Rann into a swamp."

The ghost light drifted closer. It was larger now, shaped like a woman—a woman made of blue fire. Irinya tore her gaze away from it and blinked, trying to get the afterimage out of her eyes. A memory sparked in her mind. She'd seen this phantom before. It looked like her mother. And with that thought came pain, deep and familiar, tugging at her gut. Urmila ran across the Rann, and Irinya followed, trying to catch up on her stubby legs. But she couldn't; she just couldn't.

Imshan Khan gazed at the figure, his face full of longing. "That's the only light for miles around. It makes sense to follow it."

She swallowed her pain. Had that been a true memory or a

made-up one? No matter; she couldn't afford to lose focus. She shook the wazir's arm. "Can you hear yourself? You said it was a natural phenomenon. Why would you follow it? You have observed it long enough. Come with me to the rock; we will sit there, and I will tell you a story."

"I am not a child, flower hunter," said the wazir, authority returning to his voice. "I wish to follow Chir Batti, and I will. I understand I am hallucinating. I am clearheaded. I need to know why this is happening. There is magic at work, and I will get to the root of it."

Drops of water splashed on Irinya's head. She raised her head, inhaling sharply. Lightning split the black sky, and thunder boomed, distant but menacing.

"See? It is only rain. You shouldn't let the weather upset you." He took off after the ghost light.

Irinya gave a sob of frustration and ran to catch up with him. The rain fell harder, faster. "Huzoor, you know what the rain means," she panted. "This entire place will become a marsh. We need to get to that rock or find a hill to climb."

"We have hours," said Imshan, striding ahead of her, his gaze fixed on the phantom. He jerked to a halt, and she nearly collided with him. He clutched her arm. "Do you see that? By merciful heaven, it is the sacred lotus!"

Coldness flooded her core. *Not the lotus. Not the sacred flower that must never be found.* Was it another of his hallucinations? "Where?" She squeezed her eyes shut so she would not see it, real or imagined.

He gave a tremulous sigh. "In the heart of the ghost figure. That is where it is taking us. The lotus blooms only in the monsoon, and it has just started to rain. Everything is coming together for me at last."

"Everything is coming together for your doom," she cried.

But he did not hear her. He let go of her arm and resumed his stride. Lightning forked across the sky and lit his face: water trickling down his cheeks, mouth open with childlike wonder, eyes staring at a vision she refused to see.

If she wanted to, she could fall into the illusion. Chir Batti would show her what she wanted to see. And then, perhaps, they would both die in the Rann. Irinya willed herself not to succumb to the temptation.

She must stay alive; she must return to Fardan with the jasmine. She kept her gaze on the ground, watching where she was putting her feet.

"If I could manipulate time, I could change everything," said Imshan Khan, his voice crackling with excitement. "I would be all-powerful."

"You are already the most powerful man in Gujarat," she said, trying to match her pace with his. Thunder sounded in a deafening crack overhead, and she jumped.

He scoffed. "That kind of transient power means nothing. Anyone can claim it."

"*We* are transient," she said, exasperation welling up in her. "You cannot change what has happened, and you should not try."

He didn't answer. The rain came down in sheets, and it was impossible to see where they were going. The dupatta clung to her face, limp and wet. She removed it and tied it around her waist. *Nightmare,* she thought, shivering. Except there was no waking up from it. The wazir kept walking, his pace quick and sure, and she followed him as best she could. The ground became mushy, and she lost her footing.

"Steady." The wazir paused to grab her arm. "Use the light of Chir Batti."

No. She knew who she would see if she looked at the ghost light. But it wouldn't be real. It was Fardan who was real, who needed her. Tears started in her eyes, and she dashed them away. "I don't want to." She struggled to stand up and pushed away his hand.

"What are you afraid of?" asked Imshan Khan, his brow knitting. "What do you think you will see?"

"My mother." *My mother, dead these twelve years. Why did you leave me, Ma?*

My darling, Urmila whispered. *I have been here all along. Why else do you think flowers speak to you?*

A sob racked Irinya's chest, and she raised her gaze to the one light that remained in a world of dark and driving rain.

Urmila turned around and blew her a kiss. Her mother, made of fire and light, an expression of tenderness on her face.

Irinya's heart squeezed in a vise. "Ma," she breathed. "Ma."

"I see my parents," said the wazir. "And my grandfather, whom I never met."

"It's not real." But, oh, how she wanted it to be.

"Reality is a function of sense and perception," said the wazir. "Why should we disbelieve the evidence of our eyes?"

Was he going to lecture her on the nature of reality in the middle of a storm in the Rann? She took a step forward, and her feet sank into several inches of mud. "Huzoor, we should stop. It's getting marshy."

He walked ahead of her. "Chir Batti will show us the way."

Urmila gave her a conspiratorial smile and beckoned with one finger. *Why have you stopped? Come on.*

Irinya closed her eyes and tried to center herself. It hurt to look at this replica of her mother, to know she was dead, that this was an illusion taken from her own mind.

Urmila drew closer, her outline burning through Irinya's closed eyelids. *You've forgotten that night. But it's time to remember.*

The words were a knife, slashing through the layers Irinya had built up inside herself. She put her hands to her ears and shuddered. "No."

Remember, if you want to stay alive.

Thunder boomed like the opening of a sluice gate, and memories flooded in. Irinya gasped at the onslaught.

The night her mother had vanished, there'd been a freak storm, just like this one. It was too early for the monsoon, and the kul hadn't moved yet from the grasslands.

But it hadn't yet started raining when Urmila kissed Irinya good night and told her she was after a prize. It had been a still night, moonlit, with thin tendrils of mist swirling above the ground.

Irinya had tossed and turned, unable to sleep. It was dangerous to go into the Rann at night, especially if it was misty. Even for her mother, who seemed as much at home in the salt flats as she was in her own tent. Then thunder had rolled across the sky, making Irinya cry out in alarm. Rain was even worse than the mist; it would change the ground to marsh and suck you underground—so said the elders. This was why they spent every monsoon safely in their village. She'd crept out of the tent and hurried after her mother as the first drops of rain began to fall.

But Urmila had a head start and was bigger and faster than her. By the time Irinya reached the edge of the salt flats, the rain had quickened, and she could barely make out her mother's figure, glimmering in the distance. She'd run after her, sandals flapping on the damp, cracked earth. "Ma!" she'd shouted, but Urmila had not turned around. No matter how fast she ran, her mother never got closer. Hours later, when she was ready to drop from cold and exhaustion, the figure had finally turned and smiled at her. Her five-year-old heart had squeezed in fear. Because this wasn't her mother. This was a being of fire and light, flickering blue and red in the rain. The figure had beckoned, and she had followed, because what other choice did she have? She was lost, and her mother—her *real* mother—was nowhere in sight. The rain slowed to a drizzle, and the moon peeped out once more from behind tattered clouds, revealing a landscape of desolate beauty, the wet earth gleaming under a ragged sky, reflecting the moonlight. *The sky is your father; the desert your mother.*

The figure stopped, and Irinya stared. Before her glittered a small pond with a beautiful pink lotus floating in the middle. Even through her fog of fear and fatigue, she knew she was seeing the impossible.

At the edge of the pond, lying facedown, her hand outstretched as if trying to reach the queen of flowers, was Irinya's mother. Irinya had rushed to her, crying. With great difficulty, she'd managed to turn her over. What she saw made her reel back in shock. Her mother was cold and stiff, her eyes open and unseeing, her damp face fixed in a small, disbelieving smile, as if she'd glimpsed heaven before she died.

Irinya had tried to drag her away from the pond, but Urmila was too heavy for her. *Help me,* she'd pleaded the figure made of fire and light. But the figure had turned its back on her.

Irinya had sat by the edge of the pond, shivering and weeping, clutching her mother's hand, begging her to wake up. Finally, the figure had walked up and crouched beside her. It reeked of decaying fish and rotten eggs, and the smell jerked her back to her senses. *Do you want to die, too?* it had asked. *Stay here then.* Looking, sounding so much like her mother.

It had risen and walked away, and this time, Irinya had followed. By the time dawn broke across the sky, and the figure melted into daylight, she was within sight of the camp, with no memory of the night that had passed. She went to her tent and lay on her bed, filthy and exhausted, just as her aunt was waking up. "Where's Urmila?" Bholi had asked, puzzled. "Has she left already?"

"She went out last night," Irinya had said, remembering her mother's good-night kiss.

Bholi's face had collapsed. "And you let her go? Fool!" She'd run out and alerted the others. A search party had gone out into the Rann. Irinya sat on the edge of the salt flats, waiting for her mother to return. But the search party had come back without her. She never saw Urmila again, and she never forgave herself for letting her go.

A rolling boom of thunder brought Irinya back to her senses. Her knees buckled, and she fell to the ground. *No, Ma, stop. Don't go tonight.* That was what she should have said. Tears slid down her cheeks, washed away by the rain.

Her mother's skin had been cold to the touch, her smile frozen. She'd died happy. Was that any consolation? She'd been trying to reach the lotus. She should have known better.

A shout broke through the fog of Irinya's grief. She scrambled to her feet and wiped her face. The rain had slowed, but it was impossible to see anything in the dark. In the distance was a faint glimmer. Chir Batti? She flinched away from it. It had broken through her walls and shown her how her mother had died, and that was punishment enough for being here tonight.

"Help!" came the wazir's voice. She stumbled toward it, her feet sinking into the wet mud, keeping her movements slow and cautious. It was difficult to make out where he was. His voice seemed to change direction every time he shouted. Was she going in circles?

Lightning crackled across the sky. In that split second, she glimpsed the wazir, barely thirty paces away from her. Her throat constricted. He was waist-deep in liquid mud, his face holding the first hint of alarm she'd ever seen on it. She'd warned him this might happen, but had he listened?

She dropped to her hands and knees and crawled forward in the direction where she'd seen him. A breeze blew, clearing a patch of ragged sky, and he resolved into view, arms flailing. Her hands sank into mud, and she backed away.

"Get me out before I drown," he shouted, sinking another inch.

"Take deep breaths and stop moving." She peered at him. Mud streaked his face and hair and clothes.

"Hurry up," he said, a note of appeal in his voice.

Her pulse sped up. For the first time ever, she had the wazir in her power. No matter what else happened, he still had a flower he didn't deserve, that belonged to her kul. And this was her chance to get it back. Fardan would have applauded. She dug her nails into her palm. *Fardan, Jai, Pranal, Ayush: This is for you. I wish you could see him now.*

She narrowed her gaze at him. "Give me the spider lily."

"What?" he stared at her, his face slack.

"The price of my help," she said calmly. "I will get you out, but you must first toss me the box with the flower."

"I will not," he snapped. "That's as good as asking me for the throne."

"Much good will the throne be to a dead man," she said, sitting back.

He gave a brief laugh. "You'll sit and watch me get sucked in? I didn't know you were capable of such coldness. I have underestimated you all this time."

She suppressed a bitter smile. For all his learning, the wazir of Gujarat didn't know that he couldn't get sucked into liquid mud much farther than he had already gone—unless he panicked and struggled. "Hurry up, huzoor. You don't have much time."

Chir Batti darted up to the wazir and then away, as if in agreement with her words. She averted her gaze from it.

Imshan Khan glared at her. "How do I know you won't take the flower and leave me here?"

"You don't," she said. "But I give you my word. I will get you out."

"Isn't there something I can give you that would be worth more than the spider lily?" He tilted his head, his eyes gleaming in his mud-streaked face.

"There isn't," she said, her voice flat. He'd stabbed Fardan with the same sword that had killed Deven. She wouldn't bargain with him. "Not all the gold in your treasury can buy it."

"Not all the flowers in the Rann can give you what I can," he said. "A royal title."

She stared at him, uncomprehending.

"Marriage," he clarified. "As my wife, you would be the sultana. Irinya Sultana. Do you like the sound of that?"

Surprise pooled in her stomach, cold and disorienting. She took a deep breath, centering herself. "Being close to death has robbed you of your senses, huzoor."

"On the contrary, it has sharpened them," he said. "You are quick and clever and have a gift for finding the rarest flowers. With you as my helpmate, I will take over the entire subcontinent. It will be the end of all our enemies. Think, flower hunter. I am offering you more than a kingdom. I am offering *myself*."

He really seemed to think he was worth a silver spider lily. She didn't know whether to laugh or to cry. "No, thank you," she said. "I don't want you. I want the spider lily."

"Mercenary little creature." He narrowed his eyes at her. "Have you no feelings?"

"I left them bleeding with my friends in your hall." *Friends who I pray are still alive.*

And if they were not? If Fardan was already beyond the reach of her jasmine?

She suppressed a shiver. No, she wouldn't believe that. She couldn't, or she'd fall apart. She held out her hand. "Be careful. If you let it fall into the mud, I'll walk away."

The wazir grimaced and removed the box from his pocket. "I should never have trusted you."

The little box flew in an arc toward her hand. She caught it deftly and pried it open. The spider lily glowed silver on a bed of blue velvet. She closed it again and tucked it into her pocket, her heart lifting in relief and triumph. At least the spider lily was safe, even if none of them were. This meant there was still a chance it could be used to drive the Portuguese from India. "You never did trust me, huzoor. You desired my skills, that is all."

"I desired *you*." He gave a mirthless smile. "I had you in my power, and yet I never laid a hand on you."

Her cheeks heated. Fardan had suspected as much; she just hadn't wanted to admit it to herself. She was glad of the darkness, so the wazir could not see her expression. But it didn't matter what he wanted. All that mattered was that she make it back to the palace with both flowers intact so she could save those she loved. "You need to slowly bend backward."

He stared at her. "What?"

"You must spread out your weight," she told him. "That will help you float. Once you're on your back, you can free your legs by making small movements." Something any child of her kul would have known.

He gritted his teeth but obeyed, bending backward, his arms out.

"Now move your legs. Tiny movements only."

It seemed to take forever. The rain stopped, and the wind picked up, chasing ragged clouds across the inky sky, revealing the stars. The air smelled of salt and wet earth. Chir Batti glimmered on the edge of Irinya's vision, waiting, it seemed, for her and the wazir. She ignored it, gazing at the horizon, thinking of Fardan. All her life, she'd taken his presence for granted: hunting flowers, eating his lunches, picking berries with him, laughing at his awful flute playing, admiring his beautiful drawings, ignoring his ridiculous flirting. Never once had she dreamed she might lose him. Her eyes stung. *Please don't leave me, Fardan. We're going to make a book of flower stories, remember? I need to tell you how much you mean to me. I want to sleep in your arms again. I want to hold you and be held by you every night for the rest of my worthless life.*

"My legs are out," gasped the wazir, forcing her back into the present.

She wiped her face with the back of her hand. "Good," she said. "Now sweep your arms back and forth, as if you're swimming. That will take you to the edge of the mud, and you can roll over onto the hard ground."

Five minutes later, he stood before her, exhausted and enraged, covered in sticky wet mud from head to toe. He had lost his shoes and waistcoat. What clothes were left were stuck to his body, outlining his muscular shape.

"I should kill you," he rasped. "Take the flower and throw you into the mud."

"Are you sure you can make your way out of here without me?" she said, her voice even, although her heart drummed inside her chest.

He glanced at the sky. "Probably, although I don't know how long it will take. No, flower hunter. I don't spare you out of fear, but charity. We have yet to see the lotus, and you may yet prove to be a worthy guide. Look, the ghost light beckons."

In the distance, a blue glow hung in the air, rising and falling, as if impatient. Her heart sank. He was still in Chir Batti's thrall. She'd hoped that his struggles in the swamp had knocked some cold sense into him. "Huzoor, you fell into the liquid mud because you were following Chir Batti. No telling what it will do next."

"It will take us to the lotus," he said earnestly. "I know, because it told me." He wiped his face with a sleeve—not that it made much difference—and took off toward the ghost light.

She cursed under her breath and ran behind him to catch up, her feet sinking into the wet, soggy ground. They were going farther into the Rann, and she still had no idea where they were or how long it would take to get out. She needed to return to the palace, and whether she went on foot or was able to make one last door, she would still lose time. *Ten minutes,* she told herself. *That's all I'm giving him before I leave.* "You're hallucinating," she panted. "Just like your men were."

"You just don't want me to find the lotus," he said, his tone that of a petulant child.

"Neither do you," she assured him. "Nothing good will come of it."

But she may as well have not spoken. The wazir strode across the marshy ground, leaping over pools of water, and she followed, filled with misgiving. Her mother had found the lotus and died for it. Irinya could not afford to share that fate. Lives depended on her: Fardan, Jai, Pranal, Ayush, and more—all the people who suffered under the yoke of the Portuguese, who'd had their land and livelihoods stolen and become refugees in their own country. *Five more minutes,* she thought, watching the wazir, *and I'm turning my back on you.*

Chir Batti darted ahead of them, undimmed. The wazir gave a joyous laugh, and she wondered what visions he was seeing in the ghost light. She could have found it in her heart to pity him, if not for the fate of her friends. He'd put his sword through Fardan's chest. *Too late to run,* he'd said in that cold, satisfied voice. Well, it was too late for the wazir now. The Rann had him in its grip.

The moon slipped out from behind the clouds. In that moment, a pond manifested before them. Imshan Khan gasped and lurched to a halt.

A large, moonlit pool of water, circular in shape, perhaps thirty paces across. In its center, glowing like the moon itself, a perfect pink lotus. She stared at it, transfixed. It was just as beautiful as she remembered. The only thing missing was her mother's corpse. She gulped back the sob rising in her throat. *Ma, did you get washed out to sea? Or are you still here, as Chir Batti said? Are you in the salt, in the water, or in the lotus? Are you the one who speaks to me through the flowers?*

"Perfect," whispered the wazir, his tone full of awe. "The sacred lotus. I have been led to my destiny."

She clutched his sleeve, her chest tight. Despite everything, she didn't want to watch him die. "You have been led to your death. Don't venture into the pond, huzoor."

He shook her hand off. "I wish to cleanse myself of this unholy mud. Surely you don't grudge me a bath. In fact," his eyes gleamed, "why don't you shed your inhibitions and join me?"

She took an involuntary step back from him.

He smirked. "So be it. I go alone to my destiny. You can be my witness." He tugged the muddy kurta over his head. She averted her gaze as he removed the rest of his clothing and tossed it aside. But she could still see him from her peripheral vision. Naked, he was magnificent, but also vulnerable, and her heart clenched. He stepped into the pool and waded inside until he was waist-deep in the water.

"It's cool and pure. Are you sure you won't change your mind?" He cupped his hands in the water and washed his face and hair. Beyond the pool, Chir Batti gave one last glimmer and faded into the night. She rubbed her chest, aching at the loss. What had she expected? That her mother would reappear? It had been an illusion, nothing more. The ghost light had done its work; the rest was up to her.

She crouched by the edge of the water and forced herself to look at Imshan Khan. "Come back before it's too late. Before you end up like my . . ." She stopped, unable to go on.

He turned to face her, his brow furrowed. "Your mother?"

She closed her eyes and once again saw her mother's body, her hand outstretched in supplication or surrender. She opened her eyes to find the wazir staring at her with a mixture of concern and speculation. "Yes," she said evenly. "My mother. She died because of this flower." Even as she spoke, she knew it was more than that. Her mother had broken the rules and chosen this path, knowing how it might end.

I'm after a prize tonight.

And what will you do, Ma, if you get the prize? What will there be left for you to do?

She dashed away her tears with the back of her hand. "Please come back. Don't touch the lotus."

"Such concern." Imshan Khan's face softened into a smile. Washed off by the pond water, he gleamed as bright as the lotus itself. "Are you certain you don't want to marry me after all?"

"Not if you were the last man left on earth," she retorted.

He laughed. "I will turn back time. I will change both our lives. You'll see. My grandfather and my father will be sultan. And you—you will not be an orphan."

Her throat tightened. Oh, how she wanted her mother to be alive. But wanting the forbidden was what had gotten Urmila killed in the first place. "My mother is at peace," she whispered.

"But are you?" He waded to the center of the pond, toward the lotus, until he was chest-deep in the water. He reached his hand out to pluck the flower. Irinya could hardly bear to watch.

He froze, his hand still outstretched. His eyes widened. A slow, disbelieving smile lit his face. "It's happening," he whispered. "Just as I dreamed."

She stared at him. "What's happening?"

But he did not respond. Before her horrified eyes, a slow, terrible change came over him. Lines grew on his face. The rippling muscles of his chest sagged. His lush black hair grew gray and sparse, and then white. His eyes hollowed and lost their luster. In the space of a few minutes, he aged fifty years. Nor did it stop there. He grew older still, his head bald and spotted, his pouchy skin hanging from his bones, his quivering hand a claw. He took one last, rattling breath, a ghastly grin fixed on his face. His skin decayed and vanished, leaving a white skeleton gleaming in the moonlight. The bones crumbled and turned to dust, dissolving into the pond.

The wazir was gone. Irinya was alone with the lotus.

She couldn't breathe. All the air had been sucked out of her lungs. She tried to control her breath, to slow her pulse, but it was impossible. The lotus glistened, beautiful and serene. She wanted to run away screaming. But she couldn't move.

"Sorry," she said at last, her voice shaking. "Sorry they broke the rules. Try to understand and forgive them if you can."

Time stopped. And then it rewound so fast she could not process it. She was five years old again. She heard her mother's silver laugh, felt her hand ruffle her hair. Her mother stood before her, a smile on her beloved face. *I am going to tell you a story.* Irinya slipped her hand into her mother's and listened.

The scene switched. Now Urmila was telling her about flowers, using the two poems as teaching tools.

Now she was showing her how to use the blowpipe.

Now she was showing her how to pick the best phalsa berries.

Earlier still. Irinya was three, sitting sleepily on her mother's lap by the fire while Chinmay told stories and someone played the dholak.

Earlier still. She was two, strapped to her mother's back, going into the Rann for the first time.

"Have you taken leave of your senses?" Bholi shouted. "That child   "

"—belongs in the Rann," her mother replied, cutting Bholi off.

Earlier still. She was one, and her mother was singing a lullaby while Irinya held her finger with her chubby fist. Her eyes closed, and her mother planted a kiss on her forehead. "I love you forever," Urmila whispered.

Time stopped and snapped back to the present. Irinya trembled. *Me too, Ma. Love you forever.* She wiped her face with her dupatta, but it stayed wet, tears flowing from her eyes as if they would never stop.

At last, she rose and turned away from the pond. The wazir was dead. *Dead.* That strong, beautiful, arrogant, lost man. She hoped, for his sake, that he had lived a lifetime in those moments that passed so quickly before her eyes. Perhaps he had gone to a different timeline. It was possible. Anything was possible with the lotus.

But she was still alive, still here. She hadn't made the same mistake as her mother. She cast a last look back at the lotus. In the first hint of dawn, it already looked ephemeral, as if it were not all the way there. As if she looked at it through a curtain that got thicker with every passing moment.

She glanced up, and her throat caught. Dawn light flooded the sky, permeating the striated clouds, making bands of gray and pink. The Rann was beautiful in every season. When her gaze returned to the pond, the lotus had vanished. A small breeze ruffled her hair, and a few drops of rain fell. She held her hand out to catch them, and a tiny winged seed drifted onto her palm.

She stared at it. An ordinary seed, surely. But it felt like a gift. "Thank you," she said, tucking it into her cloth bag with the jasmine.

She struck out across the Rann. The rain had transformed it into a wetland. A flock of pink flamingos flew overhead, their wings gleaming in the early-morning light. She stood and watched as they descended into a lake in the distance. How majestic they were. Like everything else in the Rann, they had a place, and they knew it. Humans were the only ones who didn't know their place, didn't keep to the boundaries.

Ma, you should have known better. The thought that she might have lost Fardan, too, was unbearable. Tears started once more in her eyes. She opened the locket, letting her tears slide down her face and trickle into it.

Would it be enough? She brought the locket to her lips and sipped. The taste of grief, loss, and death. The black chrysanthemum never brought happiness.

The door appeared, light and silver, ten paces ahead of her. The last door she'd ever open. She swallowed and walked toward it. *Fardan, I'm coming.*

CHAPTER 21

The door brought her back to the palace, not far from the sultana's chamber. The guards shouted in alarm as she appeared on
a landing, apparently out of thin air. They drew their swords
and surrounded her, their faces tense with fear, their hands shaking.

"Where is the wazir?" demanded the one with the captain's insignia.
"What have you done to him, witch?"

"Take me to Zahra Sultana," she said, making her voice loud and
firm. "I will tell her."

"Move." The captain jerked his sword toward the stairs. "And no
funny tricks, or I'll slice your limbs off."

She turned around and walked down the stairs, her head held high,
not letting her exhaustion show. But her limbs trembled and her eyes
burned. How much time had she lost? Had her friends received the
medical aid she'd demanded?

Zahra was in a small hall located off the inner courtyard. She sat
on a divan, surrounded by courtiers on cushioned seats, her face par-
tially veiled, her eyes narrow with tension. The noblemen's voices were
raised in argument. Tarana stood behind the sultana's chair, her head
bowed. On either side of the sultana was a woman soldier with a sword
on her belt and a spear in her hand. They stood straight-backed and
silent, their faces expressionless.

"Your Highness," burst out the captain with a perfunctory bow. "We have captured the witch who kidnapped the wazir." He beckoned, and the guards pushed Irinya forward.

Zahra shot to her feet, her eyes widening. "Are you all right?"

Irinya bowed, hoping she wouldn't keel over. "Yes, Your Highness."

"Shouldn't you be asking about your nephew's health and where-abouts? Why are you concerned about the witch?" snapped one of the noblemen.

Zahra cut her eyes to him. "She's not a *witch*. She's a flower hunter. She used infusion of black chrysanthemum to make a door, as I have been telling you repeatedly."

"That is unbelievable," said another.

"Oh yes, so much easier to believe that she is a witch, is it not?" said Zahra with contempt. "You men are all the same. Frightened of any woman who is capable, who is powerful."

"You have no power without our support," said a courtier in an oily voice. "At least half the court backs the wazir."

"You would be backing a dead man," said Irinya in a flat voice. She should have felt something other than impatience as she spoke the words, but she burned to know how Fardan and the others were doing. The sooner this conversation was over, the sooner she could find out. "He drowned in a swamp in the Rann." It was close enough to what had happened. They'd never believe the truth.

Hubbub broke out across the hall. Men rose to their feet and beat their chests in a theatrical display of grief, which she knew was all pre-tense. Zahra grasped her chair with one arm and leaned on it, her eyes wide, her face frozen. Tarana bent to whisper in her ear.

One of the noblemen pointed a quivering finger at Irinya. "Throw her into the dungeons. We'll torture the truth out of her before be-heading her."

Rough hands grasped Irinya's arms and shoulders, and she stumbled. Fear clamped its icy fingers around her neck. She couldn't afford to be imprisoned, not now. She had to save her friends.

"Let her go," snapped Zahra in a cold voice. "Or you'll be thrown into the dungeons yourself."

The hands released Irinya at once, and the guards stepped away. She rubbed her arms and straightened, trying to slow her breathing.

"Was this all your plan?" asked the nobleman who had demanded her arrest. "Did you have your nephew murdered so you could take the throne?"

"I had no need to do any such thing," said Zahra, glaring at him. "To even suggest it is treasonous. I am my father's chosen heir."

"We'll never support you now," proclaimed the nobleman, standing up. "Come, brethren. Let us leave this nest of lies and deceit." He stalked out, followed by the rest.

Zahra collapsed on the divan, rubbing her forehead. She frowned at the guards. "Leave us."

The guards bowed and backed away, leaving Zahra, Tarana, and Irinya alone in the hall but for the two women soldiers, who looked like they'd been carved from stone.

Tarana hurried forward and grasped Irinya's arm. "Come, sit. You look like you'll fall down any moment."

"I'm all right," repeated Irinya, but she allowed herself to be led to the divan and sat next to the sultana. Too late, she remembered her damp, muddy clothes. She scooted to the edge of the divan, hoping she hadn't ruined it. Then she wondered why she should care about a divan when her entire world had turned upside down. Imshan had died before her eyes, crumbling to dust. She hadn't been able to save him. She hadn't been able to save her mother, either. She didn't even know if Fardan and the others were still alive.

And she was worrying about a divan? She giggled.

Zahra gave her a piercing stare, poured water into a cup from a carafe, and offered it to her. Irinya drained the cup, fatigue seeping into her bones. She fought to keep her eyes open. Why had she been laughing? She couldn't remember. Tarana sat on her other side, holding her grimy hand as if she might vanish once more.

The sultana refilled her cup. "Tell me what happened. How did my nephew meet his end?"

"I will tell you everything, but first, please, I must see my friends." Irinya drank more water before setting down the cup. "I left them wounded last night in a music hall, surrounded by guards."

Zahra and Tarana exchanged a glance. The blood thundered in Irinya's ears. "What's the matter? Are they all alive? What day is this?"

"Four days," said the sultana somberly. "That's how long you've been gone. The entire palace is in an uproar. You walked through the door with Imshan, and both of you disappeared. You told the guards to get your friends medical help, and they didn't know whether to fetch a physician or throw them into the dungeons. By the time I was woken and consulted, it was too late for one of them. We gave him the last rites yesterday. I'm sorry, but it couldn't wait any longer. The other three are still alive. Two are in reasonable shape and will probably recover, although they drift in and out of consciousness. One lies at the threshold between life and death and may not make it through the night."

Darkness came before Irinya's eyes. One dead, one dying. Who had died? *Not Fardan.* It seemed a betrayal of all her friends to think that, but she couldn't help it. *Not Fardan, please, or I will not survive.* "Jasmine?" she asked, her voice sounding distant to her own ears.

The sultana shook her head. "The royal pharmacist says his stock is finished, wasted on my own dying father. Nothing can help him, but that doesn't stop him demanding tincture of jasmine every night. Even the flower market has run out." Her voice shook. "I will be glad when he's gone, liberated from his failing body."

"Once he's gone, there will be nothing to stop the noblemen from seizing power," murmured Tarana.

"The Royal Women's Guard will stand true to the sultana," said one of the soldiers, scowling.

"The Royal Women's Guard is only five hundred strong." Tarana sighed. "We may have to flee, my lady."

The sultana's face hardened. "I will not flee my home. I will die defending it."

Irinya swallowed the lump in her throat and tried to focus. "Your Highness. I bring two flowers: one for my friends, and one for you." She took the box from her pocket and held it out.

Zahra leaned back, her eyes widening. "Is that . . . ?"

Irinya nodded. "He gave it to me before he died, in return for helping him. I . . . it's a long story and I will tell it to you later. Take this, Your Highness. Use it to expel the Portuguese from India. Use what is left to cement your position in the palace. But be careful. The spider lily will steal the honor and soul if a person is greedy."

"Is that what happened to my nephew?" asked Zahra.

"It's more than that, but yes." Irinya took a deep breath. "Use it for the good of your people, and you won't fall under its spell. And never, ever, try to find another."

Zahra swallowed visibly and accepted the box. "I swear I will use this only for the good of my people." She opened the box and gasped. The silky white petals of the spider lily glowed, giving the sultana an unearthly aura.

Irinya summoned a smile. "The spider lily is where it belongs. And I must make tincture of jasmine for my friends." She got to her feet and swayed, her head swimming. Tarana rose and grasped her arm. Irinya rubbed her head, trying to stay conscious. She couldn't afford to pass out, not now.

"Tarana will go with you," said Zahra, pinning the spider lily to her tunic. "I don't trust anyone else in the palace."

The sultana marched out of the hall, a soldier on either side of her, Tarana and Irinya behind. The guards waiting outside stared in wonder at the flower on her tunic. "Summon the generals and the minister for defense," she commanded. "Have them in the audience hall in fifteen minutes. Send for Malik Ayyaz as well. I think he's still in the palace."

Tarana glanced at the sultana as they walked down a corridor along the courtyard. "What are you planning, my lady?"

She gave a savage smile. "War, my darling. It's time to send the invaders back home." She touched the petals of the spider lily, her eyes sparkling.

"I will accompany you," said Tarana.

"Like hell you will," snapped the sultana.

They continued to argue as they walked along the inner courtyard. Their voices washed over Irinya. She needed to make a tincture as fast as possible. She went over the steps in her mind, wishing it didn't need twenty-four hours for the magic to seep into the mixture. Guards and servants passing by bowed low. She barely saw them. *Fardan, are you alive? Are you all right?*

The royal infirmary was a long, low building that stood in the middle of a garden behind the palace, near the banks of the Sabarmati River. A series of latticed windows let in light and fresh air. The windowsills were covered with pots of sacred basil, brahmi, gotu kola, and other medicinal herbs.

Zahra squeezed her shoulder. "I must go to the audience hall. Tarana will get you anything you need."

Irinya nodded, her steps faltering as they entered the hall. A row of pallets stretched from one end to the other. Only three of them were occupied. She closed her eyes. The moment of truth had arrived. She walked over to the first and bent over it.

Ayush. His eyes were closed, and blood seeped through the bandage on his forehead. But his chest rose and fell, and he was breathing normally. She checked his pulse—a bit fast, but regular. He had fever, and they would have to ensure his wounds didn't become infected, but he was young and strong. He would make it.

She rose and walked with unsteady feet to the next occupied pallet.

Pranal. He was in worse shape than his brother. His chest and left shoulder were bandaged, and his left arm was in a sling. His eyes fluttered open while she was taking his pulse.

"Irinya," he said in a cracked whisper.

She squeezed his hand and gave him a reassuring smile. "I am here. You're going to be fine."

"The others?" he asked.

"All fine," she lied. His eyes closed again, and she made herself get up, made herself walk to the last occupied pallet. *Please, please, please let it be . . .*

Fardan. She swayed, and Tarana rushed up to her.

"Sit down, my lady," she said urgently. "Tell me what to do, and I will do it."

Irinya swallowed. "I need an earthen pot, boiling water, some spirits, and a mortar and pestle. That is all."

Tarana dragged up a chair for her from the corner of the wall and pushed her down on it. "I will have them sent at once." She flew out of the room.

Irinya stared at the man lying comatose by her feet. His face was gaunt and bruised, his breath weak and shallow. Still alive, but only just. Jai, poor Jai, was gone. Given the last rites by strangers, far from home. *How will you tell stories to your children and grandchildren now?*

A raw, ugly sound escaped her throat. She bit her knuckles. *Get yourself together. You have to keep him alive until the tincture is ready.* Hadn't the jasmine said it? *There are three I will heal.* That meant it would save Fardan.

Tarana returned to the hall, followed by palace servants carrying the items Irinya had requested. She wiped her face with a sleeve, washed her hands in a pitcher, and retrieved her precious jasmine from the cloth bag. She set to work, grinding the jasmine with the mortar and pestle. Its fragrance filled the room, calming her. On her instruction, one of the maids poured a golden liquor into the earthen pot and mixed it with the boiling water. Irinya scraped the ground jasmine into the pot and stoppered it.

"What now?" asked Tarana.

"Now we wait." Irinya gazed at Fardan's still figure. "It will be twenty-four hours before it's ready."

"I will guard the tincture and keep watch over them," said Tarana. "You should retire to a room and rest."

Exhaustion welled up in her, and she rubbed her eyes. "I can't leave him."

Tarana rose. "Then I will get you something to eat and drink and a change of clothing. You can lie on one of the pallets here."

She beckoned to the servants, and they left, two soldiers remaining on guard outside the infirmary.

Irinya perched on the pallet next to Fardan and grasped his hand to take his pulse. What big, thick hands he had. And yet they produced the most elegant drawings and the most delectable rotlas. She bit back a sob. His pulse was fast and irregular. He had high fever, just as she had suspected. One of his wounds must have been infected. She braced herself and drew down the sheet that covered his body.

A sick smell of something rotten mixed with the antiseptic smell of neem rose into the air, nearly gagging her. His chest and stomach were covered with bandages. Blood and pus seeped out of them. Irinya tied her dupatta around her nose and mouth, willing herself not to faint. She rose and went to the shelves that lined the walls, searching for fresh bandages. Tarana returned, carrying a platter of food. The sight and smell nearly made Irinya throw up.

"Later, please," she said, gently pushing Tarana out of the room. "I must change his bandages and reapply salve."

"I will send for a nurse, but you must eat," protested Tarana.

"After I've taken care of them," she promised.

She found a fresh roll of bandages and scissors, as well as jars of neem paste, dried madder roots, and turmeric powder. She arranged the jars next to Fardan's pallet and grasped the scissors, trying to steel herself into removing those terrible, blood-soaked bandages.

"It's no good," came a gloomy voice from behind her. "He won't last the night."

She gritted her teeth and turned around. Behind her stood a lugubrious-looking man with a walrus mustache and white overalls. "Are you a physician?"

"Merely a helper."

"Then help me remove these bandages."

With the sad-looking nurse's assistance, she managed to cut away the wet, disgusting bandages around Fardan's chest and stomach. The wounds that were revealed made her cry. He had a gaping stab wound that had been stitched together but was oozing pus and blood. No wonder he was running a high fever. At least the sword had missed his lungs.

She cleaned off the pus as best she could with damp cloth. Once his wounds were clean and dry, she made a paste of turmeric by mixing the powder with a bit of warm water. She applied the turmeric paste to his minor cuts and bruises, reserving the neem paste for the worst injuries. When she was done, the nurse helped her wrap fresh bandages around his wounds.

The nurse left, carrying away the dirty bandages and cloths. Irinya spooned sugar water into Fardan's mouth. Most of it trickled out, but she hoped some drops went down his throat. Then she did the same for Pranal and Ayush.

Tarana entered with clean clothes for her and a pitcher of water to wash her face and hands. Once Irinya had washed and changed, the maid forced her to take a break in the garden outside. But although Irinya tried, she could not eat anything. All she managed was a cup of tea.

"You can do no good to your friends if you fall sick yourself," said Tarana, looking at the untouched plate with disapproval.

"I'm fine," Irinya lied and went back inside. There was no change in Fardan, although both Ayush and Pranal looked a little better. She sat by his side, keeping vigil, willing him to fight the infection that raged through his body.

The sultana arrived that evening to check on her and give her an update.

"We leave for Junagadh in two days," she told Irinya. "The minister tried to make excuses, but the generals agreed. We will mobilize what is left of our navy in Junagadh and attack Diu in ten days' time. Malik Ayyaz will lead my forces. I'm taking all the Royal Women's Guards except the ones on watch outside the infirmary. I want you to make tincture of silver spider lily for me."

"Me?" Irinya's head reeled. "Your Highness, the palace apothecary would do a better job."

The sultana pursed her lips. "I don't trust him. I trust no one. Make the tincture in secret. I am appointing you the Royal Flower Manager of Gujarat in front of the full court tomorrow morning. No one will be able to question you after that."

Irinya found her voice. "Royal Flower Manager? I didn't know such a post existed."

Zahra smiled. "It does now." She unpinned the spider lily from her tunic and gave it to Irinya. "Use the palace apothecary equipment if you wish. I will send guards, so you don't run into any trouble."

Irinya accepted the spider lily with shaking hands. The sultana was showing great trust in her. "They'll never stop thinking you planned the murder of your nephew," she warned.

"I don't care what they think. That's exactly how their minds work." Her gaze went to the occupied pallets. "Can you tell me what happened to Imshan?"

Irinya nodded. "Please sit, Your Highness."

The sultana perched on a chair and listened as Irinya described what had happened. The telling hurt, forcing her to relive that terrible night. But she told Zahra everything except the part about her mother. That was private and did not concern the sultana.

When she was done, Zahra reached forward and squeezed her hand. "I'm sorry about the way he died. But I'm glad you are out of his power." She rose. "I must speak with my father. If he is blessed with a lucid moment, I would like to tell him about Imshan before he gets a garbled version from one of the courtiers."

She left, and Irinya returned to her vigil by Fardan's bedside. Tarana rejoined her a little later and forced her to eat a bit of khichdi with pickles. To her surprise, Irinya felt better after eating.

"Are you going to make the tincture in the apothecary's quarters?" asked Tarana, pointing to the spider lily in Irinya's hand.

Irinya considered and shook her head. "Get me the same items I used for the tincture of jasmine. The process is the same. This way, no one will suspect what I am doing. They will think the spider lily is still with the sultana."

Once again, Tarana rushed out and returned with the items Irinya required. Irinya ground the spider lily into a paste, struck by how casually she was treating this flower for which she had risked everything. "I'm sorry," she whispered as she scraped it into the steaming pot. "But I think you're going to be used for the good this time."

She stoppered the pot and gave it to Tarana. "Guard it until tomorrow. Then we can strain it into a bottle for the sultana."

Tarana grasped the pot, a determined look in her eyes. "I'm going to sleep with my arms around it."

Irinya's lips twitched. "As long as you don't spill it."

A long and difficult night followed. Tarana slept on a mat on the floor at one end of the hall, her arms around the precious pot. The nurse slept on one of the pallets in case Irinya required his help. Pranal and Ayush had periods of wakefulness, and she was kept busy spooning medicine and thin gruel into their mouths, applying wet cloths to their foreheads, and soothing them when they moaned with pain.

But Fardan did not move or make a single sound. As the night progressed, his pulse grew more erratic, his breathing more labored.

She held his hand between her own, pressing it. "If you die, I'll never forgive you," she whispered fiercely. "Stay with me, Fardan."

All through the night, she stayed by his side. At dawn, she fell asleep sitting up, only to jerk awake in a panic that he would have slipped away from her through the door of death.

But he was still alive, painfully so, each breath a rattle in his wounded chest.

In the morning, Irinya was summoned to the court. As promised, Zahra gave her the title of Royal Flower Manager and announced that she would be answerable only to the throne. Anyone interfering in her duties would be tried for treason. The announcement was met with dead silence, the courtiers throwing looks of suspicion and fear at Irinya. The stories of what she'd done to Imshan would get worse with time. Irinya bowed to the sultana, too numb to speak, her mind on Fardan. What did any of this matter unless he recovered?

The rest of the day passed in excruciating slowness. Tarana and Irinya stayed at the infirmary, guarding the tinctures. From the windows, they could see the guards who surrounded the building. Irinya hoped they were loyal to the sultana. In the distance, around the palace, they could see more guards, servants, and courtiers hurrying to and fro. The palace was a hive of activity. Tomorrow, the sultana would leave with her soldiers and generals for Junagadh. And it was Irinya's job to ensure she carried a bottle of genuine spider lily tincture with her.

"I'm going with her tomorrow," said Tarana suddenly, gazing out of the window at the palace.

"She's allowing you to?" said Irinya in astonishment.

Tarana grimaced. "She doesn't get to decide everything. I have a right to be with her, and she knows it."

"I think she would prefer it if you were safe."

Tarana shook her head. "I will die of worry in her absence. I'd rather live and die beside her."

Irinya could understand that.

When the twenty-four hours were up, Irinya removed the stopper from the pot containing tincture of jasmine. A delicate fragrance permeated the air, and she smiled in relief. It was ready. She started with Ayush, because he was easiest to wake, followed by Pranal. One teaspoon each, and they should be fully recovered by the next day.

Fardan she kept for the last. He was still unconscious, although he moaned from time to time, as if his pain penetrated the depths of his slumber. She put a hand below his head and gently raised it. "Wake up, Fardan; time to take your medicine."

His eyes fluttered, and her heart leaped with joy. "Open your mouth," she ordered.

He didn't respond, but she managed to slide a spoon of tincture inside. He swallowed it and she laid his head back down, her heart lighter. He should be better soon.

But as the day passed, there was no change in him at all. Ayush was the first to wake and get out of bed, confused and famished. Pranal was next. She sent them both off to the bathhouse to wash and change their clothing, because they stank of sweat, blood, and medicine. By the time they returned, plates of food and glasses of lassi had arrived for them, thanks to Tarana.

"Where's Jai?" asked Pranal, looking around. "Why is Fardan still asleep? What happened?"

"Eat first," said Irinya, pushing the plates toward them. "Talk later."

They didn't need a second invitation. They fell to, eating as if they'd never seen food in their entire lives. When they were done, she took them to the garden and told them that Jai was dead. It was hard telling them, harder still to see their grief, which mirrored her own.

"And Fardan?" asked Ayush, wiping his eyes.

She tried to give him a reassuring smile. "I gave him the tincture. He should recover soon."

They went back inside and joined her in her vigil by his bedside, talking in hushed tones. Irinya gave them a brief gist of what had happened.

"You saw the sacred lotus?" Ayush looked at her in awe.

Irinya flinched at the memory. "It's not a flower that is meant to be seen. I'm lucky I made it out alive."

"Luck has nothing to do with it." Pranal nudged her. "You're the kul's storyteller now. The flowers can't take you, or who'll tell their stories?"

She laughed and looked at Fardan. *Please wake up,* she thought. *How can I tell stories if you aren't there to listen to them?*

Zahra arrived a little later. Irinya rose and hissed at Pranal and Ayush, "Get up. It's the sultana."

The boys shot to their feet and bowed to her. She smiled at them. "Thank you for the help you rendered Irinya in recovering the spider lily. I'm going to use it wisely, and I will pay you well for it."

The boys exchanged a meaningful glance. "Our kul is in debt to a moneylender who takes all our flowers," said Pranal, a note of appeal in his voice.

Irinya started. With everything that had happened, she'd forgotten all about their debt. Good thing the boys had remembered.

The sultana cast a warm glance at Irinya. "Not anymore. I will send men to your kul. They will settle your debt and deal with the money-lender."

Warmth bloomed in Irinya's chest at the sultana's words. At last, her kul would be free of the baniya.

"It was Jai's dream to start a cooperative," blurted out Ayush. "So we could set our own prices, deal directly with the apothecaries, and never be in the middlemen's power again."

The sultana did not hesitate. "If that was his dream, and if it is what you want, I give my blessing. It's time we dismantled the structure that keeps you and other flower hunters mired in poverty."

Ayush gave a subdued cheer, and Pranal pumped his arms. Irinya hugged herself, her heart feeling as if it would overflow. They'd never be in debt again. They'd start a cooperative—one way of honoring Jai's memory, and Deven's, too.

The sultana turned to Irinya, her face alive with anticipation. "Is it ready?"

"It should be, Your Highness." Irinya beckoned Tarana.

Tarana fetched the pot she'd been guarding, and Irinya removed the stopper. She strained it into a jar, using a soft white muslin cloth. The liquid was a pale gold—the color of victory. She transferred it into a glass bottle, stoppered it, and handed it to the sultana.

"How much am I supposed to drink?" asked Zahra, turning the bottle over in her hands, her brows knitted.

Irinya shrugged. "I think you'll know, Your Highness. There are no records, no rules. Not for the rarest flowers."

Zahra nodded. "I'll figure it out." To Irinya's surprise, the sultana drew her into her arms and hugged her. "Take care while I'm gone. I hope he recovers soon."

Irinya smiled, her eyes blurring. "You too, take care. Conquer your enemies, but do not lose yourself."

"I'll remember." Zahra glanced at Tarana. "We have much to prepare."

Tarana went up to Irinya and squeezed her arms. "Thank you for everything. Stay safe and well. We will leave loyal guards around the infirmary so no one gives you any trouble." She planted a kiss on Irinya's cheek and left with the sultana.

The days and weeks that followed were hard and long. Every morning, Irinya gave a teaspoon of the jasmine tincture to Fardan, but it made no difference. He continued to suffer. Ayush and Pranal proved to be an immense help. They did all the running around for her, fetched her whatever she needed, and sat by his bedside when she took a break to sleep.

But she could see it wearing them down, bit by bit, as Fardan refused to improve. Every night, they would talk of Jai in quiet voices, remembering all the times they'd hunted flowers together or the times he'd gotten them out of trouble. The eldest and wisest of them all, and he was gone. Then they would look at Fardan and back at Irinya, mute appeal in their eyes, as if asking her what was wrong, why she couldn't help him.

Sweet white jasmine will betray you in the end. The words cut into her every night as she tossed and turned on a pallet near Fardan. There was always a cost. Hadn't she known it? It hadn't stopped her from using the flower. But it never helped those who needed it most. Had it lied to her when it said it would heal three people?

It doesn't matter, she thought. *I won't let him die.*

Life and death are not in your hands, flower hunter. The jasmine sat opposite her in the lotus position, its face and voice unbearably serene.

She blinked. *I am asleep and dreaming. Otherwise, I'd throttle your pretty little neck.*

It gave a gentle, derisive laugh. *And that will help, will it?*

What will help? Tell me!

You are already doing everything you can. The flower closed its eyes. *Perhaps it will be enough.*

She woke to swollen eyes and a raw feeling in her throat, as if she had screamed the whole night long. She wiped her face and got up. She wouldn't give Fardan the tincture anymore. It wasn't helping him. It might even be hindering him in some way. She bent over him, smoothing his hair back from his forehead. How thin and wasted he'd become. How slow his wounds were to heal. Every day she applied fresh dressings and changed his bandages. Every day she prayed for a miracle that did not come.

His eyes fluttered open. "Irinya?" he whispered.

Her heart leaped. He'd called her by her name. "I am here." She stroked his head and he sighed, closing his eyes again. Was it only wishful thinking that he was breathing easier? She did not allow herself to hope, to relax her guard in the slightest.

News of the outside world filtered in via the soldiers who had been stationed outside the infirmary. The sultana had reached Junagadh. The sultana had roused her navy and launched an attack on the Portuguese in Diu. The Portuguese had abandoned Diu and fled down the coast to Goa. The sultana's navy had chased them and sunk dozens of Portuguese caravels. They had attacked Goa and captured the Portuguese commander, Francisco de Almeida, along with hundreds of his men. The Portuguese were suing for peace. The Portuguese were *leaving* the Malabar Coast.

"Good riddance," said Ayush with a triumphant smile.

"They'll be back," said Irinya, checking Fardan's pulse. His fever had finally broken, and that was of greater importance to her than all the battles in the world. "Men like them are never satisfied with what they have."

"But the sultana has the silver spider lily now. She will be prepared for them," said Pranal.

One day, the tincture would run out. One day, the sultana would be no more, and who was to say if her heir would have her courage and strength?

But the future was not in anyone's hands. All that was in their hands was the present.

Fardan opened his eyes and croaked, "Water."

A jolt went through Irinya. It was the first time he'd asked for water. Ayush sprang to get him a cup, and Pranal helped him sit up. Irinya placed the cup to his lips and tilted it, allowing the water to trickle into his mouth. She wiped his mouth with the edge of her dupatta, trying not to cry.

"How are you feeling?" asked Ayush.

He leaned back against the wall, exhaustion on his face. "Like I was beaten by Bholi to within an inch of my life," he rasped.

Pranal and Ayush laughed, their tension dissolving like salt in the rain. Irinya's eyes blurred, and she bent her face so they would not notice. Fardan squeezed her hand. "I'm sorry," he whispered.

She smiled at him through her tears. She knew what he meant. *Sorry for getting stabbed. Sorry for almost dying. Sorry for not having your back.*

Don't be, she wanted to tell him. *You always had my back. I just didn't know it.*

That night, while Ayush and Pranal slept, she sat by Fardan's side and told him all that had happened. She left nothing out, not even her memory of the night her mother died. He listened to her with grave attention, his face emaciated, his hazel eyes as bright as ever. When she was done, he grasped her hand and said, "You did it, Irinya. You saved us."

Her eyes stung. "I couldn't save Jai." Or Imshan or Deven.

The pressure on her hand increased. "He knew what he was getting into. It's not your fault."

She couldn't help but think it was. None of this would have happened if she hadn't plucked the spider lily. But then the Portuguese would still be in control of the Indian Ocean, capturing trading ships and killing innocent fishermen and pilgrims. Did the sacrifice of a few justify the greater good?

No, she couldn't make herself believe that. Each life was precious. But what had happened stayed happened. There was nothing she could do to alter it. Regret would poison her waking hours; it wouldn't bring back those who were gone.

Fardan recovered slowly but surely. It was not the miraculous recovery promised by the jasmine, but the slow healing from constant care. At the end of the month, the day before Zahra returned in triumph to Bhadra Fort, he was able to get up, eat, and walk with some help. It smote Irinya's heart to see him so gaunt and weak, but he would recover his strength. She'd make sure of that. She plied him with tasty morsels of food, buttermilk, and herbal tonics until he laughingly protested that she was fattening him up for Bholi Masi to chew on.

The sultan finally gave up his tenacious hold on life and passed away.

The sultana was crowned the very next day. No one argued or told her she should marry one of the noblemen so a man could rule in her stead. Her defeat of the Portuguese had cemented her power in a way nothing else could have.

They stayed for the sultana's coronation, but as soon as it was over, Irinya requested an audience with her and told her they would be leaving for home.

"I look forward to seeing you when next you have a beautiful flower to share," said Zahra warmly. "Your kul's debt has been settled. The baniya will not bother you again." From behind her, Tarana gave Irinya a dimpled smile. "Here—take this." The sultana passed Irinya a tightly folded parchment affixed with the royal seal.

Irinya accepted it, puzzled. "What is this, Your Highness?"

"A royal edict," said Zahra, "stating your title and your powers. Organize the flower hunters and come up with a management plan. No one can stop you."

Warmth flooded Irinya's chest. Here, finally, was the chance to better the lives of all the kuls as well as replenish the magic of the Rann. "Thank you for everything, Your Highness," she said, bowing.

Zahra grasped her shoulders, raising her up. "No, thank *you*. I owe you so much, and I can never repay you."

"Then pay it forward," said Irinya. "Be the best ruler Gujarat has ever seen."

Zahra gave a rueful laugh. "Well, I have to live up to your expectations, don't I? I'll try my best, flower hunter."

"And I will scold her if she doesn't." Tarana gave Zahra an affectionate glance. Irinya left the chamber, feeling as if she were walking on air. The sultana's position was secure. No one would threaten her, or the relationship she had with Tarana, ever again. And India was safe as well—at least for now.

Irinya and the boys set off the next day after retrieving Veerana from the stable. The boys rode on horses that had been gifted to them by the sultana, laden with food packed by Tarana and a fat purse of gold mohurs to pay for the spider lily, stitched into Irinya's skirt. Someone from the Revenue Department had arranged for them to travel with a caravan until Bhuj.

"I'm so glad to be going home," said Ayush fervently as they passed through the Delhi Darwaza to join the caravan waiting outside.

Fardan laughed. "And here I thought you wanted to open a sweet shop and live in the city forever."

"I've had enough of the city," said Ayush. "I want the wide-open spaces of Banni."

Irinya looked at him in astonishment. "What happened to you?"

He shrugged. "Don't know. Maybe it was the month we spent cooped up in the palace."

Or maybe it was Jai. He'd said he didn't want to be hemmed in by brick walls, that he'd rather sleep in a tent or out in the open. As they trotted after the caravan, she turned her head for a last glance at the beautiful cityscape rising beyond the walls. *Goodbye, Ahmedabad,* she thought, her throat catching. *Goodbye, Jai.*

CHAPTER 22

The kul had returned to their village near Bhuj for the monsoon. There would be no going to the grassland until the rains were over. It was a drab, drizzly day when Irinya and the others left the caravan in Bhuj and made their way to the village. A shout went up as they halted near the village well under the peepal tree. People poured out of huts and sheds to greet them.

"They're back!"

"Fardan? Are you alive? You look awful."

"Pranal, Ayush! Just wait until I get my hands on you."

The two brothers ducked behind their horses as their mother, a large, scowling woman, bore down on them. "Where were you?" she screamed. "I've been worried sick." She grabbed them by their collars, shook them, and burst into tears.

"Where is Jai?" Jai's mother, Amba, scanned the little group, her eyes large with anxiety. "Didn't he go with you?"

Irinya's heart shriveled. Now for the most difficult part. She went up to Amba and grasped her hands, willing herself to look into the older woman's eyes. "I'm sorry, Amba. He is no more." Cries of distress broke across the crowd.

"What do you mean?" Amba dug her fingers painfully into Irinya's flesh. "What kind of horrible joke is this?"

"I'm sorry," she repeated, wishing the earth would swallow her up. "There was a fight, and he got injured. I could not save him."

Amba shrieked, a sound that shattered Irinya's fraying self-control, and fainted. Her husband, Jai's father, caught her in his arms, his own face torn by grief and bewilderment. Amba's sisters and cousins surrounded them and led them away to their hut.

Irinya crossed her arms and hugged herself, feeling cold. Fardan laid a hand on her shoulder and squeezed. "You've got this," he whispered. She took a deep breath, his touch anchoring her.

A familiar voice broke through the hubbub. "Where is she? Tell me so I can kill her!" Bholi Masi fought through the crowd that surrounded them and seized hold of Irinya.

"You bad girl," she said, shaking and crying, "how could you put me through this?"

Irinya wiped the tears away from her aunt's cheeks and summoned her strength. "I'm sorry, Masi. I'll never leave without telling you again. I promise." Bholi gave a sob and fell on her neck, nearly crushing her in her embrace.

"You have an explanation to give us," said Miraben in a voice like granite, standing with her arms akimbo. "If I am not satisfied with it, you will be exiled from the kul."

Bholi stiffened and thrust Irinya behind her. "You'll be exiling her aunt and uncle as well."

"I *do* have a good explanation." Irinya ripped out the purse of gold mohurs from her skirt and held it up. "I got back the mohur and the mohur's cousins as well. Just like I promised."

Suspiciously, Miraben opened the purse and peeked at its contents. She gasped and closed the purse again, her eyes round. "Where did you steal this from?" she said in a faint voice.

"We didn't steal it," said Ayush indignantly. "We were paid. Tell them, Irinya."

"Not like this. Properly," said Irinya. "I want a fire and a cup of tea, as befits a storyteller. Then I will tell you the story of what happened."

Miraben gave her a measuring look. "Are you ready to take Chinmay's place in the kul?"

How was that possible? Irinya remembered the sweet-natured, garrulous elder and swallowed the lump in her throat. "I don't think anyone can take his place."

"But if anyone could, it would be you," murmured Fardan. "It's what he would have wanted."

And wasn't it what she wanted as well? She squared her shoulders. "I'll tell you the story, and you can decide if I'm worth keeping on."

Miraben nodded, her lips stretching into an unwilling smile. "Tonight, we will hear your story and determine its worth." She walked toward Jai's hut to join his grieving relatives.

Irinya watched her go, her heart squeezing. She was back where she belonged, but nothing was the same. Jai was gone, and Chinmay, too. She'd seen the sacred lotus, remembered her mother, and witnessed far too many violent deaths. But she still had Fardan. She sensed him standing protectively behind her, solid and dependable, and her heart lightened. *Beloved,* she thought. *We are home.*

She turned to her aunt. "How is Gopal Masa?"

"He'll be better now that you're back." Bholi eyed Veerana, who stood behind Irinya and Fardan, placidly chewing his cud. "And his camel."

"I've brought special medicine for his lungs from Ahmedabad," said Irinya. The jasmine had not lied to her. There was a third it would heal. She cut her eyes to Fardan, and her voice sharpened. "*You* need to rest and recover from the journey."

"I'll take care of him. He looks like the wind will blow him over." Shweta, the kul's healer, laid her hand on Fardan's arm and led him away, Fardan protesting that he was fine and didn't need any special care. Irinya bit back a smile. The healer would make sure Fardan rested and ate something.

"What happened to him?" asked Bholi Masi as they walked toward their hut, one of the many mud-and-daub dwellings that surrounded the peepal tree.

"He was injured in the same fight that took Jai," said Irinya. "It took a long time for his wounds to heal." Goose bumps prickled her skin at the thought of how close it had been, of how she'd nearly lost him, too.

Bholi gave her a piercing stare. "Anything going on between you two?"

She gave her aunt an innocent smile. "What do you mean, Masi?"

They arrived at their hut. "Later." Bholi Masi shook a finger at her. "You'll tell me everything." She poked her head inside. "Look who's here with special medicine!" She tugged Irinya inside, her hand firmly closed around her wrist, as if Irinya might run away again.

Gopal Masa lay on his pallet, his breathing labored, his eyes closed. "Tell Shweta her concoctions are useless," he quavered. "I refuse to be subject to them anymore. Let me die in peace."

Irinya came forward and sat next to him, her heart clenching at the sight of his emaciated face and scrawny neck. "Please don't die just yet," she said, keeping her tone light. "I still need you. And Veerana would miss you terribly."

His eyes flew open, and he stared at her in disbelief. "Irinya? Is that you?" He reached up a bony hand to touch her face.

She pressed his hand to her cheek, tears starting in her eyes. "Fardan told me you were ill, and I got you some medicine. I'm sorry I took so long."

His face relaxed into a smile. "I don't need medicine now. The sight of you alive and well has cured me completely." He tried to get up.

"Humor me, Masa. Take one spoon, please." Irinya removed the stopper from her jar and carefully poured a spoon of jasmine tincture out for him. There was very little left, but he shouldn't need more than the single spoon to feel better. Bholi helped raise his head, and Irinya tipped the spoon inside his mouth.

He smacked his lips and lay down again. "Where have you been? Your aunt has nearly hounded me to death."

"Fool," muttered Bholi, wiping her eyes. "It is you who has tormented me with your illness."

"You both torment each other equally well." Irinya closed the jar and slid it beneath his pallet. "Honestly, you two are a walking advertisement for staying single."

Bholi fixed a beady glare on her. "You've been gone *months*. And you've spent a lot of time with *that boy*."

You have no idea, Masi. "Don't worry, I spent more of it with Veerana."

"How is he?" asked her uncle anxiously.

"He is well and looking forward to being reunited with you." She tucked the sheet around her uncle's chin. "Close your eyes now; let the medicine do its work."

He clutched her hand. "Are you leaving again?"

She smiled. "I'm not going anywhere. I'm going to sit right here and tell you stories. Would you like that?"

He gave a happy sigh. "Yes, please."

She began to speak, telling him the stories she knew about the jasmine, the hibiscus, the chrysanthemum. All stories they'd heard before, but every teller brought something new to the tale. He listened with a smile on his lips while Bholi embroidered in one corner. Only when her uncle fell asleep, his breathing quiet and even, did Irinya rise from his side.

That evening, the entire kul sat around a fire and sipped tea as she told them the story of the spider lily, how it fell into the wrong hands, and how she brought it back. When her voice grew hoarse, she paused to take another cup of tea. But no one interrupted her. None of the boys tried to tell any part of the tale. Because this was *her* story, and she was being judged on its worth.

By the time she was done, it was late at night, and the children had been packed off to sleep. All the adults sat staring at her wide-eyed as if she were Chir Batti.

"You did all this," said Miraben in a tone of wonder. "You are responsible for the sultana's victory over the Portuguese."

Irinya gazed at the dancing flames of the fire, uncomfortable with that assessment. "I am also responsible for Jai."

"We will hold the last rites for him tomorrow," said Jai's aunt, Seema. His mother was too grief-stricken to join them. One of her sisters was watching over her. "There must be recompense."

"I know." Irinya swallowed. "What would be fair?"

"You must take care of her," said Seema. "Jai was her only child."

Irinya nodded. It was a fair ask. "I will do my best."

"And you will take Chinmay's place," said Tammi, the priestess. "The story was worthy."

The elders murmured agreement. "But the mohurs," said Miraben, chewing her lip. "What do we do with them? It is too much. We can change one of them tomorrow, and that will be sufficient to see us through an entire year. But there are over thirty!"

"Bury them in a chest," said Rishabh.

Shweta snorted. "Why, so they grow into a tree of mohurs?"

"Buy more cows and buffaloes," said Devesh.

"We should only buy as many as we can take care of," said Miraben, frowning. She turned to Irinya. "What do you think we should do?"

Irinya started. They were asking *her*? But she knew what to tell them. "I think," she said slowly, "we must be careful not to take more than we need. And we don't need all these mohurs. You know who does? All the other kuls in debt to moneylenders. The sultana has given us her approval to form a cooperative. We need to connect with the other kuls, one by one, and buy their debt. Only then will they be free to form cooperatives of their own. And only then can we place limits on the number of flowers each kul can harvest."

Miraben stared at her, her mouth turned down. "These are a lot of mohurs, but they're not enough to free every nomad in Banni from debt," she rasped.

"I know," said Irinya. "But we must make a start. Once we organize ourselves and start getting higher prices for our flowers, people will be able to pay off their debts faster."

"That makes sense," said Tammi approvingly.

"Will you still go into the Rann?" asked Miraben. "None of you need to hunt flowers any longer."

"No, we need to *manage* them," said Fardan. He exchanged a quick smile with Irinya. "Off the top of my head, we should harvest no more than three flowers per kul per season."

"People won't listen to you," said Rishabh.

"They will," assured Fardan. "Once they are free of debt and they see how much they can get for a single jasmine, they will listen."

"I would like to join the cooperative and meet with other kuls," said Vimal, Miraben's son, and this time, she did not object.

They began to plan for the coming months. Miraben needed someone to go into the city with her the next day to change a mohur, and Vimal and Fardan volunteered. At first, the elders didn't want to let

Fardan take a single step out of the village, but he managed to persuade them that he was strong enough to make small trips.

After a while, Irinya slipped away and went to their hut. Gopal Masa was still asleep, but it was the sound sleep of the healthy. In the light of the flickering candle, she could see that his face was relaxed, his breathing easy. Relieved, she stepped out of the hut and strolled to the vegetable garden at the back, dominated by a large tamarind tree. The moon shone through the branches of the tree, and cicadas called, filling the night air with their chirping. It wasn't as good as being back in Banni, but it was still home. She leaned against the trunk of the tree and thought about how lucky she was to be here, to be alive, her kul safe and sound.

"Irinya?" came Fardan's voice from the front of the hut.

Her pulse quickened. "I'm here."

He walked over to her, stepping carefully between the vegetable beds. He'd regained some of the weight he'd lost during his long illness, but his face was thinner, his chin sharper. His eyes, dancing in the moonlight, were as mischievous as ever. "Got tired of the old geezers, did you?"

She gave him a small whack on the shoulder. "Don't be rude to your elders."

"Ouch." He grimaced and clutched his shoulder.

Alarm coursed through her. "Did I hurt you? Is it an old wound?" She stood on tiptoe and pushed away his hand. "Let me see it." Gently, she pulled up his sleeve to reveal the skin.

But his shoulder was unblemished. Come to think of it, none of his many wounds had been on his shoulders. But his face was scrunched up in pain, his lips pressed together.

"What is it, Fardan? How can I help?" she asked anxiously.

He gave her an innocent, wide-eyed look. "You could kiss it and make it better."

Why, the absolute *monkey*. Well, two could play the game. She pulled the sleeve up a bit farther and planted a soft kiss on his shoulder.

She let go of his sleeve and gazed into his face. He was staring at her wide-eyed, like she'd grown horns.

"Is that better?" she asked sweetly, even as her heart pounded inside her chest. "Or would you like me to kiss it some more?"

"Irinya," shouted Bholi. "Where are you?"

Fardan's expression changed to alarm. He scuttled away from the garden, taking the long route behind the tree to avoid her aunt.

Irinya bit back a giggle. "I'm here, Masi. Just enjoying the moonlight."

"It's time to sleep," called Bholi. "Don't forget, you have to get up at dawn to milk the cows."

Irinya groaned and trudged back to the hut. Odd, how everything could change and yet stay the same.

The next day, after an exhausting morning of chores, she planted the winged seed the Rann had gifted her in an empty space between the tamarind tree and a pumpkin patch. She surrounded it with a circle of sticks to protect any seedling that might emerge and tried to forget about it. It would grow or not. It would be magical or not.

Gopal Masa woke late in the morning, hungry and querulous and as healthy as he'd been a decade ago. Bholi was so happy, she didn't quarrel with him for a whole ten minutes while she served him the best meal she could rustle up. After eating, Gopal Masa went outside to fall sobbing on Veerana's neck. Veerana hummed in delight to be reunited with his old master.

Irinya didn't see Fardan all day because he'd gone with Miraben and Vimal to a money changer in Bhuj. They returned late in the evening in triumph, leading a donkey laden with supplies. Miraben had splurged on rice, grain, oil, pulses, candles, and even rolls of cotton for them to make new clothes. The supplies would be divided among all the kul families. As Fardan unloaded the donkey, Irinya whispered in his ear, "Come to the tamarind tree tonight. I have something to show you." His ears went red, but he didn't say anything.

After the evening meal, while the rest of the kul chatted around the fire and as Ayush and Pranal regaled them with stories of Jai's valor, Irinya slipped away to the garden behind her hut. She crouched over the patch where she'd planted the seed. Was it her imagination, or was a tiny shoot already thrusting valiantly out of the damp earth? She would have to check in the morning. The moonlight made everything magical.

A soft footfall sounded behind her, and she turned. Fardan stopped a few feet away from her, an odd expression on his face.

She beckoned. "Come closer."

He stepped closer, refusing to meet her eyes.

"What's the matter?" she said, puzzled. "Look here. See that patch surrounded by sticks?"

He cast a suspicious glance at her and gazed at the ground.

She stood. "I planted the seed I got from the Rann. I'm not sure, but I think it's germinating. Or maybe that's a weed. Too early to tell."

He stared at it, then back at her. "That's why you called me here?"

Why was he behaving so strangely? "Of course. What did you think?"

He huffed a laugh. "I thought you wanted to kiss me again."

Her cheeks heated. "Fardan Hajani, I'd rather kiss a frog than kiss you."

"You did it yesterday," he pointed out with an injured expression.

"Only out of pity to make you feel better," she said with a grin. "You're better now, aren't you?"

He tried to summon a pained look. "Now it's my cheek that's hurting."

"Oh, is it?" She reached up and brushed her knuckles against his cheek. He'd shaved that morning, but it was still bristly. The thought of placing her lips on it was both alarming and unbearably exciting. "You're too tall for me," she said, her tone flippant.

Helpfully, he bent toward her until his face was right above hers. "Is that better?"

She grasped his shoulders and brushed his lips with hers. It was only the briefest touch, but it sent her heart racing. His lips were so soft, so yielding, so kissable. He made a startled sound in his throat.

She released his shoulders and stepped back. He was staring at her with a stunned expression, as if she'd hit him on the head.

"Fardan," she whispered.

"Hmm," he said, dazed.

She giggled. "Are you okay?"

His gaze dropped to her lips. He bent his face and fastened his mouth on hers, grasping her hands and pushing her against the tamarind tree. His rough cheeks grazed her skin, and she gasped, inhaling his sweet, familiar scent. She tugged her hands free and slid them around his neck, pulling him closer, pressing herself against him until his heart beat like thunder against her own. All the horrors of the last few months faded away in his embrace, and a deep feeling of rightness came over her. She was where she belonged. And she was never leaving again.

GLOSSARY

arrack: Distilled alcoholic beverage produced in South and Southeast Asia.

Baluchi: A West Iranian group from the Baluchistan region of West and South Asia, which includes parts of Pakistan, Iran, and Afghanistan.

baniya: An occupational community of merchants, traders, bankers, and moneylenders, or an individual from this community, mainly in northern and western India.

brahmi: *Bacopa monnieri,* a medicinal herb native to India and commonly used in traditional Indian medicine.

charpoy: Literally "four-foot," it is a traditional woven bed used across South Asia.

Chir Batti: This "ghost light" has been reported in the Banni grasslands for centuries. The round or pear-shaped balls of light hover two to ten feet above the ground and can move very fast. Locals believe that if followed, they can mislead travelers off the road, into thorny bushes, or to the salt flats.

choli: A short, snug blouse that covers the front and is tied at the back.

darwaza: Door.

Devanagari: A writing system based on the Brahmi script, developed in ancient India. It is currently the fourth most widely used writing system in the world.

dholak: Popular folk drum of Northern India.

dhoti: A large rectangular piece of cloth tied around the waist, it is the lower garment for men in the Indian subcontinent, forming part of the traditional national costume.

Dhruva: Polestar.

dupatta: A long scarf or shawl worn by South Asian women around the neck, head, and shoulders, often with a salwar kameez.

ghagra: A long, loose, embroidered skirt worn with a choli, tied at the waist with a drawstring, and usually made of cotton.

gotu kola: *Centella asiatica* is an herb that is used in traditional Chinese and Indian medicine.

Gujari: I have taken it to mean Old Gujarati, as spoken by the Gurjars—a pastoral and agricultural community—between the twelfth and fifteenth centuries in Gujarat, Rajputana, and Punjab.

hariya: An alcoholic beverage in parts of India and Bangladesh, made from fermenting rice. I have taken linguistic liberties here and used it as the name for the fermented beverage made from kharijal fruit pulp.

huzoor: Used as a term of respect for a high-ranking person, it can be translated as "Your Excellency."

Jadeja: A dynasty that ruled the Kutch region of India between the sixteenth and twentieth centuries.

jali: Means "net" and usually refers to a perforated stone or latticed screen. Jali work is a common form of decoration in Indo-Islamic architecture.

-ji: A gender-neutral term attached as a suffix to names or titles to denote respect in many languages of the Indian subcontinent.

kameez / kurta: A long, loose tunic worn in many parts of South Asia, it has Central Asian nomadic roots. The word "kameez" is derived from Arabic and the word "kurta" from Persian. They are often used interchangeably.

kharijal: *Salvadora persica* is a salt-tolerant evergreen tree found in arid regions. Its twigs have been used by people for centuries for cleaning teeth.

Khawaja: A Persian title that translates as "Lord" and is used as an honorific.

Khojki: A Brahmi-based script used primarily by Sindhi and Ismaili communities between the sixteenth and twentieth centuries.

kul: Family, home, or parentage. I have used the word to denote the groups of families that migrate together across the Banni grasslands.

Kutchi: May refer to the region of Kutch, the Kutchi language, or the people of Kutch. In medieval times, the Kutchi language was written in the Khojki script.

lehenga: Ankle-length skirt, tied around the waist with a drawstring and worn with a choli. The lehenga has a larger flare and is more elaborate than a ghagra.

loonuk: *Salsola baryosma,* a salt-tolerant shrub found in Kutch.

Malik: A Semitic term or title that means "king." The term has also been used for lower ranked officials, noblemen, chieftains, and princes. In the Gujarat Sultanate, it was a title bestowed on those of the nobility just below the sultan. Malik Gopi and Malik Ayyaz are both historical figures from the Gujarat Sultanate. Malik Gopi did indeed collude with the Portuguese and, while he was not blown from a cannon, he fell out of favor with the sultan and was quite likely murdered following a rather sordid affair involving a dancing girl, a man beaten to death, and relatives bent on revenge.

Masi / Masa: Masi refers to one's mother's younger sister. Masa is her husband.

pachisi: An ancient Indian game, it is played on a board shaped like a cross. Players move their pieces across the board according to the throw of cowrie shells.

potli: A cloth bag that can be closed with a drawstring, it originated in ancient India.

purdah: The practice among some Muslim and Hindu women to live secluded from public view, behind a curtain or a screen or a high wall, and to dress in a manner that conceals themselves from the gaze of strangers. In modern times, purdah has largely disappeared among Hindu women.

Rann: Derived from the Sanskrit word "irina," which means "desert." The Rann of Kutch is as I have described it (apart from magic flowers and killer wasps!) with one crucial difference. The salt desert didn't come into existence until 1819, when a powerful earthquake forced the seabed to rise, creating an embankment and diverting the course of various rivers. The Rann of Kutch submerges for four months of the year in the monsoon season. In October, the water recedes, leaving behind white salt, which is farmed by locals. But in the sixteenth century, at the time of the Gujarat Sultanate, it was underwater year-round.

safa: A turban consisting of an unstitched cotton cloth tied manually around the head. The style, color, and size vary depending on the place, the climate, and the occasion.

salwar kameez: A traditional South Asian dress consisting of a long tunic with side seams that are open below the waist and loose-fitting pants held up by a drawstring (salwar).

sarangi: A bowed string folk instrument popular in South Asia.

sarraf: A money changer or banker.

sitar: A plucked stringed instrument that originated in medieval India.

tabla: A pair of twin hand drums essential to classical Hindustani music.

taluka: A unit of administrative division; a subdistrict.

wazir: A chief minister, second only to the sultan in power and status.

zamorin: The ruler of Calicut. The term is derived from the Malayalam word "samuri," which in turn is a shortened version of a much longer term that can be translated as "August Emperor."

zenana: The inner part of a house reserved for the women of the household.

FOOD

chakri: Crunchy spiral-shaped snacks

dal: Split pea or lentil curry

dhokla: A soft, savory snack made from fermented batter of chickpea flour, wheat flour, and rice

handvo: A spicy rice, lentil, and vegetable cake

jaggery: Traditional cane sugar consumed on the Indian subcontinent

jungli jalebi: Fruits or pods of the *Pithecellobium dulce* tree

karonda: Berries from *Carissa carandas,* a drought-tolerant shrub

ker: Berries from *Capparis decidua,* a small, thorny tree found in arid parts of India

khajur: Dates

khakhra: Thin cracker made from dew bean and wheat flour

khichdi: South Asian dish of rice and lentils

khirni: Sweet golden yellow berries from *Manilkara hexandra,* a slow-growing evergreen tree

lassi: A blend of yogurt, water, and spices or fruit

pakora: Crispy, deep-fried fritters made from vegetables, spices, and gram flour

phalsa: Fruit of *Grewia asiatica,* a small tree native to India

rashbhari: Cape gooseberries

rotla: Flatbread made from pearl millet flour

saag: A leafy green vegetable dish

ACKNOWLEDGMENTS

This book would not exist without the help of several amazing and talented people. First and foremost, my wonderful editor at Wednesday Books, Mara Delgado Sánchez. Thank you, Mara, for making me dig deeper into my world and characters, helping me make this book stronger.

Thanks also to the team at Wednesday Books for all their hard work in making this book possible.

My deep gratitude to my agent, Mary C. Moore of Kimberley Cameron & Associates, for believing in my stories and being such a great advocate for my work in all the years we have been together.

My heartfelt thanks to beta reader Keyan Bowes, who read the worst possible version of this book and helped me make it fit for editorial eyes.

Thanks to all the other friends and fellow writers who have been with me on my writing journey: Ariella, Charlotte, Kari, Katie, Phoebe, Suzan, and Vanessa. I am so grateful to know you.

Much love to my parents, grandmother, and sister for their encouragement of my creative pursuits, and to my children for being my rocks in an unsteady world.

Lastly, thanks to you, dear reader, for picking up this book. I hope you enjoy it as much as I did.